GILDAS

HERE AND SOON

A Prophecy

by

Chris Thomas

Wuggles Publishing,
Clydach, Swansea, South Wales.

Copyright © Chris Thomas
May 2008.

ISBN 978- 1- 904043- 10- 2

This book is also available in e-book format, details of which are available at www.authorsonline.co.uk

This one's for all the staff and regulars at the Mond club who helped me through a really rough patch in life just by being their normal, decent selves.

Thanks!

For DENNIS
in appreciation

CHRIS THOMAS
MARCH 2009

CHAPTER 1

It was as hot as the anteroom to Hell. Poor old Icarus wouldn't have got to first base; his crummy DIY wings would have fallen to bits before he even got off the ground.

Heat haze softened a line of low, ashen mountains to the north. Shimmers of overheated air danced over the valley floor sending small spirals of filmy dust and the exhalations of a million lungs into a clearly-defined layer above a slow seethe of human activity. The very air itself blistered.

Then there was the river ... or what was left of it.

The river: uncaring; turgid, moving with a sullen lethargy, foul and discoloured, between low-lying banks towards the estuary and through the city of Town before joining the Bristol Channel. The waterway looked far too wide for the pitiful trickle of stinking fluid between its bare levees; there wasn't a healthy green bush or clump of grass to be seen anywhere.

Not a single drop of proper rain had fallen for a long, long time.

Broad and shallow, the surface only averaging a few inches above the muddy ochre-stained bed, a once proud and vigorous river drifted listlessly downhill.

Nearly overhead a harsh sun blazed pitiless and indifferent, filling the dusty valley with a suffocating furnace atmosphere that was often difficult to draw into the lungs without conscious effort. Dust-devils swirled above the superheated tarmac of the elevated motorway a few hundred yards downstream.

At this section of the river, about thirty yards wide and no different in any significant way from elsewhere in this part of its course from mountain to sea, hundreds of people were in the water as far as could be seen up and downstream. Eyes searched the stony bed, hands and feet

5

scrabbled through mud, pebbles and slime in the faint hope of finding something - anything - which could be used, exchanged, burnt or possibly eaten. The river was the only place such finds could sometimes still be made; an old tin, a plastic bag or occasionally the prize of a sick, immature eel covered with raw, cancerous growths. Besides, it was something to do to ease the grinding boredom of life as well as providing the only remaining way of keeping relatively cool.

Near the centre, a man, stooping to run his pallid, wrinkled hands over the stones, found a possible treasure. Soft clouds of red-brown mud billowed sluggishly under the surface. With trembling fingers he traced the exposed outline of the object; water-soft nails probing on the outside edge for the anticipated groves. Yes, there they were, shallow but definite. He stood up, put one of his feet on the object and looked about him.

Tall and thin, he was, with a long, sensitive face topped with greying, wispy hair held in place by a length of dirty rolled towelling, which he wetted with foul river water whenever his head became too hot. Not having any sun-glasses, he kept the sun behind him as much as he could and peered through slitted lids whenever forced to face the glare. So far he'd managed to avoid both heat-stroke and cataracts.

Fifty feet or so away he spotted his two children downstream near the edge of the river, splashing brown water over each other, uncaring of the risks from the filthy fluid. God knows he'd warned them enough times about the dangers of infections and disease. His life's work had been dedicated to that end, after all.

But how many kids listened to their parents any more? When had they ever? He needed their help to get a message to his wife.

She was only a couple of minutes' walk away at their camping pitch, keeping watch over the few possessions they'd managed to retain from the thieves and bully-boy

6

gangs roaming arrogantly at will among the swarms of the dispossessed.

The dispossessed!

From far and wide they had come. From the heartlands of Africa, accustomed to drought and famine; from the shores of the Mediterranean, home to playboy and slum dweller alike; from the steppes and mountains of the continent where traditional virtues of toil and thrift no longer provided a return. Alike in their hunger they instinctively took the historical routes to the north and west as other migrations had done throughout history - until they could go no further. There was nowhere to go! On this island at the edge of the Atlantic Ocean they were forced to stop. There could be no going back.

They came in their many, many millions. More tramped the dusty tarmac thread of the motorway every day, always heading west until the realisation dawned that this section was the last outpost where food of a sort might possibly - just possibly - be obtained. Those who still had the strength walked back; the others simply sat down and died.

A huge encampment had sprung up in this valley - the furthest west that could accommodate several millions within reach of occasional food supplies. From side to side of the valley and from a few miles north of the motorway to the coast, a shanty-town of ramshackle shelters covered almost every bit of solid ground among industrial buildings and sheds. Swarms of people were packed into rows of shattered, roofless houses flanking the flood-plain; in their gardens and on the roadways. In favourable places the shelters clustered the hills on each side, disappearing over the top to meet with others encroaching from the next valley. Filth and squalor were everywhere.

'Robbie!' he called as loudly as he dared, watching the single-track bridge a little way upstream. Rows of men lined the sides, a few even sitting on the scorching sun-seared girders of the curved metal arches sweeping in a shallow arc above the roadway. 'Robbie! Janet!' He looked towards his children again. They hadn't heard him and continued their splashing, squealing and laughing. He envied them their imagination.

He didn't dare call too loud in case one of the watching men on the bridge heard him. They would then send one of their number to investigate and the inevitable result would be that they would take his find away from him. If he resisted he could be seriously hurt, even casually killed.

He had to get help to excavate the object: if it was still in one piece then it would be set very deep among the slimy pebbles. Protection, too! He needed the assistance of others to retain possession even though that would mean sharing the spoils with any helpers. Still, as the original finder, he would get to keep the biggest share. Even in the midst of anarchy there had to be some rules, if they could be enforced.

Heat blasted the back of his neck; he fought down a sudden surge of nausea and faintness borne of frustration. It faded slowly. Undecided, he looked about him, searching for a familiar face. Stooped figures topped by bronzed, unsmiling features were everywhere but nowhere could he see anyone he knew. It seemed a few of them were giving him more than a perfunctory measure of attention so he pretended to stretch his back and resumed an appearance of searching under the water, glancing occasionally to see if there was a chance of attracting the notice of one of his children.

The noise of heavy engines rumbled from the east. It must be the arrival of the supply trucks from the docks! Only two deliveries a week lately, and never at a predictable time. Others reacted to the sound; a general downstream movement commenced. The Man once more looked about him, trying to fix the position of his find by the alignment of objects on the banks so that he could locate it again. He had read somewhere this was the way sailors at sea used to fix a point in coastal waters. Satisfied, he sloshed through the stinking, ankle-deep water to his children.

'Come on Robbie, Janet; let's get back to your mother! The trucks are coming.'

At a rapid trot they negotiated the unmarked route through a shambles of plastic-covered abodes. A short journey brought them to the tiny covered enclosure they called home. 'Jennie!' he called, and pulled aside the flap of stained cloth serving as an entrance door.

Jennifer, his wife, sat huddled behind the small pile of plastic boxes and suitcases containing their only possessions, hair in a mess and crying silently. At his entrance she flinched convulsively, covering her face with grimy hands. The Man felt his stomach turn to jelly. He stooped and put an arm around her shaking shoulders. She shrank from his touch, from his helpless concern. Turning her face away she covered her eyes. Resentment replaced concern; resentment at her unconscious confirmation of his status in her eyes. He spoke gruffly.

'He's been here again, hasn't he?'

She said nothing. Tears seeped between her straining, bony fingers.

'Talk to me!' He shook her lightly. She snuffled and brushed away an errant wisp of hair in an instinctively feminine action.

'Leave it! Don't do anything! I haven't been hurt; it's just he scares me so much'. She rubbed her blotched face with dusty hands and tried to smile. Her voice changed to a cheery and patently false lightness. 'Listen, I've been thinking it might be best if we did as he suggests. It's not going to hurt me, not really, and we'll be part of a fair-sized group, at least. Better chance to survive'.

'Forget it!' Resentment combined with anger. Both emotions directed themselves towards the woman; she was here, the enemies were not. 'Being slobbered over by that cretin is bad enough but what happens when his cronies want a share after he gets tired of you? No, not that. Never! I'll try to kill him first.'

He clenched his thin, sensitive hands into small fists; trembling, impotent. A part of him watched and listened to their words, aghast at how such a conversation could come from their lips. The Man felt more of himself drawn into this phantom consciousness. For a few moments it forced an ephemeral memory of another place and time into his receptive mind.

Not so long ago...

... a house, large, grey and dignified. Tall beech trees laden with the black, untidy blotches of crow's nests formed a halo over the roof; green ivy and reddening Virginia creeper hugged the poll-stone walls in an affectionate embrace at odds with its gaunt Victorian lines. A classic gentlemen's residence in truth, with sweeping lawns, a pond with fountain and a curving line of neat gravelled driveway dappled with shade as it followed the trimmed tunnel cut through the woods on its way to the road.

Home! Until it all went so terribly wrong.

Three people on the lawn. His wife, Jennifer of the quiet voice, which could create such musical pictures when she sang. She was singing now. He listened carefully but could identify neither the music nor the song. Graceful in a long summer dress, she was entertaining her children, his children, their children, as they idled away a golden afternoon.

The Man could not see himself. He was probably at work; as usual!

A cloud passed over the sun. The woman and her children looked up. She smiled and held out her arms. The children ran to her, one each side, clasping her dress as they returned to the house.

Don't go! Please stay! The cloud thickened.

The mental picture faded to an amorphous grey then lightened to a glaring yellow. The Man realised his eyes were tightly shut. Reluctantly, he opened them to reality and the hot sweaty stink of the camp. A blaze of hatred came and went in an instant. He remembered what he had been doing and tried to banish the harshness from his voice.

'I know I'm not much of a husband or tough guy but I've made up my mind I'm prepared to die to protect my family. There's nothing left at all, otherwise.'

Jennifer averted her eyes once more and said nothing. That only made it worse.

The Man pushed his daughter forwards and stood her in front of his wife. 'Who'll they want after you? This little girl; your daughter? Think about it! I've got to go out again. The trucks are here so you'd better look after her while Robbie and I see what's on the menu today. Back as soon as we can.'

'Your turban's dried out. Take the hat!' She took a tatty, broad-brimmed Panama from her head and offered it to him. 'I'll stay out of the sun.'

'No, you keep it! We won't be very long.'

Leaving the shelter, his anger increasing rather than abating, he roughly jostled through the crowds heading for the motorway a few hundred yards downstream. A short convoy of large, assorted vehicles was trundling westwards; slowly to avoid obstacles in the roadway but fast enough to discourage any attempt at an ambush. Anyone stupid enough to get in the way got crushed. The main convoy never stopped.

At the rear of the last truck surged a crowd of people; ragged scarecrows, panting, limping, straining to keep up. The wiser ones travelled at a steady sustainable pace to make sure of having enough energy left to hold a place in the queue when the trucks stopped. Clouds of dense, black smoke issued from the last vehicle in the line and drifted slowly over the edge of the embankment. Fewer people chose to follow on this side.

More people were climbing the embankments to join the throng and teeming hordes could be seen making their way through the shanty-town, on to the feeder lanes towards the motorway junction, where the handout would take place. At the exit slip-road the last three trucks peeled off the back of the convoy and pushed slowly though the crowd to the roundabout under the junction. The rest of the convoy continued along towards the west.

The Man and his son started to run, pushing past the weaker and older followers, who were beginning to flag and drop out of the race. Some had collapsed with the exertion and their limp bodies tripped up those not quick enough to avoid them. Losers! Soon to die because they couldn't keep up. So what was new? Just the same in the society they'd lost, wasn't it? Competition? Hah! Only on *their* terms. *This* was the ultimate test! Doggedly, the Man ran faster hoping his son would be able to keep up with him.

In a cloud of oily smoke the trucks entered the roundabout, slowing to take up position at the edge of the central island. It was a large roundabout with a stream flowing through the middle below road level. At least, there used to be a stream. Now completely dried up, there wasn't even any mud left, but the steep gully slope gave partial protection to one side of the trucks. Uniformed men holding a variety of weapons leapt to the ground from inside the cabs and off narrow platforms bolted to the sides.

The running crowds stopped several yards from the trucks. Engines continued to run in case a fast getaway became necessary or a battery went flat. Diesel stank.

Two of the trucks were ordinary commercial five-tonners. The third was big, old and tired - so *terribly* tired. Unlike its colleagues it originated from army stock and had since been reconstructed to a different design entirely to suit a particular role. One of the rear axles had been removed and an extra wheel fitted each side of that remaining. The driving cab had been extended backwards to accommodate an additional row of seats used for escort guards, and the exhaust pipe had been lengthened to project from the rear.

Choking clouds of smoke issued from where the pipe had broken apart half-way under the floor. Fumes were seeping into the interior cargo space through gaps in the timber flooring; thereby ensuring all the food inside would acquire a rich diesel flavour. The old truck rocked slightly as its abused engine struggled to remain ticking over.

Feeling a tug at the hem of his tattered shirt the Man looked down into the eyes of his son. Panting, pale, the growing cataract in his left eye more pronounced in the direct light of the sun, the boy was looking weaker by the day. His skin was dry and dusty. Dehydration; he should have been sweating. A surge of pity and misery swept through the Man's whole being. His son simply wasn't designed for this sort of life, if you could it that, and he, as a father, couldn't even obtain a pair of sun-glasses to help keep off the ultraviolet solar rays blasting almost unchecked past what little was left of the ruined ozone layer. Too proud or afraid to steal; too much of a coward to snatch goods by force. He ruffled the boy's untidy hair and tried to smile.

'We'll see if we can get a bit closer if you feel up to it, OK? Put your hat back on or the sun'll make your eye worse!' He knew it was past the point of no return. That eye would never see the beauty that could have been, before long. The other eye would probably go soon after that without the type of medical help that no longer existed - at least for the likes of them. 'Ready?'

The boy nodded. 'Ready, Dad'. They began to slide between packed sweating bodies - along with a few hundred others. The leading edge of the crowd was pushed slowly towards the trucks. At the rear of the first two trucks a small flap fell down to reveal an opening to the interior. Engines revved and the two rear vehicles moved forwards to touch the outer edge of the flaps. It was now only possible to pass under the flaps to get to the other side.

Armed men moved into position; two at each end of the aisle between the trucks, two on each bonnet and two more climbing a set of iron rungs to each roof. A heavy-set man with a loud-hailer leaned from the cab of the leading truck.

'All right. Listen up!' he bawled. Silence, overlain only with a background murmur and a couple of screams of frustration from the back ranks. The loud-hailer howled with overload. He turned a knob on the side and resumed. 'You all know the procedure. Them that don't, watch the others. Come forward! Slowly now, or someone might get shot.'

The crowd moved forwards. The Man and his son headed towards the closest truck, the middle one of the three. The first person in line passed the armed guards, ducked under the flap, turned and seized a brownish-coloured cube, about four inches to a side, which was pushed onto the flap as he passed underneath. Without comment or thanks he passed the next two guards and disappeared from view.

Minutes passed. A stream of people followed each other through the gaps and emerged clutching their block of compressed food. A four-inch cube to last half a week, no matter how many had to share it. As they shuffled forwards, the Man pondered how he was to resolve his wife's problem.

The boss of a gang of thugs camped near their shelter had designs on her. Not that he was such a bad bloke; many would simply have disposed of any opposition and taken her. The trouble was this kind of thing was accepted, these days. The strong took and the weak lost - as always. He pondered as they moved slowly closer to the truck. In his original line of work he had been used to making logical decisions but it wasn't so easy when the sheer survival of his entire family was at stake. A conclusion was reached: there was only one thing to do. They would have to move camp if a living-space could be found within walking distance of the supply route.

Decision made, the Man turned his attention back to the truck, now near at hand. Seen from this close it became obvious how near to total collapse the whole supply system had become. Not enough transport, too many people, and more pouring into the country all the time. The end couldn't be far away now.

The state of the trucks was evidence enough. Dented, battered, dust-covered oil and grease marks everywhere, scarred tyres with cracked and perished rubber, body paint faded and discoloured around areas where some rough, hastily-parched welds had been applied. How they kept going at all was a miracle. No proper servicing could be done any more. When something went wrong it was repaired in the quickest way possible and when a really major repair was required the truck was scrapped and cannibalised to keep the others going. How much longer could this last?

Forget it! Get the grub and let tomorrow look after itself. Their turn at the hatch.

The Man ducked, swung round and seized the block of food. He passed the guards and waited for his son to join him with his own food block. All they had to do now was get back to the shelter without being mugged and the food stolen. He glanced idly at the guards manning the lead truck.

A familiar face! No, not so much a face as a shape; no two people could be built like that, surely! Short, massive shoulders and torso, long arms, and if he turned to face them he would be ugly as hell. The Man hesitated then approached. 'Gildas? Hey Gil!'

The guard heard and slowly turned to face him, hand moving towards a hip holster while keeping the rifle in the other hand trained just over the heads of the steady stream of people issuing from the aisle he was guarding. He wore a forage cap with a long peak and a stout pair of anti-UV goggles with side panels. Leaving the hip holster alone, he removed the goggles and regarded the Man with a pair of sad brown eyes.

'Calling me? Don't come any closer! Who are you?'

`You're Gil! Used to work at the abattoir? Don't you recognise me?'

The wide-set brown eyes studied the Man. 'You used to be the foreman, right? Kicked me out. Can't hardly recognise you under all those whiskers. That your boy?'

'Yes. Listen, you know you were one of the last to go, just before I was kicked out myself. Had to be that way because there simply weren't any animals coming in to be processed. You know why. Surely you don't hold a grudge against me?'

'Nothing personal. I just can't stomach anyone who thinks they've got some authority; it's a matter of principle. You know that! I told you often enough.'

The Man felt relieved, Gildas hadn't changed; they'd always got on fairly well. 'True, but then, I never argue with a man who's holding a gun. Any chance of a quick chat?'

Gildas nodded amiably. 'Sure. Just hang on till this truck's empty and they start on the last one, but don't come any closer. I won't shoot but I'm not the only one here. Understand?'

The Man nodded and moved a short distance away to the shade of a redundant road sign. He sat down, pulling his son with him and concealed the two precious blocks of compressed food between them. An hour passed. The glaring sun moved a little way across the sky. It became hotter than ever.

A babble of shouts and cries erupted from the other side of the trucks. Gildas and his companion raised their rifles. The shouts became louder with a hysterical edge and a couple of shots blasted out. Gildas passed out of sight down the aisle.

The rear truck gunned its engine. Dense clouds of smoke poured out of the broken exhaust pipe from burning oil deposited in the muffler by worn engine cylinders, injectors long overdue for replacement and the seized and shattered piston rings. The two front trucks moved forward; the big one travelled to the front. Its serving flap banged down and the other two tucked up tight behind it. People began to filter through the new handout point, many gasping and choking from the effects of the exhaust cloud. A few minutes later the other truck closed its serving hatch to the accompaniment of more yells of rage from disappointed customers and Gildas emerged once more. He walked towards the Man tucking his rifle under his arm and pulling a small tin box from his pocket.

'How's things with you? Family still together?' Gildas opened the tin and began to roll a cigarette. 'Fancy a fag?'

'Love one. Thanks.' The Man accepted the tin, aware of his body eagerly anticipating the pleasure of tobacco-substitute in spite of the parched dryness of his throat. 'So far we've been lucky.' They rolled their cigarettes and lit up in reverential silence. The losers standing idly in the dried stream bed at the centre of the roundabout watched enviously. Nobody came near. Nobody begged off an armed man.

'What's it like out there?' Gildas raised his chin to indicate the shanty-town to the north. 'Getting worse, I suppose. More people crowding in?'

'Too true. It's total anarchy. Ruled by local bunches of bully-boys just like everywhere else. Bodies disappear, and after dark the nearest gang holds a barbecue. Saves having to find a spot to bury them, though the collectors do their best.'

'Hah! That's only because they get a bonus when they deliver a fresh corpse down the docks. They wouldn't bother otherwise. Those that have gone off a bit have to be dumped out at sea. No profit in them. You've worked in an abattoir, like me. Work it out for yourself! You know the score.' Gildas' tone was bitter.

The Man glanced doubtfully at the two blocks of protein he and Robbie had collected and decided to change the subject. 'You get around much with these trucks?'

'This convoy only delivers about ten miles around the docks. I mostly do the run to the trading estate on the other side of the rail line. You think things are bad here? Just try living in one of those units they converted from the shops. Hot! It's like an oven inside some of them. They're killing each other for room and even the body collectors can't make a living there. No fuel, see? Nothing to cook with so everything's got to be eaten raw before it goes off. Tide's getting a bit higher every week, too. Won't be long before some units'll have to be abandoned. They'll all have to come up here then.'

The Man pondered. Another good reason for getting out. Fragrant tobacco fumes trickled from his nose. He was beginning to feel light-headed from the combined effects of the cigarette, hunger and diesel smoke. 'Truth is I'm in a bad situation where I am. Got to move. Do you know anywhere there's a place we can go to?'

Gildas shook his head slowly and took another drag. 'Where you are now is about the best area but that won't last for long. You're not only going to get a lot coming in from down there but they're expecting another big convoy of ships in with more refugees from the hot countries in a few days and the so-called authorities are going frantic trying to think of a place to put them. Can't stop them; they'll get ashore somehow. Stay put, that's my advice.'

'Can't.'

'That's a pity.' Gildas looked genuinely sympathetic 'Wish I could help more, but there it is'.

The Man indicated the rifle lying across Gildas' lap. 'Ever had to shoot anyone with that?'

Gildas gave a slow smile. 'Never. I don't think I'd ever be able to actually kill anyone. Couldn't if I had to, anyway. No bullets! I've had to use it as a club a few times though.

Only Regular Army are issued with ammunition. They don't trust the rest of us.'

A shout came from the cab of the lead truck. Turning his head Gildas saw an imperiously waving arm and a red face scowling at him. 'Got to go.' He waved back and rose to his feet. 'Listen. Hide your food blocks and let the lad come with me to the truck for a minute!'

The Man moved his body to conceal his food. 'Sure. Why?'

Gildas looked embarrassed. 'Look, you always treated me decently in work. Not like most others. I can't help you with your problem but I'd like to give you a bit of extra grub. Just you wait here and I'll fix it.' He held out a large hand. 'Good luck"'

The Man reached up and shook Gildas' hand. The sad brown eyes in the ugly face regarded him for a moment as if there was something more to be said, then Gildas turned to the boy. 'Come with me, lad!'

They walked to the driver's door of the truck. The engine gasped and rumbled. Gildas knocked on the window and the driver wound it down.

'What?'

'My extra ration. I'll take it now.'

'Suit yourself! Get back with the others, I feel nervous.' The driver reached behind his seat and produced two food blocks. He tossed them carelessly out of the window and closed it again to keep the stinking diesel fumes out of the cab. Gildas picked up the blocks and pressed them into the boy's grubby hands. 'Take care of your dad, son. I hope we'll meet again.' He turned the boy around and pushed. The boy ran to the Man. Gildas gave a small wave and rounded the front of the truck to help with controlling the crowds. There was always trouble when all the food had gone. The unlucky ones sometimes got suicidal and tried to storm their benefactors. If there was any shooting it would happen then.

May God's deputy help them all, he thought. God himself had obviously given things up as a bad job.

The Man approached his shelter thinking of who he could trust enough to enlist in the retrieval of the worn tyre casing he'd found in the river. Old tyres made good footwear and what was left could always be burned to heat some food and keep warm at night for a change. It could get pretty cold after the sun went down.

Last night around here. Tomorrow they'd move on.

Down the final alley between rag and plastic hovels he could see a small crowd of people standing in the gap his home occupied but there was no sign of the scrap of green cloth he had attached to the apex to mark its position among the others. He broke into a run pulling the boy along with him; there was a sinking feeling in his guts that had nothing to do with hunger.

Pushing standing watchers aside, he broke through the ring and viewed the ruins of his shelter with dismay. A woman clutching a small blue plastic box suddenly bolted into the crowd. The movement momentarily attracted his attention and he recognised the box as belonging to his wife; it was the one in which she kept her little bits of jewellery and small kitchen implements. The matter left his mind as quickly as it had entered.

Most of the materials they had used in the construction had already gone, the little space was almost clear, but on the few bits of dirty cloth remaining, a couple of women were bent over a still form lying on the ground covered with a ragged sheet of semi-transparent plastic. He turned to the boy 'Wait here son!'

The Man knew with a flash of insight what had happened here. He nudged one of the women, recognising her as being from an adjoining shelter. She looked up at him, an expression of intense misery on her sun-scorched face. With a slow shake of her head she struggled to rise and allow him access to the body. He helped her to her feet and gently set her aside. The body wore familiar clothes.

His wife! Dead to the world; or just dead?

He pulled away the plastic sheet and lifted the piece of heavily bloodstained cloth someone had placed over her face and upper chest. It came away stickily.

She was dead, that was obvious. Death had not come easily. The Man forced himself to look. He felt the pain of his eyeballs bulging.

A huge cut gaped wide. A heavy and very sharp blade had sliced at an angle from the right shoulder across and down nearly the whole way across her chest. It went deeper than he imagined a cut could ever be made by a hand-held weapon. The clean white paddle-shape of a divided collar bone stuck out from her shoulder. Coin-sized cross section ends of her ribs made a neat line of pale dots amid the clotting gore. Flies dived suicidally into the mess in a frenzied determination to ensure the continuity of their species. The ground beneath her was the colour of fresh liver.

The Man was aware of the approach of his son and made no effort to shield him from the ghastly sight. The boy made no sound. Perhaps the sight of death was now so familiar to him, even viewing the savagely butchered body of his own mother made little impression. The Man asked of the crowd, now beginning to disperse. 'My daughter. Where is my daughter? Who did this?'

He knew who had done it. The woman he had nudged away from the body touched his arm and proved him wrong.

'Not the ones you think.' She was aware of their harassment by the local gang boss. 'Not them. Another lot. Strangers from over there somewhere.' She pointed in the direction away from the river towards the hills. 'Never seen 'em before. One had a bit of sharpened steel - looked like a bit of old car bumper. He did it when she tried to drag the little girl away from him. The others got mad and took the steel blade off him. Then they went back the way they came. Took the girl with 'em.'

21

'How many?'

'About a dozen. Ugly lot. All over in a couple of minutes before anyone could react. Couldn't have stopped them anyhow. Too many. Sorry.'

'Thanks, I would probably have done the same thing.' The Man fought an urge to collapse and never wake again. He passed a shaking hand over his forehead then turned to the boy. 'Stay here, son. Won't be longer than I can help. Don't let anyone touch your mother and look after the food!' He covered the body, now nearly covered with a swarm of fat black flies, with the few pathetic bits of cloth he could find. They buzzed madly underneath. More arrived and settled on the cloth, searching for a way in to the bounty.

The crowd had dispersed by now. All over; nothing to be done. Not that they were callous - just helpless and apathetic. His son still had not said anything so he sat him down near the corpse and set out on the trail of his daughter with not a single idea in his mind on what he would do if he caught up with her captors.

All the rest of that day he searched eastwards through the sprawling camp that murmured and suffered in all directions. He was lucky to begin with.

Within a few hundred yards he came across another small scene of carnage; he asked a question, somebody pointed, he carried on. Soon, another. An old man clutched a woman's body covered with a smart coat. The Man asked his question but the old man didn't seem aware of his presence. A neighbour overheard and pointed the way he should go. As he left he kicked a wide-brimmed hat. Lifting it he found an ornate pair of unbroken sun glasses. He looked at the old man but received no acknowledgement. The hat, folded, went onto his head and the glasses over his eyes. At least he now had a chance to preserve his eyesight from the blasting sunlight. He went on . . .

... high up the hill to the top where he could see into the adjoining valley and coastal plain with its unending vista of plastic and rag shelters; the industrial estate occupying the site of an old oil works standing on its hummock against the setting sun as a monument to vanished industrial might. The whole valley floor here was covered with foul water by the steadily rising sea. Only the sharp line of a dual carriageway, lined the whole of its length with shelters and people, raised above the flood at high tide. An ancient ruined abbey, survivor from a vanished and indisputably happier age, hunched weary, crumbling shoulders above the water rising several feet above its slowly subsiding foundations. Further on, a petrochemical complex watched its own reflection in the surrounding tide and in the distance the skeletal remains of a steelworks lay stark and defeated at the foot of the mountains. How he wished he had a pair of binoculars!

He couldn't find her. Hadn't really expected to but he had to try. With steps wobbly from hunger and thirst he made his way back to the riverbank and gulped down a few mouthfuls of muddy water ignoring all the suspicious lumps and slime floating slowly downstream. Then back to where the shelter used to be. Another family in the process of erecting a home of thin metal rods and tattered plastic sheets occupied the space and stared at him in silent challenge. They knew! They had heard and they didn't care - or couldn't allow themselves to. He'd been unlucky. Tough, go away! - or unspoken words to that effect.

His wife's body had gone. So had the boy. So had the food blocks. In despair the Man sat down close by, too tired and weak to cry although sometimes he whimpered softly for minutes at a time like a hungry, lost puppy. No one approached or spoke to him. He sat there for two days before moving on; up into the dusty, barren hills to the north where the food trucks never went; where only those desperate for space would even consider taking their chances.

INTERMURAL 1

The planet was in trouble - real trouble. All sentient life (and any other form, for that matter) teetered on the razor-edge of extinction. Not that anyone would admit it.

They'd been fouling things up for far too long, you see; as long as it took to become an unbreakable habit and they weren't about to change now. Stuck in the old "How to borrow your way out of debt" hang-up, the only way to proceed seemed to be to increase the rate at which they were "progressing", despite the fact it was obviously going to be ruinous.

All the conventional doomsday symptoms were in plain view. The prognosis was definitive. Most of the inhabitants were helplessly aware of the obvious end result but nobody in a position to do anything about it was really prepared to put their own neck on the block. A comparatively few individual entities - giant conglomerates, the super-rich and some governments - could have used their overloaded bank vaults and/or political muscle to offset the worst of the inevitable march of events ... but it would cost. How it would cost! And the cost would come out of their pockets! So leave it alone! Maybe everything would work out all right in the end and it wouldn't cost them a penny. If it didn't, well, they'd probably be long dead and buried before things got completely out of hand, in which case it still wouldn't cost them a penny.

That's right folks, politicians, businessmen, religious leaders and the like. Put your brainless collective heads back under the sand as usual! Wait and see!

But entities the size of planets don't often actually die completely unless their luminary, that source of all life, packs up first. They just get rid of as much irritation as possible, purge themselves of the disease then start over with a new cast of characters on the global stage. `Oops! Sorry! Didn't work out that time. Let's have another go!

It had happened before. Not just once but several times. Ancient bony records buried in the rocks bore mute testimony to that.

And that's the way it should be! If you make a mess of things, try again with a clean sheet.

But this planet was really dying.

Not the basic structure, of course; sterile rock, air, water. Just the myriad flecks of life swarming on its skin; the parasites struggling to wrest a living from the current position of their evolution; feeding upon any life weaker than .itself and organising into temporary alliances with other species to attack and feed on weaker groups (definition of a competitive society). Squandering the minerals torn from Earth's outer surface on unnecessary and meaningless trinkets to sell to each other, then dumping the unwanted products of all this wasted effort into their atmosphere and oceans (definition of a consumer society).

Sounds familiar? Wait, there's more!

The ability of this particular planet to maintain the profligate, wantonly over-breeding multitude of its most powerful species had been stretched way beyond the limits of what was reasonable. Natural processes lurched blindly into action to redress the balance. Those greedy, selfish parasites had to be expunged in order to attempt a more rational mode of existence. To get rid of them the planet would have to give them a little help, then allow them to complete their headlong rush towards mutually agreed suicide.

It shouldn't be difficult. Nothing need consciously be done. The natural basic forces of entropy and evolution would follow their rules and complete the job. Systematic and deliberate destruction of the atmosphere and oceans would ensure a disastrous enough climate change to destroy many millions of square miles of previously fertile

25

croplands. Poisonous wastes would kill enough aquatic life to make matters many times worse and the dominant life-form's stubborn refusal to limit their procreation in keeping with the available resources would put the lid on things. These were Entropy's part of the job, wielding the twin weapons of starvation and decay.

Mother Nature would help, of course. There were lots of lovely new diseases she could cook up to help things along for people, animals and crops. Then, as social and economic disintegration continued accelerating at close to an exponential rate, it would become ever more difficult, and finally impossible, to counteract them. This was the responsibility of Evolution; the ultimate biological war machine.

Mind you, they'd come far in a short time. For well over five thousand years human civilisation had struggled to develop in a dignified manner from an assorted gaggle of nomadic tribes into a species able to send sophisticated data-gathering probes far beyond the bounds of the solar system - and had even landed representatives on their nearest planetary neighbours.

From Sumerian desert sands to the stars on a trail littered with the mangled corpses of failed political and religious ideologies.

CHAPTER 2

Who would have believed that it required a time-span of only fifty-odd years to bring about the total demolition of global civilised structures? But some suspected it could come to pass within their lifetimes; one man in particular.

When it became obvious that the African continent and all other lands within the same latitudes were in terminal decline because of a string of devastating droughts, he began making his plans.

At the time when the ozone layer abruptly disappeared over those same latitudes, destroying plant life and the ocular tissues of food animals, he contacted others of his kind, only to be rebuffed with derision and dire warnings not to rock the boat.

Not long afterwards, when all diurnal animals died, cows with over loaded udders and sheep unable to forage for widely scattered patches of desiccated grass, animal tenders in no better condition to care for their charges, his peers hastened to contact him and ask for further particulars.

And when the mass migrations of starved, sickly human dross began, the panic really took off.

They had good reason. More than six thousand million people on the move can create unreasonable demands on the lands to which they migrate. By road, rail, air and ship they fled - until the fuel ran out. Then they walked. Humanitarian attitudes rapidly gave way to mighty efforts to keep refugees away. 'Go and die somewhere else!' they said. 'We cannot support you.'

Nobody took any notice. It was too late and there were too many of them with nowhere to settle. They kept moving, those who were able, and overran more fortunate lands.

The killings began.

Millions died.

It made no difference. Things were past the point of no return. People with nothing to lose kept travelling in order to survive. As they travelled, they overloaded local distribution systems already stretched beyond the limits of what they were designed to cope with. Order collapsed. New lands filled up, were stripped of what was available, and in spite of ever-increasing deaths from disease and warfare, a greater number moved inexorably on.

Hundreds of millions more died.

But due to the far-sighted efforts of one man some order remained in one particular corner, and vast resources began to be channelled into an ambitious rescue plan to salvage something from the mess.

This man now conversed with one of his minions who appeared to be out of his depth. Neither of them was very happy or in full control of the situation.

'Don't give me that! Find him right now and get him to call me back! Don't argue, I said *now*!'

Red-blotched jowls quivering, eyes glaring, Lemuel Quorvis leaned over his desk and snatched at the "off" switch on his conference phone. Too fast and too hard! The plastic toggle snapped off at its base a fraction of a second after his middle fingernail broke and exposed a section of raw cuticle to the chilly air-conditioned atmosphere in his luxurious office deep underground. He gasped and closed his eyes, unable to look at what damage he'd done,

An extremely rare event occurred. Lemuel Quorvis's patience snapped completely.

'Damn it! Damn him! Damn them!' he howled, sticking the wounded digit between his rosebud lips and sucking. The pain hit within a few seconds: he moaned softly and bent his head low over the desk.

He sat for a few minutes waiting for the sharp pain to abate. It did, to be replaced by a dull throbbing. With his good hand he reached for the intercom.

'See if you can find the doctor, please, Wendy, and ask him to bring his little black bag. No, nothing serious, only a scratch, thank you. Oh, and get someone from maintenance up here after the doc leaves will you?'

He settled his vast bulk more comfortably in the wing-backed chair, willing the doctor to come quickly yet wanting time to prepare for the pain he knew was to come. Lemuel Quorvis had been aware since childhood that he occupied the bottom line in any index of pain tolerance.

At least his momentary burst of temper was back under control, he thought. Not good for his image, let alone his blood pressure. Anger only made things more difficult. In the last couple of minutes he had not only managed to upset his best agent on the ship and broken his phone but he had also succeeded in wounding himself and would probably suffer pain for several days as a result.

Worse, he prided himself upon his normally placid disposition. That was how he had achieved his present status; remaining calm while others panicked, then picking at their corporate remains when their defences had been sufficiently weakened.

Good business procedure, that!

The doctor, resident on the premises, was not long in arriving. He breezed through the soundproofed door without ringing the bell or even giving Wendy, Lemuel's long-time secretary, a chance to announce his arrival. A fat, stinking cigar stuck out of the middle of his mouth like a lance, producing dense clouds of pungent smoke.

Thin lips stretched and a big smile appeared around the cigar. 'Morning, Lem! Need my professional services or just a chat?'

Lemuel sighed and put his finger back into his mouth in case he became snappy again and said something offensive. Doc was good at his job; he just wouldn't recognise the existence of a pecking order.

He sucked, felt an extra-large twinge and removed his finger, pointing at it with his other podgy hand,

'This. Broke the nail on a switch. It hurts. Fix it!'

'Ouch!' Doctor Ian Payne flipped to sympathy mode as if a button had been pressed. This ability to instantly respond in the correct manner was one of his most important assets as far as Lemuel was concerned. 'That looks painful. Is it?'

'It was. Not so bad at the moment but that won't last long; I can feel it.'

The doctor opened his bag and passed a tissue to his mortally wounded employer. 'Here, dry it with this and don't put it in your mouth again.' He rummaged deeper into the bag, ignoring the gasps and winces of pain as Lemuel delicately dabbed saliva from his fingertip. 'How did you manage to do it?'

'Accident with the phone. Broke a switch. What are you searching for?'

'Got to sterilise under the nail. On to the ship again, were you? Things going well up there?'

'Lousy! They're nothing but a bunch of idiots. If they see anything working properly they get an uncontrollable urge to alter it. Will it sting?'

'I was under the impression that was how proper management is handled these days and of course it'll sting. I can sterilise it in one of two ways. Either use this,' and he held up a bottle of clear fluid, 'or soak your finger with petrol and apply a match. Your choice. So what's the latest?'

Lemuel's large bald head shrank back into the folds of his neck, eyeing the inoffensive bottle with a deep instinctive suspicion. 'Use that! Bit of a rebellion blown up 'cos the gangs working on the lower storage decks have found out theirs is going to be the last one constructed. They don't see why the officers have to be catered for first.'

'So? Why should they be? What are you going to do about it? Finger dry? Good, prop it on the edge of the desk and stick the bad finger up in the air!'

Lemuel did as he was told, averting his gaze as the doctor poured an inch of fluid into a glass tube with a wide, flat base.

'Hell, it's not a matter of whether the officers should be sorted out first. Besides, they haven't realised that any unforeseen problems in the installation will be cured by the time the steerage holds are started. No! The fact is, this upset is only the latest in a long line of hitches and they're all slowing things down. It's up to the managers and agents to foresee these problems and solve them before they get out of hand; not come grizzling to me every time some supervisor or other tries to make a name for himself.   Oy! Careful!'

30

This last was prompted by the doctor seizing the hand stiffly held against the desk and raising it up to be viewed through a pair of magnifying spectacles.

'Hm! Bet it hurts more, now.' It did. Lemuel tried to be brave. `I'll have to cut away a bit of the nail or it'll keep catching in the cover I'm going to put on.' He placed the glass with the sterilising fluid on the desk top and produced a glittering pair of scissors. 'So what are you going to do?

'Ah! Aah!' With a loud click the scissors performed their legitimate function and a bit of beautifully manicured fingernail painted in a tasteful shade of green hit Lemuel's cheek. He struggled to continue talking to take his mind off the major surgery being undertaken without even the balm of general anaesthetic. 'Lay down the law, that's what. Tell those moronic so-and-sos it's up to them to ensure their own survival, think of way to do it and then do it without bloodshed in what time we have left. Do you know how bad it's getting out there?' He jerked his chin in the general direction of the ceiling.

'Pretty rough last time I looked. Haven't left the premises for at least a month but it seems I'm having to patch your army up a fair bit more often than I used to. Hm! Looks clean. No blood coming out.' Lemuel felt faint. 'Stick it in the glass and don't knock it over or it'll burn a hole through the plastic veneer.'

Hesitantly the injured man inserted his finger into the glass and barely repressed a howl of pain as the doctor pressed down to submerge it up to the first joint. Ruined nail varnish instantly began to fall to the bottom in a pale green cloud. Tears sprang to his eyes. 'It's not plastic, it's real wood and a lot older than you are.' He hissed between gritted dentures, 'And you damned well know it.'

A sympathetic look was his only reply. Was there just a hint of amusement on the doctor's face? It was hard to see through a veil of tears no matter how hard he blinked. The finger was held under for about a minute before being removed, coated with a pleasant-smelling pink paste and

31

dressed. Fitting a flexible protective sheath completed the treatment. There was no pain now, only a subdued throbbing.

'Thank you doctor,' invariably polite, Lemuel.

They looked at each other.

'Something more, doc? Only I'm expecting maintenance to fix the phone then I've got a lot of calls to make.'

'My fee.'

'Sorry. Got a lot on my mind. You know where to find it.'

The doctor crossed to a disk cabinet, pulled open the second drawer and extracted a bottle half full of pale liquid and two tumblers from a recess at the rear. 'Join me?'

'Why not?' Glass clinked. The intercom buzzed. Lemuel pressed the switch with his bad finger, winced and said 'Yes?'

Someone from maintenance here. OK to come in?'

'Wheel 'em through.'

The door opened and a short elderly man in a filthy brown boiler suit entered carrying a small toolbox. He eyed the bottle pointedly before speaking. His voice sounded like grit scratching under a coal-shed door.

'Something wrong, Mr Q? Got a job for me?'

'Broken switch on the conference phone, here.' Lemuel waved a fat paw towards the mutilated machine. 'I'm expecting an important call from the ship so could you get it done quickly as possible?' He picked up the bottle. 'Another glass, if you please, doc.'

Lemuel poured out a generous measure for the old mechanic as he removed the front panel from the phone. Within a few minutes the switch had been bridged, an unused switch transferred across from another section of the array and the whole thing reassembled. The glass was proffered and the contents rapidly poured into a leathery neck, which responded with increased activity of its prominent and withered Adam's apple. Up and down it went like a lift in a shaft. With an appreciative smacking of lips and a slight belch the glass was handed back.

'Thanks, Mr Q. I'll get another part and fit it when you're not so busy.' He picked up his toolbox and turned to leave.

'Before you go, do you still look after Emma's car?'

'If you mean her battle waggon, yes Mr Q.' The old man grinned, exposing dazzling twin rows of teeth. 'She won't let anyone else touch it; only me'

'Is it in the garage now?'

'No. Haven't seen it since she went out on another one of her jaunts a few days back. Had me check out all the weapons and load it up fully with supplies and ammo before she went. She's still out there somewhere, far as I know. Want me to give her a call; find out where she is?'

'Please. Just want to make sure she's all right. I'm always the last she bothers to inform as to her whereabouts. Let Wendy know, will you?'

'Will do.' The door closed behind his stooped form. Lemuel turned to his doctor.

'Those teeth...?'

'All his own without any help from me. He's over seventy years old, would you believe?'

'Good God! He's in better condition than I was when I was in my teens.' He slapped his hands on the desk top and paid the price of inattention as a savage pain shot up his damaged finger. `Anyway, I've got work to do.' The intercom buzzed once more. Wendy spoke.

'Excuse me, sir. Can you tell Doctor Payne he's wanted up on ground level in the casualty block? His first customers are coming in.'

'Another attack?'

'Yes sir. Major Spode didn't want to bother you but this one looks as if it's rather bigger than usual. He's sure it can be contained between the first two fences, though. The lorry they used to break the gates open stalled and they weren't able to get it started again. The mob's using it as a springboard to get in. The major says he'll inform you if things get serious.'

'Thanks, Wendy.' He turned to the doctor, who was helping himself to an extra large slug from the badly depleted bottle. 'Looks like you'll be needing that, doc. Better get going.'

'On my way.' and the doctor puffed his foul cigar back into renewed life before rushing out of the room.

Lemuel sighed once more and heaved his massive bulk from the chair, replaced the bottle in the drawer and sat on the edge of his desk near the phone. In his chair he exuded an air of benevolent confidence and power. On his feet he was just a fat old man with a large, soft-looking head and small feet, the exact opposite of what one would expect the potential saviour of a small part of the human race to look like. Neither impression bespoke the truth. Born into and trained in the commercial ethics of a huge family business empire. Lemuel Quorvis possessed all the ruthlessness and ability to make tough decisions - and make them stick - necessary for the survival and profit of any successful tycoon. Secure in his isolation from the battle raging at ground level three floors up. Lemuel Quorvis sat and waited for the phone to ring.

CHAPTER 3

The attack on the bunker was only the latest in a continuous string of assaults dating back to the time when the underground complex was no more than a collection of wooden stakes connected with rope and wire. It had barely begun when Emma topped a rise in the ground and saw the small artificial mountain for the first time in over three days of travel.

Twenty-two years previously she had been christened Emma Sun Quorvis by decree of her adoptive father, Lemuel. He had to "arrange" an adoption because he had

34

been unable to produce any home grown offspring by virtue of a catastrophic failure of his breeding equipment which not even the resourceful Dr Payne had been able to reverse. Thus thwarted in his desire for a son, he had accepted the situation in bad grace by giving her the middle name of "Sun" and having her brought up as a boy. The compromise had never fully satisfied either of them.

'Now what?' A few puffs of white smoke caught her attention. They seemed to be coming from the outer perimeter close to the main gateway, about three miles from her position.

She disengaged the clutches and slowly drew to a halt using only the brakes. Powerful motors mumbled under the floor. The whisper of the air conditioning diminished as generator voltage dropped slightly, then stabilised. Emma sat and watched for any further activity. Several more plumes of smoke drifted up from the same place.

In this familiar territory, close to what passed for "home" these days, she didn't consider it necessary to have the armoured panels covering the windows; the locals should had received enough painful lessons to keep out of the way of Emma and her mobile fortress. Even so, the signs of conflict were a long way away and it was hard to make out exactly what was happening. Rotating the periscope from its normal rear view position, she centred the cross-hairs on the smoke and upped the magnification.

A drab scene of moving figures filled the screen; skinny sunburnt arms waved, men and women ran through drifting dust clouds towards the main gate of the bunker compound. Smoke drifted, partially obscuring the scene, but the rear end of a tipper lorry could just be seen securely wedged between the thick metal pillars supporting the hinges of a pair of heavy steel gates.

. A stepped ramp crudely constructed from bits of scrap led from the ground in front of the bonnet up to the cargo floor, which was tilted level with the driving cab.

Up this ramp climbed a steady stream of people clutching primitive weapons. Slipping, sliding back, pushed up by the press from behind, they reached the cab roof, hesitated and jumped or slid down out of Emma's sight. She increased the gain of the forward microphone, reduced its receiving cone and matched its directional function with the periscope targeting. A faint crackling (gunfire?) and generalised mob sounds came from the sound disc.

Another stupid raid. Emma snorted with exasperation. They never learned. They collected around the bunker, starving, weak and desperate, until someone worked them up enough to attack against impossible odds. Sticks and stones against modern weaponry and well-trained guards. Flesh versus steel. Flesh always lost.

Clutches were engaged once more. Twin engines growled and Emma turned the vehicle to mount a small hillock to one side of the shallow valley she had been following. Track drive retracted, the eight-wheeled vehicle leaned to one side and began to scrabble up the slope.

From the top, on a small plateau of hard-baked yellow clay, she had a much better view of what was going on. The artificial hill covering the bunker complex had been built on level ground in the centre of a wide, shallow valley. In the dusty distance she could just make out a darker line where the once mighty River Severn lay sullen, salty and polluted in its historical bed.

The choice of site had been a good one, she had to admit. Dad didn't make any mistakes that mattered, even now. Flat, not too far from a city and good local transport routes, yet far enough away from population supply routes to discourage all except those who had lost their way. More importantly, it was easy to gain access to a large clean aquifer unlikely to dry up totally during their stay. This had clinched the selection of the site: without water nothing else was possible.

During construction, water pumped from below had been used to fill a moat inside the perimeter fence. The bunker had been built in a huge hole gouged into the clay and rose two stories above ground level. The excavated earth had then been piled over the top to create a four-sided mound, similar to the ziggurat of ancient civilisations. Its flat top served as a helicopter pad complete with hangers and defensive artillery. Small recessed balconies, accessed from within the mound, served for sniper and machine gun posts.

At first, many of the people turning up at this isolated spot had been welcomed as extra labour and defenders; the promise of a chance to leave this dying planet representing an irresistible inducement to ensure their absolute loyalty. Most would have sold their souls for one square meal a week but the driving force behind the project, one Lemuel Quorvis, had always believed in treating his employees with a loyalty equal to that which he demanded of them; an almost unknown trait among twenty-first century industrial tycoons.

The great yellow construction and earth-moving machines were now sited in various places about the wide compound surrounding the ziggurat. A few were kept fuelled and in operational condition to provide auxiliary power and assault capability if required; the rest served as miniature fortresses from which small-arms fire could be directed. Two more fences, electrified from the main nuclear generator, had been erected at fifteen-yard intervals within the original barrier: the spaces between were mined and bristled with alarms and booby traps. The moat had dried out long ago.

Emma opened a bottle of cherry-flavoured mineral water and took a long drink while watching the familiar drama unfolding around the cross-hairs of her 'scope. Her first assessment was that poor old General Spode was having a hard time. There appeared to be many more people involved than she'd seen during any previous attack.

At some time during her absence their numbers had increased considerably. Disease in the city, maybe? More likely the rumour she'd heard about the drying up of food supplies, such as they were, was true. These folk had almost certainly come from over the river. From the state of some of those she could see it was a miracle they were still standing, let alone able to mount an attack.

Fools! Why didn't they just lie down and die decently instead of waiting for someone to get rid of them the hard way? Emma snorted again, inadvertently drawing a stream of fizzy cherry pop up her nose. In the distressing sneezing fit that followed she failed to hear the slight sounds coming from the rear of her vehicle.

Taking another swig from the bottle she decided to wait until the conflict around the gates had abated. She was pretty low on ammunition and fuel for the flame throwers; it had been a hard trip, but at least she had a full load of essential supplies for Doc Payne and the refectory.

Another tiny slithering sound came from overhead. This time Emma heard it. At the same moment there was a shattering bang and the right-hand door window exploded inwards showering her with small pellets of armoured glass.

A normal person would have shrunk away and been slow to react to such a sudden assault. Emma was not a normal person. She screamed, not with fear but in a false rage designed to provoke fear in others. Cherry pop splashed everywhere. She grabbed the ten-inch double-barrelled shotgun from its holster alongside the steering wheel as a pair of legs in tattered blue jeans swung through the window from above.

The twin-barrelled roar of such a lethal weapon in a confined space was terrifying. Rapidly-spreading BB shot under the impetus of a magnum load does not recognise any form of compromise; it blasted through the midriff of the unfortunate assailant, almost cutting him in half. Without any sound other than a pair of soft thuds, his upper half fell limply, struck the outside of the door and hung there held by his legs inside the cab acting as a counterweight. His exposed spine and bottom two pairs of ribs, garlanded with red fleshy tatters and scraps of dirty, ragged denim, was bent nearly double over the edge of the shattered glass. Blood pumped.

Emma continued to move like a striking snake. She swung the periscope to the rear of the vehicle, catching a quick view of a pair of blazing eyes set in a blotched and bearded face as it rotated. They were on the roof, some of them. With one hand she snapped down a large switch and the rising whine of a generator came faintly from under the floor; with the other she pressed the button which would raise the armour plate over all the windows. Only the one covering the right hand door failed to close properly. The corpse rose with it and held the top open by a couple of inches.

This lot must be strangers; nobody local would have been stupid enough to tackle Emma's waggon no matter how many or how desperate they were. She bared her small teeth in delight. The generator noise rose to a scream and a warning light glowed on the dashboard. The capacitors were fully charged.

Emma instantly pressed another button. A heavy relay closed with a click, the generator began to slow down and the fully loaded capacitors discharged their deadly voltage across a raised grid extending all over the external body of the vehicle, even under the floor. Faint screams came from the speaker disc and a drumming noise sounded along the roof.

It was her own fault, of course. All screens had been switched off; she'd driven the last few miles using only the windows. Memo: don't do it again! Always keep the screens on from now on even if they did distract from her driving.

Silence. Now to finish them off! This was the bit Emma liked best. Gently, almost reverently, she selected a medium reverse gear, engaged eight-wheel drive and the clutches, then floored the throttle pedal. The twin injection engines instantly howled and the heavy machine lunged backwards, all eight wheels spraying dust and stones.

The prospective bandits, about twenty of them still standing, were gathered at the rear of the vehicle staring in shock at the six bodies of their comrades lying on the ground. They were still twitching, shuddering, as motor reflexes overloaded by high voltage tried to obey the last commands given by their dying brains. The waggon's sudden movement caught them completely by surprise. Another six were crushed under the tearing wheels and several more sustained multiple broken bones as Emma swung the vehicle into a tight loop to avoid tipping down the slope.

She gave them no time to recover and attack once more, even if they were still in any condition to do so. The two front window shields dropped down and a series of blue sparks snapped across the mouths of a pair of holes drilled into the bulky bumper-bar. A thin stream of searing flame, angled slightly upwards, sprayed out of each hole like water from a hose. Seeing that she was aiming at the centre of the transfixed group, she reversed the waggon slightly, still in full lock, to ignite those to the right then went forward again, spraying burning fuel over the whole group as they belatedly woke up to their fate. They were miles too late.

'Got 'em!'

Slightly disappointed that the whole thing had taken less than ten seconds, she scrabbled on the floor to retrieve the bottle. It still contained a bit of liquid, which she poured down her throat while watching her barbecue burn itself out. Nobody had survived the onslaught; only now could she discern that there were at least a couple of children in the group, which meant there were almost certainly some women as well.

Emma didn't care. It was their own stupid fault for allowing non-combatants to take part in an attack. Serves 'em right! Dropping all the armour from the windows she leaned across and lifted the pair of legs still inside the cab over the top of the window frame. They quickly dropped out of sight. Then she switched on all the view screens. A bank of eight small pictures appeared above the windscreen.

What about the bunker?

Emma drove to her original position, deliberately travelling across the pyre. Charring bone popped and cracked; fluids splashed, hissing in the dying flames.

Nothing had changed. Moving the periscope to a forward position again showed people still clambering over the jammed lorry, although a large number had managed to reach the inner gate. Some had been electrocuted or shot and lay uncaring on the ground. A milling crowd clustered close to the steel mesh, many were carrying roughly-hacked sheets of steel in an attempt to shield themselves from bullets fired from within the compound. As she watched, several of these shields came together at a point where the twin gates met. A large individual carrying what looked like a woodsman's axe and wearing a pair of roughly-made gauntlets began to hack at the lock.

Sparks flew; the lock held. Furious blows continued to batter it. Several more people fell to the ground as the defenders realised what was going on and increased their fire. A heavy machine gun began to cough from one of the terrace pill-boxes.

This was looking serious. Emma swept the compound with her periscope. Stretcher bearers were running. Several bodies lay in the dust. They could only have been put down by firing from outside. This meant there were either guns or crossbows among the attackers.

Emma was getting hungry and that rabble was keeping her away from her dinner. Curse them all! Perhaps she'd better go and sort it out. Changing back into four-wheel drive she descended from the charnel plateau and headed over the plain at cruising speed towards the unequal battle.

Her approach was observed. As she entered the ramshackle camp clustered around the approach road people scattered out of her way and threw anything to hand at the waggon as it tore through all in its path. She didn't have to use force on these nearly defenceless people, being safe inside her impregnable killing machine, but she did so, anyway. First she switched on a recording of an interminable, tortured scream, obviously of human origin, and blasted it from the external sound discs, hugely amplified. Then she activated the flame-throwers to the front and sides to clear her path. A blackening trail of burning hovels lay strewn in her wake.

Few opposed her: those who did died without even a passing glance from the young woman at the wheel. Right up to the back of the lorry she drove. People fled, hands holding their ears closed against damage and pain from the shattering scream. It was so easy she didn't have to use any of her guns and waste precious ammunition. She switched off the front flamers and lit those to the rear to discourage the brave and the foolish.

Placing her right hand into a flexible metal-braced glove at the side of her seat, she twisted it and pushed forwards. With ponderous ease a massive hook welded to the end of a thick, heavily-greased shaft slid from the front of the waggon. Emma twitched a finger inside the glove. The hook straightened with a clang to become a thick, blunt spike. She raised her hand. Servos buzzed, hydraulic pumps took up the strain and the spike rose above the bed of the lorry. Moving the waggon forward a few yards, she brought her hand sharply down.

From then on it was easy. The spike fell, slammed, pierced the rotten flooring and continued downwards to embed itself in the chassis. Emma reversed; the lorry twisted and was slowly withdrawn from the gateway. The axe-wielder, a massive man with brawny arms and a face

42

contorted with hatred, burst into sight and reached up with his axe to smash against the front window shutter. A quick burst from one of the front flamers sent him tottering out of sight in a ball of fire.

Men ran across the compound and set up several machine guns to cover the entrance. With studied nonchalance Emma dragged the lorry backwards in a wide loop through the shelters, using it as a sweep to clear away everything near the gate. She continued reversing in a full circle to enter through the gateway until the lorry was blocking the entrance once more, facing outwards this time. The rear flamers had finished off those unwilling or unable to vacate the entrance passage.

Disengaging the spike she retracted the arm, cut the flamers and scream, drove through the now open inner gate and crossed the compound to the accompaniment of a ragged chorus of cheers. The people from the camp moved towards the outer gate once more, defeated, apathetic. Some began to collect the corpses.

'Nice job, Miss Quorvis, excellent work!' Daniel (General) Spode offered a hand to help Emma from the vehicle. She ignored it and jumped down, wincing a little at the stiffness in her legs.

General Spode paled suddenly. 'Good God! You're wounded. Stretcher! Quick, over here!'

Emma looked down at herself, at the ugly splash of redness all over her chest, waist and lap - then she laughed. 'No stretcher. It's only cherry pop. The washing machine will be of more use than a transfusion. Where's Josh?'

'Are you sure? Thank goodness!' Spode switched back to jovial briskness. 'He's probably in the garage ma'am, Want me to call him?'

'Never mind, I'll go over there myself. Get those gates locked up; there's no fight left in that lot out there now. It's quite safe.'

'Right away, Miss Quorvis.' and the "General" left on the trot. Emma watched him chivvy a few reluctant recruits into action with a look of distaste on her face. He had been just as toadying and sycophantic when he was Chief of Extraordinary Personnel for her father's industrial empire. He loved being referred to as "General" even though he'd never served in any armed forces.

Still, she had to acknowledge he was good at his job. She walked towards the garage entrance trying not to show how stiff her legs were.

Old Josh was in the back of the workshop scratching among a pile of cardboard boxes. Now *here* was a man she really respected and even asked for advice, sometimes. Probably the only one. She tip-toed quietly towards him.

'Morning Josh.' she said giving him a small push and causing him to tip forward and flatten the box he was peering into, 'I'm home.'

The old man rolled onto his back and looked up at her, eyes twinkling.

'Welcome back Emma. Had a good trip? Find any tyres for me?'

Vehicle tyres of the right sizes were among the most difficult items to get that they really needed at the moment. Emma's waggon wheels, with their armoured and plated casings wouldn't need to be replaced for another ten years, at least. Even then it still had the tracks to get around on.

'Only a few. They were jolly difficult to get, too. 'She didn't mention how difficult. She said nothing of the virtual massacre of a small community living on the brink of starvation, who'd taken up residence around a tyre depot; burning the precious casings as fuel for cooking and warmth. It wasn't so much she thought Josh would disapprove; to her, it was just a normal method of obtaining vital goods. Kill and take.

'As long as you've got us a few to carry on with. Give us a hand up, will you? He extended a thin arm ending in a large, heavily-veined hand. Emma clasped it firmly. The next moment she was in among the boxes and the old mechanic was dancing about just out of reach, cackling and grinning. 'Gotcha! Never thought you'd fall for that one.'

'I'm just tired. Now help me up.'

'A big healthy girl like you? Use your own energy! I'm too old to risk a strain. Any damage to the waggon?'

Emma struggled to her feet and brushed herself down. 'No damage except to one of the windows. Ammo's low though, and the flamer fuel is just about out. I don't expect to be going out for a few days but maybe you'd better get it up to scratch as soon as possible in case they try to break down the gates again.'

'Yes, I think that bunch out there are just about at the end of their tether or they'd never have tried it on. Digging under the fences or trying to climb over is one thing, but using a lorry to break open the gates is something else. Can't understand where they managed to find the fuel to get it moving, either. Anyway, roll it in here and I'll get started on the job. Should be ready this time tomorrow.'

'Thanks Josh.' Emma moved quietly away: see father next. Then eat, then sleep.

CHAPTER 4

It was easy; every bit as easy as Dave said it would be. Even the initial entrance to the apartment block posed no problems, just like Dave had said.

In full view of three of three other blocks they dismantled the flimsy barricade to the lift-shaft basement inspection door, a small entrance about three feet square at ground level. Nobody was patrolling the outside of the building and nobody bothered to come and check on what they were doing; it only took a couple of minutes, anyway, and they made no noise. The block guardians hadn't even bothered to make the access secure; all they'd done was conceal it behind an old door - just leaned it up against the wall across the grille. Move the door, use the shaft of

Shinks's "Basher"- a short length of scaffold tube, flattened, bent and filed to a chiselled jemmy-edge at one end with the head of a builder's lump hammer bolted to the other - to lever the grille away from the wall and climb in. The grille and door were then put back in place to assist in a quick getaway by a fifth member of the gang, a young boy, who promptly ran to hide in an abandoned ruin a short distance away to await their return.

From the bottom of the lift shaft, all they had to do was climb the metal latticework bolted to one wall. Quietly, very quietly. All exit doors were tightly closed until the climbers reached the eighth floor. There was no chance of someone using the lift; the power drain required was way over the limit of what was available and the control boxes had been removed, anyway. Nothing that took more than five amps to work was allowed in the block, and even then only one floor at a time, or the fuse would trip.

The lift doors to the eighth floor were damaged, just like Dave had said they'd be. There was a gap at the bottom large enough to get the jemmy through for leverage, but the sliding doors met correctly at the top. Shinks hung onto the lattice and listened. Faint sounds came from the other side of the doors. Shinks and his motley crew clung to the metalwork like a troupe of great slovenly spiders, trying to breath without gasping until they got their wind back from the exertions of the long climb in the suffocating heat.

There were guardians behind the door. Every floor had at least two - except at feeding time when one of them would leave to assist with distributing the grub delivered by the daily supply trucks. He would only return when this had been completed, bringing both his own and his companions' supplies with him. Shinks figured it wouldn't be long before there would be only one guardian to deal with. About ten minutes later voices were raised in conversation on the other side. Shinks strained his cauliflower ear, the only one working properly, to catch what was said. One of the guardians announced his intention to go downstairs. Shinks made out footsteps, the sound of a door slamming - hopefully the one to the stairwell - then silence. He tried unsuccessfully to see through the gap and almost lost his balance on his perch. But there was nothing to see, either. Count ten to go! He signalled to his companions. Ready? Nods all round in the gloom.

Shinks braced his booted feet against a vertical rod and dribbled saliva on to the end of his hammer handle before quietly inserting it in the gap at floor level and pushing. The metal penetrated a couple of inches without a sound. He wished he knew where the remaining guardian was located - hopefully there would only be one. With a practised twist and thrust he wrenched the hammer head and levered hard. The doors flew open as they were designed to do. Shinks kicked powerfully, plunging into the hallway and altering his grip on the hammer as he skidded on his side across the floor.

The guardian, a poor specimen of his ilk, was taken completely by surprise. He had propped himself up against the wall next to the lift doors to take advantage of the draught rising up the shaft and through the gap near the floor. The pack of greasy playing cards he had been riffling through scattered as he tried to throw himself towards the stairwell door. He didn't stand a chance and he knew it. He opened his mouth to yell a warning but before any sound issued forth the head of Shinks's hammer caught him under the lower jaw and drove most of it through his palate and up into his nasal cavity together with slivers of splintered, crushed bone and a couple of the sparse teeth still in his possession.

Within seconds they were all through the doors and out into the hallway, weapons at the ready. Nothing happened. No one came to investigate the sounds of the scuffle. So far, so good. Shinks approached the nearest door and lifted his freshly- bloodied hammer once again.

For the third time Wuggles circled his red plastic food bowl, searching in vain for a particularly savoury portion he *knew* was there - he could smell it - but was unable to locate no matter what he did. It was most frustrating. His stomach growled as he pushed at the small pile of food in the bowl with his nose, overturning a few drying scraps without success. Since he'd taken the trouble to search, and was here already, he might just as well eat something. He selected a bit of crispy, unidentifiable material from the bottom of the bowl and gnawed at it, choking a little.

Now what? Sitting back on his haunches he gazed across to the woman sitting on a rickety chair in front of a mis-matched table in the centre of the small room. She appeared to be studying a sheet of paper. Likely to be unavailable for some time, he decided, no diversion there. May as well try to go back to sleep. Wash face first.

A few licks of a paw followed by a desultory wipe across the muzzle completed his toilet - Wuggles was not the most fastidious of creatures; dried food still clung to the side of his mouth - and stood up, stretched, yawned and slowly wandered across to his basket in the corner under the window. More than half a day to wait before the man would come in. A long time, but perhaps things would look up then and he could have a game of some sort to exercise his muscles. Succumbing to another bored yawn he curled up in the basket, put his nose under a smelly paw and tried to sleep.

The woman read the news sheet, unaware of her disgruntled pet trying to pass the time of day. The news printed on the single page of many-times-recycled brownish paper bore no relationship to what she knew was really happening out there in what was left of the world, or to the gossip she picked up on her daily visit to the wash room downstairs on the first floor. Still, the cheery propaganda hype sometimes helped to create a faint mood of optimism, even a cynical chuckle when a particularly outrageous statement or claim was earnestly put forward.

The so-called news was obviously fictitious rubbish but it was better than nothing. At least someone out there was trying, for what reason wasn't clear.

With a sigh she folded the sheet and crossed to the door. A quick glance through the spy-hole revealed only the two guardians sprawled on the floor engrossed in a card game. Sliding the draw-bolts across she went out and knocked at the next door along. A thin, pale woman answered after a short pause.

'I've finished with this now, can you pass it along?'

The woman bent her scrawny neck in some sort of a nod, grabbed the news-sheet and slammed the door shut all in one quick, smooth motion. The first woman returned to her apartment, bolting the door behind her. She crossed to the only window the apartment possessed and looked out at the city baking in the midday heat, sprawling untidily down to the docks. The depot where her husband worked could just be discerned at the edge of the river, perched on a mound of rubble out of reach of high tides. A small tug trailing a long line of barges floated motionless downstream of the barrage across the river, waiting for enough water to spill over the lip before hauling its cargo up to the food depot. Two body-carriers were getting ready to leave the dockside.

The only activity to be seen within the perimeter of the food depot was around a beaten-up lorry, where a gang of ragged men were struggling to hoist what looked like an engine into the open bonnet. As she watched, one of the men slipped and fell. The heavy engine tilted to one side and rested on top of a plank supported by scaffold poles. For a few moments the scene held motionless then the plank snapped and the engine fell to the ground. The men just stared at it, their postures suggesting a mixture of hopelessness and apathy. The woman turned away from the window, pity filling her. They tried so hard, some of them. Oh God, how they tried! But it was useless. Everything was

49

useless. Why did they bother to carry on? No help would ever come - there was nowhere for it to come from.

She sat again at the table. Too soon to think about preparing some food for Gildas. He wouldn't be home until just before dark, at the earliest. At least six hours yet, and she'd already cleaned through their tiny one-roomed apartment as well as she could. Maybe she could switch the radio on; the battery should be nearly charged up by now. Undecided, she remained seated, resting her head on one elbow; a small woman, nearly past the first flush of middle age and starting to put on a little weight at last thanks to the extra food rations Gildas was able to bring home. Neat in appearance, tidy in nature and even-tempered, the last fifteen years since they had married very tolerable in comparison to the muddled carnage all about them. Gildas could justly claim responsibility for that with his determination to maintain his own idea of civilised standards even if it meant doing things the hard way. Not that he would have agreed with such a flattering assessment. It was just his way. Thank God she'd ended up with him! Not much to look at, true (neither was herself, she had to admit), but an oasis of strength in the midst of a desert of defencelessness.

A high-pitched wavering sound intruded upon her musings. Then several more, ending each time with a soft snort. Wuggles was snoring! The woman glanced at the basket in the corner. Yes, he was sound asleep. How long had they had him now? There was so little to mark the passage of time. At least five years, it must be. He lay curled inside the worn wickerwork, oblivious to the world; a perfect specimen of his race. Short, smooth creamy fur all over except for brown ears, tail and the lower parts of his legs where his socks would be if he wore any. The only other discoloration was across the face; a brown mask pierced by two electric-blue eyes - when they were open. They were closed in deep slumber now and his long white whiskers twitched in response to frantic activity within his dreams. The woman wondered how he found anything to dream about.

Wuggles was a Siamese cat, pure-bred more by accident than intent although he possessed no piece of paper to prove his immaculate heredity. Neutered, a bit corpulent and carrying a floppy bag of loose skin between his stomach and hind legs like a broody marsupial; a perfectly normal Siamese cat, at that. Playful, good-natured and often suffocatingly affectionate with those he liked. He slept on.

From the other side of the door she heard a sudden scuffling followed by a muffled bang. The woman looked up, concern on her face. Any unusual noise was potentially dangerous and should be investigated - investigated from a safe distance, Gildas had instructed her. She felt strangely reluctant to do so. She listened. No further sounds came but some instinct told her things were not as they should be. A sense that something lurked the other side of the door gradually grew upon her. Look, she must.

Uncertainly, she approached the unpainted door not knowing why she should feel so afraid at a single unexplained noise. Any problems out in the hall should be dealt with by the guardians, shouldn't they? And they were eight floors up, besides. She looked at the basket. Wuggles hadn't heard anything, he still languished in the gentle arms of a feline Morpheus, but then he'd always led a protected life. His survival instincts would have been eroded away to the point of extinction at his age.

In an abrupt change of mood at her own silliness she put her eye to the peephole just in time to see a blocky object swinging in a distorted arc across her field of view towards the door-handle side, shutting out the tiny glimpse she caught of a huddled form slumped against one wall of the hallway. A massive bang shook the flimsy door. The top bolt flew from its seating, the hardboard cladding slammed against her forehead and Wuggles leapt out of his basket with a screech. Another violent bang came from lower

51

down and the door crashed open, spinning the woman round, trapping her against the wall behind its swing. There was a rush of feet, and the door rebounded, allowing the stunned woman to sink to the floor. She moaned in shock, closing her eyes in response to the pain in her head.

Silence. No, she could hear breathing. Better keep her eyes closed until whoever it was went away. Something hard struck her side. She convulsed, barely managing to suppress a shout of pain. Silence again, then...

... 'Well?' asked a voice, slightly effeminate.

'Have a look around!' said another. More authoritative, this one. 'I'll keep her quiet.' There came the sound of tearing cloth.

They're going to gag me, she thought. No! No! With a desperate surge, ignoring the sharp pain in her side, she rolled sideways and opened her eyes. A glimpse of dirty shoes and trousers, then the floor. Another glimpse of Wuggles crouching beneath the redundant cooker, eyes wide, black, with white showing at the sides. She was grabbed, her frantic rolling stopped, and somebody fell on her. She screamed and thrashed her legs trying to get to her feet. No chance. Quiet again, she looked around as far as she could see, trying to judge what was happening.

Four men were in the room with her, one standing against the closed door. So much for getting out. They were all looking at her. Thin, ragged and with the universal look of bestiality she associated with the swarming masses of sub-humanity on all sides. Seasoned killers without doubt. Terror threatened to engulf her tiny grip on self-possession.

'Take what you want and go!' she managed to say in a trembling voice.

'Don't worry, girl, we will.' said one who seemed to be in a slightly better condition that the rest. 'Where do you keep the grub?'

'In the oven over there. Take it and go!'

The scruff nodded to one of the others, who opened the oven door exposing the small cache of food; a few tins and a pile of protein blocks. He produced a cloth bag from somewhere among his rags and started to throw the supplies into it. In his haste, a couple fell on the floor.

'Clumsy slob.' grumbled the irritated legislator. 'Pick 'em up quick and let's get out of here before the other sentry gets back or we'll have to take on the whole bunch downstairs.'

'No need to worry about that,' the clumsy slob reassured him, bending to retrieve the food blocks. He looked under the cooker. 'Hey, Shinks, There's a cat under here. Didn't you tell me you knew someone ready to pay well for live dogs or cats? A bit of exchange goods would be handy. Better than skinning it and putting it in the pot.' He reached for Wuggles who spat at him and crouched further in as if trying to press through the wall.

'Leave it till we go!' Shinks ordered. 'We'll have to tidy up at least one loose end first.' He nodded at the woman lying on the floor.

The clumsy slob caught on fast. He wasn't really a bad bloke. He'd just fallen on hard times like everyone else. He decided to register a token protest.

'She can't do us any harm, Shinks. Let's take what we want and go before we're trapped in here. We get caught, we're dead. You know that. Where do you keep the medicines, if you've got any?' This last to the groggy woman.

'I know that ... Dave. That's what I was going to do ... Dave. You're the one who fouled that idea up ... Dave. Get the picture ... Dave?'

'Aw, hell. I didn't think. Perhaps if she gave her word ...?'

'What the hell are you talking about? Want to take the risk? I sure as hell won't. What about you two?' he turned to the others. 'Well?'

The one by the door strolled across to the table and leaned on it. He regarded the woman through hooded eyes. 'Gag her, then we'll have a vote.' He grinned, revealing an

53

irregular row of yellow stumps. The woman looked wildly around. She had a bad feeling about this. With no-one to stop it, the door began to swing open slowly.

The one called Shinks crouched down to tie a strip of cloth across her mouth. In panic the woman reached up and clawed his face with her nails. Shinks fell over, roaring. As the others began to move forward she scrabbled to her feet and backed up against the small sink. A tiny knife lay at the bottom. The only weapon available to her! She grabbed it and threatened them, waving it around uncertainly.

They backed off, but no-one went near the door. The woman rushed for it, extending the little knife in front of her. They split up, all moving further away. She saw the opportunity and took a couple of swift steps towards the now fully open door.

Shinks tripped her up. Somebody kicked hard at her wrist until she had to let the knife go; several broken bones saw to that. Somebody else closed the door. A savage blow to the head caused her to lose consciousness for a few minutes. When she became aware once more she found she was on the bed, only able to see to one side because of the jerking, gasping body lying on top of her. She tried to scream but only tasted rancid cloth. No sound came. It didn't take long before the expected grunt of release and lessening of pressure as her violator rolled off, helped to a large extent by the eager hands of the next customer. She saw the knife at his belt. She snatched at it. Broken wrist bones grated and sent waves of pain up her arm. She used the other hand. The knife came free and she stabbed blindly up. Instant reward came in the sound of a screech of mortal agony and shock.

That was her last conscious action before she fell onto the floor. All she was aware of after that final surge of resistance were thudding blows, kicks and sharp slicing sensations as a thick, bloodstained knife pierced her ribs again and again. The final picture before the termination of her agony was that of a small, defenceless cat still crouching under the cooker; frightened and helpless to prevent her death even if it was aware of what was occurring. Her closing thoughts, just before Shinks bought his ghastly hammer into play, removed all aspects of her plight but instead held to a concern of the probable fate of her pet, and just before the final blackness overtook her, a certainty that Gildas would be home soon to set things right again.

Didn't he always?

CHAPTER 5

A rare darkening sky scattered a thin film of sparse mist onto the streets of Town; millions of microscopic tears. Gutters trickling with just a thin flow of filthy water left from the last high tide tried vainly to empty themselves down drains blocked with trash and decaying organic debris, failed, and spread out into sullen pools over the crumbling tarmac, containing all manner of discarded material. Elsewhere it disappeared immediately into the parched earth.

The whole city assumed an even more forbidding aspect than usual during this kind of highly unusual weather quite in keeping with the emotional condition of the lonely figure trudging towards the suburbs, splashing unheeding through the refuse-laden squalor.

What a ghastly day it had been! Overcast, grey; a light wind steadily blowing a fine, mist through the shallow canyons of the city, swirling in sudden miserable confusion at every street corner; soaking, damp, unhappy.

Gildas wandered blindly, allowing instinct and mental auto-pilot to guide his way home, the thin mistiness mingling with the tears flowing unchecked, unnoticed and unashamed to drip down onto his dampening top-coat. The incoming tide followed him relentlessly through the dockside streets, sometimes almost catching him up, sometimes impeded temporarily by little dams of debris in the roadway, always striving towards the high water mark some seven feet up the sides of the gutted and crumbling buildings, increasing a little bit more every week that passed.

It was done! Over! Finished! A sudden gap had been created between now and whatever future there may be. Was there really any future worth having? Was any future required, necessary or even desirable? At the moment it didn't seem likely and Gildas allowed this trend of thought to continue - as it had done for the last three days.

Three days? Only three days since the outside world had invaded and destroyed his final defence; his private sanctuary; his retreat from what was horribly real: invaded, desecrated, assaulted and killed nearly all he held dear. Not a lot to hold dear, true, but all he had, and *they* had done it, taken it away. Probably laughed and joked when they were doing it, too - had a good time - got away and would almost certainly go unpunished for their crime.

Slowly he moved out of the city centre into the dormitory suburbs still safely above high tide, his tormented mind progressing from misery to utter despair as he entered the twenty-acre apartment-block enclave built on a narrow strip of flat land at the side of the valley. There was another and bigger site on top of the hill. Monolithic living structures; functional, soulless and uncaring. Built fast and cheap, all financial corners cut in a panicky last-ditch effort to house the teeming millions of ruined refugees fleeing for their lives from hotter countries.

It was a terrible place to live, to have one's home. There seemed to be a sort of unseen barrier, almost a cultural threshold to be crossed between the old city and the shabby new tenement ghettos. Shutters protecting the few remaining shops still managing to make a living by selling home-produced goods were stronger here, cruder, much repaired and presenting a defiant challenge to the often-mounted attacks of local gangs when they had nothing better to do. Not a good place to walk alone. Especially in the state Gildas was in.

His sense of danger had become eroded with grief and as a result he failed to notice the two figures sheltering from the light drizzle under the remains of a small tree in the garden of a burnt-out ground-floor living unit.

As he approached, one of them abruptly stepped out in front of him with a hand raised.

'Stop! Wait a while!'

Gildas hardly knew the man was there until he bumped into him. Then he stopped. The despair increased.

Oh no. Not now, for God's sake, he thought, aware that a second figure had stepped quietly out behind him. He began to feel afraid, a sensation somehow at odds with his previous depression.

'What you want?' he muttered.

'Don't be scared, you're among friends. Friends should be happy together and share things. Have you anything to share with your friends?' The man's voice was mild and cultured. He did not fit with the type normally found around here. He smiled insincerely and put his hands into his pockets.

Gildas just wanted to go home, or to what was left of it. Defiance flared and was immediately regretted. 'I'm never scared among friends but today's the wrong day. I'm empty. How about you share with me?'

The implied challenge appeared to be unacceptable to his new friends. He heard the movement from behind at the same time as he saw the smile disappear from the face in front of him and he allowed his legs to collapse. The bludgeon swung from behind at his head knocked his hat off. He rolled onto his back, bent his stubby legs and kicked upwards - hard. A pained shout and that one was down; now for the one in front who was already coming forward with a thin knife in one hand.

Gildas was still on his back. He rolled to the left and lashed out viciously with his right foot. More by luck than anything else, the steel toe-cap of his boot stuck the man on the side of the knee. He fell, dropping the knife to clutch at his leg, which seemed to be bent sideways. Quickly Gildas leapt to his feet and kicked him hard in the side of the head - then did it again to make sure. He stood for a moment to make sure both his attackers would remain on the ground long enough for him to escape, saw the knife on the ground by his hat and picked them both up.

As he began to walk away he felt his legs begin to shake and the panic, which should normally have occurred the moment he became aware of any danger, welled up in his chest. His nerve suddenly snapped and he ran as fast as his wobbly legs would allow.

It wasn't very far to the block where he lived but as he approached the panic and unsteadiness handicapped him so much he didn't think he was going to make it.

The battered door to the block suddenly loomed in front of him but before he could pass inside he was seized by a group of ragged hoodlums who had been hiding behind a screen of junk and desiccated bushes each side of the door. They half-carried him inside and threw him sprawling onto the hall floor; a floor paved with large tiles, chipped, cracked and smeared with stains; some dark and ominous like those on the walls. Many a pitched battle had been fought here without quarter or mercy, and it showed. The scars and terrible stains were prized as trophies of past victories and served as a warning to strangers that the resident guardians of this apartment block had a worthy track record.

Gildas lay shivering and gasping while his scruffy crew of captors (or saviours) formed a tight ring around him. These were not exactly friends, rather they were allies to whom every tenant of the block paid in cash or kind to keep things as safe and secure as possible. Nobody had much choice; it was pay up or else! If you fell in with a good and well-organised gang you were lucky. This was a pretty good bunch who'd done a fair job - until recently.

Panic ebbed away. Someone said 'It's the guy from floor eight, y'know, the one that had the trouble.' The voice rose. 'Hey, Jeggs! Out here!'

Noises of agreement sounded as several others recognised their erstwhile victim and turned away. A man came out of the former caretaker's office: Leo Jeggs, the temporary gang leader - all gang leaders were temporary. His dark, hooded eyes surveyed the bundle on the floor without interest.

'Yeah, I know him. What's he doin' on the floor? Hey, you! Get up!'

He prodded Gildas gently with a table leg he carried. A thick, moulded table leg with nails, hooks and screws driven into the squared-off thick end. Dented, splintered and coated with a congealed stickiness. A frightening weapon. 'Hey, I said get up! What the hell happened?'

'Mugged. Empty. Tried to hurt me.'

'Stand up, man!'

Gildas rose shakily from the floor. Nobody offered to help him.

'You're not hurt or cut, even. They just left you alone, did they?'

It was meant to be a type of joke. A couple of the more sycophantic scruffs responded with a snuffle of derision. It just wasn't done. If you were empty you got hurt. Everyone carried an offering for when (not if) they got mugged. Even having something to hand over was no guarantee of safety - not all muggers followed the rules.

'I made them let me go.'

'How?'

'Downed them both and ran like hell.'

'Sure! Weak, were they? Starving, eh? Two of 'em? Where'd you leave 'em?'

'Back towards Town centre outside where the folk got torched last month.'

Jeggs rubbed his chin as if deep in thought; purely a gesture of indecision. Jeggs had a great deal of trouble stringing two corresponding coherent thoughts together. With his muscles there wasn't much need for high intelligence. 'Suppose we'd better check it out.'

'You're damned right you'd better check it out.' Gildas shouted, surprising himself as well as the onlookers with a sudden surge of anger. He felt secure now, and besides . . . 'You owe me, Jeggs. The whole lousy bunch of you owe me. About time you did what we pay you for.'

Even as he said this he knew he was being unfair. They did a good job on the whole, except for last week. It would take a long time before he let them off the hook for *that.* All the same, better not antagonise them too much. He needed them more than they needed him

Jeggs didn't seem to mind. One thought at a time, that was Jeggs. He motioned to a bunch of thugs blocking the stairs to the upper floors. 'Go check it out. Anyone there, bring him in. Know where to go?'

A few nods and mumbles drifted from the motley crew as they moved outside into the dark, automatically spreading out into a defensive pattern, their marked lack of enthusiasm due to the very real dangers of leaving their home patch at night. They were only breaking the habit because, as Gildas had forcefully reminded them, they owed him.

He was kept near the door and told to wait. Jeggs went back to his office and switched on the outside floodlight mounted on the fifth floor. Four whole levels of apartments blacked out to compensate for the sudden power drain. The rest of the gang resumed their vigil behind the barricades flanking the front door. Gildas waited.

Shortly, the investigative patrol came into view, shoving one of the muggers - the one with the modified groin - in front of them. Gagged with a piece of cloth torn from his own shirt he was brought into the hall and Jeggs called. Jeggs looked him over. 'Where's the other one?'

'Other one's a goner. Head all pulpy; bit of brain out one ear. Slung him in the torched unit.' The speaker pushed the captive closer to Jeggs. 'This one just laying there.'

Jeggs waved Gildas over. 'This one of `em? Y'heard y'killed the other?'

'Didn't look at their faces. If he was there then he was one of them. Pity about his mate, not that I could care less.' Gildas managed to keep an impassive face in spite of the shock coursing through him.

The gang boss studied Gildas' face carefully. 'Trouble is he now knows you an' where you're staying. He'll have to go as well to be on the safe side in case he's a new recruit in one of the other local blocks. Doesn't appear to bother you much. Maybe you'd like to go back with them and see to the job yourself?'

Gildas thought rapidly. He had never been directly responsible for a death before today and now he was being asked if he wanted to do another one. His recent attacker was doomed whether he did the job or left it to the gang. If the gang performed the deed as a matter of sensible security against possible reprisals against the block it would mean that they would no longer feel any obligation to him and he could ask for no more favours.

Jeggs wasn't always as stupid as he looked. He occasionally had a good day.

'I'll do it.' said Gildas, feeling in his pocket for the knife he had confiscated. It had pierced the fabric of his pocket and cut his leg. He could now feel the trickle of blood and to make things worse he sliced his hand trying to get it out of the pocket. It was horribly sharp and it was only fitting that it should be used against one of those who would have murdered him without hesitation. This guy was only a stinking mugger! He concentrated on thoughts of hatred to brace his courage and pressed the slender blade into its slot then tried to open it again from the side of the blood-slicked (his *own* blood) handle. It wouldn't budge! Cursing under his breath he struggled with the stubborn blade until

61

one of the female gang members, reached out and took it from his hand, saying, 'Here, give that to me!'

Gildas recognised the voice. It was Clare, one of the women in the gang, reputed to be their most experienced fighter. Even Jeggs treated her with something approaching respect, or at least, deference. 'Watch this!' she said, pointing to a feature on the handle Gildas hadn't noticed. A small seven-pointed silver star was inset flush with the wood surface close to one end. Clare pressed it down with a fingernail and Gildas barely heard a tiny click as the blade was released. Still nervous, he opened the blade fully and nodded his readiness to continue.

They dragged their stumbling victim back to the burnt-out unit. Inside, by the weak light of the security lamp adorning the nearest block, they slammed him upright against a wall for Gildas to perform the job.

A thought occurred to him. 'I'm going to remove the gag. If you yell, I'll kill you instantly, understand?'

'Mmf. Mmf.' The gag came off. 'Thanks.'

'Ever been in our unit before?'

The blank, scared look in the captive's eyes was replaced with one of hope.

'Can't remember. Why?'

'Think hard! Maybe we can sort something out.'

'Like what?' No answer. 'Tell me why you want to know an' maybe I can come up with some info for you.'

Gildas raised the knife so the man could see it. It was very thin and had evidently seen much use. The blade glowed with a yellow dullness in the sickly light of the lamp. The man swallowed and looked elsewhere.

`There was a raid on floor eight last week. A woman was raped, killed and carved up. Things were taken that meant a lot to me. The woman was my wife.' He jabbed the knife towards the man's eyes. 'Know anything about it? Anything at all? Pleeeassse.' Gildas' voice faded to a venomous, trembling hiss. Small drops of saliva spattered the victim's face.

The man flinched. He could recognise the signs of madness in the ugly runt with the muscular shoulders who had him at his mercy. Mercy? There was none evident on the face in front of him. He swallowed again, slightly surprised that such a dry mouth and throat as he had could have produced anything to swallow.

'I do know something about it, I think. Wasn't directly involved myself but I might know who did it if we can come to a deal.'

'Here's the only deal you'll get. You'd better take it. Give me names and I'll let you go, alive and in one piece. This I promise. Sell me short and I'll hunt you down and gut you like a fish. This I also promise. What's it to be?'

One of the thugs holding the mugger began to get impatient. 'Look, man, make this as quick as you can, will you? We can't leave the block for too long in case there's a raid tonight. It's perfect weather for it.'

'This shouldn't take long.' Gildas faced the mugger again. 'Come on, spit it out!'

'Four guys. Only know two names, Shinks and Dave. Freelance, like us. Don't run with any block. Kipped down here for one night last week. Needed some trade goods and decided to do your unit. Random selection, nothing personal against you. Wanted me and my mate there to go with `em.' He nodded towards the twisted bundle of clothes under the window sill. 'We said no chance, so they went anyway. That's it.'

'Fair enough. Did they say how they were going to get in?'

'Said they'd seen the inspection door bottom of the lift shaft back of the block wasn't covered with anything too heavy. Easy to shift, get in and climb up the shaft. Floor eight was probably the first one they were able to force the doors open. All they needed was a bit of luck to get in and time it for when the nosebags are handed out, they'd be able to clobber any guard quick.'

Gildas had heard enough. 'OK, let's get him back to the block.'

'You're not going to finish him?' Clare sounded very disappointed. 'You're really going to let him go?'

'Jeggs said he was mine to do what I like with. This is what I want to do. He'll live, but on my terms.' He winked at Clare.

She noticed the wink even in the gloom. Grunted in disgust she roughly pulled the mugger away from the wall, tripped him up and trod heavily over the length of him on her way out of the unit.

'You want him back, you bring him back!' She beckoned to the others and they all headed back the way they had come, growling under their breath.

Gildas helped the winded mugger back on to his feet. 'If you want to live, keep up with them and don't try to escape. I gave you a promise and I'll stick to it.'

They trotted after the gang, who ignored them entirely, and made the short distance back to the block without incident. Jeggs was not impressed. 'Bottled out, eh?'

'Nope. Got two names for you. Ones that did my unit. Dave and Shinks. Ever heard of them?'

Jeggs shook his head. Aware of his obligations he added. 'We'll look out for them and do the necessary when they're found. That suit you OK?'

Gildas knew that was all he could expect for the moment. If ever the culprits were found, revenge would be taken and the results shown to the block tenants to advertise what a good job the guardians were doing. Good PR. Looking after their own, etc, etc. 'Right. I'll get rid of this one now - in my own way. Can I borrow Clare for a few minutes?'

'Sure.' Jeggs was feeling expansive; Gildas was about to disillusion him. 'All square now, eh?'

'Not on your life.' Gildas still felt he had nothing to lose and faced up to the gang boss. 'You still owe me. I'm sorting this out myself and just asking you for a little help, is all. You still owe me, right?'

Jeggs wasn't bothered. 'Yeah, yeah. Talk about it later. Want to go with him, Clare?'

Clare didn't, not really, but although she still felt contempt at Gildas for being a wimp she was curious about how he would dispose of his victim. 'OK. Suppose someone should watch his back. C'mon, get out there!' She booted the mugger hard in the direction of the door. He fell, sprawled, adding another mark to the pitted floor. Gildas cast her a look of dislike, helped the mugger up and half-carried him outside, surprised at the light weight of the man.

The three walked to the rear of the building. All windows of the lower three floors were blocked up and impregnable against intruders. Nobody could see them. Gildas released the mugger. 'Stop!' The man stopped, turned and faced them. 'Strip!'

'Oh, come on!' The man half-turned, poised to run. Clare glided forward like a panther, hand hunting at her waist to choose the right sort of knife. The man realised he wouldn't get away if he bolted. 'No! Not that. Please!'

Gildas forced all thoughts of the probable fate of his captive out of his mind. This man would have killed him earlier if he'd been given the chance. 'I promised to let *you* go, that's all. Everything else stays here. Now strip!'

They all knew what his fate was likely to be. Without clothes or weapons he would be easy prey for any outcasts like himself. He would be lucky indeed to find any mercy among the beasts of the night-time city.

The man stripped, deliberately casting the clothes into a puddle. Gildas watched silently, intent upon suppressing any feelings of pity or even sympathy. It didn't take long; the man possessed no underclothing and finally stood before them wearing only the clothing bestowed by God. He straightened, ignoring a disparaging snigger from Clare.

Naked, he assumed an inappropriate air of dignity. 'Now what?'

'Go!' Gildas pointed towards the city.

'At least let me keep the knife. I need some kind of defence, you know that. Please!'

Gildas removed the knife from his pocket, considered for a moment and went to hand it to the mugger. With a sudden movement Clare snatched it from his grasp. 'No. It stays here.'

'Oh come *on!* We can't let him go out there without any protection at all. I just want to punish him, not be responsible for his death. Let him have the knife, at least!' He pointed to the small pile of clothes in the puddle. 'And the sheath, there.'

'Please!' begged the man, now starting to shiver violently with the cold. 'The knife. Please. You'll never see me again, I promise.'

'Get lost!' Clare's amusement disappeared. She strode rapidly towards the wretched, shivering figure. 'Over there. Get! Now! Or maybe I'd better kick you the first few hundred yards,'

The man swayed, undecided. Clare tensed. With a muffled sound, a cross between a groan of despair and a plea for mercy, he turned away, shuddering, and broke into a shambling trot across the hard-packed earth in the direction of the shadow cast by a short row of roofless houses. Gildas shrugged and bent to retrieve the sheath for the knife from the puddle then began to retrace his steps towards the safety of the block. Clare could carry the rest of the gear back if she wanted it that badly.

Half way back he heard Clare trotting to catch him up. She fell into step beside him. 'That's got rid of him.' she said with a hint of satisfaction. Gildas was in no mood to be friendly.

'Why didn't you let me deal with him as I wanted?' he said. 'You didn't have to send him away like that.'

'You got the clothes?'

'No.'

'Nor me.'

Gildas glanced at the powerful, yet feminine form striding alongside. She was not carrying anything and was regarding him with a quizzical look. 'If you've got a problem, spit it out.'

'You left his things there?'

'Sure. No good to me. It's up to him now. Depends how stupid or scared he is. If he's got any sense he'll watch till we left then wait a while to collect his gear. It's his own fault if its all wet; he put it in that puddle deliberately. Don't suppose you noticed he didn't take his shoes off?' Gildas shook his head. 'Well I did, but didn't say anything. That guy's not the survival type. He'll die soon enough on his own without any help from us.'

Gildas just grunted. With the diversion out of the way he was beginning to lapse back into the misery he'd carried from the docks. When they passed through the fortified doors of the entrance to the block nobody took any notice and Clare left him without another word. He started up the stairs to what used to be his home.

Home? Not any longer. Panting a little from the stairs he reached the door to his living unit, splintered and bent from the intrusion. It had taken him a whole day to make it secure again and able to be locked. He went inside and flopped onto the floor, spent, starting to shake and more miserable than he had ever felt in his life.

The final act had been performed earlier that day at the docks. An experience fraught with a silently howling despair he never wished to have to repeat.

Two whole days he had spent alone with the body of his wife. Two days to relive the memories collected over twenty years of companionship, comfort and undemonstrative affection. Neither had wanted to bring yet more children into an already overcrowded world and both were content with each others company in the constant moving of house in pursuit of prospects of work -

especially during the last few years. Since they'd wed, the only other members permitted to join the small family had been a succession of cats, the latest of which had condescended to remain with them from kitten-hood for a full five years until its disappearance at the time of the intrusion and the death of his wife.

Gildas had arrived home from work, exhausted after the two-mile walk, to meet a deputation of guardians in the main entrance hall. The atmosphere had been defensive rather than contrite. With an escort of three guardians he had been conducted to his unit and shown the results. They had witnessed his dry-eyed grief and anger then left him to sort things out alone.

They owed him!

After two days of mourning, nobody offered to help him transport the body to the docks - he hadn't asked, but someone should have offered. It took him three hours to carry his burden the two miles, following the ebbing tide to the dockside and waiting for the rust-smeared tugs to pull their trains of barges alongside. They were only able to operate during the period two hours each side of low tide.

They *owed* him!

At the crowded quay-side he saw a familiar face from work with a dead member of his own family and arranged to leave his wife's body in his care while he negotiated a deal with the captain of the disposal tug - the floating tumbrel train. Rumour had it that not all the bodies were dumped in the channel about fifteen miles out. It had been noticed that not enough weighting stones were taken on board after each of the two daily trips to ensure the sinking of the full load of corpses. Pertinent enquiries were answered (when they were answered at all) with the assurance it was purely coincidence that the food-block processing ships were within only a couple of miles from the dumping grounds. The fact that many of the shrouds sold to mourners had obviously been second-hand was explained by stating they had come from corpses buried on land at an undisclosed location. Waste not, want not. It made sense, didn't it?

Nobody believed it. But nobody could prove otherwise or do anything about it either.

Gildas took his place in the long line waiting to see the captain. When his turn came he collected and paid for the issue shrouds, torn and stained, then spent a short time negotiating with a tired, pale man to ensure a guarantee of certain disposal at sea. The two days of waiting should already have made certain of that but nothing could be depended upon these days. A small amount of valueless cash changed hands.

Returning to his colleague he assisted him to cover the corpse of his relative then thankfully accepted help to wrap his wife. It was a heartbreakingly messy job on a quay-side covered with stinking, drying mud left by the sea. Taking their places in the loading line they shuffled forwards, laid their burdens on a rotting pallet, said a few parting words under their breath then hastily departed the charnel dockside.

Outside they said their good-byes and parted; each knowing they would probably never meet again. Gildas had told his companion he would not be returning to work with the road maintenance gang, the latest in a long series of temporary jobs. Finding a rare quiet place he sat down. It began to rain, the first rain for over a year. Soft, light drizzle enveloped him. Still he sat, lonely and despondent until the onset of dusk and the soft plash of the tide flowing over the quay-side roused him enough to start the journey back to the block. He almost hoped he wouldn't make it alive.

Now he sat once more in the ruins of his unit. The few bits of poor furniture still lay scattered where the killers had thrown it in their search for anything worth having. The huge, ghastly stain on the floor where his wife had drained her life's blood remained uncleaned.

God, he felt wretched.

They owed him!
DAMMIT, THEY *OWED* HIM!!
Without realising it, he fell asleep.

CHAPTER 6

Soft light of a cloudless dawn filtered through a window on to a huddled shape sprawled across a section of the floor. The single-room unit looked ten times worse in daylight and it stank of decay and neglect. As the light strengthened, the figure remained motionless, making dry and softly rasping sounds from its open mouth. Gildas was lost in the deep oblivion of spiritual and emotional exhaustion.

The sun had risen quite high before a square of hot light from the window managed to creep across the floor to touch one of his eyelids. Blackness changed to red and then to yellow behind the closed lid before the sluggish brain behind recognised it could no longer ignore the promptings of enforced wakefulness. The eye opened, squinted and closed again at the onset of a sudden overwhelming photon attack. Gildas rolled stiffly over and sat up. He groaned.

He sat for a while on the floor, gradually waking. Getting to his feet he shuffled to the refrigerator and pulled it away from the wall. Retrieving a tin from the recess of the motor unit he replaced the fridge and collected a dirty mug from the sink together with a small bottle of water. A minimum amount of water was poured into a tiny heater, which was plugged into the single power socket the room possessed. Shortly thereafter a mug of black, unsweetened coffee - real coffee, a rare luxury - began the uphill journey of getting Gildas' body fit to live another day.

Oh God! He didn't want to live another day. He looked about him at the shabby room, averting his gaze from the horrible mark on the floor and lingering on the wicker basket tucked into a corner together with two small dishes and a used plastic toilet tray. The basket was lined with soft cloths, scattered with thin, pale hairs. Once the sanctum of the only other member of his little family but now empty, cold and ... Oh God! Don't think about it!

Something twisted in his brain. He actually *felt* it! Finishing the dregs of his bitter coffee he came to an involuntary decision - for better or worse.

Do it now!

Thus a turning point occurred in the life of an insignificant being that would alter the course of events far into the future. There could be no turning back now.

First he would have to endure an argument with Jeggs.

Funnily enough, Jeggs put up only token resistance.

'Four weeks only, then we're all square, agreed?'

'Agreed.' He looked closely at Jeggs' face peering at him from the huddle of blankets on his bed. 'You OK? You look like hell.'

'None of your damned business. Get out and take this slag with you!' Jeggs kicked feebly at his mound of bedclothes. With a small squeal of fright, an extremely feminine form tumbled from the bed and landed on the floor with a soft thud. Pale blue eyes partially shielded by an untidy mop of mousy hair tried unsuccessfully to focus on Gildas.

'Get out!' said Jeggs.

She got out. Stumbling, weaving and grabbing her clothes from a chair as she went. How Jeggs managed to keep himself and his "guests" in drugs was a mystery to all. Gildas turned to follow her.

'It's up to you to sort it out with Clare, though. Your problem. Don't make it mine! She's not going to like it.' Jeggs sounded a trifle vindictive. 'Talk to her right and she'll come round, maybe.' Jeggs tried to laugh. It sounded more like a death rattle and ended in a racking cough. 'I thought I told you to get out.'

Gildas got.

Clare had been on night watch so she was still asleep and would remain undisturbed that way until early afternoon at least. Nobody was prepared to risk waking her before she was ready. Bandages were not easy to get hold of. Gildas waited.

Just after midday, one of the watchers at the door reported a signal from the apartment block on the right. The food trucks were coming. The three guardians rostered for the day's collection duty left the block to liaise with three representatives from each of the other local blocks in this section of the ghetto to act as escort to the little convoy. They would all rendezvous at the entrance road and escort the trucks to each block in turn, guarding the distribution of the food and presenting a list of requirements for each of their respective blocks; repairs to be done, complaints the local guardians could not, or would not, deal with, mail for the unofficial postage service and so on. Most requests would be ignored. Needs were many, resources were pitifully slender. They would do their best. Perhaps.

When the trucks pulled up at his door Gildas helped to unload and distribute the food to the other inhabitants of the block then continued waiting until Clare condescended to put in an appearance. He had nothing better to do for now.

She bounced out of her dorm room, grabbed her share of the food and disappeared again before Gildas could react properly. He waited.

At long last she reappeared, looking fit and mean. Fully armed, she strode across the hallway, heading for the outside door. Gildas jumped up, grabbed at his leg to ease the piercing agony of an abused muscle and hobbled rapidly in her wake. He nearly caught her at the door and had to brake quickly as she slammed it in his face. Not in a very good mood, obviously. Maybe he should leave it till tomorrow.

No! Gildas was determined. He'd made up his mind completely during his long vigil and was in no temper to balk at the first obstacle. She'd either agree or she wouldn't and that would be the end of it. He pushed at the door.

Clare was leaning on one of the defensive screens gazing out over the bleak, sun-seared cityscape, one thumb tucked into her thick, bandoleered belt. Gildas stopped for a moment to gather his thoughts. How to approach her? Hadn't thought about that. He recognised he was nervous and even a little scared. It had been a long time since he had approached any woman for any reason. He and his wife had been very close and self-sufficient as a couple, avoiding prolonged associations with others whenever possible. He braced himself. 'Clare?'

'What?' Quietly. She didn't turn round.

'Can I talk to you for a moment?'

'Just a minute.' She stood still, gazing afar. Gildas, a bit to one side, thought he saw an eyelid blinking rapidly as if mopping up a tear but instantly dismissed the thought as impossible. Anyone else, maybe. Definitely not Clare.

A few silent moments passed before she suddenly rounded on him. 'Now what?' She was her normal self once more, normal in as far as their short association had taught him. 'What's wrong with the leg?' Gildas was still massaging it without realising. 'Broken it, I hope.'

'Not exactly. Just strained a muscle. Jeggs told me to wait till you got up. He's assigned you to me.' Why couldn't Jeggs have done the hard bit instead of leaving it all to him to sort out?

'Assigned to you? For what? I'm not that sort of a girl, I'll have you know.' Was that a joke? 'Tell me!'

Do it! Get it over with.

'To train me up. You're the only one I trust to do it right. The lot of you still owe me for what happened to my wife and everything else. You know it! Make me half as good as you in a punch-up and the obligation is settled.'

There! He'd said it. The bit of flattery might help. Now wait until she finished laughing herself sick then wait a bit more until she'd beaten the stuffing out of Jeggs and hope for the best after that.

Clare didn't laugh.

'OK. Let's go up to your unit.' And that was it. Gildas could hardly believe his ears. Still limping a bit he hurried after the sturdy figure.

Clare grimly surveyed the mess inside Gildas' vandalised home. 'They told me you took your wife's body down the docks yesterday. If I hadn't been asleep after my shift I'd have made sure you had some help or at least an escort. Why didn't you ask?'

'Too sick inside. Besides, that lot won't do anything unless you force them.'

Clare slapped him across the arm. 'Don't be too goddam' ready to think we're all the same. I'd have helped if I'd known about it. Still, forget that for now; looks like you've been living here like a pig the last few days. Ready for your first lesson?' She regarded him quizzically; a smile, friendly.

Gildas smiled back. His first smile for a long time. Then he wished he'd saved the energy. Suddenly he was looking at the floor which seemed to be coming to meet his face and sliding sideways at the same time. With a crash and a blinding explosion of pain he hit something and rolled over, coming to rest against the wall. Instinctively he flipped himself the right way up and scrabbled into a corner. There was no pursuit or follow-up. He became aware of Clare still standing by the entrance door. She was still smiling. Realisation dawned.

'So that was lesson number one, hey? Never trust anyone. Nobody at all. Ever.' He started to get up.

'Stay there or I'll have to do it again. Lesson number one it was. Trust anyone enough to let down your guard and you get hurt, right?' Gildas nodded. 'Here's what I want you to do by tomorrow. We'll have to use this place for practice and if you think I'm going to work in this mess you can think again. Get it cleaned up, cleared out and scrubbed! We'll need as much space as we can get so arrange the furniture so it can be moved easy. Do that and I'll call in the morning then we'll have a chat and get started, OK?'

Gildas nodded again, glumly. He knew it would be a waste of breath to explain that he hardly ever trusted anyone, anyway. Hadn't she just caught him out at it? Best to do as she said. Clare left him to it without another word.

The following morning she returned carrying a small plastic carrier bag. She inspected the small room critically and lifted the threadbare mat Gildas had placed over the stain on the floor. The mark still showed, a stain on chipboard is almost impossible to remove, but it had lost its identity. No more than a big brown patch now, anonymous, like a gravy spillage. She clucked her tongue approvingly. 'Good job. Must have taken you quite a while, not to mention how you were feeling when you were doing it. Got any fresh water left?'

Gildas shook his head. 'Used it all up cleaning. Had to borrow some from the neighbours. God knows when I'll be able to give it back.'

'Looks like you've been up all night. Feel up to it today?'

'I'll live. Let's get started.'

'Talk first. Got the water boiler handy? Good. Boil up some of this!' She opened the plastic bag and took out a bottle of water and a couple of tins with screw-on tops. Coffee. Sugar. Gildas immediately felt a lot better.

When they settled down, each with a mug of sweet-smelling beverage, Clare laid out her terms.

'Understand one thing. I'm not doing this for your sake or for some imagined sense of obligation to you for what happened here.' Her tone was uncompromising. Gildas kept his mouth shut. 'I'm doing it 'cos it's a cushy number, something different to do, and it gets me away from that bunch of morons downstairs. They're starting to make me sick with the way they talk and act. How long did Jeggs say he'd give me?'

'Four weeks.'

'Well never mind what he says, OK? I'll decide how long it'll be. If I don't think you're going to shape up - and it won't take long to find that out - I'll dump you. On the other hand, if you're better than you look like you're going to be we'll take it as far as we can. First thing to tell you; always try to get something into your stomach as early as possible after waking up, even if its only a drink of water. That's why I bought this coffee up; I needed it as much as you do. We'll start work as soon as it's finished. What experience have you had in the combat game? Army?'

'No, not actually in the army. The closest I got was as a guard on the supply trucks up the valley with the regulars. They gave me a gun but no ammo and left me to it. No training of any sort.'

'How did you manage to sort things out when you got mugged the other day, then? You killed one of them and downed the other. You must have had some practice or you'd be on the body barges by now - or a fifty-pound carton of protein blocks. How come?'

'What happened the other day was luck. Good for me and bad for the other two. These flats are built on the patch I was born and brought up. It was a rough area in those days too, and you had to be able to look after yourself or you had real problems. I survived the hard way, like most others from round here; not so much by being tough but making others think it wasn't a good idea to mess with me. Most times it worked. I watched, learned and tried to keep out of trouble.'

'Being short and ugly probably helped.' Clare would never have gained success as a diplomat. 'You've got a good set of muscles though. Natural? Or do you keep them in trim?'

'Natural. I've mostly had physical jobs 'cos one look at me automatically excludes me from any job which needs brainwork.' Gildas spoke without rancour or resentment. It was the way things were. He'd learned to accept it.

'Understandable. Physical jobs mean mixing with physical people. Had a bit of practice then, yes?'

'A bit. Enough to get out of trouble most times. I know how to look after myself in a defensive way but it's not easy to be the aggressor. That's why I need you; I've heard you know all the tricks and then a few more. Think you can teach me? I need it. Please?' Gildas felt close to grovelling but also felt he had gone far enough. There *were* limits.

'Why not? Like I said, I need a break and a chance to brush up on things myself. This way I get both as long as there aren't any misunderstandings. Finished your coffee? Right, let's get to work.'

And work they did! Clare didn't do much to begin with except to give orders and instructions. Gildas did the press-ups, running on the spot, more press-ups, shadow boxing, more press-ups ... beyond mid-day it went on with only a short break early afternoon to eat, then on again. By evening Gildas was exhausted. Clare taught him how to relax with the aid of simple yoga and left without comment.

The next morning Gildas felt as if he would never move again - ever - but his tutor proved unsympathetic when she turned up. 'You'll get used to it.' was the nearest she got to any form of pity and after the compulsory coffee the torture resumed.

This went on for four days before there was any change. His muscles and joints were less painful by then and Clare decided it was time to start on simple combat techniques. It was sheer hell! Gildas gritted his aching teeth and persevered with dogged persistence. After several days of this came a period of practice with various weapons; knife, club, staff (they had to go outside sometimes, to the vast entertainment of the rest of the gang), axe (Gildas with the weapon, Clare without), and other nasty things Clare carried on the broad belt around her waist, including the belt itself. Over a period of three weeks the activity became more advanced and violent. Gildas spent a large part of each day patching up scars and soothing bruises - there was never a scratch on Clare. The family in the unit below complained - once. Clare dealt with it. They didn't complain a second time.

In a break to gather breath after a particularly noisy session Clare let down her guard somewhat and confided how she had come by her expertise, something she had so far not told her companions downstairs. She must have been in a reflective mood, a condition she would have been quick to condemn as bad for survival. Gildas started her off.

'Just lucky, I guess.' was her answer to his guarded question.

'In what way?'

'Good parents helped a lot. They made sure I got the best education money could buy; and being an only child was an advantage. Dad was a keep-fit freak and he made sure I grew up the same to compensate for the son he never had. At least he did up until the time I got snatched.'

'Snatched? Kidnapped?'

'Let's just say I woke up one day and I was in a different place with a lot of women. They used to entertain men - for a price. Get the picture?'

'Knocking shop, eh? Were you old enough to learn the trade?'

Perhaps his tone had not been sympathetic enough; Clare gave him a very direct look. 'Just the theory, not the practical side. Not after what happened to the first customer they tried to stick me with. I was pretty big even at ten years old, and knew how to deal with things like that, thanks to Dad's teaching. They beat me up and tried again. That one I crippled for life, I hope. Got beat up again for it. Didn't stop them trying but I got away in the end. Had to look after myself for a few years then got in the Army. Treated good there; trained me good too. Got promoted to training others.' In the meantime my father tracked down and dealt with the ones who snatched me.

Gildas clucked his tongue in understanding, masking his real thoughts. There was a very great amount she was not telling him; not that it mattered. She might if he asked but

78

she probably had good reasons for holding back. It wasn't as if he were her personal confidant after all.

'Seen any action?' he contented himself with saying.

'More than most, I reckon.' Her attitude suggested fact rather than a boast. 'Abroad lots of places when the hot countries were going to hell, then defending the far end of the Channel Tunnel.' She peered quizzically at Gildas. 'Heard what happened there, did you?'

'A massacre, wasn't it?'

'Sure was.' Clare smiled nastily. 'A massacre, then another massacre, then another and another and another. Nearly every day thousands got killed. Bombed until they'd almost run out of fuel for the planes. Shelled, napalmed, grenaded, shot, hand-to-hand. Down to knives and rocks in the end, we were, and still they came trying to get through the tunnel. Didn't have a chance, of course. We had all the weapons that mattered but there were so many of them.'

'What *really* happened in the end?'

'Earth moving machines kept packing up and being sabotaged 'til there just weren't enough left to do the job. Otherwise we'd probably still be there.'

'What did the earth movers have to do with it?'

'Any idea how many bodies there were?' Gildas shook his head. 'Millions, that's how many. Only the big machines could shift enough to keep the killing area clear outside the end of the tunnel. We used 'dozers, scrapers, anything that could move piles of corpses. People used to lay among the bodies and attack the machines when they set to work, trying to disable them 'cos we used to use them as shields as well when we had to attack. In the end we blocked the tunnel entrance with the machines that were left and used the fastest one to escape over our side.

'But they could have climbed over the machines or at least moved one enough to pass through, surely. Do you mean they just let the refugees through after all that killing to try to stop them?'

'No chance. Do you really think that when they built that tunnel they didn't include arrangements to block it if they had to? Don't be daft! As it happened there wasn't any power to close the doors built into the roof and sides but the final line of defence worked just fine. All we had to do was reach out and press a button; explosives did the rest. Blew through to the sea bed, didn't they? Flooded the lot. Not that it made much difference in the long run. They kept coming across without the tunnel and they're still coming in anything that'll float. Things are going to get a lot worse too. That's why I keep in shape. I want to live - even like this.'

'My idea too.' said Gildas. 'But I sometimes wonder why.' He got to his feet. 'Ready for some more punishment?'

'Any time.' Clare bounded up like a plump grasshopper and pounded poor Gildas savagely for a full hour as if to atone for her revelations.

Later, once again nursing his bruises before sleep, Gildas pictured Clare's life as she had told it. Twenty years ago it would have been an impossible tale, but in these times ...? Gildas finally slept whilst wondering why a woman who had experienced such a brutalising life was not a fully fledged psychopath instead of the generous, sensible person now teaching him the harsh procedures of her trade. It was a question he was not prepared to ask her yet.

A few days later Clare told him he was as ready for his revenge as she could make him, pecked his cheek, wished him well and walked out. He hadn't realised she had divined his purpose but on reflection it must have been pretty obvious to anyone. She moved out of the block the same day.

Two days later Gildas set out to face a dying world on its own terms.

INTERMURAL 2

More than five thousand-odd painful, blood-soaked years! And still they couldn't get it right!

After all that futile effort it took less than a few decades to bring everything crashing back to the starting line.

From our present standpoint it is only too easy to see how it happened; speculation still continues about the exact sequence of events, but there are no dissenting voices about the primary cause - unrestrained overpopulation of a single, high-consumption species called homo sapiens, coupled with the existing natural solar output cycle and the position of Earth within the planetary system.

So what actually went wrong? And why was it not recognised and properly dealt with before a blindingly obvious danger turned into an irreversible disaster?

Today it is easy to see how Mother Nature, demonstrating her dispassionate (some would say cruel) modus operandi relieved the pressure.

Consider the moving mammalian carpets on the ice-fringed beaches of today's France, relentlessly pressing onwards to almost certain death.

This is Nature's way of solving an overpopulation problem. Unfortunately, humans are much less prone than animals to respond in such an eminently sensible manner. Instead, towards the end, they didn't simply ignore the fact there were too many people for the available assets to support. The irresponsible fools actively encouraged unrestricted breeding! Would you believe it?

Yes, they were apparently hell-bent on filling the world with as many people as possible - and then some.

There were many different reasons for this, depending on the type of society in which one lived. In most of the equatorial countries, for instance, if one did not produce a large army of wage-earners for support, parents beyond

81

breeding age simply starved to death when they became too old to provide for themselves. So high were mortality rates due to disease, malnutrition and warfare that a large number of offspring was required to ensure enough survived to provide this support. In such societies it was the lack of communal provision for the elderly that encouraged the creation of insupportable populations.

Ignorance, or lack of the basic methods of birth control also played its part. This was gleefully aided and abetted in many parts by deliberate government decision in an instinctive effort to obtain a greater share of material assistance from the richer countries, much (probably even most) of which was casually diverted into already wealthy wallets instead of feeding the masses of those it was meant to help. A further consideration was the need to amass plenty of easily available battle-fodder in case of invasion (or to invade somewhere else).

Then there was the ruthlessly selfish folly of religious belief.

Whether the dogma issued by leading zealots was to encourage large families or ban the use of contraceptive devices, the effect was the same; more children were produced than either the parents, or the society in which they lived, could reasonably sustain. The clandestine motives behind such doctrines were always the same, too; produce more believers than competing religions and eventually, given sufficient time, all others would fail in the numbers game and fade away to leave a hugely overpopulated planet all of one religion.

The only true religion, naturally.

Aren't they all?

But they didn't have enough time to do it.

Too many units of any species, each striving to acquire more than their fair share of what is available, is a guaranteed blueprint for doom. The human species was no exception. The only thing its collective intelligence and ingenuity was able to achieve was to delay the onset of the inevitable, thereby ensuring the collapse was more catastrophic than it need have been.

The more human units there were, the greater became the competition for what was left and thus the science of Economics ballooned in importance; its sole purpose being the diversion of resources from the weak to the strong despite loud and continuing trumpeting by the latter acclaiming their intrinsic and God-given altruism.

The strong became stronger and more in control of the destiny of others: the weak simply had their backs pressed more tightly against the wall in ever-increasing numbers.

No wonder there was an ecological backlash!

CHAPTER 7

The bunker had never been intended to remain in use for very long. The whole purpose of constructing it in the first place was simply as a co-ordination centre and rallying point for those selected to fill the two huge star-ships nearing completion in their four-hundred-mile orbit. After all, it wasn't much use trying to start a colony without plenty of colonists.

As a result, the decor was somewhat less than homely. In the basement, four floors below ground level, were kept the supplies necessary to fulfil the bunker's primary functions. Here, too, were sited the two main and backup semi-portable nuclear generators, each of which was capable of providing well over a hundred times what was needed at the moment.

On the next floor up, well away from the generator room, Lemuel Quorvis had his personal suite from which he directed the huge operation to which he had devoted all his resources together with those of many others endowed with the Midas and Machiavellian touch. The primary reason he was in overall charge was very simple; he was the only one they all nearly trusted, as well as being the individual who'd started the whole process off in the first place. Besides, he was capable of immense persuasion when he considered his life could be at stake.

The remainder of the complex was mostly devoted to the well-being of about five hundred men, women and children. There was sufficient room for nearly three thousand, but most of these were not expected to arrive until the star-ships neared completion.

In her own suite, as fluffy and feminine a place as could be imagined, Emma shed her travel clothes and stepped into the warm caress of a much needed shower. A clean pink dress was donned with an intense appreciation of the feel of real silk gliding over her shoulders. A comfortable pair of soft moccasins completed the job.

Even with her hair still wet and lank she presented a stunning picture - and she was fully aware of the fact. Five foot two of velvet skin, a bit pale at the moment from spending so much time under cover, enveloping a formation designed by a God in one of his more erotically-creative moments. Her face was that of an angel; heart-shaped with a small, rather petulant, mouth, an appealing snub nose donated by her sire and a pair of clear grey eyes placed slightly far apart. This totally false impression of innocent maiden purity was topped off by long, wavy blond hair covering the small ears set close to her head.

Her slim, well-proportioned body had concave curves where they were supposed to be and soft lumps in all the right places, all held off the ground by a pair of straight, slender legs.

Yes, she knew she would never have any problem attracting a mate. Not that she had ever tried, not really. She just didn't feel the need for one now and hopefully never would. Men just happened to be there; simply another irritating obstacle in the path of a fulfilling life: emotionally-driven victims to her will, with whom she had not the slightest intention of becoming romantically involved.

She would much rather kill them than bed down with them.

Now that was *much* more fun!

But she was definitely beautiful, by anyone's standards.

Then she went and ruined the entire girlish effect by replacing her gunbelt.

Emma didn't care. After combing out her hair she locked the door behind her and went to report to her father.

'Morning Wendy!' Emma breezed into the office as if she'd just returned from college instead of a foraging trip costing the lives of God knows how many hapless refugees; many of them scarcely half an hour before. 'Father in his office?'

Wendy nodded and smiled in greeting. 'Go right in. He's just had a little accident and a visit from the Doc. Oh, and something's gone wrong up on Dum. He's upset. Be gentle with him, OK?'

'Thanks.' Coding the door, Emma went in. 'Hi, Father. I'm home. Got a full load but it wasn't easy.'

'Hello Sun! It never is with you.' Lemuel eased himself from the edge of his desk and lumbered across to envelope his daughter in a hug of genuine relief. In spite of his comments to the contrary he was always pleased to see her return safely from her jaunts and even worried about her a little when he could spare the time. He released her and returned to his desk, sinking into the overstuffed chair with evident relish.

'Wendy tells me the Doc came to see you earlier - professionally.'

'This.' He exhibited his damaged finger with false nonchalance. 'Broke the nail. Nothing much really.'

Emma sniffed; a hangnail wasn't exactly life-threatening. 'What's going on upstairs? The ship, Dum, I mean.'

'Work stopped on the coffin decks as they were beginning to assemble the latest batch of units. The place is ringed with components and more are arriving all the time.

The shuttles will be working continually from now on. It could cause a log-jam that might take weeks to clear and we can't afford to wait. Could be we'll have to get under way sooner than we thought. I'm waiting for them to call me back with an explanation of what they're going to do about it. They're taking their time though.' He glared at the phone accusingly.

'Want anything? I could use a feed and some sleep.'

'You go right ahead. I'll be doing the same once I've sorted this out.'

'Just make sure that you do!' Emma crossed to the door. 'And don't go sleeping in that chair again. Have a proper kip in your bed for a change. See you later.'

At that moment the phone buzzed. Lemuel flicked the switch and a bad-tempered voice barked from the speaker.

'Lem? You there?'

Lemuel beamed in recognition. 'Manny, me old son. To what do I owe the honour? He signalled for Emma to remain. 'What can I do for you?'

'You can put the vid on for a start; you know I hate talking to someone I can't see.'

'Sorry.' He flicked another switch and one of the consoled screens glowed, flickered and stabilised into a picture of an angry face almost totally covered with straggly grey hair. Manny had really let himself go lately. 'If you could see yourself you'd understand why I keep the video link off.' He smiled at seeing some of the tension drain from the face. 'What's wrong? You look a trifle miffed.'

'Miffed isn't the word I'd use. I've just come off talking to the ship. Fitting out the coffin decks has stopped. It's spreading. There's talk of a strike. A strike, for God's sake! With all our lives at stake? I prefer to call it mutiny and you know how I deal with mutineers. You're in charge. What are you doing about it?'

Manfred Bexter had amassed his huge fortune in the realms of mineral exploitation, generally in the

86

impoverished and overpopulated countries where the promise of basic subsistence was enough to ensure constant competition for the privilege of working in his mines and open cast sites. In other words, virtual slave labour; and the slaves were grateful for it.

'They'll be calling back any time now. Don't worry, I'll sort it out. I don't think your methods will work very well out there; these are better-educated people than those you used to employ. Reason will prevail, believe me!'

The intercom buzzed. 'Hang on, Manny, this might be them now. Yes, Wendy.'

'Ship central on line five, Mr Quorvis. Shall I put them through now?'

'Please. Link Mr Bexter in on five as well, would you?'

Another screen awoke. A row of four people stood bolt upright facing the screen. One, in a dark, formal suit, complete with tie, yet, spoke. He looked worried.

'Sorry to be so long in calling back, Mr Quorvis, but it took a while persuading Jack here to speak to you in person.' He tilted his head towards a thickset man in a bright orange body stocking who was glaring into the screen with unmistakeable belligerence.

Lemuel knew Jack Bensen from other disputes he'd handled in the past. He used to be in the industrial news a lot during the days when trade unions still existed. If Jack was involved in this against his will then the grievance must be genuine. Lemuel respected him greatly as a tough, but rational negotiator.

'What's up, Mr Bensen? I've only heard one side of the argument. Will you give me yours?'

The big man looked uncomfortable. 'It's the order in which the coffin decks are being constructed, Mr Quorvis. The men don't see why the officers should be catered for first. They want to, well, to make sure their own berths are guaranteed.'

'Why shouldn't they be guaranteed? We all want to get out of here, after all, and every able-bodied person we can get will be needed when we make landfall.'

'Even so, Mr Quorvis, they're not happy, and this job is taking a lot longer than any of us thought.'

'Nobody's lied to you Jack. That's not all, though, is it? What else, hm?'

The big man looked away from the screen as if embarrassed. He swallowed before answering. It was pretty obvious he didn't want to be involved with this but he had the welfare of his crew to consider. With an effort he looked squarely into the screen once more.

'I wouldn't have thought you'd ever lie to us, Mr Quorvis. You never have to me and I doubt you ever will. Trouble is, the real trouble, there's a rumour going round we'll have to get away sooner than planned and that means the whole thing might not be completed. The men believe there's a variant of the AIDS virus down there which can be transmitted through the air and in water. Hundred per cent fatal in six days, they say. And if that's right the colonists'll have to be vetted and got up here before time and we're nowhere near ready for them in any numbers. The men just want to make sure their families are all right and won't be left behind, that's all.' His voice died away uncertainly and he looked straight into Lemuel's eyes.

'Fair enough Jack. Tell the men they can do it the way they want.' He saw one of the other men was about to speak. 'Hang on a moment Adrian! Jack, I've never lied to you because I've never had to. I won't lie now if you promise to tell the men all I'm about to tell you now. Agreed?'

Jack nodded.

'Right. Firstly, the rumour is true. There *is* an epidemic of sorts directly related to the old AIDS scare which never really caused the damage it was supposed to. They never managed to find a proper cure for that either, and now it's mutated yet again to something a lot more serious. Connect something like that to the conditions in which people are trying to survive down here and it's pretty certain not many are going to get through it. It means this - yes, in all likelihood we'll have to get everyone up there at least a couple of months before we assumed. OK so far'?

Another nod. Jack's face was grim. He didn't want to be the bearer of bad news and was contemplating how effortlessly and quickly Lemuel had talked him into such a position.

'Adrian there will keep you posted with all the information we get regarding the spread of the disease - and that's not going to be much. All right, Adrian?'

Adrian opened his mouth to speak but Lemuel got in first.

'Yes I know we decided to keep it quiet and hope it would fizzle out but truth is less damaging than rumours no matter how much it may stick in the craw. And it's all round the ship anyway. There's a similar problem on Dee, but I suppose your spies have told you that. We level with them from now on, OK?' He'd already decided not to mention the other death bugs of cholera, typhoid and what appeared to be bubonic plague, which were raging totally out of any hope of control all over the still-populated parts of the planet. And that was without the new sicknesses which had Doc Payne staying up nights. Let poor old Jack deal with the AIDS rumour first and lumber Adrian with sorting out the rest later. He felt sorry for Jack. Like himself, he was getting too old for all this hassle.

'Whatever you say, Mr Quorvis.' Adrian forbore to mention this was what he had argued strenuously with Lemuel for only recently. Not a good idea with Jack in earshot. 'I'll work out regular information meetings, probably every other day, but I'll have to have some help.'

'I'll send up some of the families, they can fill up the space in the empty coffins. We've plenty of idle help down here; it'll save constructing them on site and allow the job to be done quicker - with the necessary checks, of course.

The women can help with the admin. Just post guards on the children. It's too dangerous for kids running around up there just now.'

'Jack! Start the men assembling the pods for the officers. You're an engineer. You know damned well the officers have to be sited close to the central column. They've got to drive the damned thing. You also know you can't start on the outside pods without a hell of a lot of re-scheduling unless you want to unbalance the spin and risk a breakup. Either you'll have to work on the complete outer layer all at once or you'll have to stop the spin. You'll then have to move further out to maintain a stable temperature; that means all components will have to be transported further. Not only that, your position won't be fixed and the shuttle will have to re-programme every time they make a delivery. All this will take extra time we don't appear to have. Am I right?'

Jack nodded again. He was very unhappy.

'I'm sorry, Mr Quorvis, I didn't realise you knew so much about these things. The men are engineers too. We've talked it over and can't find any compromise they consider to be reasonable. All your suggestions were raised at the time, I recall. They're determined not to take any chances whatsoever.

'Jack, Jack!' Lemuel couldn't believe this man was so blind to the obvious solution. He had just been given the information which would point the way. It would have made Jack feel so much better if he had suggested it himself. What had happened to the sensible negotiator of yester-year? He must be tired. They all were. It wasn't easy up there.

'You've just heard me tell Adrian I'll be sending up some of the families. They'll start coming on the first shuttle available when they've been checked out. There's no disease in this depot but we can't allow even a hidden cold germ on the ship as you are aware. The obvious place to accommodate them is in the coffin decks and the easiest ones to build are those around the central column. If all goes well you should have them in place and pressurised by the time they arrive. Are you with me now?'

Jack was with him all right. If women and children occupied the officer's quarters then it would be virtually impossible to do a moonlight flit. An insurance policy had been offered. Jack was not slow to take it up. He smiled for the first time; no trace of self-denigration evident.

'That should stitch everything up very nicely, thank you Mr Quorvis. With your permission I'll go tell the men and get them to work.'

'Thanks Jack. I'll look forward to meeting you again in person before very long. Better go now.'

As soon as straw-boss Jack had vacated the office, Lemuel surveyed the three men left with overt disapproval.

'Why couldn't you lot do that? That's what I put you up there for. You're supposed to be managers. Have you got an explanation or have I got to suggest one for you?'

The manager who had not spoken as yet cleared his throat.

'I think I can speak for all of us here, Mr Quorvis. It's simply that the construction is now reaching a stage when there are not enough of us with the authority to make decisions which you reached just now. There have been plenty of other problems you've never heard about. We've dealt with them as they have arisen. It's only when something goes as badly wrong as this that we have to involve you. Our job here is to see that your instructions are carried out as best we can.'

'Get to the point!' Lemuel had a sneaky feeling he knew what the troupe was angling for.

'We would like more freedom to make our own major decisions and request you send more properly qualified people up here to take some of the load off us ... sir.'

Dangerous. But ... And what about that "sir" at the end. It seemed to contain sardonic overtones.

'Agreed.' The man registered momentary surprise at this quick answer before his training took over and his face smoothed to its customary urbanity. 'As soon as I select a few suitable candidates. Give me a week and you should all be able to get back to having a good night's sleep once in a while. Now put me through to the Commander!'

'At once, sir.'

The screen faded, but just before it went blank Lemuel thought he caught a glance of what may have been triumph pass between the men. Most would have missed it. He gave his attention to the other screen where Manny had watched with uncharacteristic silence.

'Happy now, Manny?'

'Leaving things in your capable hands, Lem. I'll carry on with the shuttles. 'Bye now.'

The remaining screen blanked. Lemuel switched off his video link with a sigh and turned to his daughter.

'What did you make of that, Sun?'

Lemuel's gonads may have been in the process of terminal decline on the occasion of Emma's conception but a full complement of his genes had passed to the daughter. Her instincts were rarely wrong-footed.

'You must be daft. I wouldn't trust that lot in charge of the ship any further than I could lift you. I didn't like them when they were running your interests down here either. Be careful of them, Father.'

'They were good organisers, Sun. They always produced the goods and I treated them well. Something's changed, though; I can sense it. Maybe being out in space, free-fall and all that, has affected their sense of friendship.'

'Friendship!' Emma sneered. 'Rubbish! It's much more basic than that. Down here, the more they earned for you, the more went in their own bank accounts. Used to be called "performance related pay", remember? Screwing the employees and customers to inflate their own salaries way beyond what was reasonable. Now money means nothing but power does. The ship will be ready soon and they're up on it and you're down here. Do I have to spell it out for you?'

Lemuel smiled rather sadly. 'No. In fact, I half-expected something like this. Would probably have been surprised if it hadn't happened. It's a shame though, but you can't always predict human nature.'

'They're a threat. When I spot a threat I kill it.'

'I know, Sun. Your little habits have not escaped my notice. Still, forget that now. Commander Danhill will be coming on in a moment. Have you got a message for him?'

'Yes. Give him my indifferent regards and tell him he can waste his time as much as he like as long as he doesn't waste any more of mine.'

'Oh come on, Sun! You told me you were going to think about it, which implied you could change your mind. Look, we need - *I* need to keep him sweet, not to mention the rest of his family. Don't make it any harder for your poor old dad. Please!'

'That's right. Got to keep the politics going, haven't we? Thought we were going to leave all that sort of thing on Earth. What did they use to call it; a marriage of convenience or of state? The guy's a slob; an arrogant mealy-mouthed slob, and I'm not going to have anything to do with him or his lousy relatives. Just keep him clear of me, father, or I'll deal with him in the way I know best.'

'He's bound to ask me. I can't tell him that.'

'Use the diplomacy you're so good at! Tell him anything you like except what you both want to hear.' Emma started for the door again. 'He can get stuffed!'

Lemuel tried once more. There was more at stake here than he was able to tell her. 'Look, you don't actually have to *marry* the man. Have an informal arrangement if you prefer.'

The moment the words were out he realised he'd made a dreadful mistake. He wanted to bite his tongue off. Emma swung round, obviously furious. Two red spots appeared on her pale cheeks as she reached the desk, slammed her hands on the top and locked eyes with her father. Lemuel looked away.

'Don't...you...ever...say...that...again!' The words were forced out through clenched teeth. 'I'm not one of your modern-minded type of slags.' Lemuel winced. 'When I want to have a family and settle down I won't have too much trouble finding a man - a real man - and doing it properly. I'm old-fashioned enough to believe in that kind of thing and proud of it. I leave screwing around and shacking up with any pair of pants that happens to be available to the dirty bimbos up in the dorms. Understand?'

Lemuel swallowed. 'I was only trying ...'

'Well don't!'

She lifted her hands from the desk and Lemuel was surprised to see they were shaking slightly. His Sun had always been a little prim but he hadn't realised the full, extent of her feelings on such matters until now. It was a bit of a shock in the light of what was going on in the world and the extent of her active participation in the extermination of her own species.

His Sun had matured and developed independent attitudes of her own, he realised. He just hadn't noticed. Always been too busy to notice. So busy! He felt a little ashamed. Emma turned abruptly and strode across the room.

'I'll come back when we've both had some sleep and we can apologise to each other then.' she snapped. Slamming the heavy armoured door behind her she swept past a surprised Wendy in the outer office without speaking. She kept her head averted so Wendy couldn't see how wet her eyes had become.

A call came in on the terminal. Wendy routed Commander Danhill through to her boss.

And because her hidden and unrewarded affection for her employer reached far beyond normal loyalty, she listened in as usual, quite unashamedly, in case her testimony or support might be needed one day.

Lemuel never knew how often she'd protected his back in this manner.

She didn't know it at the time, but this was another occasion when it really paid off.

CHAPTER 8

Gildas sat in comparative comfort in the shade of a slab of rock overlooking the docks and Town centre. It was still early enough in the morning for shadow to be markedly cooler than direct sunlight. Later in the day temperature differentials between sun and shade would be barely noticeable. "Enjoy it while it lasts" was Gildas' motto for the morning; there would be precious little enjoyment the rest of the day and none at all during the hours of darkness. Striving for the basic means of survival would ensure that, on top of trying to think of a way to track down the killers of his wife and exact a terrible retribution. The retribution had been resolved in detail but he was no nearer deciding how to find the perpetrators than he had been when he slipped unobserved out of the apartment block.

All this time to reflect on it and he *still* hadn't a clue.

From his vantage point he'd watched the unceasing struggle for that same basic survival unfolding in a continuous sequence among the ruins of the swarming city below. Three days he'd been there, just sitting and brooding during the day and sometimes sleeping on a narrow ledge of rock, which could only be approached with difficulty from just one direction. Nobody had bothered him, which was exactly the reason he'd come here after leaving the tower block. He could see his previous home clearly from here. His old unit had already been taken over by others.

At about mid-morning he roused himself enough to do something about his growling belly. He'd brought everything edible from his unit but it had only been sufficient for a couple of days on starvation rations. Time to finish what was left. Grunting and stretching he shuffled to the furthest end of his ledge, where a small can was propped up on a few flat pebbles under a very slow drip of water from the rock. There was enough for his needs. He ate the last of his provisions, drank all the water then sat back in the narrowing patch of shade, at a loss what to do next.

By the time he began to feel cooked by the searing sun, shade on the ledge now having been banished completely, he still hadn't formed any course of action. Food, however, still had to be obtained. Reluctantly he packed up his few belongings and negotiated the narrow path down to the roadside through a tumble of rickety shelters, heading for the docks. Apathetic stick-figures watched him pass by from the gloom of their poor homes. Nobody accosted or even acknowledged him except for a small gang of children, who thought he wouldn't mind having a few rocks thrown at him. Children never changed. They scattered silently when he turned in their direction. Being ugly helped, sometimes.

Picking his way along an increasingly crowded road he shortly reached a point opposite the fortifications built around a part of the quay-side where the food barges unloaded upstream of the river barrage. Realising by now it was useless trying to get close to the only entrance, he kept on the road to the far end and doubled back along the wall. Pushing through the throng alongside the wall as closely as he could in an attempt to recognise one of the guards standing on the wall, he began to lose hope. Most of them seemed to be dressed in civilian rags, only a few Army uniforms were in sight. They also seemed to be generally younger than in the days when he used to escort the distribution trucks - and much harder-faced. Gildas continued pushing doggedly through the crowds.

At high tide the ground he trod was nearly six feet under water. The food depot had been constructed on top of a flat, oval mound of rubble gathered from long-gone buildings at the waterfront. From this mound a causeway, lined by two unscalable walls, ran in a straight line from the depot to the nearest main road a hundred yards away. The compound was about as impregnable as it could be made.

All at once he stumbled into an open space. The wall had turned sharply to the left and a fifty-yard stretch of ramshackle barrier as far as the waterside was completely clear of shelters and people. The crowding began again in a rough semicircle on the edge of the open space. Gildas stepped smartly back and surveyed the scene. This had not been the situation before in the vicinity of the main gate. Only something really dangerous could keep any area free of people this close to a source of food. He examined the perimeter barrier carefully.

At approximately the centre of the cleared space a small pill-box constructed from old concrete blocks projected from the base of the wall. He could see two openings, one in front, the other to one side, the blocks close to the dark recesses blackened as if by intense heat or smoke. There was probably another opening on the other side he couldn't see, as well. The dim shape of a narrow tube ending in what appeared to be a thick sausage could be discerned at the centre of both gaps.

Gildas could recognise a flame-thrower when he saw it and now noticed the condition of the ground in the empty area; scorched, blackened and covered with sooty particles like cinders. He looked higher up the wall. Being a small man had till now obstructed his view when surrounded by a press of people, nearly all of them taller than himself.

It couldn't have been a better excuse for a double-take.

A short length of wall directly above the flame-throwers was redolent with greenery. Tomato plants, containers sprouting spindly potato leaves, radishes, lettuces and cabbage interspersed with various herbs and flowers, including what could only have been tobacco and cannabis plants: a single flourishing island in a sea of desolation.

Gildas gaped in disbelief. A large cut had been made in the wall, covered above and in front with oddly-shaped panes of glass. Bullet proof? Guessing who had ordered the arrangement, it almost *had* to be.

And there he was!

Behind the glass stretched an old car seat propped up on blocks and sitting in the seat was a familiar figure, apparently asleep.

It must have been as hot as Hell itself under that glass but it didn't seem to bother the sleeper. His eyes were concealed behind an ornate pair of anti-UV goggles. A wicked-looking revolver rested on his chest, held there by a huge, hairy hand. The rest of the visible body was built to match.

Ape-like was the only fitting description. Gildas didn't expect to get much help from this source but it was the only known face he'd spotted up to now so it had to be worth a go. But making the initial approach didn't look easy. From past experience he was more likely to get a bullet before a hearing.

The figure in the hot-house moved slightly, stretching and smacking its thin lips. The hand not holding the gun dropped down out of sight and came up again holding a glass full of a golden fluid. Home-brew, of course. A gap opened in the face and half the contents of the glass poured rapidly inside. The hand descended once more to the floor, came up empty again to remove the goggles. Dark eyes swept over the crowds of supplicants, swivelling slowly, searching, on the look-out for possible infiltrators through the small arena. Gildas sneered. It was all for theatrical effect, as usual. The eyes passed over Gildas, completed the scan, then returned to him. A bushy eyebrow lifted in query.

He had been recognised. Gildas essayed a cautious wave. The figure nodded, lurched upright and descended downhill out of sight. A sturdy, and very narrow, metal door opened at ground level and the man stepped into view holding the revolver ready for action. He pointed at Gildas.

'Hey, you. Over here!' The voice fitted the appearance. Harsh, grating, accustomed to command.

Gildas stepped forward. So did several others. The man instantly reacted, firing a shot over head level, just, and shouting incoherently. The others scuttled back. Gildas stood uncertainly but the man waved him on again with an impatient gesture.

'Come on! Leg it over here, smartly now!'

Gildas legged in haste. The man with the gun never took his eyes off the crowd. When Gildas reached him he dodged quickly into the doorway dragging Gildas after him, then slammed and bolted the door. A volley of small stones immediately clattered on the outside. The man grinned and jerked his thumb at the door.

'Don't alter at all, do they? Gil, isn't it? Come on through the back here!' He led the way through a tangle of debris to the compound inside the wall and pointed to a row of metal boxes. 'Let's sit down here.'

They looked at each other, appraising. Gildas took the initiative.

'Nice to see you again Sarge. Looks like you're still on top of things as usual.'

'You're not attached to the Army now. To all intents and purposes it doesn't exist any more. I'm just the boss here now. My name's Frank, by the way. Use it!' He gave a sudden braying laugh as though a joke had been told.

'Sure, anything you say. How's life?'

Frank stopped laughing as abruptly as he'd begun. He regarded Gildas in a friendly manner. 'Not too bad. Why're you here? Need a job?'

'Any going?'

'Couple of vacancies for them that know the score. Had a problem yesterday. Nearly lost the truck as well as the crew but we managed to tow it back in about an hour ago.

It'll be on the road again soon as we wipe all the blood off and we'll need another crew. Interested?'

Gildas didn't quite know how to respond. This was a completely different personality from the one he'd known in charge of the trucks he'd been assigned to a few months before. Going back to them would mean feeding well but at the price of his freedom. Freedom was necessary to do the things he wanted. On the other hand, with the trucks he would be able to get around in comparative safety. Hmmm!'

'Do you arm all your guards now? By that I mean do you issue ammo to go with the gun?'

'You gotta be joking. Almost impossible to get enough supplies any more. If you come in I think I can get a couple of full magazines for your personal use. Just keep it under your hat, OK? Not literally, though.' Again he bellowed with laughter at his feeble quip.

Gildas was now staring to become more than a little worried at the personality change in the man sitting alongside him. On his previous stint with the supply convoy Frank had been in charge although Gildas hadn't known his name at the time. Everyone used to call him "The Beast" when out of earshot and "Sarge" at close quarters. Beast suited him better because he was one. Rat-trap mouth, hard face, seemingly unable to smile, let alone laugh, and with a disposition to match. The stereotype barrack-square drill sergeant who only had respect for superior force - and then only grudgingly. Everybody who knew him kept out of his way as much as they could.

Something had happened in the meantime, obviously. A bash on the head, maybe, inducing some sort of benevolent brain damage? Judging by his present surroundings and evident wealth in material goods he had just as obviously fallen on good times. But surely someone of his temperament in charge of vital supplies would always fall on good times if they played their cards right. Still it was all very mysterious.

Gildas decided to push his luck. 'You got a driver for the truck?'

'Ever driven a truck?'

'Sure.' He didn't mention it was at least ten years previously.

'Job's yours.'

'Thanks. When do I start?'

'You eaten yet?'

'Not much.'

'Right, then.' Frank threw away his cigarette. 'Nosh should be ready about now. We'll get some down your neck then see if it's ready to roll. Come with me!'

Gildas followed the Beast back into the redoubt and down a short flight of steps. The walls of the passage changed from loosely-piled concrete blocks to cemented brick clad here and there with loose patches of crumbling plaster. They were descending into a building, which had been covered over with rubble to keep the depot above high-tide level, he realised. They were probably several such buildings under the elevated mound. He racked his brains trying to remember what had stood on this spot before the crash.

A savoury aroma flooded his flaring nostrils as they went through a door into what had once been the ground floor of the house. A small chandelier lit a tastefully decorated and furnished room. On the far side another door opened onto a well-equipped kitchen, where a cook - in proper cook's traditional dress (and *female*, yet) stirred a pot on the stove. The Beast thought of everything, especially for his own comfort. They washed in a tiny sink and sat at the table.

The stew was delicious, so was the dessert, a mixture of fresh and tinned fruits under a tasty shell of real pastry. Gildas had almost forgotten what proper food tasted like. He felt an uncomfortable sense of gratitude towards the Beast and was even prepared to overlook the thinly-veiled innuendoes and overt actions of a crude and distinctly

101

sexual nature performed by his gracious host towards the cook as she served them. If she didn't object, why should he care? And she didn't seem to care, either. A good-looking yet slatternly woman, it was evidently a price she was prepared to pay for living in luxury.

Afterwards, sitting in the blast of a fan, they exchanged small-talk until a deferential knock on the door signalled the convoy was ready to roll. They made their way out into the burning heat. A murmuring sound came from behind the wall; the crowd knew something was about to happen. The Beast thought it necessary to remark on it.

'Don't worry about them. They never learn. Try and attack the trucks every time they poke their noses outside the gates, they do. Flamers'll sort them out.'

'We never had any trouble like this before.' said Gildas. 'What's changed?'

'More people, that's what. They're still piling into the country one way or another. No organisation to stop them any more. It's dog eat dog now if you can find one. Won't be long before we won't get any more food coming in at all. Factory ships are about out of fuel. They'll have to be abandoned within a fortnight. After that it'll hit the fan, you'll see. I can't wait ...'

'What?'

'Never mind. Just remember what I said and make your own arrangements. Wait for me here a minute!'

He left Gildas standing on the causeway and unlocked a small hut built against the perimeter wall, closing the door behind him as he entered. In a few minutes he reappeared carrying a plastic lunch-box. The door was securely locked once more. He handed the box to Gildas.

'Hang on to this till we get to the truck. I'll tell you what to do with it then.'

A fifty-yard walk brought them to the second set of gates, which admitted them into the warehouse yard. Ten decaying trucks were parked in a straggling line outside a large shed with open doors and a few weary men were finishing the loading of the last in line. Few had any glass left in their windows; heavy steel mesh had been bolted or welded over the vulnerable openings to resist the ever-present threat of thrown missiles. Adapted for riot conditions as far as limited resources would allow.

Gildas glanced inside the open warehouse and his heart sank. He began to understand what the Beast had told him. Only a few pallets of food blocks remained in a far corner; the rest of the space was empty. He glanced sideways at the Beast.

'Not much left. I see what you meant.'

The Beast nodded and waved a hairy paw at the line of sheds. 'The shed on the right is about half full, enough for two days or so, the rest are empty. Should have another line of barges the day after tomorrow but there's no guarantee about that. I estimate a maximum of a month before we have to close this place down.'

'Best get out before it happens, huh?'

The Beast gave him a quick glance. 'Draw your own conclusions. Just do as I tell you and it'll be all right. OK?'

'Whatever you say.' *Like hell*, he thought. The nice-guy image just didn't fit. The Beast only looked after the Beast. Be careful and get in first, that's what he really meant. 'What truck have I got?'

'Number three, on the end. The one they're loading.'

Last truck. Nice. Gildas walked up to it. Drab-coloured with a large number 3 scrawled on both sides and the back in watery white emulsion by a brush with gaps in the bristles. He recognised the vehicle.

'This one had a new engine yet?'

'Know it, eh?' The Beast gave a wintry smile. 'No. We keep this one special for the tail-end of the convoy for a very good reason. Get in!'

Gildas scrambled into the cab; not an easy job due to the complete lack of steps or handholds. They had been wrenched off to discourage desperate people clinging to the sides and getting at the drivers. Inside the cab everything was wet as though a hosepipe had been used. It had, he knew, but there was still a tinge of red in some of the puddles on the floor and in the blotches scattered randomly over the seats, and sides. The smell of blood was unmistakable. This was the truck the Beast had mentioned - the one in an ambush. The Beast looked about him and shooed away a couple of guards, who were a bit too near for his liking.

'Now listen! Got that box safe?' Gildas nodded and dropped it in the cubby behind the driving seat. 'Right. Your drop will be the last one. Under the motorway fly-over. Someone will meet you. They'll have a box just like this one. All you have to do is swap over and deliver the other box back to me. I strongly recommend you do not inspect the contents unless you wish to incur my extreme displeasure. Got it?'

Out in the open at last! *This* was the reason the Beast had sheathed his claws and altered his scales especially for his old chum, Gildas. Hah! Gildas raised his hands in acquiescence. 'None of my business, Sarge. Consider it done. Shall I call on you at supper time?'

May as well give the impression he was amenable about being considered on the make. The Beast only understood this way of life.

'I'll see a place is set for you. Good luck!'

The Beast stepped away from the truck. 'All right, you lot. Mount up!'

A few starter motors whined. At other trucks amateur mechanics laboured at large starting handles. Nothing happened to Gildas' truck so he just sat there until he was approached by a grimy individual carrying a thick cable. He attached this to a massive lug crudely welded to the front chassis rail. Another truck rumbled up and the other end of the cable slipped over its rusty tow-hitch. Gildas selected second gear, the cable tightened and the bump-start began.

At the end of the second circuit of the yard the engine finally choked into life. He gunned the accelerator frantically to keep it going. Thick clouds of smoke billowed from underneath and enveloped the cab. Dimly he could see the mechanic battling to release the tow rope, a towel tied over his nose and mouth. The mechanic scuttled to the door and thumped. Gildas leaned out of the window, ducking quickly as the rope was pushed inside followed by the mechanic who jumped up and clung to the window frame. He strove to make out the muffled words the mechanic was shouting at him.

'Don't let 'er stop! Keep 'er goin' whatever you do unless you want to end up stranded like the last crew! Understand?'

'OK' shouted Gildas, jerking the clutch and dislodging the man still clinging to the door. He fell back like a slug anointed with salt and disappeared into the murk as Gildas found first gear, let out the unexpectedly savage clutch and promptly stalled the engine. The whole thing had to be done again.

Finally they got on the move, grinding through the compound gates and lining up on the causeway. Men on top of the wall on the land side began throwing down broken pieces of food blocks. Shouting began. It sounded like a battle, and very likely was. A roaring started from the direction of the main gate, or "Beast's Castle" as Gildas now thought of it. The flame-throwers had been set into ravening life. Frank, in his transparent turret, waved an arm and the gates were flung open. The convoy hastened through, running a gauntlet of hopping, galloping scarecrow figures beating on the sides, throwing rocks at the mesh-covered windows, doing anything they could to stop one of the decrepit lorries and try to loot the contents.

They failed, of course. They always failed. But that didn't stop those not lured from the gates to scrabble for crumbs thrown from the wall from trying. Nothing to lose. Go for it or die trying. And several did; crushed beneath the scarred tyres or falling in the multitude to lie trampled and bleeding by their equals.

Gildas shuddered and tried to blot the screams and pleas from his ears. Life had been rough at times inside the tenement blocks, what with the gangs and disappearances, but it had been a virtual paradise compared to this.

Tough! All that was in the past. He had a mission now, and not the slightest idea how to go about it. As the convoy growled north along the city feeder road, slowly but inexorably towards the motorway, Gildas tried vainly, as he had so often during the last three days, to resolve his dilemma.

CHAPTER 9

It didn't take long for Gildas to appreciate why his truck was kept at the tail end of the convoy.

The smoke!

He knew of this ill-fated truck from his previous stint as a guard, and hated it. Worn cylinders, piston rings and injectors, low compression and out-of-phase timing. All these contributed to the continuous manufacture of thick black clouds issuing from the broken-off exhaust pipe halfway to the rear. A great way of discouraging crowds of hopeful people from following and posing a threat to the security of the vulnerable tail-end Charlie.

Fortunately a stiff breeze flowing from the mountains kept the pall away from the cab and Gildas was grateful for that as he battled to keep the wretched vehicle from stalling or roaring away out of control. He soon found the best way to handle things was to keep in second gear with the engine running at about half revs thus maximising the amount of smoke whilst still being able to keep up with the convoy without the risk of the engine cutting out. How he was expected to cope when they stopped was another matter.

Gildas soon gave up trying to hold some sort of conversation with the guards sharing the cab with him. Six of them, a sullen silent lot. Couldn't blame them really, he thought, this truck always had a reputation for bringing bad luck, usually of the terminal variety, down on the heads of its attendants. From personal experience he knew of four complete crews who had been butchered because of breakdowns suffered whilst delivering and many more had died from ambush attacks or during escapes from tricky situations when the blunt nose of the truck had to be used as a battering ram to plough through tightly packed crowds of desperate, starving rioters. Silently resolving he would not add to their number he concentrated grimly upon keeping the thing mobile, unaware that his luck would shortly be put to the test.

The convoy ground slowly up the valley road. Trucks peeled off occasionally to deliver to the concentration camp once used as a trading estate. Gildas was shocked to note where the high tide mark now reached; over the road in places and most of the former trading units alongside the river were obviously marooned at times. Some had been abandoned; gaping holes in their cladding, where loose sheets had been savaged to be used as roofs; shades to keep off the savage glare of that great flaming eye in the sky. He could see many of the shades between the rickety structures, which became even more tightly packed together as they moved closer to the motorway.

Soon there were only three trucks left, travelling on a different course to the distribution point. This change served to emphasise the increasing breakdown of organisation. Only a few months before there had been at least another fifteen trucks available at this point to travel further afield. The next depot was about twelve miles to the west and they only delivered to further west again. This left nothing for the bit in between, packed with hungry people. Gildas decided there and then he had to arrange his future plans very quickly.

It was done for him. Halfway between the trading estate and their drop-off point the road crossed a river bridge to a roundabout over a subway which carried the main valley road. They turned right on to the slip road and eased through the masses of people, many of whom were waiting to follow the trucks to their destination in the hope of being among the lucky ones to get some food. The dense cloud in the wake of Gildas' truck, so useful in keeping crowds at bay, now revealed another important advantage.

One of the guards coughed, spat on the window and watched it trickle down. Then he spoke at last.

'About here this truck was hit last trip. Others didn't know about it till they reached the drop. By the time they got back it was too late so a little caution may be indicated. Hear me, driver?'

Gildas grunted, wishing he had a rear-view mirror. Anything could come from behind down the slope of the roundabout and he wouldn't know about it. He didn't dare poke his head out to look behind and he knew the futility of asking anyone else to do so. It was a good way of getting instant concussion.

This was a pity because even a quick, casual glance would have spotted a bulky moving object, struggling painfully into view over the rise from the roundabout, as a threat. It was not very big but what it lacked in size it made up for in weight and potential damage capability. A wide metal arm projected from the front reaching to within a couple of feet from the ground. On flapping, wobbly tyres it breasted the rise and began to gather speed down the slope, sparks and flames spewing from holes in the side of the exposed engine where the exhaust manifold should have been. The ear-blasting noise of expelled exhaust gases was itself nearly drowned by a hideous rattling as oil-starved bearings loudly proclaimed their intention to seize up at any moment.

A stretch of roadway clear of people was coming up ahead. Unusually clear! Gildas suddenly experienced an attack of nerves. His sixth sense began to yammer and he wrenched the steering wheel sharply just as he heard a roaring from behind. As the heavy truck lurched and overshot the kerb, Gildas struggled to regain control, dimly aware of a yellowish object whizzing past only a few feet from his shoulder. He slammed on the brakes. The engine lost way and stalled. Gildas released the brakes, pressed the clutch and released it again while he fiddled with the gear lever. The engine caught, stopped then caught again. In a panic Gildas pressed the clutch and throttle hard at the same time, relieved to hear the old engine roar and knock loudly in response. A loud crash sounded from up ahead.

Looking up he saw a faded yellow earth digger embedded into the rear of the truck in front. Swarms of men, many armed, were in the process of jumping off the body frame of the digger, where they had been clinging from ropes and chains, and running forward to the front of the damaged truck. The driver of that truck could not have failed to notice something was amiss and had responded by accelerating, dragging the earth mover along behind by its wide shovel, which had passed under the rear of the truck and wedged itself between the axle and floor.

Struggling to keep the rebellious engine at maximum power and slipping the clutch as well as he could, Gildas bounced the truck along the rough ground at the edge of the road trying to catch up with the depleted convoy. Stick figures scattered, survival temporarily taking precedence over energy conservation. His conscious mind, taking the elements of self-preservation into account, ordered him to get the hell out of it but a vengeful despair and hatred of the very people he was trying to help overrode this. The guard sitting behind him reached forward, wound a window down a little, rested his rifle barrel on the glass and commenced firing steadily at the attackers. He was a very good shot. Men jerked, spun round, fell. Some went under the wheels. He could hear and feel the unmistakable soft "*flump*" of flattening human bodies. He drew alongside the digger. As

109

the truck's front wing passed in front of its big rear driving wheel (flat as a pancake, he had time to notice) he pulled the steering wheel hard to the right and rammed it squarely in the middle, just under the driver's cab.

With a cracking squeal the truck's wing crumbled and dug into its own front tyre. It rasped and squealed, cutting a ragged slot through the tough tyre rubber and metal reinforcement, finally reaching the interior. The tyre exploded and the wheel rim hit the tarmac in a shower of sparks. The digger driver, caught completely by surprise, gave Gildas a shocked look before levelling a nasty-looking revolver at him. He was too late. Under the impetus of the heavy truck the digger lurched up, spoiling the shot. With a loud crash it dropped on to its four wheels once more and Gildas reacted swiftly by pressing his accelerator down to the floor. The truck howled and shuddered. A strong smell of burning clutch wafted through gaps in the bodywork and into the cab. Gildas kept his foot down.

The digger slewed sideways, tearing its rusty shovel clear of its victim. It began to tip. The driver leapt for his life and disappeared screaming under the other rear tyre, also flat, to be squashed like a bug. A red splash revolved on the tattered rubber to splash everything within reach.

With a horrendous clanging the digger toppled right over, the shovel raising the rear of its erstwhile prey completely into the air. Gildas once more wrenched at the steering wheel to avoid the shovel swinging in his direction as the digger revolved slowly on its side. The truck's ruined front wheel just cleared the carcass and he slammed his foot down on the clutch again to keep the engine roaring. The truck in front began to slow down. Sensing a further problem. Gildas drew alongside and saw its driver frantically yanking at the gear lever, mouthing to himself. Seeing Gildas, he jerked his thumb towards the back and used both hands to pantomime a push. Gildas got the message - no drive. Very likely snapped an axle shaft during the collision, he surmised. Only thing to do was try and get back to the depot. He stopped, discovered he couldn't find reverse gear and had to perform a couple of wide U-turns across the dual-carriageway to line up with the rear of the other lorry. The steering was now very heavy indeed, the damaged wheel seemingly capable of locating every small irregularity in the surface of the road and amplifying it into a bone-jarring jolt. Using his rusty front chassis rails and blunt bonnet he pushed the disabled truck forwards, praying the metal would hold enough to avoid puncturing the radiator.

The lead truck had already turned round and was standing by, bristling with the guns of nervous guards, until the linked pair did the same, then it followed behind. The crowd raged at first when it was perceived there wouldn't be any handout, but was emphatically discouraged by several fusillades from the rear truck. All, that is, except for one foolhardy attacker, holding some sort of projectile weapon, who fired wildly after them. Gildas felt the rear of his vehicle sag slightly. One of the twin tyres on the driver's side had been shot out. 'Great!' he shouted, making his companions jump, 'Just what we needed. Pushing this lump all the way home, clutch nearly burned-out, engine ready to pack in, two tyres gone and listing on one side. Just great!'

A mile further down the road the remaining tyre on the same side, unable to take the extra load, also blew out. The list increased alarmingly. Gildas ground his teeth in frustration. They made it back, though. Very slowly. Several times the little convoy was mobbed and the guns came into play. The engine knock became noticeably louder, too. Gildas' jaw ached with tension. It didn't help when the guard who'd spoken before decided to give tongue yet again.

'Beast ain't going to like this.'

'Tough! He'll have to lump it, then.' Gildas concentrated on his work, breathing in shallow puffs to escape the worst effects of the truck's smoke now thick in the cab because of the following wind.

The Beast didn't like it one little bit but Gildas was sure his disapproval, vented loudly in unambiguous language at excessive length, had nothing to do with the plight of the starving refugees deprived of their provisions. Gildas was not invited to supper after all and only received a string of instructions about getting his truck ready for another run early in the morning. This took until well after dark and that night he bedded down in one of the sheds with the others. The Beast took his little package away with him for safe keeping.

The one bright spark was that the Beat had reverted to his true, and more familiar, character. It was all to do with the package, of course. That bit of flannel earlier had only been staged to persuade Gildas to act as courier. He wondered what was in it but refused to contemplate asking. Better not to know; just do the job and await a chance to do what he wanted. Maybe tomorrow. Gildas could cope now, or he would be able to once a good night's sleep had cured a bad dose of the shakes.

A bellowing roar and stink of diesel fumes roused him quivering and disoriented from a troubled sleep plagued by bad dreams of thin, hollow-faced dwarfs swarming all over him. Two seconds later a heavy boot thudded into his ribs.

'Get up you!' Your chariot awaits.'

He looked up through crusted eyelids: no-one was in sight but he'd recognised the voice. The Beast was loose!

Grabbing his rifle he tottered towards the shed door. The air was cool; the sun about to rise. The thundering engine didn't stop and he felt like hell. Not going out yet, surely?

They were, though. As he rounded the side of the building he was transfixed by a solitary headlamp shining directly into his eyes. Squinting, he shuffled along the wall and bumped into a mattress. Well, it looked and felt like a mattress, but this illusion faded when a wide, pink slash

112

opened near the top and the grating tones of the Beast once more assailed his shrinking ears. Hairy barrel-chest and no dentures; an early-morning Beast was no sight for a weak stomach.

'Morning Gil! Have a good night's sleep? Ready to roll?' The tone was conciliatory but the words were lies except for the last three.

Gildas shuddered with nausea. 'Any chance of some breakfast?'

A steel bear-trap clamped on his upper arm and he felt himself propelled towards the light. The Beast bent his head to Gildas' ear.

'None at all, my little friend. You can feed yourself some of the supplies on the way. Take this package and get it up to the motorway junction you didn't get to yesterday!' He released Gildas' arm and opened the truck door. 'You've had two lovely fat new tyres fitted and the metal you ruined has been straightened out - well, nearly. All OK now?'

'Just a minute.' Gildas checked his pockets for the ammunition, his belt for his knives and his rifle in case anyone had stolen the firing pin while he slept. He went to the rear of the truck, trying unsuccessfully to disregard the airborne poison. 'There's only this one? Where are the other trucks?'

'Coming later. You're all on your own, son, and don't tell me you won't do it. I abhor gratuitous violence but I will, repeat will, make a deliberate, albeit reluctant exception in your case if necessary. You know it. Please don't make me do it in front of these impressionable young men.'

Gildas climbed into the cab. The impressionable young men were already on board. Six pairs of bleary eyes glared at him in the gloom as if everything was his fault. He ignored them, and turned back to the Beast.

'Look! It's not so much that I'm bothered about one truck going out alone. The trouble is you're expecting me to take this one. You know how dodgy it is to keep going, just

113

listen to that knock. It's only got to stall once and we're in real trouble if it happens in the wrong place. At least give us another one or send an escort.

'No! Get going! Dump the truck if you have to but get that package to where it's going unless you wish to incur my extreme displeasure. Try to avoid scratching the paintwork again, will you?'

They got. Gildas allowed some of his anger to be vented in the run through the usual crowd at the gates then, when they were out on the open road, he wound the ruined engine right up in top gear and literally pounded along the tarmac, weaving aside only where he had to. On reaching the site of the previous day's ambush there was no sign of the fallen digger. Taken somewhere to be used in another ambush one day, no doubt.

A mile further on they reached the motorway junction. Gildas ordered two of the guards to remain in the back of the truck, two through a trap door on to the roof and another two into the rear compartment to hand out food blocks to the men on the roof when instructed. They slowly entered the roundabout, a throng of people following behind. Without stopping, he managed to get into bottom gear and shouted to the guards on the roof to start throwing food blocks out as far as they could. The truck slowly trundled around the island, Gildas bobbing his head occasionally out of the window, searching for those he had come to meet.

Three quarters of the way round, as they were passing under the motorway bridge, he was sure he spotted them. It had to be them. An organisation of some sort was necessary for the exchange of trade goods and this bunch looked properly organised; heavily-armed and better fed then the unfortunates fighting and scrambling for the broken blocks being thrown carelessly onto the roadway from the truck roof, and banded together in an appearance of casual discipline. A typical shanty-town gang under the control of a bully-boy warlord. About a dozen of them came

114

swaggering down from the dark cleft under one end of the bridge, heading purposefully for the truck, stopped as they reached the edge of the road and stood still, weapons at the ready. People running for the food handout gave them a wide berth.

Gildas suppressed a sudden blazing flare of instinctive hatred and slowed down as much as he dared. He opened the window.

'You got something for me?' he called.

One of them nodded and produced a small cloth bag from somewhere among his rags. Handing what looked like a heavy builder's hammer (obviously a weapon of some sort) to one of his colleagues, he hurried forward 'Here! Stop the truck!' he shouted

'Not a chance. Wait a minute!'

Keeping the truck barely moving, Gildas removed the quick-release rails holding the protective window mesh in place and passed the rails and mesh to one of the guards sitting behind.

'You get up here!' He said loudly tapping the window frame. The man leapt up, jamming his elbows to each side and thrusting his muscular chest into the cab. There was no step for him to stand on and he was forced to rely on his arm muscles alone to stay in place. He knew he was vulnerable but counted on his fellow bandits to protect him. His bronzed, brutish face pushed to within a few inches from Gildas' nose.

'Show me!'

Gildas reached behind his seat and pulled out the box. He showed it to the man, who reached for it eagerly, barely maintaining his precarious balance with only one arm. Gildas snatched the box back. 'Not here! Exchange out of sight. Hang on!'

'Can't. Go round the roundabout again. One of my people come with me. Two of yours stay with you, the rest wait with my men till we get back. Do it my way or not at all and someone with a bit more bottle'll have to come.

Beast might get upset if you go back empty-handed.' He uttered a short laugh like a bark and dropped from sight.

Clare Masson had watched this brief exchange from her shaded position under the bridge. She'd held back when she'd spotting who was driving the truck but as the head thug returned to his crew she trotted down to join them in time to hear Shinks giving his orders.

' Clare and Duggy'll come in the truck with me and if we're not back in half an hour you know what to do. Let the mob take the bodies after you've stripped them and then come looking for us. If we get back OK, watch for my signal, disarm the guards if you can and secure the truck. If there's a chance to get the cargo, we'll take it. Beast won't care long as he gets his lousy truck back. Got it?'

Clare's ears twitched. Shinks going in the truck? How convenient. Now this could just turn out to be a classic case of poetic justice.

She'd become part of this particular bunch of thugs only two days before. It hadn't been very difficult for one of her experience to follow the trail of the killers who had raided Gildas' living unit and she'd traced them to this gang who tended to live a nomadic existence. Only Shinks was still with them at the moment, Dave and the other two having departed to an unknown destination further up the valley.

She hadn't met Dave, who'd departed just before she found them. The other two had left to follow him only that morning. Unable to contact Gildas she'd waited until she could be sure that they would all be together - and then they could all die together.

Now Gildas had turned up too soon, driving the very truck the gang had been waiting for. Just in time, too! A couple of her comrades were exhibiting signs of withdrawal.

'I fancy a ride in the truck.' She pushed her way to the front. 'Best not to take Duggy 'cos he gets car sick. Leave him here! I'll come along to protect your manly body from those nasty men.' She smiled at Shinks, friendly and sardonic at the same time. He was still a little bit nervous of her, having seen her in action a few times. He turned to Duggy.

'Feeling a bit bilious today Doug?'

'Well, yes, I am a bit queasy. Like Clare says, she'd be more use than me at the moment.' He was terrified of the tough, stocky woman and not ashamed to show it.

Clare smiled sweetly at him. Duggy moved back out of her reach, face twitching in an effort to restrain his bad temper. He always got like that when his "stuff" became hard to find.

The truck returned after its slow journey round the island. The door opened, guards leapt out leaving two of their number in the cab. Following the still-moving vehicle, Clare climbed into the rear seat, pressing as far into the corner as she could, while Shinks sat in front with Gildas. With his eyes fixed on the road, he hadn't registered her entrance. When the door slammed shut he accelerated, rounded the island once more and headed up the main valley road, crushing those shelters he was unable to avoid.

Two miles on, at the end of a long straight stretch, he pulled into a lay-by and selected neutral gear. The engine settled to an erratic rumble, rocking the truck slightly. No more shelters could be seen and only a few small groups of people were in sight; those heading south burdened with firewood from the few remaining desiccated woodlands to the north.

Very few people tried to scratch a living more than a couple of miles from the food distribution routes and so there was more chance of obtaining other benefits. The opportunity to find supplies of drinkable water was one. Trade in wood and other useful raw materials was another; even a couple of ancient coal mines were still being worked by those with enough strength to spare. This had the additional payoff of a water supply from deep underground where some seepage still gathered from the massively depleted water-table.

117

These trade goods could be carried or wheeled on rickety carts to the main settlements and exchanged for enough food to survive unless someone stronger took it from them. Any trade tended to be a matter of taking chances.

The engine threatened to stall. Fortunately, someone had considerately repaired the hand throttle. Gildas set it up far enough for the engine to keep going without any risk of choking to a halt. He opened his door and retrieved the package once more. He jerked his head. 'Out!'

Locking eyes with Gildas, Swinging his "Basher" casually in one hand, Shinks got out and walked several yards in front of the truck. Clare reached out to tap Gildas on the shoulder. The guard sitting beside her made the mistake of grabbing her arm in a futile effort to restrain her. Hs cries of pain attracted Gildas' attention. Turning round he goggled at Clare in disbelief. 'Where on earth did you spring from? You'd better leave that poor man alone in case he gets too badly injured.'

Clare obeyed, but only after giving one last extra twist to extract a more satisfactory squeal from her hapless victim 'Better introduce me, hadn't you?'

'This frail young lady is called Clare.' he informed the two scowling guards. 'She's a friend of mine and she's on our side, so stop playing around with her and try to be nice. I'm getting out now.' Keep a close watch, will you? I don't trust this guy.' Sling the strap of his rifle over one shoulder, he climbed from the cab, holding the box in plain view

'Never trust anyone, remember?' Clare reminded him. They call him Shinks, by the way. He's a nasty piece of work. Tell you why, soon.' Anticipating what was likely to happen, she reached down and got her rifle ready by flicking off the safety catch and raising it to her shoulder with the barrel sticking out of the window. As Gildas walked slowly towards Shinks, she loaded a round into the breach.

Although it had not been prearranged, Clare knew that Shinks believed she would protect his back and deal with any threat from the guards in the cab. At the distinctive sound of the rifle being cocked, both men in the road swung their heads towards the truck. Shinks reacted instantly. With a convulsive jerk he threw his Basher at Gildas, striking him in the stomach. Gilds folded up in pain, dropped his rifle and Shinks made a dive to seize it.

Clare squeezed the trigger and made a snap shot, hoping she wouldn't kill him. Her aim, such as it was, sped true. Shinks took the slug in his left shoulder and fell, yelling in shock and pain. Clare climbed out of the truck slotting another bullet into the breach and switching to full automatic. 'You OK Gil?' she called.

Gildas waved a feeble arm. Clare walked across and helped him to his feet, leading him back to the truck, listening carefully for any sounds behind her back. Sure enough, Shinks took the chance she'd given him.

Alerted by the scratch of boots on tarmac, she span round, gun at the ready. Shinks had already started to move and was about to escape over the crash barrier at the side of the lay-by. Unfortunately for him he hadn't enough time to snatch up his weapon lying near the front of the truck, where it had ended up after hitting Gildas.

Clare brought up her rifle and squeezed the trigger once more. Shinks jumped the barrier, jerking in mid-air under the impact of a stream of bullets, and disappeared. Clare walked over to the crash barrier, Gildas following slowly behind.

Shinks was still conscious, twitching and trembling slightly. A single bullet had got him in the side of the throat. The spray of blood here was very slight. It was a different matter down below where several slugs had taken him in the groin and right thigh. Already the arterial gushes had diminished almost to nothing and barely splattered the surface of the large pool steadily sinking into the parched soil. Clare regarded him with a total lack of compassion then turned to address Gildas.

'See this guy? He was one of those who butchered your wife so if you want him to know why he's dying you don't have much time. I'll leave him to you.' She turned away to pick up the discarded weapons and return to the truck.

Gildas knelt down beside the dying man, who was watching him through vacant eyes already dimming with the onset of terminal unconsciousness. He didn't know what to say. He felt dirty and helpless to control his own destiny let alone that of another. With an effort he reached out to clasp the other's shoulder. The movement prompted words.

'Do you know why this has happened to you?'

The man's mouth dropped open disturbing an enormous bluebottle, which had been trying to force its way between the visibly paling lips. Not much time left. Gildas spoke again.

'You killed my wife, you and three others. Back in Town. One of the tenements, remember?'

No sound, of course, but a slight flare of the nostrils and a crinkling at the corners of the eyes was an answer of sorts. If so, it could have been interpreted as an expression of amusement. Gildas took it as such.

Fighting the urge to scream at the futility of this and all of life he slid the worn gutting knife from its sheath and held it before the face of his victim. The face became very still.

'He's going.' thought Gildas. *'Do it now!'*

As the random miracle of life slipped reluctantly out of the man's body, Gildas slid his knife into the wound made by the bullet in the neck. Hesitantly at first, then with a rush, twisting so that the sharp edge faced forwards and pulling it viciously towards himself. The corpse's head wobbled loosely as the blade whispered free and a savage grin etched itself on the face as if in mirth combined with surprise. Gildas choked, wiped the thin blade on the man's clothes then, in a sudden blaze of fury slashed the face again and again to wipe out the smile. Pallid slashes opened up; there was no more blood left. Panting with emotion he sat flaccid, looking at his handiwork, then cleaned the blade once more and returned it to its sheath. He drew a revolver from his waistband.

A single shot blasted. After a pause there was a short, spaced fusillade. Gildas loped over to the truck. His cheeks were wet and his strong lower jaw worked silently as though he was chewing something. Clare stood silent and unmoving by the open driver's door.

There was nothing useful to be said. Climbing aboard, they took the guards back to the roundabout and headed further north.

It was a considerable time before any words passed between them.

CHAPTER 10

By the time they'd travelled three miles further up the main valley road Clare decided things had gone far enough. The lack of speech was bad but the look on Gildas' face was distinctly unnerving.

'Where are we going?'

Gildas gave no indication he'd heard. His gaze was fixed upon the far distance; he didn't seem to see the small gaggle of traders who had to fling themselves madly to one side to avoid being crushed by the truck's hard, scarred tyres. His face was crumpled like a wet towel.

'Gil, stop this truck! Gil. GIL!' Clare prodded her gun barrel into his ribs. She prodded again, harder. 'Gil!'

Gildas swung his head to face her. She recoiled from the fury etched into his face. All at once it collapsed and he seemed to relax, applying the brakes hard. Knocking the gearbox into neutral he allowed the worn, squealing friction pads to slow their speed and pulled off the road leading to a bridge over what was left of the river. No-one was in sight.

The truck trundled slowly forwards until the front wheels were on the narrow steel bridge. Gildas operated the hand throttle once more and slumped across the steering wheel. Clare remained silent.

After a few minutes Gildas sighed, stretched and clambered over the seats to the cargo compartment, returning with a two-gallon container.

'We need water for the radiator and I don't want to use the drinking supply. Cover me !'

Clare climbed the ladder to the roof and stood on guard while her little companion slid down the bank and crossed the bleached pebbles. A tiny trickle of discoloured water showed at intervals. At one of the deeper pools, with a bit of extra excavation, Gildas managed to nearly fill the container.

Returning to the truck he turned it around, crossed the main road and climbed a road up the side of the valley through a couple of hairpin bends. Gaunt, shattered houses lined the road, standing tired and despondent among the miniature deserts of their small, dusty gardens. In a convenient driveway he turned the truck round once more to face it downhill, locked the wheels into the kerb and switched off the engine.

It wouldn't stop. Gildas was forced to slam it into gear and stall it. With a hideous rattle and a series of violent jerks it died. Steam appeared from under the engine cover. A moaning sound punctuated with sharp cracks and clicks filled the air as the overheated power unit began to cool.

'Thought it was beginning to heat up.' He explained. 'Can't put water in yet, we'll have to wait a while. Go back on the roof and watch for trouble!'

Clare did as she was told - in her book, security came a long way before curiosity - but in the time before Gildas emerged carrying the water bottle she saw nobody. Who'd want to stay in this dump, anyway?

The radiator cap clattered. Gildas gasped as his hands came into contact with hot metal. In a few minutes the radiator had been filled and he shouted for Clare to get back inside. As soon as she had done so he struggled to swing the wheels out of the kerb and the heavy vehicle gathered speed down the hill. Fighting the floppy gear lever he managed to bump start the engine. It bellowed into life and they turned onto the main road once more, still heading north.

Gildas seemed more relaxed now, Clare was pleased to notice. Without taking his eyes from the road, he spoke.

'Sorry about that, the engine'll only start that way. If it ever stops on the flat we'll have to abandon it. There's a place further on where we can rest safely for a while and feed.'

The sun passed its zenith before they reached Gildas' safe haven close to what used to be a golf course on a side road. Only a few dead trees lined the tarmac and they could see far to the north where the mountains raised pale hunched shoulders into the heat-haze. Gildas stalled and secured the truck on a slope and they both climbed out. Clare broke the silence which had lasted since they filled the radiator.

'What was all that about back there?'

'How do you mean?'

'You've been too damned quiet. Ever since we took over the truck. Bit upset, were you? Had plans of your own that I messed up, maybe?'

'No plans,' Gildas sat on the roadside bank and patted a flat spot at his side. Clare sat, after carefully checking the mountain wasteland to the north.

Gildas thought for a moment, 'How come you were in the truck? Wouldn't have thought you'd have had anything to do with that lot.'

For some reason Clare realised she was feeling slightly embarrassed. That hadn't happened for many years.

123

'Had a bit of luck. When I left your unit I came across a rumour, followed a trail of talk - you know how it gets around, there not being much to talk about these days - and the trail led straight to the gang you were looking for.'

'What trail? What rumours?'

'Your wife. The ones that did her in. You do realise that the guy you finished off was one of them?'

'So you said.'

'Did you speak to him?'

'Yes.' Gildas did not elaborate any further. Clare decided not to pursue the subject.

'That was Shinks. He was the only one with the group when you turned up so I climbed aboard to hand him over to you.'

Gildas buried his gargoyle face in his gnarled hands and moved them up and down tiredly. 'Nice of you. You followed them? You set him up for me to kill? You did that - for *me*?' It was as if he couldn't believe it.

'Why not?' Clare tossed her head. 'I didn't have anything better to do and I was getting bored. Aren't you pleased, for God's sake?'

He looked up at her. She couldn't read his expression.

'I suppose I'd better say thanks.' He gave a weak grin, which disappeared as quickly as it had come. 'Where are the others? There were four of them; one was called Dave.'

'The other three had left by the time I arrived. Dave, the ringleader, had gone first then the other two followed him a couple of days later. Don't know where, only that they went up the valley. I've been keeping an eye out for them on our way up here, but no sign. Either they've gone up a side valley or they're still ahead somewhere. What were you doing in a single truck up at the motorway, anyway? That's a good way to get dead.'

'Got trapped into delivering a package, didn't I? Didn't want to do it but I had no choice if I wanted to stay mobile to find those I'm looking for. Don't even know what was in it.'

'Drugs.'

'Drugs?' Gildas gaped in disbelief. 'Even now? Among that lot of poor devils down there, you're telling me, are still some who think that drugs, dope, junk, whatever has any importance at all?' Gildas found this hard to take in. He got up and went to the truck. 'Not calling you a liar but I've got to see for myself before I can believe anyone has got a sense of priority like that these days. Junkies should have been among the first to die off.'

Sure enough, when Gildas opened the little package he found a couple of new syringes, several glass phials of liquid and a number of plastic bottles and packets filled with powders and pills of varying sizes and colours. He surveyed the contents with incredulity then, with a snort of rage flung it across the road. Bottles rolled, packets scattered, one phial broke, the liquid it contained immediately vanishing into the parched soil.

Gildas marched jerkily a little way up the road and stood facing the silent mountains. He seemed to be in some distress. Clare left him alone and commenced the kind of task which more practical womankind has always considered more important than tantrums - the preparation of a meal.

There wasn't much choice but what was available was there in bulk; nearly a whole truck-full of protein blocks. She set up her little solar-powered "volcano", added a couple of cupfuls of drinking water from the truck's supplies and lit a handful of twigs broken from dead trees lining the road. Leaving it to boil, she crumbled one of the grey-pink cubes into a billy-can then waited. When the water was boiling she added it to the powder and stirred it into a thick, odourless soup.

Gildas was still in the same place, staring unseeingly into the distance. Clare's call to the repast went unnoticed. The soup would soon cool down. She refused to allow her efforts to be wasted and went to him, took his arm and pulled him into the shade of the truck where the billy-can

125

stood steaming. He offered no resistance and followed like a little boy who had been soundly scolded.

'Eat!' she ordered.

He ate, without enthusiasm or comment, then promptly fell asleep.

For three hours Clare patrolled up and down the road, half hoping trouble would appear and give her the opportunity to kill something. The surroundings remained barren and silent. She picked up the drugs stolen from the scarce medical supplies entrusted to the depot and hid them in the truck. They might come in useful as trade goods. Her frustration with her moody companion increased. Eventually Gildas joined her, cracking his finger joints and stretching his limbs.

They walked together for a while, then. . . 'There is a reason.' he said.

'For what?'

'You know. Don't play games! None of this is a game to me.'

'It isn't for anyone these days. What makes you think you deserve special treatment?'

Gildas put a hand on her shoulder and tried to pull her to a stop. It didn't work. She shrugged it off and continued walking. Gildas stopped.

'Wait!' he said. 'Let me explain! Please!'

Clare sat heavily on the bank and sighed.

'I think I know. I guess I knew when you asked me to educate you in the physical arts. You're not used to having to live this way, are you? Well, neither are six thousand million others, and most of them are dead by now. You're one of the lucky ones and you're still grizzling.'

Gildas had the grace to look ashamed. 'I know that, intellectually, but ... ' he paused, then suddenly burst out, 'I don't want to die but I can't come to terms with all this.' He calmed and spread out his arms, rotating to encompass the entire landscape. 'Do you know what this place used to be

126

like? Have you ever been here before it stopped raining? Have you?'

'No.'

'It was beautiful here. Me and the wife often used to come here for a walk up those two small valleys there.' He gestured towards the mountains, then to the west. 'And over that way there's a deep valley with a rough and pretty river which we used to follow up as far as we could. Sometimes we'd bring a picnic. The wife loved it up here. Nobody around, see? I used to catch a few fish sometimes, trout, and we'd grill them over a fire to eat with our sandwiches. It's all gone now. No river, no fish, no greenery, nothing. Everything's gone and it'll never come back in our lifetimes. There's nothing worthwhile left.

Clare disagreed. 'It's just different, that's all. Take another look. It's still beautiful. Lifeless, harsh, empty maybe, but beautiful in a different way. Accept it as it is, don't grieve for it as it was.'

Gildas looked at the ground and shuffled his feet. 'A few weeks ago I might have agreed with you. When my family was destroyed it altered everything. Sometimes I wish I'd died with them but I've got a job to do now.' His jaw muscles twisted. 'Kill the ones who did it. After that, who knows?'

'Them?' Clare asked softly.

'Yes. Kill them!'

'No. No, you said you wished you'd died with them. I know about your wife. Who else was there?'

'Never mind.'

'Tell me! Did you have any children or somebody else living with you?'

Gildas shuffled again. 'I didn't find the body but I know he's dead. Probably been eaten.'

'You had a son? But you told me ...'

'No. I know it sounds stupid but please don't laugh ... we had a cat, a beautiful Siamese cat, and they took him.'

Clare had no inclination to laugh. It was easy to tell the ugly little man was close to tears and her heart went out to him. She felt an unexpected urge to clutch him to her and soothe him until he felt better. So it was true they had no children, just a cat, which was very likely doted upon and treated with more affection and love than most children still alive in these misbegotten times would ever experience.

Poor Gildas! 'I'm sorry.' Clare said, touching his arm to communicate her very real sympathy. 'Let's go back to the truck. I suppose you want to try to find them?'

Gildas nodded. 'I can take you back to the motorway first, if you like. I've got plenty of fuel; enough for two hundred miles or so.'

They began to retrace their steps. Clare feigned indignation. 'Not a chance! This is much more interesting. We can get a long way before dark. Let's go!'

'Thanks.' Gildas said. 'I could use the company as well as some help.'

The engine started easily down the hill. Rejoining the main road they headed further north. The valley became narrower as they neared the headwaters, now totally devoid of water of any sort. After another six or seven miles the road climbed steeply up a pass leading to another valley beyond the encircling mountains. Labouring hard in low gear the decrepit truck howled its agony up the narrow canyon in a thick cloud of smoke. At the top, another mile had to be covered before a down-hill steep enough to restart the engine was reached. Gratefully, Gildas switched it off again.

Up on this high ground there was not the slightest sign of life. A few isolated houses stood scattered here and there, small patched of trees and bushes thrust clawed and blackened branches to the pitiless sky and an empty reservoir far below the road lay dusty and pale at the foot of its retaining wall. No birds were to be seen or heard and even the social insects like ants had abandoned the useless fight for survival.

A holocaust landscape indeed!

The depleted radiator had to be filled again - this time with their precious drinking water. Still, they had enough for their needs. Pressing onwards, a couple more miles were covered as the sun approached the horizon.

A tiny village lay ahead at the end of a long, straight piece of road. Gildas' survival instinct began to twitch. He took his foot off the accelerator.

'I can feel it too.' Clare stated with certainty. 'The racket we're making can be heard for miles. Anyone there will be well prepared for us by now. Don't stop! I'll climb into the back. If you think they're harmless, use your own judgement whether to stop or not. I'll deal with them if they turn nasty.'

Gildas' instinct had been true, as usual, but as it happened there seemed to be no problem. As he approached the little collection of houses a figure stepped out into the road, laid down a rifle and walked towards the truck holding both arms straight out sideways. Gildas slowed the truck, passed the figure - a man - and came to a squealing halt a hundred yards further on forcing the man to trot behind. No challenge came from Clare and the man stopped by the driver's door well out of reach.

Gildas nodded, unsmiling. 'Got a problem? Need any help?'

'Well, not really. Just wondered if you've come from Town.'

'Yes. Thought I'd take a nice run in the country. You live here?'

The man grinned. 'No. Don't think anyone could make a living here. We're from Town too. Just making our way home.'

'Where from?'

'Had a, er, mission. Place not far from here needed some supplies. We were commissioned to provide the supplies. Man's got to get food and his needs where he can these days, y'know. This one of the food trucks, is it?'

'Why? And who's the Man?'

'Well, the Man's in charge of the station and they're bound to be getting a bit low on grub up there so I thought you were doing a delivery.'

Gildas thought fast. 'So we're still on the right road, then? Never been this way before and the directions weren't all that good. How far to go?'

'Only about seven miles or so. Just carry on till you come to the junction with another main road, turn left then first right and follow the lane for just over a mile. First village you come to.'

'Met anybody else on your way back here?'

'No. No-one to be found north of here except for the station. You want we should tag along with you for company and give a hand to unload? That way we can earn a lift with you back into Town. How about it?'

'No thanks. I'll be OK. Not going back for quite a while, anyway.'

'Fair enough, but if you've got a couple of food blocks to spare we'd appreciate a donation. They won't be missed.'

'We?'

'Huh?'

'You keep saying "we". Where's your mates?'

At this softly-spoken question the man realised he'd made the most stupid mistake possible. He tried to cover it up but someone else ... someone hiding in a house on the corner of a side road, had heard.

'Only a figure of ...'

'Hold it right there!' A harsh voice, running feet, a single shot, a clatter as a gun fell to the floor. All this out of Gildas' sight behind the truck. The man he'd been speaking to turned to run.

'Stop, or I'll fire!' Gildas shouted.

The man jolted to a halt and raised his arms above his head. Clare paced silently up behind him.

'Come on out, Gil!'

He jacked up the hand throttle and climbed out stiffly. At once the truck began to creep forwards. He reached inside and pressed the brake pedal with his hand.

'Clare! Get that guy to bring a big rock over here and put it under one of the front wheels!'

'Clare?' The man turned to see who was sticking a hot gun barrel into his ribs. His face lit up. 'Clare! Thank the Lord it's you! We'd never have tried anything rough if we'd known you were on board. You remember me?'

'Yeah, I know you - and your buddy. Now get the rock and do like he says. That's a nice big one over there.'

The rock was placed to secure the truck. The man dusted his hands and approached Gildas.

'Get those hands back up and see to your mate, or don't you care what I've done with him?' snapped Clare. She looked angry. Gildas strongly suspected he knew the reason.

The other would-be bushwhacker lay on his side clasping his right leg. A red puddle spread underneath.

'Why did you plug me Clare? If we'd known ...'

'Shut up! I didn't plug you, I made you leak' She handed her gun to Gildas. 'No need for names. You know who these guys are?'

Gildas nodded. 'I can guess.'

'Right enough! They're all yours now. Try not to waste too many bullets!' Clare turned away.

Gildas stared into the white faces of the two men. God, he didn't want to do this. Left to himself he might have walked away. Unbidden, a picture of a small, jolly woman holding a purring cat with a silly smile on its face came into his mind. The men before him faded into a couple of cardboard cut-outs of the type found on a combat training firing range. Colour dimmed to be replaced with black and white tones.

It was a lot easier with this in his mind. He shot the one standing. The single bullet tore a large hole in the man's groin. He fell, mouth in a silent "O" and eyes unfocussed.

The other man screamed. Gildas shot him too. In the same place but this time the bullet ricocheted from the road and emerged from his stomach after shattering his lower spine on the way.

Both would live - for a while. Gildas turned his back on them, ignoring the groans and shrill screams. With a bit of luck they would take a long time about it. It felt fitting after what they had done to his family.

Clare was waiting for him in the cab of the truck. As he climbed in she regarded him quizzically. 'So you're not going to finish them off?'

'Let them suffer!' snarled Gildas. Clare's face set into hard lines and she stayed his arm as he reached for the gear lever.

'No you don't. I'm not about to let them stay like that no matter what they've done. It's not what I led you to them for. Either you finish the job or I'll do it for you.' She opened her door.

One of the men was still screaming hoarsely, heard even over the violent knocking of the engine. 'Stop! I'll do it.' Gildas said.

He walked to the men. One had mercifully passed out; the other was sitting up frantically clasping the ruin of his smashed groin and keening miserably. Gildas reached into his pocket and withdrew the thin gutting knife he'd confiscated from the erstwhile mugger back at the tenement block. Its worn, thin blade reflected the setting sun with a misty golden sheen. His victim looked back at him, helpless, tormented, yet still aggressive. No words passed were spoken.

In sudden decision, Gildas stepped behind the man, grabbed his shock of matted hair and tilted his head sharply back. The knife descended and swept soundlessly across the throat. A harsh gurgle bubbling through a thick gout of blood, a thin squeak as the edge of the blade failed to sever a neck vertebra and the job was done. Gildas let go the hair and the body slumped flabbily onto the road. Jerky and uncoordinated now, Gildas slit the throat of the other one as well, for good measure, dropped the knife and completed the job up by throwing up over the corpse.

He sank to his knees, retching, only dimly aware of a figure approaching and strong arms pulling him back on his feet. He clung to the figure desperately, sinking his face into soft, pleasantly-smelling cloth and fought to avoid losing his last vestiges of self-control.

Clare patted his head and made soothing noises. They stood locked together for several minutes.

Gildas soon recovered enough to remember where he was. He pulled away, shuddering and looking wildly about. Without even glancing at Clare or his victims, he located the knife where he'd dropped it, cleaned and sheathed the terrible little blade and ran to the truck, almost hurling himself into the driving seat.

'Come on, then!' he shouted, gunning the engine madly.

She walked casually around the front to stay clear of the oily smoke and climbed in by his side. 'Want me to take over the wheel for a while?' she asked.

In answer, Gildas accelerated as hard as the old truck could endure.

'Where are we going now.' Clare said as though nothing whatsoever had happened.

Gildas wiped his eyes and answered in the same manner. It could be rather unnerving to observe these sudden changes of mood and emotion. To Clare, he seemed to be running on automatic pilot much of the time; the real Gildas hidden carefully away until such time as his quest for revenge came to an end.

'Those two guys just came from some sort of a place a few miles up the road.' he said in clipped tones. 'Some station or other, they called it. Maybe Dave, the last one, will be there. Might as well get it all over with in a single day.'

Clare shook her head. 'No way.' You haven't seen him. Neither have I but from what I've heard it'll take both of us

133

to sort *him* out. You're too tired. Let's find a place to camp overnight and get there first thing in the morning.'

It took a bit of persuasion but Gildas eventually realised the sense of her decision. They had to turn round and retrace their route in order to find a suitable place on a hill with a clear view in all directions. Food, then sleep in shifts; first one then the other taking vigilant and, fortunately, uneventful watches.

Mid-morning they were on their way again. Passing through the small village, Gildas discovered the two corpses had disappeared, only a large stain on the dusty tarmac remaining to show where they had lain. So there were still a few predators left able to adapt in some measure and clean up the carrion even in these parched, barren environs, Clare thought. It was a warning. She felt no desire to investigate where the corpses had gone or find what had taken them.

Following the directions Gildas had been given they came to a bridge over what used to be a sparkling river in a lush valley, now dry and dusty. The radiator was filled once more from a small, filthy pool in the river bed. Up the hill, down the other side and there was the station - or what was once a tiny hamlet evidently still occupied.

There wasn't much; a few nice-looking houses, a farm and a chapel nestling in a narrow valley with a masonry arch bridge straddling the bed of a dry stream. Other newer buildings had been erected to enlarge the total area and the originals linked together by means of windowless corridors. A helicopter pad marked with a large white cross was laid out in the hard-packed dust of an adjoining field. Two people in white robes stood near the landing pad watching the truck draw near.

And, wonder of wonders, a tiny patch of green! Trees! Grass! Flowers! All growing close about the shores of a small pool of open water in the stream bed just above the bridge. Gildas stopped the truck by the first house in the village. The two people in white crossed the edge of the field and the dry stream bed, stopping at the roadside.

One of them nodded affably. Gildas returned the silent greeting and tried to smile. The man, for man it was, said 'Lost your way or have you anything for us? You are not expected.'

'Got a full load of food blocks if you want them. All we want in return is some information.

The man smiled. 'That depends on the information, but well do our best to help and we could certainly use the supplies. Deliveries from our regular sources have become rather erratic lately. By the way, that house on your left has several armed men watching you. No offence, it's only a precaution. We've got to be careful nowadays.

Clare hunched down in her seat and snapped her gun to fully automatic fire. Gildas saw no immediate danger and felt no resentment. The back of the truck could have been filled with heavily armed and nasty bandits for all these people knew. 'We'll have to park this truck on a hill or we'll never get it going again.'

'No problem. To save carrying things twice, park in the farmyard up ahead and we'll unload there. We can always use one of our own transporters to get you going again. No need to be worried, we're not aggressive here.'

It was already too late to back out, Gildas knew. Two men, both with machine pistols and one clasping a small missile cradle, emerged from the house. From their look and bearing Gildas suspected they were professional soldiers.

Clare didn't suspect - she knew for certain. 'Those are trained army men.' she said. 'SAS copycats, for a bet. We should be safe from them as long as we don't start anything. This must be a Government establishment. Thought all that nonsense had gone by the board. How come this place is still functioning?'

'We'll find out as part of the deal for the food.' Gildas replied.

The soldiers checked the cab and opened the rear of the truck. No stowaways would have had a chance with that missile trained on the opening. At their signal, Gildas engaged gears and moved slowly into the farmyard. At another signal he switched off the engine.

When the rattling and knocking had finally ceased, a breathless calm descended over the hamlet. For better or worse they were here.

Now where was Dave?

CHAPTER 11

With a ruthless, yet surprisingly gentle efficiency, they were totally disarmed and politely asked to stand in the shade of the barn until someone in charge came to speak to them. The interior of the truck was also thoroughly inspected, all discovered weapons piled up in one place, but nothing was removed. Clare was accustomed to this procedure and offered no protest whilst Gildas muttered and shuffled his feet. He'd never taken kindly to anyone ordering him around and felt aggrieved at the fact even his little knife had been taken from him.

Only one of the soldiers remained to keep an eye on things and he stayed close enough for conversation to be difficult. He seemed amiable enough but Clare's trained eye recognised the signs that signified his potential for immediate, and possibly fatal, response to any untoward action. Even at mid-morning it was already stifling hot.

Another man (they hadn't seen any woman so far) in white robes sauntered across from the direction of the pretty whitewashed chapel over the dried-out stream. He was whistling. Catching sight of the pair waiting in the shade the whistle ceased abruptly and his pace increased. Coming closer he stopped and put his head to one side as if to see more clearly.

'Gildas? It is, by God! What on earth are *you* doing here?'

Gildas was nonplussed for a moment. Then a wide grin split his creased face into two unequal sections. 'You! I could ask the same thing. Hardly recognise you in the spook outfit.' He turned to Clare. 'I know this man. We used to work together. Everything's OK.' He stepped forward holding out his hand. The sentry instantly came on the alert and lifted his rifle to point at Gildas.

The Man noticed the warning movement and waved a casual hand at the guard, who lowered his aim. 'It's all right, Hal. He's an old friend.' Then, to Gildas, 'But I don't know your companion. Is she safe?'

'Safe, nervous and thirsty, like me. It's good to see you.'

'You too. I can't do much about your nerves; these army boys won't allow anybody near the station to carry weapons in case the heat and stress send somebody round the bend. Not even me, and I'm in charge of the place. Don't worry, you'll get all your toys back when you leave. But I can do something about the thirst. Fancy a cup of tea? *Real* tea!'

'Tea?' Gildas had to restrain himself from howling with joy. He hadn't tasted a proper cup of tea for nearly five years and he'd always loved his teapot. His wife had always conjured up a delicious brew and ... STOP!. Don't think about it! He blinked his suddenly watery eyes. 'Lead me to it, quick!'

It *was* real tea, too. How had they managed to get hold of it? In the small, neat refectory the Man performed the mandatory rituals of electric kettle, teapot and pouring with evident relish as though this was a special occasion for him as well. Carrying the steaming mugs on a tray he joined them at a table and confirmed the fact.

'Very little left. We only bring it out for VIPs and this will convince everybody here of your status more than any words of mine would do. It's one of the few decisions I really like to make. Cheers!' He lifted his mug in salute.

For a minute or two there was a reverent silence only broken by the occasional slurp. Gildas resumed the conversation.

'So you're in charge, eh? Where's the family; I've only ever met your boy, y'know. And how did you manage to get up here and take over the place?'

Family's gone.' The Man's face took on an expression of barely suppressed grief. 'All of them. I'd rather not talk about it. It's a familiar story these days.'

'Sorry.' Gildas buried his face in his mug to hide his discomfiture. 'But not so long ago you were struggling to make a living down at the camp just outside Town. You asked me then where would I recommend you to move to and I remember telling you to stay put. How did you end up here?'

'I simply headed up the valley to end it all in the mountains. A man can go a long way without food; it's water that's the problem. By the time I reached the main river bridge just down the road a way I was just about finished but there was a little pool there - not fit for drinking as I found to my cost - bad gut for three days - then carried on. Fifteen minutes later I was stopped by the guards here. Been here ever since. That's it.'

'And they quietly let you take over a place like this because you're a nice guy, yes?' Clare was sceptical. Clare was always sceptical with those she didn't know really well and she didn't like tea, anyway. 'A government establishment run by a government that hasn't existed for a long time, research I'd guess, and you walk in out of the wilderness, get welcomed with open arms and hop into the top job just like that. Come on, Professor, there's more to it than that!'

The Man took another sip of tea, smiled and said 'Does sound a bit like a fairy story, I'll admit, but that's the way it was. It's true - absolutely.' He turned to Gildas. 'Remember when we worked together?' A nod - yes. 'Well, I can't recall what I told you then but did I ever mention what I used to

138

do before working at the abattoir?' A shake - no. 'I worked for a government research facility just like this one. How about that? Even knew a couple of the staff here.'

'So how did you get the top job?'

'I was far more qualified in the field than anyone else here and it was my speciality. They were pleased to get me. No animosity, nothing. Just shows how times have changed. I wasn't sacked from my former place, you know. The unit was taken over by a private company and I was one of those chosen to go. That always happens when a new firm takes over; cost cutting, doing the same things on the cheap and expecting better results. Out of the question! If they hadn't moved me on I would have left none the less. I could see society beginning to collapse, the inevitable end of all that extra solar heat and radiation, so other priorities were at the front of my mind. I moved the family into Town and used my biological and management clout - and called in a few favours - to get some sort of job with accommodation which would also help keep the family well fed. I make no apology for that, either. Then when the food animals stopped coming in we were kicked out of our flat by a bunch of hoodlums when I refused to pay tribute to them. Wish I'd knuckled under to them now. At least we'd still have been together.'

Gildas knew what he meant. 'That's what I did, but it still went wrong. So what are you working on here and how do you manage to keep going?'

The Man held up a placatory hand. 'Afraid I can't talk about our work - even to you. Hope you understand and won't take offence. I can tell you it's biological and to do with the star-ships up there. Research into better methods of doing things never stops. Going back to how I got this job: once I was recognised by a couple of my old colleagues they wouldn't let me go again even though I simply wanted to keep walking north until I dropped. Apparently the type of investigation I used to be involved in had suddenly assumed top priority and I was the only

139

one who could provide access to the data links. Too much security has its down-side. Would you believe they'd shipped all my old files and disks in and even bought my old computer terminal here. I told them to go to hell.'

'Yet here you are. How did they persuade you?'

'Easy. They fed me with supplies they could ill-afford, then the resident psychologist devoted her whole time to my well-being and everyone was so friendly. I began to get interested again and stopped resisting. I'm in charge simply because I'm doing the most important work and nobody else wants the responsibility. Besides, given the choice between topping myself and doing important work I'm interested and which might benefit the whole of what's left of mankind, there is no sensible choice. It might make the future a bit better than what's going on out there at the moment.'

Gildas could think of no rejoinder to this. Clare was less impressed.

'So you landed on your feet. Good for you! How do you get your supplies and why set up this place just here?'

The Man nodded towards the window. 'Out there is a clear-water spring. The only one we know of for miles around. There's not enough to flow downstream, it all evaporates, but here we found a well-hidden oasis and a helicopter comes in twice a week with essentials. We're in constant radio contact with our masters and what we want, we get - eventually. It's a pretty good set-up, considering.'

'Nobody else delivers, then?'

Gildas woke up to where Clare was heading. How could he have forgotten the very reason for their presence here? 'Any local suppliers?' he asked.

'You must be joking. There aren't any locals. At least ...' He trailed off, thinking. 'We do get a couple of thugs coming up from Town but they only appear every so often. I've only seen two of them, just for a moment. Yesterday, in fact, but I didn't speak to them. They delivered a pack of things we can use and we paid them with some chemicals

140

we've got plenty of. They seemed to know exactly what they wanted but, as I said, I wasn't involved myself.'

'Junkies, huh?'

'I'd imagine so. Did you meet up with them on your way here?'

'We did. Don't expect them back.'

The Man regarded Gildas' set face solemnly. 'I understand. Don't go into details, I don't want to know. How about you, though? Why are you here? Doing some trading of your own?'

'In a way. You're welcome to most of the food we've got on board and all we'd like in exchange is some information. Is there a regular person here who deals with the thugs you mentioned?'

'Well, the steward handles that kind of thing. He got lumbered with the job because he was once a professional cook before he started studying the assembly of crystal proteins. When you think of it, that's not so very much different from cooking; at least at my level of the art.'

'Can I have a talk with him? I'll volunteer for the washing up if it'll help.'

'Certainly. I'll see if he's busy at the moment.' The Man brought a small communicator from his pocket and pressed a few buttons. The machine began to buzz. 'Not available He's probably busy at this time of day but we'll catch up with him later. In the meantime you're welcome to whatever hospitality we can provide. State your needs and if we can supply them, they're yours.'

Clare pushed away her nearly-full cup of tea. 'We'll get the blocks off the truck first. Can you detail a few strong arms to do the lifting? Then it's a hot shower followed by a cold one and a visit to the laundry. After that I'd like someone to lead me to a soft mattress and then leave me completely alone for six hours. Gil can do what he likes.'

The Man grinned; his face resembled that of a small boy. 'You're welcome to all that and a great deal more.' He called across the guard who had been hovering near the door and gave him some instructions. 'Follow him and he'll sort you out. If you need to speak to me just ask your escort, otherwise I'll see you here at the evening meal.' With a languid wave he left the refectory.

Clare slumbered, dreaming of floating in a warm white cloud. A heavy thumping noise woke her, followed immediately by a harsh hectoring voice. 'You in there, time to eat. Can you hear me?'

'Right! Coming!' Clare shouted and rolled off her cloud, feet-first onto the floor. Damned sergeants, they were all alike; nothing but a mouth surrounded by a fringe of uniform. The thumping resumed, forcing her to cross to the door and open it. She swung it wide. Sure enough, a sergeant with stripes and full uniform she smiled sweetly. 'Thank you for calling me, sergeant. Time for din-dins, is it? Just give me a few minutes and I'll be ready. Would you like to come in and wait?'

Eyes popping, the way sergeant's eyes sometimes do, he shook his head and watched her meaty buttocks perambulate across to the wardrobe like a set of old-fashioned latex dumbbells. Clare dressed without the slightest hint of embarrassment, pranced over to the sergeant, who stood stiff and disapproving with his back to the open door, and linked arms with him. 'Lead on, Sarge!'

Oh it was lovely being able to take liberties with one of the officers without the fear of a come-back.

Gildas and the Man were already having their meal. It was a self-service arrangement. Piling a plate with whatever was available, she joined them.

'He'll be joining us as soon as he can - the steward.' Gildas said through a mouthful of something pink. 'Eat up before it gets cold!'

By the time the room had nearly emptied of diners Clare had counted about ten soldiers and sixteen staff. That meant there had to be about another dozen or so on the premises if it kept going on a twenty-four hour basis as the sergeant had told her. This place must be of some importance, then, if all these people were being supported by an outside agency. It proved some organisation was still in existence among, but hidden from, the total anarchy which was everybody else's lot. She had a shrewd suspicion of who was at the back of it, too.

A chubby smiling man she'd spotted at intervals behind the food counter came across, sat down and shook hands with them both. Clare disliked him on sight.

'Name's Chessel. The Man here tells me you've cut off most of our unofficial supplies and want to know where Dave has gone to. That right?'

Gildas nodded. Even in that small action it was evident he didn't much like the cook, either. 'There's a good reason, believe me. We have to find him to get ... something from him.' *Yes*, he thought, *his life*.

'Well, he arrived here four days ago. Didn't have much to trade this time but we gave him a couple of meals, a bed for the night and a couple of boxes of bullets along with his usual medicine then off he went.'

'Not going back towards Town or we'd have seen him. Did he say where he was going?'

'Yeah. Not to his normal stamping ground.' The cook smiled as if at a secret joke. 'He said something about being king of the castle somewhere else for a change. I remember him rattling on at length some months ago about this castle. Seems he had a bit of a thing about it. He even described it to me, though he never told me where it was, but there's only one in this part of the country which fits the description - spires and turrets and such.'

'That one by the motorway outside Cardiff.' Clare said immediately. 'It's the only one I know like that. You think that too?'

'That's right.' The chubby man agreed. 'He's got ambition, that one. Don't know about a king but he'll make a perfect tyrant. I don't think we'll be seeing him again, anyway.'

'Why's that?' The Man broke into the conversation. 'I owe you more than one favour, Gil. Listen, for your own good, stay well clear of any area where there may still be enough people to do you some damage. That means the towns, cities and any supply routes.'

'Things getting worse, eh?'

The Man looked sombre. 'Far, far worse than you could ever imagine. We estimate it'll only be a matter of weeks before there'll only be a few human beings left in this country and those'll be the ones who are outside the mainstream in places like this. I can sense this will make no difference to why you're going after Dave but you'd better realise you're heading towards almost certain death.'

Gildas seemed a bit shaken. 'Can you expand on that? I don't see how things can get much worse than they are.'

'We're in regular contact with our main base and they are in contact with other similar bases scattered all over Europe and Australasia. The southern hemisphere's all right at present but up here, well, for want of a better word, it's the plague.'

Clare laughed out loud. 'Tell us something we don't know. Cholera, typhoid and all sorts of nasties have been sweeping the camps since this whole thing started four years ago. It can't be controlled, sure, but once the population drops to a level where the food supplies can be sustained, the situation should stabilise. So what's new?'

'Two things. From now on you can virtually forget about any food supplies. Think about it! The only supplies there are come from the processing ships at a few places around the coast. It's common knowledge they use whatever sea produce - seaweed, algae, fish, and so on - they can get but the primary raw material is human bodies. That's almost all that's left! Now there's a new virus started up. Nasty one, too! You don't think the people who control the processors are going to handle corpses contaminated with a bug that's got a hundred percent success rate, do you? Anyway, most of the ships have stopped production and those with enough bunkers left are heading north away from us. Maybe they'll be able to start a new life somewhere else. Who knows? Good luck to them! They'll need all the luck they can get when their fuel runs out.'

The Man had access to outside information. Clare knew nothing about bacteriology but she'd had basic training with the warfare side of the business. 'What's this new bug like?' she asked.

'A form of our old friend HIV. Since it reared its ugly head in the early eighties it's mutated and modified itself to meet all we can throw up against it. Some cures worked for a short while then the virus found a way round and we were back to square one. We never did find a vaccine which lasted more than a year. At least, up to a short while ago, it could only be transferred by exchange of body fluids.' Gildas screwed his face up in disgust. 'But now one of the latest changes has the ability to infect by water-borne droplets. In other words, you can breath it in. It doesn't lay dormant for years, either; within a couple of days the body's defences are overrun and the victim begins to die.'

That was it, for Clare. Time to rejoin the family and get the hell out. Luckily they were going in the right direction. 'Can you supply us with masks and filters when we leave?'

'Willingly. We've already had our mechanic look at your truck and topped up the tank from our stores. Mind you, he almost burst into tears at the state it was in. He's very sensitive about vehicle abuse, is our mechanic, but he's done the best he can. When do you want to leave? We can put you up for a few days at least.'

Gildas stood up and offered his hand to the cook who shook it and left in the direction of the kitchen without another word. He addressed the Man. 'Thanks for the offer but we'd like to leave now. We appreciate all your help.'

'At least spend the night. It'll be dark in just a couple of hours.'

'We can get a long way in that time. Any word about what the route is like?'

The Man got up from the table. 'If you're sure. Let's have a chat with the sergeant.'

The sergeant couldn't advise Gildas about anything he didn't already know. 'Don't advise you go back the way you came and use the motorway.' he said.' Your best bet's to go back to the first main road down there - he gestured to the south - turn left and then right at the first roundabout after nine miles or so. That'll eventually lead you onto a dual carriageway to Cardiff going right past this castle of yours. Best to keep on a wide road like that 'cos there's less chance of it being completely blocked anywhere. I've heard there are still a lot of people down that way in the old mining valleys and now the supply situation has gone critical there's no grub getting up that way any more so there'll be a lot of hungry and bad-tempered people who'll think your truck is coming to feed them. You'll be stopped and killed for sure.'

'Ta.' said Gildas, reaching for another doorstep of a sandwich and stuffing it into his mouth. 'That's very reassuring.

The truck stood close inside the gate, ravaged and shabby yet still imparting that peculiar air of indestructibility. Their weapons were returned, intact and with extra ammunition. The masks and filters Clare had requested were on the front seats. Gildas faced the Man in the white robe.

'Thanks for everything.' he said as they shook hands. 'I hope you're wrong about what you think's going to happen but we wish you good luck whatever turns up.'

The Man seemed a bit abashed. 'It'll work its own way out whatever we do.' he said. 'I've got this strange feeling we'll meet again and I've learned to trust my feelings. So long for now.'

He stood for some time listening to the noise of the truck engine battering at the calm evening air, shook his head and paced slowly over the little river bridge to the little chapel. Passing through the twin doors designed to

146

keep the interior atmosphere as cool and clean as possible, he donned his heavy working harness and went to check on the progress of his charges.

In the centre of the old chapel stood a translucent tent lit from within by a pale pink glow. He entered. Two banks of cages stood on metal legs; twelve cages in all. In all but two of the cages lay what appeared to be the carcass of a skinned animal, mostly cats and dogs with one solitary monkey, perhaps the last of his species in the country - if not yet the world. The last two cages contained extremely small human babies, both with wide eyes and decidedly un-baby-like expression on their faces. Their black piggy eyes followed the Man as he moved to the cage containing the latest of his acquisitions, donated (for a price) by a certain Dave a few days before. It had not seemed appropriate to mention the matter to the two recent guests.

The animal in the cage was a cat, completely devoid of fur yet lying quite still without a shiver in the icy atmosphere. The skin was a mix of pink and pale blue over most of the body except for the face, lower limbs and the tail, which had a brownish tinge. On top of its head and extending a little way down the neck an oval section of skin had been removed and replaced with a, hard partially transparent covering patterned with microscopically thin silver wires which emerged from tiny holes drilled in the skull and congregated at a small connecting plug near the centre. Wires led from this plug to a monitor hung over the cage. Other connections and thin plastic tubes led from other parts of the body to a series of life-support devices and other miniature monitors.

The Man check all functions in his normal meticulous manner. He made notes and drew lines on charts. He spoke softly into his communicator-cum- dictating machine. This animal would be the culmination of his efforts in this place. He had to get it right this time.

All was well.

Satisfied, he left the tent to speak with the assistant who kept watch over the experimental longevity tanks ranged along the walls of the nave. A brief exchange and the Man sat in front of his computer. He selected a disk, switched on the machine and resumed his endless search for the impossible.

Behind him, in the pink light that seemed to emanate from the very air itself (which, in a sense, it did), the small Siamese cat once called Wuggles pranced through his endless dreams. He leapt, ran, bounded, tussled playfully with a short, ugly man who he knew loved him, and did all the things a cat in the prime of life cannot help but do. His body remained inert, but even if he died right now in the cage he had lived a full life - in his feline dreams.

Gildas hadn't known. There was no reason why he should have been told.

Luckily for him, the Man wasn't aware he owed his very life to that single fact.

INTERMURAL 3

Extreme poverty and starvation became widespread as more and more resources were diverted into fewer and fewer pockets. Civil insurrection became the normal way of life in many countries leading to bitter and prolonged civil wars as regional administrations weakened or collapsed.

Conflict spread. War zones increased in number all over the planet. Religious differences, political aspirations, historical hatreds, boundary disputes; people fought each other for all sorts of reasons. Manufacturing barons rubbed their hands in glee at the prospect of increased profits from sales of weaponry - including one by the name of Lemuel Quorvis. War is always good for business.

And rebuilding countries afterwards is even better.

Unfortunately the number of conflicts increased faster than they were resolved - and they took a lot longer to resolve because heavily-armed guerrilla groups were able to keep going for a very long time after the main hostilities finished.

A wide band to both north and south of the equator gradually deteriorated into an almost permanent war zone.

And just because the combatants couldn't find ways to live peacefully alongside one another they tipped the balance of survival for everyone else past the point of no recovery.

Man evolved in Africa, so they tell us. It was only fitting he should end his story there.

CHAPTER 12

At least the reconditioned fuel injectors had partially reduced the volume of smoke, but the engine still knocked as loudly as ever. It didn't really matter, though; they only wanted one last journey out of the battered wreck and then they could lay its weary, bloodstained bones to rest.

A trip of about nine miles brought them to the outskirts of what used to be a bustling market town, now nothing more than a clutter of masonry and brick carcasses. The buildings, once so full of activity, sat pale and silent in the once-fertile valley, overlooked by the sun-baked mountains and the ancient castle brooding on its knoll. At the roundabout where the town by-pass began, Gildas turned sharp right onto the road leasing to Cardiff. Clare couldn't resist a snort of amusement.

'Why do you always go right around a traffic island like that and why do you insist on keeping to the left hand side of the road? I've noticed you don't even cross over what's left of the solid while line on the bends. You afraid something's going to come and bump into us or scared you'll get a ticket off a traffic cop?'

'Habit. You never know what's round the bend.'

'Oh! No harm in that, I suppose. Talking about being round the bend, the Sarge told you to avoid this route. But you know better, yes?'

'Maybe I know the roads better than him in spite of the info he gets. This way is quicker and shorter with only one major hill coming up and the road's a lot wider. If we went the way he said it's narrow and there's more chance of an ambush 'cos we'd have to pass through a lot of villages. It's really only one big by-pass once we get over the mountain.'

'Fair enough! Doesn't matter to me. All I want is to get this vengeance thing of yours out of the way then get the hell out of the way of what's coming.'

They clattered past a small village and began the long climb up into the mountains. Burnt pine forests each side of the road formed a vertical landscape of blackened devastation.

'Get out of the way? How? There's nowhere to go!'

Clare grinned. 'I'll find a way, don't worry. If you're nice to me I might just take you along. Pretend I know something you don't.'

A sceptical grunt was the only reply. The head of the pass came into sight. They had left the ravaged pine forest and now travelled in deep shadow, the sun having descended below the mountain tops. It still shone brightly on the matched twin peaks above and to their right, though. Bright pink from underlying sandstone rock, devoid of any of their original stunted mountain grasses, the rounded scarp summits seemed to float in the air. Gildas had to drop down a couple of gears as the old truck laboured up the incline. Smoke increased, blowing into the cab from behind, and he was forced to open a window in order to keep breathing.

Clare had never passed this way before and found the scenery spectacular. What had it been like when there were still green growing things to be found? she wondered. And all those little gullies corrugating the steep sides of the valley; they must have been full of the sound of bubbling water, once. Chuckling, laughing water, clear and bright, tumbling from the heights under a normal sun. And clouds. Whatever happened to clouds? Bushes, berries, birds ... ah, yes, birds. All gone now. All gone. Even the hot-country birds hadn't been allowed the time to successfully migrate to this parched island.

Clare shook herself to banish the insidious ghosts, with only partial success. The summit of the pass was close at hand and a single large building, the only one in sight, loomed on one side. Gildas pulled into a car park opposite. A few abandoned vehicles were lined up against the fence. From their elevated position they could see into one of the cars. A scatter of bones lay on both front seats, smaller ones in the back. The hosepipe from a vacuum cleaner led from the exhaust pipe in through the driver's window, the remaining gap plugged with faded rags. Clare directed her companion's attention to the sad tableau.

'Did he have the right idea or simply a lack of guts?'

Could have been for either reason. Not something I could have done, though. It's a posh car. Maybe the losing of more possessions makes the loss worse, I don't know. Hope they're resting in peace.' He averted his eyes and pointed. 'That there's the old mountain hostel. We'll sleep there under cover tonight and get an early start.'

In spite of the knowledge there could be no possibility of anyone turning up, Clare insisted on them standing watches as long as they stayed. 'A good habit to keep.' she lectured, firmly overriding his sullen protests. 'Besides, you never know.'

With a bit of manoeuvring, arms aching from having to turn the heavy steering wheel while the truck was nearly stationary, Gildas backed the vehicle up against a doorway giving access only to a small storeroom with no other door and no windows. It was in the centre of a roughly-built wall erected with apparent haste and no regard to appearance in a gap between two small buildings north of the main structure. A good view of the road and the opposite side of

151

the pass clinched the selection of this place to spend the night: even the road was sloping downhill in the direction they wanted to go so there shouldn't be any trouble starting the engine when it was time to continue.

After a thorough search of the other buildings and immediate surroundings, they opened the truck's large rear door. It was getting dark, Gildas was hot and tired, but their security was not sufficient for Clare's liking. With merciless goading she kept him at it. Between them, enough of the equipment carried in the cargo bay was stacked on the floor to thwart anyone who tried to get in by crawling under the truck. It was a long job and black night had set in by the time Clare approved the arrangements.

Whoever was on watch only had the choice of sitting in the front seats or stretching out on the roof. Still, it was as safe as it could ever be.

They found that quite a large pile of food blocks had been left inside. A large note was taped to the wall. 'Thanks for the grub.' it read. 'We've left you some in case you need it to barter your way through any road blocks. Good luck' There was no signature.

'Thoughtful of them.' murmured Clare. 'I reckon we may as well have some supper before we settle down. Any volunteers for the first watch?'

The hint was enough. 'I volunteer you.' said Gildas nastily. 'I didn't have a siesta this afternoon and I've found out killing makes me sleepy as well as sick.'

'So be it. I'll get some wood for a fire.' and she started ripping up some of the floorboards in the main building with quite unnecessary force. The brittle, desiccated timbers made a good fire for their night-time picnic. The sky to the east brightened. A full moon was on the way.

With Clare on guard it seemed to be a good idea to completely strip off all his clothes; the air in the storeroom being hot and stuffy in the absence of any outside ventilation. Two hour sessions had been agreed. It was good to slide beneath the dusty blankets free of the sweaty

152

clothes he'd worn for days on end. A couple of food blocks topped with a folded blanket served for a pillow.

As soon as Gildas' head touched basement level he fell into a deep, dreamless sleep. A clattering noise dragged him back to a state of semi-consciousness. It sounded exactly like a machine pistol being kicked over the concrete and was followed immediately by a muffled, incoherent curse. He raised his head and gazed about with muzzy eyes.

No night is ever completely dark; there is always some light even though it may only be that of a solitary star behind clouds - and there were plenty of stars about that night with no clouds. The moon was full and well up above the mountain. From the amount of light entering the room through the rear door of the truck it must have been almost as bright as a cloudy day outside.

Close alongside him a large rounded object swayed and wobbled. Black against the pale silvery light of the moon, the jerky silhouette raised bumps and protrusions which sank back into the mass only to reappear elsewhere. A puffing sound, interspersed with muted grunts emanated from it. Gildas felt the hair on his head begin to stiffen and raise up. Dim memories of childhood nightmares sprang into his mind.

All at once a large section detached itself from the top and fell to the floor. 'Phoof!' blew a soft feminine whisper and Gildas saw the outline of a human head, which tilted sharply up to send a spray of long, thick hair up, over and down the back. He relaxed; it was only Clare removing her jacket without bothering to go through the lengthy process of buttons, studs and zip-fasteners.

Must be time to change the look-out. Just a few seconds more. His eyes close in an attempt to recapture the bliss of sleep albeit only for a few seconds. More movement and soft grunts. Strange for her not to wake him before getting ready to sleep - not Clare's military correctness at all. A whiff of scented soap drifted past his nostrils. His consciousness began to fade ...

153

... to flare up quiveringly alert as the blankets shifted, lifted, and the unmistakable touch of warm, soft flesh drifted up against his back; a large area low down and two others, a bit smaller, higher up: a pneumatic, rubbery pressure like three tepid water bottles. The blankets dropped once more.

Silence and stillness for a couple of minutes. Touching skin warmed up.

'Gil? I know you're awake. Turn over!'

Oh no, he thought. *How do I get out of this?* Clare shifted slightly. Something furry tickled his buttocks.

'Gil?' A muscular arm slid over his shoulder and rested on his chest. It felt like warm silk. 'Gil!'

He dared not tense his muscles, she would sense the movement. Move his legs slowly to the right positions, that was it; very slowly, as if getting ready to turn over as she demanded.

Now!

A sudden frantic leap propelled by a panicky flush of adrenaline, and he slipped from Clare's loose grasp to roll over onto the hard concrete floor. Jerking upright he leaned against the wall he'd cannoned into, looking wildly around for his clothes. He couldn't remember where he'd left them. Ah, yes, there they were - on the other side of Clare. He focused bleary eyes upon her.

She lay where he'd left her, one arm propping her head up over the pillow. He could dimly make out a lazy grin on her face. With studied sensual invitation she slowly pulled back the blanket exposing a shadowy full-frontal in the process. Gildas was only human; his traitorous body reacted in the manner Nature intended even against his strivings to counteract it.

Damn her! What the hell had got into her? Despite his embarrassed anger a smile flickered across his face - to be instantly erased as his normal (to him) principles once more resumed control.

Clare assumed a phoney drawl. 'Wanna mess around?' She moved slightly. The overall effect of this tiny motion was intensely erotic - as she'd meant it to be, of course. It had worked often enough in the past but, then, she'd never tried it on her present quarry.

'No!'

At this emphatic monosyllable, deliberately spat out loudly in a tone of mixed distaste and resentment (and some other indefinable emotion akin to reproach), something changed in the demeanour of the woman offering herself on the makeshift bed. Her expression remained as before and not a muscle in her body tensed or relaxed but something fled and left behind a greatly altered interpretation of her designs.

She was not accustomed to rejection, Gildas realised. Good! Now retain the initiative!

'Who's on guard? A whole army of rabble could be creeping in on us right now while you're swanning around in the nude trying to prove you haven't lost your touch. Get your clothes back on for God's sake! I've still got some principles and decency left even if you haven't.'

He had been right. The smile slowly left her face to be replaced with a look of disbelief. She studied him in the gloom, saying nothing.

'Throw my clothes over here! If it's my watch, the sooner I get out of here the better. Even if it's not, I'm going anyway.

Clare flung the blanket completely off, reached over to the wad of clothing and threw it hard at Gildas. He could no longer read her face and ignored her as he found, and climbed into, his pants.

'Something wrong?' Her tone was scathing; the instinctive modulation of the woman scorned. 'Haven't got what it takes, eh?' She sat up, remaining on her knees. 'Bit funny, are you? Queer, like?'

Gildas kept his mouth shut. Whatever he said would only give further umbrage and inflame the situation. He

155

donned the rest of his clothes and stood up. Clare tried again, conciliatory, as though he hadn't understood what was happening and only needed another chance to come to his senses.

'There's nobody out there, you can see for miles. We've got plenty of time and I'm not feeling a bit tired. Neither of us has had much fun the last few days; it'll help us both relax. Come on, shed the rags and climb in here!' She suddenly giggled. 'And you can take that any way you like.'

Gildas compressed his lips, not daring to speak. Two steps brought him to the side of the bed. Clare misinterpreted his intentions and raised her arms to embrace his hips. With a quick movement he swayed to one side, reached down, grabbed his knife-belt and the two clips of ammunition he'd hidden under his pillow. Clare's arms dropped to her sides once more.

'I can make you.' He voice turned hard once more.

'Don't be stupid! That's impossible.'

'Want to bet?'

Gildas froze. Maybe she could. If any woman could, it would be Clare. Up to now she'd proven exceptionally competent at whatever she tackled.

'Made a habit of it, have you?' He tried to keep his tone light and bantering. 'Old hand at male rape, huh? The world's only one-woman gang-bang? Go to sleep! I'll try to forget this ever happened.' He crossed to the far corner where his rifle stood propped up in the angle. Check the magazine! One already up the spout? Good, now get out, fast!

Before climbing into the back of the truck he turned to look at her once more, now more fully illuminated by what little light there was. She had swivelled round, but now with both hands among the folds of the blanket. Instead of acting chastened she was obviously furious, her whole body posture advertising the fact.

'There must be something wrong with you.' she snapped.

'Why's that?'

'Well ... it's not natural.'

'Talk about it tomorrow if you want.' He suddenly felt tired of the whole sordid incident. 'I'd rather let the matter drop. Put it down to a matter of principle.'

'To hell with your prissy principles, what about my feelings? I've got feelings, you know.'

'OK, OK, so you've got feelings. So what? Now get some sleep! I'll wake you in a couple of hours.' and Gildas turned, clambered through the truck and left her there, seething, frustrated, dugs drooping pathetically in hurt rejection.

A full moon bathed the stark landscape in a silver glow. Clare had been right about being able to see for miles. All was still.

The night passed without further problems. Two more watches were exchanged in strained silence and towards the end of his second spell Gildas gathered some more floorboards from another part of the building and re-lit the fire. Reluctant to use more clean water than necessary he made a breakfast out of one of the food blocks and dumped in the contents of a small tin found in the gift donated by the research station. It was unlabelled and looked exactly like chunky cat food in gravy. Smelled like it too, but in it went to make a hot, savoury paste dotted with meaty bits. He went to rouse (delete that word, he thought) Clare.

Breakfast was consumed in a stony silence. Camp was struck and a nasty few moments endured when the truck refused to fire up until over half a mile of downhill had been traversed. Start it eventually did, the entire valley echoing in confirmation.

Clare looked terrible. Slack-faced, pale, with frizzy hair sticking wildly out from under the fringes of her bush cap. Either she hadn't slept much the previous night or the cat food may have been a bit off. Tough! Gildas decided to lighten the mood.

157

'With a bit of luck we should be able to get all the way today.' he blabbed cheerfully.

First mistake of the day! 'You're probably incapable of getting all the way with anything if last night's performance is anything to go by.' Clare sneered. 'Now shut it and keep it shut till I give you permission!'

No answer to that! The old truck reached the head of the next valley and barrelled down a long hill into a heavily built-up area, once a major stamping ground of the Kings of coal and iron. The road became a dual-carriageway. Suddenly Gildas stamped on the brakes as hard as he could.

'On your left.' he shouted. 'See it?'

Clare grabbed her gun convulsively and peered out of the window. 'No. What am I looking for?'

Gildas jabbed a finger. 'On the old main road down there! We've passed it now. Oh damn these brakes!' A harsh metallic screech came from one of the front wheels as the remains of the friction material shredded and tore loose. The truck gradually came to a noisy stop. Gildas wrenched at the hand throttle just in time to stop the engine from stalling. 'Get out!' he barked. 'Quick! And don't forget your gun!' Another stupid thing to say - Clare never went anywhere without a gun.

They stood by the crash barrier looking down on the town. Something moved. Gildas pointed. 'Down there, near that row of shops.'

There was nothing to be seen.

'What?' Clare snarled irritably. 'There's nobody left here; just look at the place.'

It was silent. Not a breath of air moved. Already the sun had risen enough to hammer the parched valley like a malignant God armed with a club. A flicker beside the nearest shop; the merest hint of a fleeting shadow. 'I see it.' said Clare. 'You keep the waggon going and I'll deal with it. How many do you want?'

'One will be enough. Any more'll only waste in this heat 'cos we've got nowhere to keep it.'

It only took one bullet and a ten-minute wait then Clare was back at the truck throwing the burden from her broad shoulders into the rear door. She climbed in after it. Already the flies had appeared from nowhere and were assaulting her catch.

'You drive on while I sort this out!' she said, pulling out a horribly sharp knife. She seemed happier now she'd killed something. Gildas closed the door and got the truck moving again.

'What I can't understand is how these things are able to live there. There must have been at least a dozen in that flock. Goats do collect in flocks, don't they, or is it herds?' She had to shout above the bellowing engine. A ghastly, cloying smell swept into the cab forcing Gildas to accelerate.

'Herds, I think. Goats can survive where other mammals can't. This is an old mining valley and the mountains both sides have been wrecked by open cast pits. The natural water table has been shot to hell. Maybe there a few seepages left. As for food, there must be some sort in a few places or the goats wouldn't be here. Let me know when you want to stop.'

'Just keep going!'

Gildas kept going. The wide road clung to the side of the valley high up; empty except for an occasional abandoned vehicle easily seen soon enough to avoid. Clare stayed in the back, engrossed in the art of butchery. Rounding yet another long sweeping curve a section of straight valley stretched ahead. Away in the distance a column of smoke reached into the stagnant, overheated air. Gildas stopped the truck once more.

'Clare! Up here!'

Inside of two seconds she was by his side watching the pillar of smoke.

'Where there's smoke there's trouble.' she stated. Gildas nodded in agreement. 'Nothing we can't handle. I suppose. I'll find a place to stop where we can get a good view!'

159

A side road provided a perfect vantage point. Thankfully Gildas climbed out. Deep breaths of hot air cleaned his lungs, although goat smell still hung about him like a shroud. Clare had the additional benefit of goat's blood decorating her clothing and arms. Precious water was expended to remove the worst.

'I'm tired.' she said. 'Watch what's happening down there and wake me in two hours!' Laying in the shade of the truck she instantly fell asleep.

Bossy broad! Serves her right! Gildas found the binoculars and did as he was told.

The smoke disappeared in a while and all he could see was an infrequent movement among the clutter of buildings comprising an old industrial estate. It almost filled the valley for a couple of miles. The smoke had issued from about the centre of the complex. After two hours he woke Clare.

'We have to go right past that spot. What do we do?'

'Eat first, then simply carry on. Any nonsense and we start shooting. Don't be so negative!'

It was goat for dinner, of course. Gildas discovered a deep loathing for such strong- tasting flesh, if it could be called a taste. Clare tore into the charred steaks with typically unfeminine gusto.

'Eat it or I'll ram it down your throat.' she growled between hyena-like bites. Gildas ate, snapping and gulping.

He checked the radiator water and put in more fuel while Clare used one of her knives to remove shreds of goat meat from between her strong, white teeth. The truck engine started easily this time and they swung back on to the main road.

It was easy travelling as they approached the remains of the old trading estate. The road was clear and nobody showed. People were there, however. Gildas had seen them. He hoped they would keep under cover.

Unfortunately the natives had other ideas. Clare spotted it first. 'Get over to the other carriageway if you can and stop in a couple of hundred yards!' she ordered.

Gildas saw it too. A break in the central reservation appeared conveniently and he swung the wheel, battling with the useless brakes. They stopped and surveyed the obstacle ahead.

Across both carriage-ways stretched a line of vehicles; lorries, cars and even a caravan; a double thickness of barricade in most places. Directly overhead the barrier a pedestrian footbridge reached right over the road and a few crouching figures were scattered along its length. As they watched more people appeared and others popped up on the high concrete walls that lined each side of the road. Clare used the binoculars. Several more faces could be seen peering from the windows of the caravan.

She inspected the caravan carefully. It was one of the smaller touring versions, raised from the ground about four feet or so on pillars of concrete blocks with a rough staircase of more blocks ascending to the doorway.

Vulnerable! A weak point. The *only* weak point.

'Even if they hadn't been able to hear us coming from miles away there's no way in which we'd have been allowed to move that lot without being gunned down.'

'They've got guns?'

'Just a figure of speech but we'd better assume they have until proven otherwise. Hmmm, how many vehicles do you imagine come from this direction?'

'None for a long time, I'd say. There's nobody back there unless one of the goats holds a drivers' licence, or hadn't you noticed?'

'And how many drivers have you seen lately who drive on the wrong side of the road and behaved as if the rules still applied?'

Gildas thought. 'None, now you mention it. Habit, I suppose, like me.'

'That's what I thought. Notice how the caravan is on this carriageway? They must use it as a hidey-hole so they can storm any vehicle the barrier stops, while their cronies keep the guards and drivers occupied and distracted from the footbridge and walls. They're not geared up for someone coming from the other direction. Pull out to the centre of the road and keep an eye on that wall up there. If you see any heads, knock them off!'

They both got out of the truck. Clare walked round the front while Gildas guarded against any threat from the wall. Signalling him to do the same, she got back inside.

'That's a solid looking front bumper. Think it'll hold up long enough to batter a way through?'

Gildas eyed her in horror. 'No way! It's not that solid and what happens if we hole a tyre on those concrete blocks or puncture the radiator? Lets find another way round.'

'Is there one?'

'Not without going back for miles but that's better than running such a big risk.'

'And go along the narrow roads - which are far easier to block off than this one. Think about it!'

Then, after a few minutes of silence, 'Right! If we head for the caravan there are bound to be a couple of gaps so the storming party can get through quickly. That's likely the weakest point. Come on Gil, go for it!' There was a metallic click as Clare set her gun to fully automatic fire.

Gildas reluctantly started the truck moving. Then he floored the accelerator and geared up as fast as the worn transmission would permit. The caravan raced towards them with frightening speed. Thin ragged figures poured from its door, fighting and pushing each other aside in their haste.

The truck hit.

CHAPTER 13

The truck was heavy and moving fast; the caravan was light and standing on stilts. As the blunt nose of the truck crumpled the thin aluminium wall and splintered the floor, the caravan roof tilted towards them and the whole thing reared up nearly reaching the roof of the truck. Gildas could see through one of the caravan windows. A face streaked with blood fell down behind the glass shards to be impaled through the chin on one of them. Screams and shouts of pain came from all sides.

Clare's tactical guess had been correct. It *was* a weak point. Lowering his head to peer under the caravan, Gildas spotted a solitary wrecked car facing him, originally hidden behind the caravan. Ten yards further on a lorry obscured this weak point from the sight of anyone coming from the opposite direction. To each side of this lorry a wide gap yawned invitingly. Crashes and thumps came from the roof as missiles thrown from the bridge and walls found their target.

Clare's gun began chattering. Gildas concentrated grimly on steering towards the gap nearest the wall, fervently wishing he had a reverse gear to shed the obstructing car and caravan, which now decided to topple down and lie across the car's roof, obscuring his vision completely. Gildas wrenched the steering wheel to the right, the caravan fell away; shrieks of unbearable pain still coming from its ruined windows. Now steer left, then right, fast! Away went the car to the side, clattering and banging against the side of the truck. A huge cloud of steam erupted in front of him.

Radiator punctured, as he had feared. Keep going! Should be able to make a couple of miles before the engine seized up completely.

It felt strange driving on the wrong side of the road. Even stranger when he finally stopped at a sloping entry slip-road. Breaking the primary rule of the road just didn't feel right. But he *had* to stop because the steam had gradually faded away to be replaced by a blacker, oilier smoke. Gildas killed the engine.

The front of the truck was a twisted tangle of rusty brown metal. The bumper bar was missing, the two thick rails that once supported it now projecting from the wreckage. One wing had vanished completely and the other had bent sufficiently to foul the tyre when on nearly full lock. Gildas tugged at it in a straining rage before his adrenaline glands ran out. He sat down defeated, sweating and gasping for breath.

Clare had climbed on to the roof and was watching for danger. She shouted down. 'What's the score?'

'We only want a new radiator, that's all.' Then with heavy sarcasm, 'Oh, and a fully equipped body shop to make a place to put it. We're finished.'

'Well there wasn't any other way, was there? It's your lousy driving. On our toes from here on then, is it?'

As Gildas searched through his large stock of expletives for a suitable reply a heavy stone struck the side of the truck just above his head. 'Oh, oh!' commented Clare, snapping off a couple of shots. A howl of pain issued from behind a low wall at the roadside. 'If you can get this thing started and move a little way further I would be greatly obliged. Would you believe those idiots are following us? They seem rather upset.'

Gildas leapt frantically for the open door and took the gear lever out of neutral. The truck gathered speed down the slope of the slip-road. A yell from Clare reminded him she was still on the roof. Never mind, there were plenty of hand-holds up there. The engine growled into life with no fuss.

At the roundabout under the junction it became apparent why they still had company; the slip-road to get back onto

164

the main drag had been barricaded, too. Not so thoroughly this time, just a single tractor unit towing a high-sided trailer deliberately jack-knifed across the tarmac to discourage anyone wanting to get off at this exit. There was no way a head-on collision would shift *this*. Besides, Clare was on the roof and the shock would certainly throw her off with dire results - to Gildas too, if she survived. What to do?

Only one way out. Push!

Selecting the lowest gear the truck possessed, Gildas steered it towards the concrete wall supporting the main road. The rear end of the trailer almost butted up to this wall and the angle was such that Gildas' truck approached as if entering a wedge-shaped canyon. With a tearing of metal the truck edged slowly along the side of the trailer until its other side - the wheel devoid of a protecting wing - touched the concrete buttress. The truck stopped momentarily.

A loud thump sounded from the rear. Looking quickly into the rear cargo space Gildas saw Clare standing to face backwards through the open door, legs braced wide for balance. She must have swung down from the roof. Gildas prayed fervently there wasn't a heavy load in the trailer. He gradually increased the throttle pressure.

Nothing happened except for a swaying of the metal wall hanging over him. More throttle! A slight movement - then stop. What Gildas couldn't see was the trailer wheel on the wrong side of the kerbstones impeding its sideways motion. Stones and pieces of metal began raining down from the wall overhead. He heard Clare shouting.

In a sudden panic he pressed the accelerator pedal to the floor. The truck lunged forward, metal shrieked, a loud bang erupted as the trailer tyre exploded. Shocked, he lifted his foot and the truck moved back. Clare shouted again. He looked behind once more and saw a sea of faces close behind. Clare stooped and threw some things out of the

165

door opening. Whoops and cheers broke out; an alteration in mob voice. People dropped from sight.

Of course! It was food they wanted and Clare was supplying it. Food blocks, goat meat and entrails, even bits of skin; out the back it went and a fight for possession commenced. The truck had stopped; now grab the grub! He heard Clare scream. 'For Pete's sake, Gil, get going!'

More traction was needed. What about the four-wheel drive, if it was still connected? He engaged the front axle and floored the pedal once more. Six scarred tyres gripped the ground, raising the cab a few inches. The rear pair, which had come off the tarmac, began to spin but the trailer had moved a bit more. Release pedal, roll back and do it again! Amid a bedlam of metallic groans the mangled truck slowly pushed the trailer to one side. The drive-wheels span madly, worn tyres squealing, scattering rocks and pieces of broken concrete, causing consternation and an anguished roar from the swelling crowd. The gap widened and the truck shouldered the barrier aside, the engine now sounding very peculiar.

They were through! Engine clattering loudly in a cloud of hot smoke and decomposing tyre rubber burning on tarmac, the old truck freed itself and shot up the slip-road. In the back Clare fell over and only just managed to grip the edges of the door frame. One of her legs suddenly stung and went numb. As the rate of acceleration slowed down she scrabbled her way back to the comparative safety of the interior.

A mile further on Gildas halted on another sloping slip-road, the engine clanking to a stop by itself. Shakily he climbed from the cab and tottered to the rear door. Inside, Clare was trying to get her trousers off. One leg was stained with fresh blood. From the goat?

It hadn't come from the goat; she had been hit with several pellets from a shotgun nearly at the end of their effective range. About a dozen of them had penetrated the skin and the wounds bled profusely. Clare finally managed to remove the trousers with a minimum of teeth-grinding and surveyed the damage gloomily.

'Have to get these out.' she said, gently touching the skin. 'Any sign of pursuit yet?'

Gildas looked back the way they had come. 'Not yet. They've probably given up.'

'More likely it's the end of their patch and we can expect a visit from the next bunch down the valley if we don't look sharp. Pass down the first aid kit, will you?'

There were plenty of bandages, not new, but clean. Gildas gently covered the bleeding area, trying to ignore the sardonic smile on Clare's face as he was forced to touch her leg. 'I think it'd be a good idea to find somewhere to hide.' he said. 'Any suggestions?'

'Let's get down into the trading estate. Think our gallant chariot will make it?'

'I'll see. You keep watch out back!' Gildas rolled the truck down the slope more in hope than anything else. The engine started, to his intense surprise and relief, and he steered it down the slope. At the roundabout beneath the fly-over he turned into the estate and pulled up at the second building he came to. Large double doors gaped open. Driving inside to the centre of the hangar-like building he switched off the engine and ran back to close the doors. They slid easily on their tracks and he threw the securing bolts into place. Safe! For a while, at least. Silence descended like a fog.

Lighting a fire was too much of a risk; Clare's "volcano" had to be used to boil some water with the assistance of a wide shaft of sunlight slanting through a shattered skylight. Clare's wounds were cleared of shot, anointed with antiseptic cream and dressed properly with fresh bandages from the medical kit. White-faced, she endured his clumsy ministrations, not a sound escaping her compressed lips. They rested, half-expecting a visit from the locals at any minute.

At least, Clare rested. Gildas still felt exposed even under cover. It made him jumpy; unable to settle down. 'I'm going to have a look around.' he said at last, getting to his feet. 'You OK?'

'Be careful! If I hear shots I'll come limping.'

Gildas grinned. She must have forgotten all about last night, he thought - and that nicely summed up his knowledge of female mental processes, as he was to find out before very long.

As it happened, he didn't even leave the building. Several peripheral rooms, storage and office areas, attracted his attention and invited inspection. The second room he checked provided a partial answer to their problems.

The building appeared to have been a depot for a haulage concern as evidenced by what could only have been engine oil scattered over the floor of the main hall. Every transport depot had to have some sort of workshop for basic maintenance of its vehicles and it was this workshop Gildas was fortunate enough to discover.

Most of the portable equipment had been removed long ago, but in a locker against one wall he found the remains of a tool-kit, sadly depleted, but with enough tools, he hoped, to enable the truck to continue travelling. With high hopes he lugged the box over to the truck and set to work.

The radiator was the first problem, and the most serious. When this old warrior had been designed nearly seventy years previously, someone had the bright notion of placing the radiator outside the protection of the bodywork for extra cooling in hot desert conditions. This proved very useful for Gildas. In a remarkably short time he had disconnected the unit and removed the hosepipes.

The radiator was finished; a severe buckle bent it completely across the middle; the top hose connection had snapped and the bottom one was flattened beyond repair. Gildas kicked it hard across the floor.

'That's that! We need a replacement and only an army depot is likely to have one.'

Clare limped over and peered into the dark cavity left by the radiator, wrinkling her nose. 'I don't know too much about engines, but looking at that lump in there do you really think it's worth trying to get it mobile again?'

'Course it is! Got us here, didn't it?'

'Up to you. You're the mechanic. Are we carrying any spare oil?'

Gildas, alarmed, stuck his head into the front of the truck. The whole engine was covered with oil and a sizeable pool lay on the floor beneath. He hadn't noticed it in his excitement at finding something useful to do. His heart sank.

'Maybe I could find a radiator on another vehicle and cobble it in.' he said. 'It's worth a try. Did you notice any outside when we got here?'

'Several. You'll have to do the work, though. I'll watch out, if you like.'

'Let's go!' Carrying his toolkit Gildas cautiously opened one of the entrance doors. 'All clear. There's a lorry over there. Cover me!'

That lorry proved too difficult to work on. He couldn't tilt the cab to gain access. However, behind the lorry a large saloon car lay on its side. Doors, bonnet, windows and engine were missing but a big radiator sat at the front of the engine compartment.

Of course, it wouldn't be a direct fit; even the correct radiator could not have been properly positioned inside the bent and broken cavity. Gildas' only fear was - would it hold water without leaks? Used radiators only rarely remained watertight after being left empty for a long while. He tested it as best he could, bashed holes in the sides of the truck's bonnet, bolted the radiator in place and connected water-lines with the aid of odd bits of metal and rubber pipe scavenged from several vehicles close at hand.

'That's the best I can do.' he said with evident pride. 'Now I'll check the engine oil.'

169

Several gallon cans of oil were located in the cargo compartment. Two went in the engine. It had lost more than Gildas realised because of the severe overheating it had suffered. Badly abused oil seals and gaskets were succumbing to their age. Still, now they were ready to go. Clare ruined his plans.

'How are you going to start the thing without a hill to run it down?' she asked innocently.

Gildas looked at her, then at the truck. 'I don't know.' he confessed.

'Well I'm damned if I'm going to push it. Let me know when you think of something!' and she lay down to have a nap. A rushing noise came from outside and loose metal sheets covering the warehouse began rattling. Dust spilled in through the broken windows.

Dust-devils stirred up by pockets of overheated air were common, but they didn't happen at night. Strong winds didn't come often in these desert days, either - and when they did it was every bit as unpleasant as the average Sahara dust storm. The sky darkened and the temperature increased. Gildas had plenty of time to figure out a way to start the truck but came up with nothing. He couldn't even attempt to fix the starter motor; a brief foray under the truck provided the information that there was no starter motor there at all; just an oily hole caked with equally oily dust where it used to be bolted. Cannibalised to keep another truck going! He gave up.

As night fell they warmed up more water over a small fire and ate another meal. Nobody would notice the smoke through the clouds of dust scouring through the industrial estate. Clare had first claim on sleep because of her wounds.

Three hours into his second watch Gildas thought he heard something over the noise of the storm; a distant crash like a roof blowing off. Coming on the alert he wondered whether he should wake Clare. Ten seconds later the decision was made for him. The windows on the northern

170

side of the warehouse glowed with a white light that strengthened rapidly then faded again as if a powerful torch had been swept across them. Running into one of the rooms on that side, he looked out. Whatever it was had just moved beyond his sight behind an adjoining warehouse and he could see the roofs of several more further away bathed in a harsh light before plunging back into darkness in sequence as the source travelled away from him. A subdued rumble could be heard over the thin scream of fast-moving air.

Clare objected strongly to being prodded awake. Gildas could only make squeaky noises round the wrathful hands encircling his neck until she realised who he was. She released him with the simple expedient of throwing him sprawling on the floor.

'You should know better than that.' she snapped, hands clenching and opening. Gildas kept an eye on those hands as he lay on the ground, massaging his throat.

'Something big just turned up.' he rasped. 'Gone up the valley. It might be looking for us. Gotta get out of here.'

'What was it?'

'Couldn't see.' Gildas' voice began returning to normal as he staggered back on his feet. 'Only it was big. Come on! Grab what we can and find a place to hide.'

Clare wasn't having any of it. 'We're as safe here as anywhere else. Still sounds like a storm out there. Collect your weapons and we'll wait in the room nearest the door. If they come in we'll have the drop on them.'

Reluctantly, he complied. They waited, alert for any sound not caused by the wind. It didn't take long for something to happen.

A tremendous explosion shook the warehouse, followed immediately by the stutter of a heavy machine gun. Faint shouts and screams carried on the wind. A pale orange light lit the room. They looked at each other, wondering.

'Shall we take a look?' Clare was already heading for the main door. Without waiting for an answer she found the

171

handle, pulled it open and disappeared in a cloud of dust. Choking, she pulled it shut again. Gildas joined her.

'Let sleeping dogs lie.' he advised.

'No! That's transport out there, in case you haven't realised. I haven't got much faith in our own so maybe we can pinch someone else's. Find a cover for your face and follow me!'

It was lighter outside than any summer night should be. A strong smell of burning assailed their nostrils through the makeshift dust masks. Keeping close together they ran to the traffic roundabout.

The main artery through the major part of the industrial estate began at this point and they could see its course for about half a mile. Half-way along this section a large building was burning furiously on the left side, the flames occasionally being obliterated by thick smoke pouring from the roof. As they watched another section suddenly started burning along a wide front as if soaked in petrol. Small figures lurched jerkily in and out of sight. The machine gun stammered again. Some of the figures fell and stayed down.

'Come on!' Clare ran across the road and a stretch of open ground to an intact factory unit. Gildas followed, asking himself over and over; why the hell was he doing this? He knew, all right! This was Clare's speciality and he was safer close to her than by himself. He ran faster. Together they moved up the road using as much of the scant cover as they could find.

Soon they had moved close enough to see into the compound where the fire burned at its fiercest. From the shadow of an abandoned office cabin they had a good view. Gildas whistled softly in surprise.

'Whew! What kind of waggon is that? Army, you reckon?'

'Yes and no. I think we'd better find something a bit more substantial to hide behind. The slugs from those guns'll penetrate twenty of these cabins without slowing down. There, that wall over there.'

From the shelter of the low concrete wall they observed the action. Two groups of about fifty people were engaged in a totally ineffectual attack on one of the strangest vehicles Gildas had ever seen. It stood in a car-parking space facing the main building; massive, grotesque, like a huge slug daring the attackers to come closer. The people stood on either side; to the rear lay many bodies. The front could not be seen but many more bodies were strewn in the glare of powerful lights, which lit up a red brick wall. Eight thick wheels supported its hulking body.

Clare grinned. 'Watch this! Any moment now. They're nearly all in the right positions.'

Gildas looked again and noticed the attackers were getting bolder. The waggon simply sat there, making no hostile overtures. Perhaps it had run out of ammunition.

Stones, pieces of metal and lumps of concrete rained on the waggon. The people slowly moved closer. All at once several of the bolder ones ran forward and began climbing the sides in an attempt to gain the roof. The others surged about, using metal rods and girders to hammer on the sides. The waggon rang like a bell. Armour plate, Gildas thought. It sounded very heavy.

'Come on girl! Now! Now!' breathed Clare beside him.

Her unheard instructions were obeyed. Jagged blue streaks clothed the waggon. Men and women screamed in an extremity of pain as they were flung from the machine. Those on the roof fell and jerked like baldly-handled string puppets. A moment later a huge flare of flame burst from both sides to completely engulf the two lines of people.

Within seconds the screaming had ceased. Two mass funeral pyres blazed freely. The sound of the dying wind and the rumble of engines were the only things to be heard beside the crackle of flames. Clare gripped Gildas' arm to hold him in place. Minutes passed.

A circular cover opened on the roof of the waggon near the front and fell with a loud crash. A small, dimly-seen figure silhouetted against the floodlit wall cautiously rose

173

into view, the head turning to survey all sides in turn. With a quick hop the figure leapt up onto the roof, a large gun under one arm questing for targets, circling. Satisfied, the figure walked along the roof rolling and kicking corpses over the side. Clare raised her hands to her mouth in preparation for a shout.

She never got the chance. In one of the windows of the factory a tiny flicker of fire spurted. The figure on the roof of the waggon must have seen it, too. It fell flat even before Gildas heard the shot, for shot it was, a scatter-gun rather than a rifle. Another shot blasted out. The figure wriggled rapidly towards the hatch cover and raised it as a temporary shield.

'Trapped!' Clare murmured. 'We'll have to help out. I think she's been hit.'

'She?'

'Wait and see! If only I can get a clear shot! There can't be that many scatter-guns around here and goodness knows how they've still got any cartridges. It could be the same guy who peppered me.' She shook Gildas' shoulder. 'Stay here! I've got a score to settle with that one. Don't come out into the open unless you see I'm really in trouble and be careful of that one on the waggon. She's very, *very* dangerous.'

'She?' Gildas repeated. 'Who is she?'

I said wait and see. Now don't fire unless you absolutely have to and whatever you do, don't ask her for her name!' With a sign to keep alert, Clare glided along the wall away from him.

Shortly, Gildas saw her flitting across the road at the limit of the dying fire-glow and disappear into an alley. No more shots were fired at the waggon. Whoever was firing was apparently waiting for the driver to make a desperate effort to get back inside. Only one good shot would be required then.

He had faith in Clare and she did not disappoint him. A flurry of shots came from the ambusher's window and a staggering figure showed to straightaway topple out and crash into a broken heap at the base of the wall.

Silence. Then something white waved from the window. Flag of parley? He heard a shout.' 'Ma. 'Ma. O...oot! 'Are. It... 'lare! 'Ear me?'

Very slowly the figure on the waggon roof moved its gun barrel to point at the window. A high-pitched voice called out. A short conversation ensued ending with Clare showing herself at the window. Apparently recognised, she rushed back downstairs, clambered up a ladder bolted to the side of the waggon and assisted the figure back through the trapdoor, which was then closed from the inside.

Gildas stayed where he was.

CHAPTER   14

Amazingly, he fell asleep! Perhaps not so amazing when one took the events of the previous day into account. Still, to slumber at all in the present surroundings took a bit of doing.

Someone else thought so, too. A painful kick in the ribs immediately followed by two bellowing blasts from a heavy-calibre rifle wrenched him from the gentle arms of unconsciousness to awake and freeze in a spasm of fear as the first thing he saw was a large figure blotting out the sky and holding a gun. A second bash with the same heavy boot bought home the reality.

'All right. Stop that! I'm awake.'

Too late. The third savage kick thudded into the same rib. Even with the normal distortion of the senses that occurs on awakening, Gildas could have sworn there had been a significant pause between his plea and the third kick. He blinked blearily at the silhouette; it was Clare. That clinched it! There must have been a pause.

'Moron! Asleep at a time like this? You must be crazy. Get up! Do you know how close you were to getting your throat slit?'

'Sorry.' He struggled to his feet, winced at the sound of cracking joints and grabbed unsuccessfully at his rifle as it clattered to the ground. Clare lashed a boot out at it in annoyance. She was definitely in a kicking mood.

'Say sorry to yourself, not me! If I'd been two minutes later you'd have been dead. A couple of the locals were stalking you along the wall. Idiot!'

Gildas peered into the flickering shadow cast by the nearly extinguished flames behind the wall. There were no corpses. He glanced at Clare.

'I shot over their heads.' She appeared to be making an excuse. 'There's been enough killing here already. Besides, we have to leave a few to look after the kids and women; not that there's many left of them, either. Follow me and keep alert!'

Retrieving his gun, Gildas trotted after her as she found a path through the scattered corpses towards the mobile death-machine squatting among its recent victims. As they drew near he experienced a strong sense of instinctive fear; and not without reason. It was understandable. Seen close up in the half-light of an approaching dawn, the machine resembled something from a nasty dream - like a saurian monster from aeons past with its scarred, blotched scales, luminous eyes and vast breaths feeding mighty lungs.. Such a physical nature seemed more tangible than the reality of dusty, riveted armour plate, headlamps and the great cooling fans for the engines. Unnatural power and malevolence radiated from every part of its hulking, angular mass. He studied it in awe as Clare hammered on a door high up near the front.

The door opened. Harsh white light blazed from the interior. Clare threw in her gun, mounted two recessed steps to the threshold and waved Gildas to do likewise. Reluctantly, he obliged. The door swung quickly closed behind him, pushing him sharply inside. He just managed to get his fingers out of the way of the frame before it slammed shut and locked automatically with a loud snap of solenoid-driven bolts.

Unsettled, he sat down on the leather - leather? - seat and tried to look across to the other side of what was obviously the control cabin. Clare had her back to him and obscured the view. He leaned forward.

The seat was wide enough for two to sit comfortably. There was a similar one on the other side of the cab. Between them, a softly upholstered chair at a slightly higher level faced a semi-circular console of controls. At the rear of the chair a strong metal frame supported a steel mesh festooned with quick-access boxes, holsters with protruding gun and knife handles and a large selection of grenades, AP mines and other weapons he could not immediately recognise. This fleeting first survey quickly focused itself on the occupant of the chair, and for a very good reason. Either a late-adolescent girl or a young adult woman sat facing him, stiffly upright. She dominated the cabin, and not only because she sat at a higher level. It was the total ease and familiarity with which she sat. She appeared to be part of the machine; flesh and blood cohabiting with dispassionate steel, separate yet combined in a symbiosis of purpose.

She belonged there! One with the growling motors, the murderous armaments, the vicious demeanour. All the more surprising because she was also the most beautiful creature he could ever remember meeting - save one. Gildas was smitten. He had instantly fallen in love in spite of the fact she was regarding him with a most belligerent expression - and had a small revolver levelled at a spot he knew would be exactly at the centre point of his eyebrows. Despite his sinless intent, he froze.

'Your rifle. Turn it to face the other way and give it to Clare! Nice and easy, now.'

177

Even her voice was music to his ears. As if in a trance he did as he was bid. Clare grinned openly into his face. Emma always affected men like this. Lucky bitch!

Emma lowered the gun, slid it into a small holster at the side of the control console with a smooth practised motion and addressed Clare with undisguised contempt.

'So this is your precious Gildas, huh? God, isn't he ugly? You must be getting old if you can't do any better than this.'

Clare shrugged. 'Any port in a storm. At least he doesn't smell quite so bad as most of them out there and who cares in the dark, anyway? It's quality that counts as you get older and he's well blessed, believe me. Or have you still got to find out about all that?'

'You'll never know, will you?'

Both girls smiled sweetly at each other. Gildas felt a sharp twinge of injustice overlain with resentment.

'I never ... we didn't ... Aw, hell.' He met two innocent and inquiring stares. 'Forget it!'

Emma's face hardened. 'Right, lets get to work. Their stores must be around here somewhere. You!' she jabbed a finger at the unfortunate Gildas. 'Don't speak until you're spoken to from now on and don't pull any sort of weapon out when you're in here,' Clare sniggered, 'And when I tell you to do something you'll do it without question or delay! Give me any problems and I'll kill you. Understand?'

Gildas nodded, shocked at the abrupt change in her mood. Emma flicked a few switches and clasped a small lever directly in front of her. The engines woke up, snarling, and they began to move. Small bumps signified a single corpse, the bigger jolt meant they had crossed a heap of them where the mass barbecue still smouldered. Gildas leaned across to Clare.

'What's up with her?' he whispered. 'Got some pellets in her butt, has she?'

The waggon slammed to a stop. Gildas felt the revolver lined up on exactly the same spot between his eyes before he had time to look up.

'Get out!'

'Huh? What'd I do?' he appealed to Clare.

'Still here, ugly? I'll give you one more chance because Clare here seems to be rather fond of you for some reason beyond my understanding - and also because you may be rather deaf.' Emma's voice rose to a shout. 'Get out!' She touched a button. The door clicked and swung ajar; the revolver didn't waver a millimetre.

Clare leaned forward to block the line of fire. 'Come on, Emma. Don't be so touchy. I know you're hurting but don't take it out on him; he doesn't know any better. Put the gun away and we'll get the gear and vacate the premises. OK?'

'Out of the way! He's leaving.' Emma pushed Clare's shoulder. Clare didn't budge. Emma pushed harder.

Wiry arms grabbed Gildas around the shoulders and pulled him back. He saw an inverted bearded face above him and a large crude knife grasped in a grubby hand poised to descend into his chest. Clare sat upright; there was a huge explosion and the face disappeared leaving a deep bloody pit between the twin tangled thatches of hair and beard. A slobbering scream came from the mess, spraying Gildas with warm blood. The body relaxed, dropped out of sight, and the door slammed shut. He stayed down, shaking with reaction.

After a moment he was pulled up once more by Clare's strong hand. She was holding Emma's revolver in her other fist. Emma sat stiffly in her chair, weaponless. Clare popped the gun back in its holster, produced a scrap of rag and proceeded to wipe the worst of the blood off her little companion.

'Come on girl, get us moving before they gather enough courage to rush us again! Gildas'll thank you later for saving his life instead of snuffing it out. Get going!'

Petulantly, Emma operated controls. The waggon lurched into motion. Lips compressed into a thin line she guided it along the factory wall looking for a big enough entrance.

It was sealed by a sliding door. A tight turn, a howl from the engines and a shattering crash solved what could have been a problem with access. The metal monster simply burst through the door and entered the building trailing thin metal sheets and bars.

Feeling slightly more forgiving and relaxed by her unnecessary exhibition of powered violence, Emma dropped the window shields and peered into the gloomy cavern of the old factory. Much of the machinery had been removed from its original positions and arranged to form small courtyards within which could be seen mattresses, bits of furniture and other tatty household equipment. Each habitation appeared to be about the right size to house a couple of family units in relative comfort and independence.

Emma set the waggon to trundle down a wide passageway through the "housing estate", as Gildas thought of it. At the entrance to one of the homes she halted and surveyed the interior. Stretching his neck, Gildas was able to see through the far window. Two very elderly people, possibly a man and a woman, lay on a double mattress covered with a thin, and very dirty, sheet. With a quick movement she flicked a switch on the console. The faint squeal of a servo sounded from somewhere in the waggon. Emma reached for a small red button.

Before she could press the button her arm was stayed in an implacable grasp as Clare grabbed it.

'Don't do it, girl. It's not necessary; they can't hurt us. Just look at them!'

Two frightened faces stared at the waggon over the top of the sheet, eyes black in the absence of direct light. The sheet was jerked up and the faces disappeared.

'I'm beginning to feel sorry I picked you two up. Any survivors could cause trouble. Let go my arm so I can crisp them - they won't feel a thing, I promise.'

'You're not thinking. Kill those two old folk and it may prompt what's left of the local population to have a go at us again. We've got to get out to load up the stores when we find them, remember. We don't require more trouble than needful.'

'With this waggon I can handle anything they could do.' Emma's boast was well-founded, but she stayed her hand from the trigger button, none the less. Not that she could have done anything else; she knew she wouldn't be able to move her arm as long as Clare didn't want her to. With her free hand she flicked the "flamer active" switch back to "off". Clare released her arm and the waggon continued.

Still shaking a little, Gildas wondered what motivated their homicidal driver.

Mesh-covered floodlights mounted on the waggon lit the factory interior brighter than daylight; pitch black shadows travelled in the opposite direction. It wasn't very long before they located the community stores in a large annex just off the main industrial hall. There was a substantial stockpile; far too much to get inside the commodious storage space at the rear of the waggon.

Emma rotated the machine so that the front faced the way they had come - it was the only practical means of entrance. She snapped out her orders.

'Just select the most useful gear! Concentrate on food and medical supplies! You two are more fitted for the manual work so get out there and start loading! You'll find a forklift in the back I'll keep watch for any unwanted attention we may attract because of your squeamishness.' The door opened. 'Get going and don't pass in front of the waggon if you want to go on breathing.'

They reached the rear of the waggon to find the door ramp already descending. Clare began to search the stacks of goods for useful provisions while Gildas unstrapped the gas-powered forklift from the side stanchions and struggled to operate the unfamiliar controls. Driving it out onto the annex floor, he shut off the engine and awaited instructions. He felt very vulnerable and found himself searching the shadowy metal roof braces high overhead in case one of the

181

locals was about to drop something heavy and terminally painful on his head. They had already demonstrated their "social attitude to strangers" curriculum vitae.

A muffled murmur of voices began close at hand and gained amplitude as if an argument was in progress. It burst into a medley of shouts.

'Stop him!'

'Don't do it, Nye! They'll kill you.'

'Come back here, you stupid old goat!.

And a woman, resigned. 'Leave him! He's not going to listen to anybody, as usual; he's always been pig-headed. Jack, come back here, good boy! No point in you both being shot.'

The voices ebbed away. Unseen faces watched and awaited developments from the shadows. Shuffling footsteps accompanied by a sharp tapping came closer. Into the glare of the headlamps moved the small, stooped figure of a very elderly man clad in a dark, heavy overcoat, which clashed sharply with the pure white patches of his thick mop of hair and long bushy beard. Immediately he came into the direct glare of the lamps he stopped, sensing the pressure and warmth of a light he could not see. A pair of milky eyes bespoke his total blindness as did the ornately-carved white stick with which he tapped his way. He painfully drew himself up to his maximum height, which wasn't much. Yet despite his lack of physical stature, his obvious frailty and his ragamuffin apparel, he radiated a presence Gildas could not deny as he sat on the forklift waiting for what might happen next. Tangled white whiskers moved as the man opened his mouth to speak, using his stick to point behind him.

'Leave us! Do you have to steal our food as well as destroy so many of our number? Will you leave the survivors, women, babes and the old, to starve? We deny you our provisions. Go from here at once! Leave this place!'

The voice suited the man; it was full, resonant, almost oratorical; this was a man of learning, of breeding. From the still-open door of the waggon came a trill of soft, sardonic laughter. Gildas feared for the man's safety. An incoherent babble of shouts sounded from the shadows. The man ignored his companions; his stick shook with passionate emphasis. The rich tones continued.

'Go! You have forfeited the right to our hospitality, which we would freely have given.' Even Gildas was forced to smile at *that*. The voice boomed louder, shaking with age and emotion. 'Instead of coming in a spirit of friendship you have burned, killed, laid waste our community. What kind of people are you? Murderers! Killers! Go! Let us be!'

A faint whine came to Gildas' ears from somewhere out of sight. It sounded vaguely familiar. *Oh no!* He leapt from the forklift and began to run to the front of the waggon, shouting. 'No, no! Stop!'

A woman screamed from the darkness. Jack! Jack, don't! Oh my God!' Running footsteps clattered on concrete. A young man appeared, bent low and moving fast with outstretched arms; heading straight for the patriarch, who was taking a deep breath for his next outburst, stick held high. There was a flash of white light from the front of the waggon a and a clicking noise. Gildas slid to a halt.

With a sound like that of an ancient gas boiler coming to life, a thin jet of flame shot towards the old man, enveloping him in fire. His would-be rescuer, unable to stop, ran right into it in an attempt to knock him clear. Too late! The searing spray got them both. They fell to the floor, locked together. The flamer stopped.

The terrible screams, old and hoarse, young and shrill, and drumming of thrashing limbs were mercifully short-lived; that wonderful, confident voice had been stilled for ever. A short, shocked silence followed by shouts and wails erupted from the shadows of the main industrial hall. Emma's voice came from an external speaker.

183

'Get on with it, you two!'

Gildas couldn't believe it. She sounded so calm. 'You didn't have to do that.' he yelled.

'I'm not telling you again. Get loading!'

Averting his gaze from the guttering flames and melted human fat spitting and popping on the blackened concrete, Gildas struggled onto the forklift and attempted to start the engine. He failed.

He tried again and failed again. Spreading his hands over his face he rested his head on the horizontal steering wheel.

It had been a hell of a morning so far.

Someone shook his shoulder. He looked up into Clare's concerned face. 'You OK?' she asked.

He nodded, unable to respond.

She leaned across and pressed a button; the gas engine thudded into life. 'Get over there, then' she gestured. 'Those big containers. Sure you're OK?'

'Why did she have to fry the old man and that boy?' Gildas asked, trying to keep his voice level. 'She didn't have to. Is she crazy, or what?'

Clare glanced towards the waggon door. 'In a way, yes. I told you she was very dangerous, remember? But in this case I would probably have done the same. That old man could have wound the survivors up into another attack and even more would have been killed; perhaps us among them; we're exposed out here. They had to be discouraged for their own sakes. And I'd've used a flamer rather than a gun, too.' She anticipated his next criticism 'It scares people more.' She paused, then added, 'Mind you, I don't think that particular consideration so much as entered her mind. She just likes killing people. Never forget that! Start loading now before she gets nasty.'

'Gets nasty!' But he got loading.

It took more than an hour even with the fork-lift but at last they clambered back in the cabin. Emma was reading an old comic. 'Finished?' she asked.

Clare flexed her arms. 'The cargo space is full but there's a lot left. Pity we can't take it all.'

They had discussed it earlier. Gildas acted on cue.

'We can if we really need to.' he chipped in.

Emma reacted as expected. 'What do you mean? I need to get as much as I can; this is likely to be the last foraging trip I make.'

Clare explained. 'We've got a truck. It'll take most of what's left. All we ask in return is you accompany us in a short diversion before we hit the motorway. You are heading for Gloucester I take it?'

'Yes. Why the diversion?'

'Gildas has a score to settle. It may be his last chance.'

'It may well be.' Emma remarked grimly. 'And he might need the fire power in this waggon as a bit of insurance, right?'

'He might. All OK, then?'

Emma grinned. 'It might be a bit of fun to watch him in action. I've always enjoyed watching the antics of circus clowns. But I reserve the right not to interfere if I don't want to.'

Fat chance thought Clare. But she said aloud. 'Whatever you say. It's his fight. Go back out of the gates and turn left.'

Clare leaned back in her seat and quietly sighed with relief. The thought of travelling in the waggon trying to stop Emma from shooting poor old Gildas had filled her with dread. Why had he found it necessary to antagonise her in the first place? She'd made a point of telling him Emma was dangerous. But for now she could relax.

Getting the truck started was easy. Emma simply drove the blunt, armoured front of her waggon up behind and pushed - then moved quickly out of the way as her view became obscured with black smoke.

Back in the factory community stores they loaded the truck with all it could carry safely. No-one was to be seen;

185

the inhabitants had evidently decided to keep their heads down until the "all clear".

By the time they were back on the main valley highway the sun had risen half-way to its zenith, hazy and indistinct in a dusty sky. The heavily-burdened tyres pressed sand and dust from the previous night's wind into the softened tarmac, leaving a permanent record of their passing. There wasn't far to go. A journey of less than a mile brought the little convoy to the correct exit slip road and the two vehicles followed a minor road up and around a high rock buttress; one idling easily, the other bellowing in mechanical agony at being forced to climb in its lowest gear.

An easing of the gradient brought relief to the ears. The castle came into view. Gildas almost wept at the destruction.

Gone were the graceful spires, the neat gardens, the tall surrounding trees. Most of the walls still stood, topped by a tangle of blackened timbers sprouting like an insane hairdo from equally blackened eaves. Each window had its own crown of soot plastered above the empty frame.

A great fire had raged here - and not so very long ago. Never steeped in significant historical associations, never the scene of important battles or the signing of far-reaching treaties, the building, relatively new in the march of history, had never presented an impression of might or age ... but it was, or had been, beautiful to gaze upon.

But no more. Castell Goch - the Red Castle - stood in ruins.

The former car park contained a bewildering array of plastic sheets of different colours, some still managing to cling on flimsy frames or lines, hanging limp and hot in the calm air. Most had been blown flat and wrapped around some of the more substantially-anchored structures. The immediate area appeared deserted. Lamenting silently inside, Gildas coaxed the truck closer to the main building.

'Look!' said Clare, pointing.

At the main entrance to the castle building stood two figures dressed in cloth sheets that touched the floor. Each wore a broad-brimmed hat which, upon closer inspection, proved to be simply a brim and nothing else. Neither moved. Gildas stopped the truck.

'I'm going over to talk to them.'

'No you're not.' Clare grabbed his arm. 'There may be another hundred of them in there out of sight. It's a bit too deserted around here for my liking and it was damned stupid of you to switch off the engine like that. If you want to talk to them get them to come over here.'

Gildas checked his gun. 'I haven't come all this way to argue over protocol. If Dave is still here I'll find him and then destroy him if I can. Don't try to stop me!'

Clare let him go without further argument, checked her own armaments and made sure their little first-aid kit was within easy reach.

As Gildas approached the figures one of them held up a hand, palm facing out, in a gesture that said "stop". He did so and addressed them.

'Where has everyone gone?'

They stared at him, gaunt and apathetic. For a moment he thought they would ignore him; then one of them spoke.

'Elsewhere. A few days ago. Many have died, only a few are left. They are hiding. They are afraid. What will you do to us?'

This guy must be a relative of the old man back at the factory, Gildas thought; the richness of tone and vaguely bardic delivery had to have a common root, at the very least. The last phrase, the question, was the most important. Gildas responded in kind, not without a certain difficulty.

'Why, nothing! All I require is the location of one man. He is called Dave. I do not know his second name.'

'I am familiar with the names of all who are left. There is no-one called Dave among us.' Another figure in a shroud joined the two at the door and whispered in the speaker's ear. He nodded and continued. 'A man who called

187

himself Dave came two days past. It was at his urging that many left to scatter as they willed. He was only here a matter of hours before the helicopter arrived to transport him, we know not where.'

Helicopter? Only VIPs would warrant a helicopter. Who the hell *was* Dave?

'Do you remember the direction it travelled?'

The man gestured to the north-east. 'We were not told his destination.'

'Thank you.' Gildas turned to leave. The bard called out.

Do you have news of the disease? How much time is left to us?'

Gildas turned back. 'What disease? There are so many. It is all about us.'

'The man Dave told us of a new and deadly strain. Unfamiliar. The helicopter brought the news.'

That explained the reluctance to allowing him to get too close. He shook his head. 'I don't know anything of that. I must go now. Goodbye.'

'Do you have any food to spare us? We have water, but we have not received a food supply for some weeks. Those who are left will not leave here, there is nowhere to go, but we would rather die quickly of the sickness when it arrives than slowly of hunger. Please! Anything you can contribute will be accepted with our grateful thanks.'

'I shall leave what I can.'

'And if you find your friend Dave, please thank him once more for what he did for us. Without his help we could not have survived for even these few extra days.'

Certainly, just before I kill him very painfully.

No more words were exchanged. Working hard, he unloaded supplies until Emma began to get fractious. Bump-starting the old truck, they retreated from the doomed community; the castle its mausoleum before too long.

His eyes felt a bit damp for some reason.

CHAPTER 15

For Emma, the journey home was surprisingly uneventful; only twice was she able to use her armoury against attacks and even then the numbers involved were few. It was all very boring. The small travelling groups of weak, haggard creatures hardly had the strength or will to throw a few stones let alone do enough damage to halt the two-vehicle convoy. Their extermination was nothing more than merciful, as even Gildas was forced to agree. Stories of the sickness were true, all right. Emma would shortly have to find some other way to pass the time.

The battered old truck trundled along wonderfully. Knocking, clattering and belching huge clouds of smoke, true, but it kept going. Even with her lack of mechanical knowledge Clare found herself in awe at its staying powers and felt impelled to express her surprise to her companion at the wheel.

'How is it possible?' she ended the question, shouting above the din. There were travelling east along a wide dual-carriageway at the time; flatter land spread out ahead. The high mountains had been left behind.

Gildas spread his hands across the steering wheel, palms up, the equivalent of a shrug.

'Darned if I know. Some just won't give up. My grandfather used to be a bus driver after the last big war and I remember him telling me about one he worked on. It was old when it came into the depot. After working in Town and up the valleys for years and years, they decided to put it on a route that had several hellish steep hills, and not many passengers, to work its guts out till the end of its days. But it just wouldn't die! Year after year it slogged up those hills, summer and winter; nothing went wrong with it that routine servicing couldn't sort out. It was unbelievable! In the end the company got so ashamed of its obvious age and appearance they sold it overseas. Last my granddad heard it was still going strong somewhere in Malaya. He read a bit about it in a trade magazine. I wouldn't be surprised if it wasn't still rattling around out there somewhere if there's anybody left alive to drive the thing. Machinery sometimes throws up something unbreakable in spite of the best efforts of designers and engineers to turn out rubbish that has to be replaced as soon as they can get away with it.

'Yes, but this thing?'

'Don't knock it! This is an old army truck. They made thousands of the things. According to the Beast, my old boss, this one originally came from an army scrap yard. It's one of the early ones and has very likely seen more than its fair share of action and killing in different parts of the world. It's a survivor and as long as we keep putting the right liquids in the right places it'll see us all right.'

At that precise moment, as is so often the case, the engine lost power and wouldn't respond to the accelerator. Coasting to a stop, Gildas felt his ears go red. The waggon pulled alongside. 'What's wrong?' Emma snapped through the loudspeaker. 'Why have you stopped?'

'Broken down!' yelled Gildas, furious at the amused grin on Clare's face.

'No need to shout, you'll damage the microphone. I'll pull in front and tow you. Can't afford to leave the cargo behind. Just stay sitting where you are!'

Emma's waggon could drive in reverse as easily as forwards. The extending arm emerged, its hook located around the main cross-chassis girder, and they were off. It took all Gildas' nerve and skill to keep in a straight line at the speed Emma drove. Within an hour they were in sight of the bunker.

None of the former inhabitants were to be seen in the ramshackle camp by the main gate. There were only a scatter of people in protective suits loading a lorry with plastic-covered objects. They looked suspiciously like makeshift body bags. A faded yellow digger was engaged in the excavation of a deep hole some distance away. One of the workers ran towards them waving his arms. Emma stopped; this looked serious.

'Welcome home, Emma.' General Spode - who else? 'Be careful how you drive in. Try not to run over anything in your path and stop as soon as you get inside the gate. I'll explain later.'

Definitely something wrong! It was safer for her to do as requested until she knew enough about what had happened to make up her own mind. Spode was a fool but he wasn't crazy. Their arrival had been noticed by observers on top of the ziggurat. A reception committee had been scrambled and now awaited them inside the entry to the compound: four steam-cleaners - their entire complement - and twenty people sweating in silver total-cover suits. One approached.

'Please don't open your doors and stay inside till we've finished steaming down your vehicles. We'll be as quick as we can.' The figure waved the others on. Two steamers were positioned to each side of both vehicles and sterilisation began.

It didn't take very long but by the time they had finished Gildas felt he had been parboiled by steam blasting through the missing windows and gaps in the body panels. When the all-clear was signalled by the sweating sterilising teams frantically discarding their protective clothing, he leapt from the truck and hammered on the door of Emma's waggon.

'Let me in, quick! I'm cooking.'

'Cook, then! I'm not opening up until I find out what's been going on here. Anybody going to tell me?'

Gildas slumped in the shadow cast by the waggon. He felt faint with the overpowering heat and strong disinfectant odour from the dripping vehicles. One of the team approached, now disrobed and wiping his brow.

'God, it's hot in those suits. Can you hear me, Miss Quorvis?'

'Yes. What's happened. Why is the outside camp empty?'

'Disease. It was nasty. Only took a couple of days to wipe most of them out; the rest took off the way you came in. Doc says the steamers'll help make things a bit safer. You can get out now if you like. It's all right. Doc slapped on a quarantine soon as he realised what was happening.'

'No. I'll drive right into the stores to get unloaded. There's a full load in the truck as well.'

'I wouldn't advise that, Miss Quorvis, the stores are loading up all the transport we've got. No room for you in there at the moment. Besides, you'll probably have to take a load, like all the rest. May as well get freshened up and let Josh check the waggon out before the trip.'

"Moving out, huh?'

'Right. Your father gave the order right after Doc told him about the quarantine. He's still here. Wouldn't leave until you got back. We tried to make him go but you know what he's like.'

'Thanks. Josh is waiting for me over the garage. You can return to your duties.'

The man saluted sloppily and raced for the air-conditioned relief of the bunker. Loyal though he was, the combined effect of heat and bug-killer were too much to bear for long.

Gildas felt the same. He leaned against the hot side of the waggon fighting to avoid passing out. The waggon lurched forward almost knocking him under one of the heavy tyres.

'Hey! Wait till I'm out of the way, you stupid idiot.' he yelled.

The waggon stopped abruptly. A servo motor whined and a hatch opened in the plating to reveal a malignant little tube turning in his direction. Gildas watched it, too paralysed to move.

'Drop, you fool!' Clare screamed. 'Emma, don't! We need him.'

'I don't need him. Nobody needs him.'

Gildas dropped. The gun fired. Miniature slugs tore the air above his head. Groggily he was aware of a rush of feet. A shadow passed before him and a loud bang was followed by a clicking noise. Rough hands grasped him, pulled him around to the lee side of the truck and cast him on the ground. His head span.

'You brainless moron.' It was Clare. She was not happy. 'Get in the truck and stay on the floor. I'll take it in.'

He used his hands to crawl up one of the wheels. His sight was dimming, legs buckling. As he fumbled his way to the door he caught a brief glimpse of Clare rounding the corner. There was blood on her cheek, fresh blood. He opened the door and dragged himself behind the front seat to lie gasping on the floor. His goggles had disappeared. Clare sat behind the wheel; the truck lurched into deep shade and cool air. Gildas finally gave up and passed out.

He couldn't have been out for long. Voices penetrated the thick fog surrounding him and he became aware of Clare leaving the truck. She left the door open.

'A man's voice: 'Emma! I've been trying to get through to you. Don't you ever switch the radio on?'

'Can't stand the noise, Josh. It irritates me. For heaven's sake, Clare, what have you done to your face? I'll get Doc up here.'

Gildas began to feel a little better. Trying not to groan too loudly he stretched out, slowly closed the truck door then lifted himself on to the seat and raised his head above window level.

He looked straight into Emma's eyes. A wintry smile appeared fleetingly on her face and she spoke into a communicator.

'Can you come to Josh's workshop, Doc? Got a cut here for you to repair. Might need stitches.'

The com squawked in reply. The truck door swung open almost tipping Gildas back on the floor. Clare dragged him out gently and sat him down.

'Thanks.' he muttered. 'Your face. How did you get cut up like that?'

'The waggon's machine pistol barrel exploded when I bashed it with the butt of my own gun. Got hit, that's all.'

That's all? 'Thanks again.' He was feeling hot again. Vertical lines swayed. Suddenly he vomited. Surprised, he surveyed the mess over Clare's boots and did it again. His stomach stabbed at him. Dimly aware of rapid footsteps travelling away from his vicinity, his eyes glazed over and he passed out once more.

He saw a face. It spoke to him. 'Here he comes! Don't try to sit up! Drink this!' The words reached him after apparently passing down a long earthenware pipe. They were out of phase with the lips, reaching his ears before the lips moved. It was all very peculiar.

He drank. There was no taste. He drank some more at the insistence of his benefactor. Then he closed his eyes. Sound ceased and he slept.

His feet felt cold, his body was warm. Someone was talking to him.

'Wake up, son! Come on! Speak to Uncle Josh!'

He was lying in a cot against the wall of the workshop. A very old man was bending over him, but moved back on seeing his patient recover consciousness and regarded him with bright, lively eyes.

'Feeling any better? Fancy a cup of something? You'll have to come over to the machine to get it. I'm not going to be a nursemaid.'

Gildas used his elbows to prop himself up. A thick blanket covered him - all except for his feet. No wonder they'd woken him up, the air cooler was going at full blast. He swung his legs over the edge of the cot, tried to stand and swayed badly until the old man clasped his arm and began to lead him across the floor. He collapsed into a

194

heavily upholstered chair by the side of a wall-mounted drinks dispenser and tried to express his thanks. Josh waved his hands in dismissal.

'Never mind all that! You want a hot or cold drink? Don't take any notice of what's on the menu; they all taste the same 'cept you can get it cold or hot.'

'Hot, please.'

With a plastic cup of a hot, rather pleasant-tasting fluid on the arm of his chair and several gulps inside his belly he felt better able to take an interest in what was going on.

'Do you know what happened to me?'

The old man's withered face opened to flash twin rows of gleaming teeth. He laughed.

'Gawd! You should've seen the panic you caused. Even the doc went pale. We all thought you'd brought one of the diseases in with you.'

So had Gildas, just before he went under. 'But it wasn't?' he asked.

'Nah. You were pumped full of everything the doc could think of - so were the rest of us.' He rubbed his arm suggestively, then his buttocks. After that the doc asked some questions and poked around in the mess you made with a metal rod. Turns out you got some bug from last night's supper. Goat, Clare said.'

So that was it! Simple food poisoning, if you could call burned goat meat food. Gildas summoned up a weak grin. 'Sorry about that. It's not as if I enjoyed swallowing it, either. I'd better apologise to the others.' He set aside the now-empty cup and made as if to get up. Josh leaned forward and gently pushed him back into the folds of the comfortable old chair.

'Not a good idea, 'specially as far as Emma, Miss Quorvis, is concerned. Seems she's got a bit of a grudge against you. Know why?'

'Not a clue. I've tried to be as nice as I can but it simply doesn't work. She tried to kill me out there in the yard, y'know. With a machine pistol, no less! Said nobody

195

needed me. Maybe that's true but it's not a good enough reason to snuff me out. There's something wrong with that girl.'

Josh stood up and retrieved the cup for further use. With his free hand he patted Gildas on the shoulder.

'Don't feel too bad about that, son. Mind you, the jabs she got from the doc didn't exactly improve her feelings for you one little bit. Still, when you get to know her you'll find she's a pretty good sort. Trouble is, she doesn't know you and those she don't know are a threat to her. I've had a chat to Miss Masson and she's asked me to look after you for a while. Keep you and Emma apart, in a manner of speaking. Feel well enough to stand up now?'

Gildas grunted and managed to get on his feet, relieved to find he felt very much better. He tried to ignore the stinging sensations in his arms and butt.

'Miss Masson? Who's she?'

'The girl who steered your truck in here. Don't you know her name or who she is?' A bushy eyebrow lifted in mild astonishment.

'Oh, Clare. Never knew her other name. Never asked. Who is she, then?'

Josh opened his mouth then closed it again. He rubbed his chin. 'Friend of Emma's. Ever since they were both little tots. I've known her nearly all her life.'

That's not what he was going to tell me, thought Gildas. There's more. 'Anything else I should know?'

'Best ask her yourself.' Josh turned away. 'Come and tell me 'bout what happened to your truck; haven't seen one of these for years.'

An hour later Gildas found himself in the company of a very large and uncommunicative guard being guided through a labyrinth of passages and stairways. Many other people of all ages thronged the walkways, chattering and purposeful. An atmosphere of expectancy and anticipation was in the air - just like Gildas remembered as a child on

196

the day his family set out on holiday. The base was getting ready to leave - somewhere.

He had left Josh busy with re-equipping Emma's waggon while his assistants did their best with the old truck The fault which had immobilised them had already been dealt with; a simple blockage of the main fuel pipe by a shred of paint peeled off the interior of the fuel tank. The tank had been cleaned, the pipe cleared and work had commenced on the jerry-rigged cooling system. They had even found an old starter motor they though might fit with a bit of modification. This procedure included the highly descriptive comments of the mechanic detailed to do the job in the absence of Gildas, who had been summoned downstairs at just the right moment.

The guard halted before a heavy door. An intercom bleeped, words were exchanged and the door clicked. Entering, they approached a desk behind which sat an attractive middle-aged woman. The guard left.

'Gildas, yes?' The woman, cool and poised, gestured to a chair. 'I'm Wendy, Mr Quorvis' secretary. Have a sit down until the others arrive; they shouldn't be long.' She smiled, at once reassuring yet in complete control of her little domain; the perfect receptionist. Gildas felt at ease for the first time since he'd caught sight of this intimidating place.

Clare and Emma arrived together. Emma looked right through him. Clare winked. He felt the return of the familiar nervous stress, a natural consequence of being in the presence of Emma, as he was to discover. For now he distracted himself with a round-eyed inspection of her. She had changed into proper woman's clothing and tidied herself up. Her appearance was that of a beautiful young woman. Gildas was captivated; all memories of her natural disposition fled from his mind.

Later he was to remember this moment as the point he *really* began to fall hopelessly in love with her: to have something to live for once more. He gawped like a love-sick calf. Clare recognised the signs; it always happened

197

when men caught sight of her companion. She didn't laugh. Instead she smiled mirthlessly and signalled him to get up

Emma ignored him completely.

The door to the inner office opened and they all trouped in, Gildas hanging back. A small fat man got up from behind a desk at the far end of the room and minced forward to clasp Emma, peck Clare on the cheek and shake hands with Gildas. He beamed at Gildas.

'Nice to meet you. I'm Lemuel Quorvis. Thanks for helping my daughter out of a jam. I am obliged.' His nose twitched and wrinkled. 'Excuse me a moment.'

Returning hastily to his desk he touched one of a row of buttons. Scented air wafted from overhead grilles. Gildas became miserably aware of the state and aroma of his clothing and body.

'I'm sorry, Mr Quorvis, I ...'

Lemuel waved them to the desk, where three chairs had been placed for them. 'Please! I don't mean to offend, but my digestive system is too delicate for compromise. I'm well aware of what you've been through and I bet Josh never even suggested you freshen up. You can sort yourself out as you wish after we've had our little chat. It's not going to be as long as I'd like because you may have noticed we're in the process of pulling out.' His head tilted up in enquiry. Gildas realised he was expected to comment.

'Er, yes.' What to say next? 'Where to?'

'The ship, of course.'

'Ship?'

Lemuel glanced at the wall clock and settled further into his chair. 'Obviously Clare's not seen fit to mention the matter. Hmmm, perhaps I'd better explain briefly. You can get the rest of the details from Clare here. We're getting off the planet. I and several others have nearly completed two interstellar transports which can carry about ten thousand people each to a pair of planets in a nearby system. They've been probed and we think they can both support our kind of life.'

'Gildas' jaw dropped. 'I've heard rumours. They're true? I thought it was just wishful thinking.'

'It's true. The old storyline cliché out of the bag again. Y'know, the one about the dying planet and the wealthy industrialists. I used to think it was a joke, too, until I began to discover all the reasons for making it happen were already with us and well advanced. We started work just in time - about twenty years ago.' He grinned. 'Makes me feel like a character in a corny science-fiction novel except they always seemed to live exciting lives. All I've had out of it is ulcers, years of paperwork and screaming arguments with people who have to be verbally flogged before they'll lift a finger to save their own skins, let alone the skins of others. Still, maybe that'll alter once we get going.'

Gildas couldn't think of anything to say. Lemuel tapped the desk lightly with both hands in a "Right, let's get on with it" gesture. He looked levelly at Gildas.

'I'd like to invite you to come along. There's plenty of room; we're having to go sooner than we'd arranged for and a lot of those who were invited won't be able to get to the shuttle base in time. (*Shuttle base?* thought Gildas weakly). Lemuel's face saddened. 'And a lot will fall to these bugs that are going around. Think about it and let Clare know. She'll organise things. Just one thing I'd like to request as a sort of condition, though I freely declare you've earned your place.' He tilted his head once more, inviting some kind of response from the ugly, smelly little man sitting opposite. Gildas simply nodded, overcome. There was simply way too much information here in one lump for him to handle.

'I'd like you to act as a bodyguard for my daughter, here.' added Lemuel. 'Stay with her always, as far as propriety allows, and keep her out of trouble if you can. Deal?'

Gildas looked wildly at the two girls to his left. Clare was openly grinning. Emma snorted and pretended to take an interest in the pattern on the carpet. In shock, he nodded.

199

Lemuel took this as an affirmative. Glancing at the paging monitor on his desk he rose to his feet and extended a podgy hand to Gildas once more. He got up and accepted it limply.

'I doubt whether we'll meet again till planet-fall. If you need to contact me ask Emma. In the likely event of her telling you where to go.' he ignored another scornful snort from his daughter, followed quickly by a muted raspberry. 'See Wendy, my secretary, Doc or my security chief, Mr Spode.'

He retrieved his hand, which Gildas had been gripping with an increasing pressure as he spoke, thankful it wasn't the one with the damaged finger. 'I'll have to ask you all to excuse me now. My paging monitor is almost at capacity with folk who can't make up their own minds and need somebody to tell them what to do.' He glared at the offending screen with mock annoyance. 'And once more, thanks for your assistance to my daughter because *she'll* never admit she needed it.'

Leaving the control office with a cheerful wave and smile from Wendy, Gildas halted in the corridor, uncertain what he was expected to do next. Emma flounced off, ridiculously high heels beating an aggressive tattoo on the painted concrete floor. He stood there watching till she rounded a corner and out of sight. A strong, gentle arm surrounded his waist.

'Come on.' said Clare softly. 'I've ordered up some grub for you. It only needs heating, then we'll get you settled.' He allowed her to lead him away like a little lost boy - which was exactly how he felt.

The meal was a wonder. *Real* vegetables and even a portion of fish. Fish! It had been so long since he'd eaten any he had difficulty in recognising it at first. Sitting with Clare in the huge refectory, nearly empty at the time, he consumed enough for two, trying not to think of the effect on his recently-abused digestive system. It went down and stayed down. Whatever the doc had given him, it worked with no after-effects. They didn't speak much, and only then of everyday matters.

Tiredness set in with a vengeance. He followed Clare along a passage and halted at one of the recessed doors.

'You can kip down in here for tonight.' Clare informed him. Unlocking the door she pressed the key-card into his hand and pushed him inside. The room was large, though sparse on furnishings. 'Bathroom over there behind that curtain, bed there.' She pointed. 'You'll find fresh clothes in the drawers. I've told the stores your approximate size. I'm in next door, that way. If you need anything, pick up the phone, I've routed it direct through to my room. I doubt whether anything I've got to offer will appeal to you though, judging by the state you're in. See you in the morning.' She left.

Gildas stood alone in the centre of the room, blinking and wondering at the events of the day. From a ruined castle standing in the midst of death that morning to safety, comfort and civilised company in the evening. A dream? And what about the offer of a new life, conveyed there in a ship built to travel between the stars?

It was all too much for him. He lurched towards the bed, fell across the soft linen fully clothed and instantly succumbed to the gentle yet insistent embrace of Morpheus.

CHAPTER 16

He was soaking in the bath when Clare called for him. True to her nature, she simply opened the door he'd forgotten to lock and headed straight for the bathroom. Gildas had been wallowing contentedly in the tub for so long that the water had lost almost all its heat. It was the second lot of hot water and he intended finishing off with a shower. It could be a long time before this luxury would be available again.

The huge piles of fluffy suds had dissipated too, which gave rise to a certain amount of fluttering modesty when her head popped unannounced round the corner of the bathroom curtain.

'Want me to scrub your back?'

Water splashed. Clare ducked back in the nick of time.

'I'll take that as a "no thank you very much". Shall I wait? Your clothes are all out here, you know.'

'Aw, Clare. Give a chap a fair deal, will you? Can you come back in twenty minutes?'

'Have it your own way, Mister Bashful. I've seen all I want to. I've recovered your goggles and got you a few more pairs from the stores. I'll leave them on the bed.'

She left, leaving the door to the passage wide open.

Reluctantly, Gildas slithered out of the bath and spent five more minutes wriggling and gasping under a cold shower jet. He entered the bedroom tingling with a glorious sense of well-being he hadn't experienced for many months, humming under his breath and prepared to tolerate whatever the future had to offer.

A perfectly executed wolf-whistle issued from the direction of the doorway. He spun round, completely forgetting his nudity. Two grinning young girls stood in the doorway watching him. Giggling, they turned and raced away down the passage. He rushed to the door and angrily slammed it shut, all feelings of well-being abruptly shattered.

In a jerky rage he rummaged through drawers and the wardrobe, found suitable clothing and began to dress. Half way through he stopped and sat down hard on the bed as he felt a sudden change of mood sweeping through his mind.

Mister Bashful?

Maybe he was.

Relax!

He forced himself to do so. Deliberately. He searched his body, finding and erasing all the tension he could find inside. He sat very still.

Mister Bashful!

Question: Was he the odd man out?

Answer: Yes, apparently.

Question: Why?

He couldn't find an answer. Only random reactions to emotions which seemed out of place in the context of others.

But wasn't everyone like that?

Or was it caused by the total experience of a lifetime? Tracing recent history, it seemed something had changed within him at the time of his wife's murder.

OK! Wasn't that enough to alter anyone's outlook on life? And hadn't he thought only a short time ago that he hadn't felt so good for months?

There was the connection! Since his personal tragedy he simply hadn't been able, or even wanted, to get along with another human being. He had set himself apart, bottling feelings and emotions: hiding his natural personality from others.

And the reason for this shift? It had to be trust - or lack of it, rather. It just wasn't possible to trust anybody out there. Not if you wanted to live.

It was out of place here in the bunker, though. These people had something to look forward to. They worked for the common good. They were organised.

Hah!

No good. *There* was the classic contradiction in terms. People who strove for the common good had no right to be organised. Being organised meant a small group had to be doing the organising and that in turn meant they were doing it for their own benefit - not for others. Like it or not, that was how human nature worked. Spontaneous mass altruism had never existed.

Such thoughts were strange to Gildas. He'd never been a philosophical person or a man of decision - or action either, come to that. Happy to bumble along the path of existence and always taking directions supplied by others. Having to think for himself wasn't easy.

He couldn't even take a joke any more.

Clare breezed in through the door without knocking. He looked at her vacantly, still enmeshed in the thrall of unfamiliar thought processes.

'I'm sorry.' he said.

'What? Sorry for what?'

'Never mind.' He shrugged into a coverall and began to transfer his weapons to a line of quick-release shackles around the waist.

'Never mind those.' Clare pulled at his sleeve. 'Let's get some breakfast. Lock your door!'

Gildas said nothing, engrossed in his own thoughts, until they joined the queue at the serving counter. He was still trying to order his mind to this new attitude - but the old one wouldn't go away.

'Do you think I'm weird?' he blurted.

'That's a funny question.'

'Yes it is. Forget it!'

Clare regarded him thoughtfully. They collected their trays and found a table in the crowded dining hall. Breakfast was consumed in silence. Before drinking his tea substitute, a new thought intruded on Gildas' whirling mind. He seized it gratefully as a way of breaking free.

'Don't suppose there are any fags to be found around here?'

Clare jerked a thumb at an unmarked box attached to the wall close to their table. 'Just press the button and wait!'

Free cigarettes! Oh, bliss! Oh, happy day! The small pack of white cylinders with a book of cardboard lighters attached brought Gildas back on course. He sprawled back in his chair and savoured the moment. Clare regarded the metamorphosis with some amusement.

'You look better. Every junkie does after a fix. Now perhaps you can tell me what you were sorry about.'

'Huh?'

'When I came to collect you, remember? You said you were sorry. Why?'

Gildas took a deep drag and considered before answering. 'I got mad with you, that's all, but it was really my own fault.' Just recently I've got so I can't take a joke any more. Sorry again.'

'What joke?'

'You left the door open, deliberately, no doubt.'

'And someone looked in?'

'Caught me standing there starkers. I got mad instead of laughing it off. Then I got to thinking. Do you think it's really safe here?'

'As safe as it's possible to be these days but don't get too used to it. We won't be here long.'

He'd forgotten! He pumped more strange-tasting smoke through his bronchial tubes. Tissues shrank. Enzyme production raced into high gear in a vain attempt to limit the damage.

'And I've got a job to do, I recollect.'

'Really fallen on your feet, haven't you?' Clare looked as if she were genuinely pleased for him. 'Look, I'll be leaving here in a few hours. The chopper's booked for about fourteen hundred. Uncle Lem's given me the job of bringing you up to date but there's not much point showing you around this place 'cos you'll be leaving in a few days yourself. What do you want to know first?'

Chopper? Uncle Lem?

Gildas looked her right in the eye. 'Who are you?'

'Clare Masson, at your service.'

'That's all? What about the "Uncle Lem" bit? He's the king-pin around here, isn't he? And how come you rate a ride in a chopper? Only VIPs get that and there's hardly enough fuel left to keep them flying, for a bet.'

'He's not my real uncle, not in the family sense. He and Father have been cronies since long before I was born. Emma used to be like a younger sister to me till she went

205

bad. She's still a very close friend. Ever heard of Universal Commodities?'

'Never. Some company or other?'

Clare gave a short laugh. 'You could say that; it's what most people think - those that have heard of it. Not listed on any stock exchange, though. Much too big for that. Call it a confederation of large organisations all linked to a family dynasty. The Quorvis family.'

Gildas was impressed. 'That chap I saw last night is the boss of all that? And Emma's one of his kids?'

'Those two are all of that family that's left. Uncle Lem's not really the boss of anything any more. How many factories have you seen working recently?'

'I remember him saying something about space and interstellar craft. How can that be done without working factories and paid staff?'

'No need to pay the staff; a berth on one of the ships is enough for them. They're fed and sheltered as well. Many places are still turning out what's needed. Spread out, all in isolated places, even some research to iron out the wrinkles of what is basically a last-ditch leap into the unknown. I wouldn't mind betting that research station we found just after we left Town was one of them. Even with what they've achieved so far it's still a hell of a risk, y'know. Plenty of things could go wrong and we could all end up heading for the far boundaries of the universe stone-cold dead in what's left of our coffins.'

Gildas was not convinced. 'Even with all that it's too much to believe. Surely at least one national government must be involved. At least the United States.'

'Forget about national governments. They all cut and run when people stopped taking any notice of what they were doing. Soon as they lost their power to enforce, their reason for existence evaporated. Simply too many people, see? What we had out there just before the Channel Tunnel was flooded was the ultimate enterprise society. Take what you want from anybody you like as long as you're strong

206

enough to do it. Simple as that.' Clare stared at the table-top and wrung her powerful hands together; a rare sign of emotion had been triggered.

'So Uncle Lem did it all, eh?'

'Him and a bunch of his colleagues. All powerful people with resources to use. My father's one of them.'

'What does he ... did he ... deal in?'

'Weapons. Guns' tanks, missiles. You want a nuclear sub - he'll get one for you. He's probably still got a few in stock somewhere.'

'That figures.'

Clare looked up. 'Sure it figures. I went into the war games just to annoy him. We don't get on, never did. Don't jump to conclusions. Come on, let's get you organised! I haven't got long.'

'Hang on a minute and let me enjoy this fag! It's been a long time since the last one.'

Two cigarettes later, his head buzzing slightly with a wonderful nicotine-induced euphoria, Gildas allowed Clare to lead him from the refectory.

The first call was back to his room where he selected the weapons he wanted to carry. Foremost was the slim gutting knife in its self-sharpening sheath. Ever since it had been commandeered from its original owner he had felt an odd, yet comforting affinity for the sliver of thin, dull steel. Old, probably antique, its slender contours projected an aura of competence; a no-nonsense efficiency that sat easily in his shovel-like hand. His mind balked at the contemplation of how many individual lives it had released from the body during its lengthy, and no doubt active existence. The worn handle and razor-thin blade bore mute testimony to this fact. It was a weapon to be used, not a curiosity to be displayed.

Clare waited with badly concealed impatience while he made his choice, mulling over each item for minutes at a time. She was in a hurry, not realising he was still fighting the remains of his philosophical diversion.'

'Come on! You can sort yourself out in the armoury after I've shown you the layout. We've still got to see if we can persuade Emma to put up with you yet. That's not going to be easy if I know her and I'm getting on that chopper, no matter what! Come *on*!'

She showed him the armoury, the barrack rooms and the hospital, where Doc Payne unceremoniously grabbed him and extracted various fluids from his shrinking flesh with quite unnecessary force, growling 'Got to be sure, y'know.'

And that was all he said. Gildas didn't complain. He'd spotted the mountain of papers on Doc's desk and the long queue outside the dispensary. Doc had a lot on his plate. He was being given priority treatment.

It still hurt, though.

Throughout the bunker they roamed, from the helicopter landing pad, ringed with artillery on the roof of the ziggurat, to the nethermost caverns, where great black pumps groaned and wheezed to extract water from the underlying rocks far below. Gildas fell into a lengthy conversation with the crew manning the nuclear generator complex and had to be dragged away bodily by his testy guide, shouting he'd be back.

It was when they reached the stores that he dug his heels in and refused to leave until he was ready.

The place was the size of an aircraft hangar. It was full of people busily pushing barrows and trolleys or carrying boxes and barrels. Gas-powered forklifts scuttled between rows of shelving and racks, which reached to the ceiling high above. All routes converged on a line of vehicles beginning at the closed main doors and extending back to a ramp that disappeared under the floor. More identical vehicles could be seen on the ramp, their roofs descending like steps below the opening.

And what vehicles! Were they even vehicles at all? They looked more like shipping containers. If they were such, where were the tractor units and overhead loading gantries? Gildas goggled and took a closer look. They were very different. Maybe Clare could explain.

'No wheels, no skirt, no fans! They can't be hovercraft, can they?'

Clare flashed her strong teeth in a huge grin. 'Thought you'd have a shock when you saw these. No, they're not hovers. Those are much too expensive to run and maintain. Nobody uses hovers to carry loads any more. Any more guesses?'

Gildas walked around one of the vehicles. It was nothing more than a steel box. The shipping container analogy was perfect, but these were only three-quarters as high. There was no sign of any means of propulsion or suspension. The almost-featureless lump sat squarely on the concrete floor; he could see small ridges of dust where the weight of the thing had gouged shallow grooves in the unyielding material. In front, two thin windows no more than horizontal strips of clear plastic allowed whoever was driving to see ahead. Steel shutters had been fitted above the windows, poised and ready to drop at the first sign of flying-lead trouble. A line of lamps stretched across the front just below the roof line, each with its own steel mesh protection.

The lower part of the front was severely recessed and angled back nearly forty five degrees. It appeared to be faced with a series of plastic louvres. The same sort of cover lined the sides which, he now noticed, were also angled inwards slightly for the bottom four feet or so. At the rear a similar recess extended far underneath. A strong, hinged ramp sloped from the top of the recess giving access to the cavernous interior. A continuous stream of goods vanished within, transported by arms, grabs, wheeled trolleys and powered lifting gear. People sweated from their labours despite the air conditioning in the hangar. Nobody was idle.

'Well?' Clare had dogged his puzzled peregrinations. 'Any ideas?'

209

He regarded her with rounded eyes. 'None, unless someone's come up with some sort of gravity repulsion. It can't move, otherwise.'

Clare clapped him on the shoulder and ruffled his hair. It came as such a surprise he was unable to react. 'Good boy. Right first time.'

Gildas pulled away, frowning. He hated people doing that to him. 'I'm not a dog. How can I be right? That hasn't been invented yet. It's impossible!'

'Wait and see! Let's have a cup of coffee. It looks as if this batch is ready to leave soon and you can watch them for yourself. We've only got to pay Emma a visit before I go and there's plenty of time for that.'

At the "coffee" dispenser Gildas demanded an explanation. 'So it has been invented. When? Who by?'

'About twenty years ago. One of the Far East concerns.'

Gildas sneered. 'Vested interests, of course. Too much to lose on existing assets. Inventors disappear, processes get filed away under lock and key until the time comes to rip off future generations. Then comes the switch-over in a blaze of hype - at a price. How close am I?'

'Spot on, but naive as any other Joe Public as far as considering the implications is concerned.'

'How come?'

'Well, take the push plates fitted to the transporters over there ....'

'Push plates?'

'Easier to say than gravity repulsion units.'

'Oh! Carry on, then!'

'Imagine what would have happened if they'd been put on the market overnight - and that's just how quick it could have been done. They're easy to make and power. Cheap, too. All transport would have been virtually free. Think of the consequences!'

'Yeah. Great for the punters and disaster for the fat cats. That's why they couldn't allow it to happen.'

210

'Idiot! You're not thinking far enough ahead. The overland transport industry is - was, rather - the biggest in the world. Ships, planes, lorries, trains, countless millions of cars, vans and motorbikes. The whole global economy would have collapsed. Thousands of big industries closed, hundreds of millions on the dole queue with the biggest cash providers no longer in business and not able to pay the taxes which provided that welfare. Can't you see any further than your nose?'

'I can see the greatest polluters ever seen on earth being killed off. I can see millions of people deliberately being kept in a state of semi-starvation and poverty to keep prices up. I can see fat cats manipulating the development of the whole world for their own benefit, to make sure they stay the only fat cats on the block. It's the way it was, is now, and always will be. It stinks!'

Clare nodded, took a swig of cold "coffee" and threw the empty mug into the recycling bag. 'We're obviously poles apart. It's just as obvious we can't both be right. They're finishing up over there, ready for the next convoy. Let's watch them leave before tackling Emma. We can extend this interesting discussion some other time.'

Gloomily, Gildas followed her across the hangar. There was nothing to discuss. How could she possibly justify such a system? On the other hand, she'd always been level-headed in his estimation up to now. Hang on though! What about that night in the abandoned hostel up on the mountain? Or had she also been right then - and *he* was the oddball? Self-doubt popped up again to haunt him and he concentrated on the activity going on around the containers in an attempt to side-track his thoughts.

Doors slammed, feet pattered on concrete, the area cleared except for a single man, who walked down the line and up the other side looking carefully at the vehicles. Apparently satisfied, he faced the lead vehicle, waved and lifted a silver whistle to his lips in the manner of an old-fashioned railway station-master, blew a long blast and sauntered unhurriedly to a cubicle just inside the main exit. Closing a transparent door behind him, he did something to a row of oversize buttons. The hangar exit began to open smoothly. Gildas moved forward to get a better view, only to be grabbed and pulled behind a pile of large packing - cases. Shrugging off the clutching hand - Clare's, of course - he tried to move to his original position only to be stopped once more.

'Stop doing that!'

'I wouldn't go out there if I were you. Look around! See anyone else close to the vans?'

Gildas looked. Nobody was in sight. 'Vans, you call them? What's wrong, they dangerous, or something?'

'Not really. Only if one of the plates isn't lined up properly. We've been told it's possible for that to happen when the shutters are opening or if there's any accident or damage of some sort. If part of you happens to be in line with the thrust then horrible things are likely to happen. I've never heard of it happening and I don't want to be around if it does. The thrust is at right-angles to the plates so just watch at a slant, as it were, OK?'

Two of the vans were in Gildas' immediate line of view. As the main doors neared the end of their travel, the lead van simply lifted off the ground without a sound and hovered about a foot above the concrete, the second van following suit a few moments later, then several more. A tiny sound, like a sharpening-stone caressing fine steel, signalled forward motion and the vans drifted out into the blazing sunlight. One by one they passed, soundless and stately like a convoy of ships on a calm sea.

Gildas was impressed in spite of himself. 'So what's the secret?'

'Ask Josh in the workshop. He hates the things and won't go near them. Diesel and petrol are the only proper engines for him but he knows more than most about how these things work. Come on, time to upset Emma!'

212

One of the vans had halted and was descending to the floor - the first of a fresh line to be loaded. Wearily the loaders came from cover and set to work again almost before the ramps had thudded down. Clare lugged Gildas out through the closing hangar doors.

Emma had hidden in the workshop, hoping to put them off the trail which, quite naturally, made it the first place Clare headed for. A quiet question to Josh caused his thumb to jerk in the direction of the tool room, where they found their quarry tearing bits off an old glossy magazine. She greeted Clare with beaming smile then jabbed an unfriendly finger at Gildas.

'Get out! Clare's welcome to stay.'

Gildas turned to go with an intense feeling of relief. He hadn't been looking forward to this confrontation and was thankful Emma wasn't waving a gun in his direction. Clare got to the door ahead of him and slammed it shut.

'You stay! Go over there behind the lockers and let me handle this!'

'I'd rather wait outside with Josh.'

'Don't you dare!' she hissed. 'Do as you're told!' A hefty push propelled him in the right direction. He caught a quick glimpse of Emma concentrating on her magazine as if nothing was happening. Seething inside from a mix of humiliation and jangling nerves he looked around for a place to sit. There was nothing. He stood.

'Hi, Emma!' greeted Clare. 'I'll be heading out on the chopper in about an hour. Thought I'd call to say so long and get your bodyguard installed.'

'How thoughtful of you.' Emma's voice dripped with sarcasm. 'And what do you think I should do with him?'

Clare sighed as if patiently trying to explain the obvious to an unwilling child - which, of course, she was.

'Look, it's no good beefing about it. Your father thinks it's a good idea and he's only trying to protect your back. There are quite a few people around who might just hold a grudge against you. You'll only be able to carry small

213

weapons from now on, you know that, and there'll be no big guns allowed on board ship.

'I can handle them.'

'One at a time, yes. But what if they gang up on you? You're dead, that's what! You're only acting like this to show your father how independent you are. That's not necessary as far as he's concerned. He's worried about you, can't you see that?'

'Tough! Take that little runt away! I don't need him.'

Gildas had heard enough. He slammed his hand hard against the nearest locker, paused a moment in sudden doubt as to whether he was doing the right thing, then strode purposefully from his shelter. To hell with this!

'To hell with this!' he shouted. 'I'm damned if I'm going to be spoken about as if I wasn't here.' A couple of steps brought him in front of Emma, lounging in her chair with a sardonic smile on her perfect face. He almost backed down then, his growing attraction to her waging war with his worry that she would simply pull out a gun and shoot him dead here on the spot.

'So you're back again, little man. I thought I told you to get out.'

'Don't be funny with me, you ... you....' He felt his lower lip quivering and lapsed into silence, his brief spell of bravado spent.

Clare said. 'If she won't listen to her father or me I don't see you can make any difference. Maybe we should simply forget the whole idea.'

Gildas' face turned even uglier than usual and he managed to find his voice again. 'No!' he exploded. 'Her Dad gave me the job and promised me a place on the ship. If she won't co-operate I'm stuck here with nowhere to go. I'll get on that ship if I have to keep her tied up until it sails ... flies ... whatever it does.'

Emma gave a theatrical yawn and waved a languid hand in the direction of the door. 'Go away, little man! Your presence is not required.'

214

No response. Gildas stayed put. Emma's face reddened and she yelled out loud, all pretence at sophistication gone. 'Get out!'

He cast a despairing look at Clare and turned to go. At that precise moment the door opened and Josh sauntered in rubbing oily hands with an even oilier cloth. He stopped short as if in surprise at seeing the room was occupied. Gildas swore later he could distinctly see the outline of a keyhole pressed into the old man's right ear.

'Oops! Sorry if I'm interrupting anything but I need a couple of tools.' Josh didn't look at all sorry. 'Won't be long. Just carry on as if I wasn't here.' He wandered out of sight behind the lockers. Tools clattered.

Emma remained glaring at her two adversaries. No word passed between them. She was building up steam for the time Josh departed.

The metallic clamour ceased and Josh wandered casually into view carrying some small spanners in one hand. He stopped at the door and cocked his head in enquiry. 'Something wrong?'

'It's all right, Josh.' said Emma. 'These two are just leaving.'

'There *is* something wrong.' Josh put the spanners in one of his overall pockets and approached her. 'What's up, Miss Emma?' Turning to kneel alongside her chair, he held onto the back with one hand. Now slightly behind her he gave a quick jerk of his head towards the open door.

Clare understood. 'Let's go Gil. We'll try again later.'

'Waste your own time as much as you like but don't try to waste mine.' Emma sneered. 'Maybe I'll see you on board ship ... maybe not. Just leave, will you?'

Closing the door behind them, they made a plodding bee-line for the drinks dispenser; Gildas in a state of resigned despair, Clare impassive as ever.

Back in the tool room Josh sat cross-legged on the floor in front of Emma. 'So what's the problem, girl?'

She leaned forward and patted him on the shoulder. 'Nothing for you to concern yourself with, old friend. Dad simply thinks I need looking after. I happen to think differently, that's all.'

'What's he done?'

Emma sniffed in disdain. 'Only wanted to lumber me with a minder, didn't he?'

'Gildas?'

'Who else? Can you imagine it? Me trailing that ugly midget like a shadow? I told Dad it's not on but he won't listen so I've had to deal with the situation myself.'

This brought a grin to Josh's withered face as he imagined how much unaccustomed restraint Emma had found it necessary to exert in order to solve the problem without bloodshed. A little cackle escaped from him.

'What's so funny?'

He's still standing instead of lining the inside of a plastic bag. Wouldn't have expected that.'

Emma indicated the room 'Too dangerous to use a gun in here. Besides, I'm not carrying one at the moment.' Josh's eyebrows lifted in surprise at this. 'I've already attempted to get rid of him twice and failed both times. He's leading a charmed life at the moment. Still, it's all settled now.'

Josh caught her tone. ' So there's something else, isn't there? Not often you haven't got a gun on you. I've got a feeling you only left it in your room in case you were tempted.'

'Well, Clare was with him, of course. She's been showing him around before she left. Didn't want to take the chance of her getting hurt, that's all.'

'Or risking her reaction?'

Emma laughed; a tinkling carefree sound; an honest amusement quite out of keeping with her atavistic nature. 'So you've noticed, too. How did you find out?'

'It would have been obvious even if she hadn't told me. Stands out a mile.'

216

'It does, doesn't it? I can't understand what she sees in that scrawny monster but I can recognise a crush when I see it. If I'd hurt him out in the open she'd have been on me like a tornado. I'm fast, but I don't think I could have fired on her. Clare's a lot bigger and good at the hand-to-hand stuff; she would have spread me all over the floor before I could blink, friend or not. Has she told you how they met?'

'Sure has. We had a long talk together last night over a few jugs of Doc's home brew. Won't you change your mind? It's not going to hurt you none. He's really a nice guy and deserves a break.'

Emma demurred. 'Don't worry. I'll see he gets on the ship, for Clare's sake, and if I can't then I'm damned sure she will, even if she has to create a vacancy with malice aforethought. I just don't want anyone following me around or getting in the way and telling me what to do.'

'I still think you should do what your father wants. I know you've got troubles waiting for you when you reach the ship and I've had an idea that might solve everything, with a bit of luck.'

Emma scowled. It's really none of your business, Josh. I'll handle that my own way, thanks. Why are you grinning again?'

Josh stretched out on the floor, folded his filthy hands behind his ancient cheese-cutter cap and wriggled until he was comfortable. This could take a long time.

'At least you can listen, unless you've got something better to do. I need a bit of a break, anyway.' His scratchy voice took on a sing-song quality. 'Hearken unto Uncle Josh and we shall banish the maddening woes of Emma together.'

INTERMURAL 4

Everything was geared to more and more production. This resulted, as it always had done, to the rich increasing their bank balances and the poor becoming ever more desperate. If overproduction of unnecessary goods was not halted, resources would be stripped - but if it was halted, then everyone would become poor and that could never be countenanced. So it went on, the system winding itself up towards the point at which it would either use everything up or become buried under a mountain of unsellable goods. Not a pretty picture either way.

Trouble was, they were killing their global life-support platform to do it. Gases rarely (more often, never) found in nature collected in the upper atmosphere in amounts too large for natural decay to render harmless. Destructive solar wavelengths penetrated to ground level causing cancers, blindness and crop failures. On top of all this grief, carbon and oxygen compounds conspired to restrict heat dissipation. The world got hotter. Deserts in the equatorial region expanded at a horrifying rate. Excess rain in the temperate zones ensured many crops rotted in the fields, thus reducing food supply even further.

Starvation, which had stalked the hot countries for centuries, finally ballooned out of all control. A mass exodus began of those who had the stamina to walk far enough: those unable to make it simply died. An expanding flood of hungry people moved slowly north into more favoured latitudes.

Things started to become nasty. As the refugees moved into other countries they were reluctantly received, at first, as a problem which would surely be only temporary - the richer countries would help out; they always had up to then. And they did, to begin with, until a couple of catastrophic harvests meant they had to make a choice between feeding their own populations at a reasonable profit and feeding a huge number of refugees at hardly any profit at all. The aid organisations howled and grovelled in vain. The grub stopped coming.

There was only one thing to do - start fighting. And they did! It usually began as retaliation when the indigenous

218

inhabitants of a host country woke up to the realisation they were gradually becoming as starved of food supplies as the fugitives they were trying to help. When disorganised fighting and looting became bad enough , the local army stepped in. The killing started in earnest then, but it didn't stop more people coming. To them, it was a choice of staying away and dying or moving in and maybe dying. No choice at all, really.

They died in their millions while the fatter countries looked on, wrung their collective hands, shed their crocodile tears and realised the threat of a nice expensive, high-tech nuclear bomb couldn't worry people who had nothing to lose; who, in fact, may have welcomed it.

Raw materials for the industrial machine became scarcer, nearly drying up, because insufficient numbers of skilled people remained over a wide swathe of the globe to extract them. Oil, a basic necessity, became very difficult to get hold of and certain countries eyed their neighbours' remaining wells with an increasing jealousy. Sabres started rattling, old territorial disputes emerged from the shadows of history and the world moved gradually towards conflict on a huge scale.

And still the increasing masses moved inexorably northwards. There wasn't much suitable land to the south, anyway. Countries became flooded with humanity bringing disease, hostility and conflict. Those who still had the strength copulated without restraint, brought forth offspring, copulated again and again, bringing yet more and more children into an already horrendously overloaded and shrinking world. It was as if each breeder was determined to preserve their own bloodline at the expense of everyone else's.

Fatal diseases, of course, had a field day. Epidemics of cholera, typhus and others had always been a scourge in the hot countries but up until then they had at least been kept within manageable boundaries. With the entrenchment of nationalistic attitudes, all that had stopped and these

219

diseases were able to thrive once more. During the previous few decades a new killer that attacked the immune system had been proliferating ever since its introduction to an isolated inland tribe acting as innocent guinea-pigs in a study to evaluate its effectiveness as a bacteriological weapon. It all went wrong, of course, and huge efforts had been made to develop an effective antidote, but nobody managed it. The carrot of mighty profits was never claimed. This disease finally put the lid on things when it began to mutate. It had to happen. One particular mutation rapidly assumed the lead. It had developed the ability to be transmitted by airborne droplets once it had taken hold of a host. Not only that, it was able to affect other warm-blooded species in a similar manner. Food animals became in short supply.

From that point everything went rapidly downhill. One particular region, a collection of two large and many smaller islands off the west coast of the largest land-mass had traditionally been the preferred haven of the dispossessed, the oppressed and the politically weak. It was a natural destination for those able to get that far. Already crammed with people, fighting for survival against a ruined industrial and agricultural base and with a non-existent economy, it tried to halt the unending torrents of immigrants. Even the tunnel linking the largest island to the mainland was finally flooded in a vain attempt to keep them out.

But still they came, in boats, ships and anything which could float; landing on the beaches, swarming up the cliffs and floundering across the mud-flats created when the outgoing tide laid bare vast tracts of previously fertile land inundated with salt water twice a day. The melting of the ice caps by increasing global temperatures had risen the high-water mark by many feet. Climate changed here too, from temperate through wet to dry, to hot, then very hot . Atmospheric damage would take a long while to revert to

220

what it used to be and the turnover point hadn't been reached yet. Not by a long shot!

CHAPTER 17

The atmosphere around the drinks dispenser could almost be cut with a knife.

Sitting on the concrete floor, a hot drink in his hand, Gildas stared across the harshly- illuminated workshop with glazed eyes. Two small lorries were in the process of being serviced by a team of mechanics and his old truck was pulled tight to one wall awaiting completion.

'Sulk a lot, don't you?' Clare flicked iced water at him from her cup as she leaned, poised and easy as ever, against the wall.

'Huh? Stop that!' He wiped his face. 'What do you mean ... sulk?'

'You're always doing it. Any little excuse and you sink into an offended silence like a big kid. Snap out of it! I'll see you get on board one way or another.'

'Why?'

'Why what?'

'Why are you always doing things for me?' Gildas appeared genuinely puzzled. 'What are you bothering for?'

Clare shifted her position in sudden discomfort, gulped the remains of her iced water and tore the cup to shreds before replying. She looked at the tool-room door, from behind which could be heard a mumble of conversation suddenly interrupted by a sustained peal of laughter. It seemed to cheer her.

'If you can't guess then it's not for me to enlighten you. Sort it out by yourself and if you don't want to go I can give your place to someone else if need be. There'll be plenty wanting it, y'know.' She gave him a hard look. 'You can be a right stupid idiot at times, y'know.'

She hurled the remains of the cup into a bin with quite needless force and stalked away to converse with one of the mechanics. Gildas stayed slouched where he was, glowering into his "coffee".

He sat there for another ten minutes before the tool room door opened and Emma marched out on stiff legs. She passed him without so much as a look and disappeared through the door leading to the stairwell. Old Josh strolled into view, glanced quickly at the gloomy figure by the drinks machine and carried on across to the lorries. Clare saw him coming. He gave her a wink, had his back patted in return and carried on with his work.

'Come on, old son!' Hauling Gildas to his feet she dragged him in the direction of the stairwell. 'It's all fixed up. Give me a hand to get my stuff up here; the chopper's due any minute and the pilot won't want to stay very long if he's got any sense.'

Gildas winced with the strength of her grip and wriggled free. 'What's fixed up? What the hell are you talking about?'

'You've been accepted as a temporary bodyguard for Miss Wonderful. Smile, for God's sake! It means you won't have to rely on me after all. That should make you happy.'

Gildas couldn't take it in. 'What happened? She cut me dead just now. Did Josh swing it?' Suspicion cut in. 'Did you fiddle things?'

She wrapped a large hand round the back of his neck, pulled him close and planted a big, sloppy kiss on top of his head. She was obviously pleased with herself. Abashed, Gildas pulled free once more.

'It'd be a good idea to have a long chat with Josh soon as you can - definitely before you run into Emma again. In fact, I insist on it for your own sake. Now don't argue, I'm not going to tell you any more. Flex those mighty muscles; I've got a lot of gear to shift and it's heavy. Let's try to find a trolley of some sort.'

Gildas stood in the shade of a blockhouse watching the helicopter take off in a swirling cloud of fine dust. He was in a good position to see the exaggerated waving from his erstwhile companion-at-arms: so did all the others who were watching. His sense of doing the right thing forced him to flap a hand in the right direction and that was as far as he intended to go. It was when she began blowing kisses at him that he gave up with a sigh and retreated down into the coolness of the ziggurat. His last glimpse of her was a laughing round face kept towards him as the chopper twisted, tilted and grabbed for height.

She resembled a happy schoolgirl more than a trained and ruthless killer. Gildas still had difficulty reconciling the two opposing sides of her nature. Or three sides ... or four?

Women!

Time to see Josh.

Josh was nowhere to be seen in the workshop but one of the mechanics gave him directions to his quarters on the same floor. Gildas knocked and waited. No reply. He knocked harder. A tired-looking old man opened the door.

'I'm sorry.' Gildas murmured. 'They didn't tell me you'd gone for a kip. I'll come back later.'

'No, no, son. Come on in! I can always get some sleep later. I'm in charge of the garage, after all. Fancy a nice cup of tea? I'll put the kettle on. Grab yourself a chair! Come in! Come in!' Prattling away he ushered his reluctant guest inside and pottered around. Gildas made small talk until the tea was poured ... real tea ... then came to the point of his visit. Firm but friendly; that was his game-plan.

'So how did you do it?'

Josh feigned misunderstanding. 'Do what?'

'You know all right! Clare told me to see you before I accidentally ran into Miss Quorvis and you'd put me in the picture. I've got a vague feeling I'm not going to like it much. Am I wrong?'

'Depends on your point of view. Miss Clare set off, then?'

'Yes, a few minutes ago. Said she was going to some place in the Midlands and would meet up with me when the convoy gets there. Any idea when I'll be going?'

'That depends on Miss Emma. You'll have to stay close to her and she'll only do something when she's good and ready.'

'So I've definitely got the job, then?'

Josh's face cracked into a grin. 'You always had it, son. What old Lem says goes no matter what anyone else says. The difficulty was to get you accepted by the body you're supposed to guard before it reared up and put a bullet in your head. She'd do it without a second thought, y'know.'

'I've seen her in action. Believe me, I know!' Gildas spoke with deep feeling. 'So what's the catch? There's bound to be one; she'd never give in on something like that. It has to be a deal of some kind. Are you going to tell me or not?'

'You'd have had to know, anyway. The deal, as you so delicately put it, involves you.' Josh's mouth opened in a huge yawn. 'Sorry about that. It was Miss Clare's idea, really.'

Gildas groaned. 'I might have guessed. What's she let me in for now?'

Twin lines of glittering teeth reflected the overhead light. Josh was smiling. 'I'm about to tell you. Sit tight where you are for a minute!'

Groaning a little in response to a series of loud cracks from his leg joints, he staggered to his feet and crossed to a set of drawers on the far side of the room. From the top drawer he lifted a large revolver, checked the cylinders, removed the safety catch and sat in a convenient chair, placing the gun on top of the drawer unit within easy reach. Gildas stiffened.

'Don't worry, son. I'm just paranoid like everyone else who intends to survive these days. I really don't expect to have to use it, honestly! I won't beat about the bush; here it is, straight. You're now officially engaged to be married to the delectable Emma. How does that grab you?'

Gildas felt his head begin to spin. Raising both hands he massaged his scalp in unconscious displacement activity while he strove to marshal his emotions.

'Oh no, no, no! If only ... why did Clare do this to me? She wanted to pay me back. That's it! She's not ....' His voice trailed away as he looked appealingly at old Josh. 'No!' Firmly now. 'It's some kind of a joke, yes? Pretty sick as far as I'm concerned. You don't know the half of it.'

'Take it easy, son! I don't pretend to understand Miss Clare's motives but I do know about other considerations which are more important to Miss Emma. That's the only reason I allowed myself to get talked into this. You want to hear the full story or not?'

Gildas nodded, not trusting himself to speak.

'Right, then. Relax and listen! Your girl-friend, Miss Clare ....'

'She's not my girl friend.' Gildas shot back.

'Suit yourself. Anyway, Miss Clare knew there was no way in which Emma could be persuaded to accept you gracefully after she'd fallen out with her dad over it. She seems to have a down on you for some reason.' He looked questioningly at Gildas but saw only an unreadable face.

'Hum, well. Those two girls have known each other a long time but I've known Emma all her life. I like to think I'm one of the very few people she trusts. Clare's aware of this. She's also aware about Emma's problem with one of the commanders on Dum - that's the name of the ship she'll be travelling on.'

Gildas became alert. 'Problem?'

'Name's Danhill, Erne Danhill. He's from a powerful family and built like Atlas, with looks to match. He's intelligent, highly qualified, knows how to manipulate people and he's a slob.'

'A slob?'

Josh shrugged. 'That's what Emma thinks and I'm prepared to trust her judgement. She absolutely refuses to even consider marrying him.'

'Marrying him?'

'Look, son. Leave off with the surprised exclamations till after I've finished, huh? I want to get back to bed. Where was I? Yes, he's stuck on her and she hates his guts. She'd like nothing better than to spread them over the floor and paddle in them. Old Lem is keen on the idea but he's got an uphill job getting her to accept it. Emma's convinced there's some sort of conspiracy going on. She once muttered something about dynasties and dictators but clammed up when I asked her what she was talking about.' He returned to the table leaving his gun behind, supped the last of his tea and poured a fresh cup. Sitting close to Gildas he continued.

'Well, Clare thought it would resolve the situation if Emma was engaged to marry somebody else. That way things would have to be left till we get where we're going and the situation could be completely different by then. Since you'd already been appointed her bodyguard by old Lem you were the obvious patsy. It would sort out both problems. To make it look good Clare said she'd have a go first, deliberately fail and at the same time hopefully goad you into annoying Emma still further so she would dig her heels in even more. I would listen outside the door and when I thought the time was right I'd come in, get rid of you two and see if I could swing it when she was in the right frame of mind. It worked, much to my surprise.'

Josh guzzled more tea to soothe his dry throat. 'Any comments? You don't look too happy about it, son.'

Gildas wasn't happy at all, in spite of his ticket off-planet being assured. Other things were important too. Things like feeling humiliated yet again. Should he confide in Josh? Why not? He felt badly in need of someone to talk to openly.

'Look at me, Josh! Then compare me with this Danhill! Who's going to believe a thing like that?'

'Huh?'

'I'm forty-four years old. Emma can't be more than twenty-three, or so. I've got used to being called ugly, deformed, even. It hasn't bothered me for years. Emma's beautiful and I don't mind admitting I'm crazy about her, but I also know there's no chance of us ever getting together romantically under any circumstances. She knows it too. I heard her screeching with laughter there in the tool room; that must have been when she cottoned on to what you were suggesting. She walked past me as if I were invisible when she came out, y'know.'

Josh looked properly sympathetic. 'All that you say may be true. I don't know why she's got a down on you and no, she didn't tell me why either and I didn't ask. Look on the bright side! You get to travel far away to a better world, we hope. Miss Clare'll see you right considering the way she feels about you.' Gildas opened his mouth to speak and Josh silenced him with a gesture. 'You're safe from Emma as long as the trip lasts and by the time we get there she'll probably have changed her mind in your favour. I know her.'

'And in the meantime?'

'What do you mean?'

'This Commander Danhill is just going to accept things, is he? There could be a lot at stake if Emma's right about dynasties and things. It's a new world without human history, remember, and most people have forgotten how democracy works these days. Politically it'll just be a slightly more civilised version of a bully-boy gang bossing the locals around.'

Josh regarded Gildas quizzically and rubbed his stubbly chin. It sounded like a wire brush on cheap carpet. 'Figured it out that quick have you? I thought you were bright, but... Wouldn't really have thought you were the type to worry over things political, though. Hm!' He paused. 'Maybe we'll have a chat about it some time in the future and I'll introduce you to a few people. Anyway, so what? Has it ever been really different when you think about it? What's it got to do with Danhill, anyway?'

'He's the boss on the ship and the crew does as he tells them. My life's not going to be worth a bull's udder once I get on board.'

The phone rang, Josh picked it up, said "right" a few times and replaced the receiver. He stood up.

'She wants to see you. Right now.' Gildas hesitated then started for the door. Josh, seeing the look of dread on his face, stayed him.

'OK. Maybe it'll be dodgy for a while, but after you've had time to think it through you'll realise it's not going to be as bad as all that. There are three captains, for a start, but we'll discuss that another time. You'll be close to Miss Emma and you know how she tends to react to trouble. Miss Clare's told me she intends to stick real close to you both; she can use her friendship credentials for that. Can you really imagine her allowing any danger to get too close? She'll be the real bodyguard, not you. I don't think that's occurred to Miss Emma yet. I won't be far away, either, not that I'll be much use if it hits the fan.'

He patted Gildas on the back and guided him to the door. 'Cheer up, son! Let's all get through this and spend the rest of our lives in peace and happiness. God knows we deserve it. Your truck'll be ready first thing in the morning. Now get the hell out of here and let me get some sleep!'

Gildas felt a little better; not quite as isolated as before. There were things going on behind the scenes he hadn't been aware of. Time to think about whether he wanted to be involved, later. 'How do I find her?'

'Go to Wendy, Lem's secretary, and she'll take you there. See you later.' He pushed Gildas into the corridor and closed the door.

The lower corridors were thronged with people scurrying in all directions. The exodus must be well under way, thought Gildas as he followed Wendy's willowy form to Emma's chambers. She pressed the intercom buzzer, smiled reassuringly at Gildas and returned the way they had come.

'Who's there?' Even Emma's intercom sounded irritable. A small camera suspended from the ceiling rotated and picked him up. 'Oh, it's you. Come on in, then!' The camera moved in a half circle, surveying in all directions before the door solenoids withdrew the bolts and the door opened just enough for him to squeeze inside.

He found himself in a tiny cubicle facing another door. The one at his back closed before the other clicked open to reveal a confusing array of pink drapes and walls. Passing inside, he stood uncertainly then jumped as an artificially sweet voice close behind him said 'Enter my parlour, little man! We are now compromised and no amount of denials will make any difference at all to the rumour machine. It'll be all over the bunker by this evening. Josh'll see to that.'

'Oh, God!' muttered Gildas. He felt his neck heating up.

Emma drifted out from behind a pair of long, pink curtains and passed close to him. Exotic perfume tugged at his nostrils and he felt them flare involuntarily. She sat on an antique chair by an equally antique writing bureau and crooked a finger at him.

'Stand in front of me here! That's right. Now what are your intentions?'

Gildas cleared his throat. He didn't know what to say.

'Come on! Come on! You're in charge; how are you going to work things?' She gave him a dazzling smile; Gildas felt no reassurance whatever. He groped for words.

'I'm sorry.' *Damn*! Why did he have to say *that*? She was only a young girl and he was a middle-aged man.

Yes, but she was also very dangerous. He tried again.

'Thanks for allowing me to take up your father's offer. I'll do my best to live up to his expectations.'

Emma's smile became sweeter and even more false. 'And?'

'And what?'

The smile vanished to be replaced by the hard, uncompromising expression he found so unsettling. 'And you're going to keep out of my way, aren't you?'

He took a deep breath. 'As much as I can. Josh has told me the score. Please believe it wasn't my idea.'

'Oh I know whose idea it was and I'll discuss the matter with her at the earliest opportunity.' She gave a genuine smile this time. 'Actually I think it's a pretty good one, if a bit far-fetched. It'll certainly put a ferret up old Danhill's nose, the slob.'

'You mean Commander Danhill, I assume. How do you think he'll respond?'

'Violently, I hope. That'll give me the chance to get rid of him permanently; then you'll be able to go your own way and get out of my hair.'

Oh, thanks, he thought. Aloud he said 'When do you want me to start?'

'Why, now, of course. I'll make sure you earn your ticket, don't worry. You can begin by guarding the door there ... on the outside.'

'There's no good reason for me to stay by the door and guard it. You're quite safe here in your own rooms, I should think. Can't you get hold of a couple of radio hand-sets so we can keep in touch?'

'Certainly I can, little man.' The light tone left her voice. 'But I'm not going to. Your job is to stay close by me and that's exactly what you're going to do at all times. It also means that when I want privacy, which is likely to be most of the time, you'll be as close as I want you to be and not an inch closer. Understand?'

'Perfectly.' There was no point in arguing. He crossed to the door. Emma followed and linked arms with him. He dared not pull away.

Outside in the corridor she swung him to one side against the wall and said in an unnecessarily loud voice 'Wait here, beloved, I'll be with you very soon.'

230

Heads turned. Whispers and not a few wry smiles passed between some of the passing populace within earshot. Emma placed her mouth close to his ear giving the impression of bestowing a loving kiss on his cheek. She was really whispering 'That'll give them something to think about. I might come out in a couple of hours if I feel like it and you'll have to stand here all that time, poor little man. Don't think of going anywhere; remember I can see you on the camera any time.'

Prancing away and through the door she gave a light-hearted laugh as if full of the joys of romance. Gildas still didn't dare to say anything; he couldn't see a microphone, which didn't mean there wasn't one on the camera. A little giddy from her closeness and the heady smell of her perfume he stood rigidly by the door, sweating profusely despite the chill air-conditioning.

He was still there much later when Josh wandered out of the passing stream of pedestrians.

'Everything going all right?' he asked mildly.

Gildas was close to the point of collapse. Only his pride stopped him from sinking to the floor on his knees in front of everyone. That and his aching bladder.

'Thank God you're here.' he blabbed fervently. 'She's kept me standing here for over four hours. I'm ready to drop and nearly starving. The nearest toilet's a long way, too. She had her grub delivered some time ago but forgot about me. I asked the waiter for something but he hasn't come back yet.'

Josh nodded wisely. 'Thought that's how it would turn out. She didn't forget about you, son, you should know her well enough by now, First things first; you run down to the gents while I stay here then we'll see what we can do.

Gildas ran - very fast.

On his return, Josh pressed a communicator and a sheet of paper into his hand. 'This is a directory of numbers to call. Anything you need, all you have to do is call the stores for whoever you want. If they start grizzling tell them it's on the direct orders of Mr Quorvis himself. If they still won't co-operate, call me. I've already cleared things with the boss. Let's get you a chair first.' He started pressing buttons.

The chair was comfortable, so was his stomach after the kitchen had responded favourably with a filling meal and an unspoken air of sympathy. Testing his new-found and tenuous authority he badgered the stores to provide a screen and a single camp-bed, which he positioned across the door frame. Lemuel Quorvis' name cut across all barriers. Clutching the worn handle of his little knife beneath the pillow he rapidly sank into a disturbed, yet satisfactory sleep.

CHAPTER 18

The servo motor operating Emma's door was surprisingly powerful and low geared: powerful enough to push the bed, its snoring occupant and the screen right out into the centre of the corridor on the second stage of its swing. The motion and grating of metal bed-legs woke Gildas up sufficiently to stare muzzily at Emma's amused face staring down at him.

'Rise, slugabed! Let's go!'

'Where?' He discovered he was still fully clothed and crawled out from under the blanket he had requisitioned when the air conditioning had started to freeze his skin during the night.

'I want to see Josh first. Get up!' She kicked the bed hard. One of the bed legs collapsed.

'What about my breakfast?'

Emma's face hardened. 'You should have got up earlier. You're my bodyguard, and I'm taking my body down to the garage. Guard it! Move!' She kicked the bed once more, breaking another of its legs, and strode off down the corridor without looking back.

Cursing, he slid off the sharply-tilted bed and stooped to get his boots from underneath. They weren't there; someone had pinched his boots! Bemused, he stared at the apparently empty space until his muddled brain recognised two dusty black toe-caps facing the wrong way to what he'd expected.

He was wearing them! Things were getting bad; he hadn't felt this disoriented for a long time - at least a week. Turning, he just caught sight of Emma's rear end swaying round a corner and out of sight. He scuttled after her as fast as his short, bowed legs could carry him.

She paced down the corridor in a stiff, purposeful manner, not condescending to acknowledge his presence when he caught up.

'I suppose you've had *your* breakfast?' Unable to keep a slightly waspish tone out of his voice, he felt a little surprised when she answered him.

'As a matter of fact, no. I never have any; just a cup of coffee or two, and I've got the makings for that in my room. I did have a peep through the camera to offer you one, but when I saw you were asleep on the job, I thought to hell with you. Maybe Josh'll be able to find a crust for you to gnaw on and you can get a drink from the dispenser in the garage.'

Josh obliged like the good 'un he was. A packet of dried-out biscuits was located and this, together with the aid of some unidentifiable slop from the machine had to suffice. Gildas found them to be almost edible. He snapped and gulped at them while the old mechanic showed Emma what he'd done to her waggon. She was smiling when they returned to the office and waved him back into his chair as he tried to get up without tipping his breakfast over his lap.

'No rush. We won't be starting until well into the afternoon so you'll have plenty of time to feed and get your things together.'

'We going somewhere?'

'Didn't I tell you? No, I don't think I did. We're taking the final convoy to the launch site later today. I'll be in my waggon and you'll be driving the truck you came in. Josh says he'll go with you in case of any problems.' One of the mechanics outside in the workshop shouted something. 'Looks like the chopper's arrived to pick up Father and his chattels. I'll go call him.'

She ran from the room. Once more Gildas began to stand up. Where she went he had to go. Josh had other ideas. Pushing the little man back down, he said. 'You look like hell, know that? Could you find your way back to your room?'

Gildas nodded round a mouthful of biscuit

'Right. Finish off the pack if you like and if you want more call in at the canteen on your way. Then go to bed and have a proper sleep - you'll need it. The convoy won't stop till it gets where its going and in the state you are now you're not going to stay the course.'

'Where *are* we going, anyhow?'

'A place this side of Birmingham. It'll be mostly motorway to get there.'

'Thanks. What about her?' he nodded at the door.

'Don't worry about Miss Emma. She'll leave you alone for a while and I'll make sure you'll be called in plenty of time. Now git!'

Gildas got. Twenty minutes later he was snoring happily in a warm bed.

As good as his word, Josh kept the intercom buzzing until it dragged him back, more bleary-eyed than before, into an unsympathetic world. He could have cheerfully killed the grease-smeared senior citizen for his consideration but instead thanked him very much before asking him how much time he had and where should he report.

'Come back up here,' said Josh, 'and bring everything you want to take with you. Miss Emma'll be along later.'

'Have I got time for a shower?'

'You probably have unless the circuit's been cut off; they're closing the place down gradually. We have to take the generators with us, y'know. Don't take too long!'

Shaved, showered and otherwise refreshed, Gildas checked and donned his weapons. Josh saw him coming at the gallop and waved him to a stop. 'She's just called. Be here soon. Coffee?'

Gildas shuddered at the prospect. 'Thanks for the offer, but I think I'll pass. I've been told I'm taking my old truck. Think it'll make the trip?'

'Old as it is, it'll probably outlive you. It's being loaded right now. Sit yourself down and wait 'til Miss Emma gets here. Sure you don't want a coffee?'

The convoy lined up against one wall of the ziggurat, ready for the signal to move off. It had been a wonderful sensation for Gildas when he pressed a button on the battered dashboard of the old truck and heard the distinctive sound of a starter motor before the engine broke into coughing, roaring life. He turned to his companion in the passenger seat.

'If you only knew how nice that feels, just pressing a button and not having to rely on a hill to roll down. It sounds a lot better too. My thanks.'

Josh nodded in calm acceptance of his due praise. 'Amazing what a couple of reconditioned parts and a little nursing will do. Don't get too happy though, we only did a rough job and this machine is old. I think it'll get us to where we want to go but treat the poor old thing gently, OK?'

'I'll be careful, but I can't help noticing I've been put at the tail end as usual.'

'It's the smoke. We couldn't completely rebuild the damned engine you know.' Josh's voice took on a note of asperity.

Gildas turned off the engine. They waited in the rippling heat of the afternoon sun, sweating, silent. Josh dropped off to sleep.

It took more than a hour to make sure nobody had been left behind but at last, with a deafening hoot from Emma's waggon at point, they began to file slowly through the gates. As the van in front silently drifted away Gildas started the truck and followed. At the outer gate waited a man in full military uniform standing by a shiny four-wheel-drive vehicle. "General" Spode - who else?

'Get a move on!' he bawled, waving a peremptory arm. 'Keep up with the rest!'

Gildas pulled to a stop between the two sets of gates and revved up the engine. The wind was nicely in the right direction; a cloud of thick smoke drifted across to envelop the unfortunate General, who continued to open his mouth and windmill his arm even faster. Gildas grinned; it must have been as hot as hell in that heavy clothing.

Opening the door he strode across to the red faced man.

'Little hitch, I'm afraid. I've got the chief mechanic with me though. We'll soon be on our way. You carry on!'

'Get that truck away from there! I've got to lock the gates up.'

That was what Gildas had surmised; it would have been characteristic of Spode. He inspected the gate.

'It's only a snap lock. We're both quite capable of operating it. Soon as we're fixed up I'll make sure the job's done.'

General Spode glared at him, red-faced and breathing heavily in an effort to avoid choking on the diesel fumes. He glanced after the retreating convoy. There was where his duty lay.

'You've got ten minutes. If you haven't caught up by then I'm coming back for you. We can do without you and the truck but we'll need the mechanic at the launch site. Move it!'

Gildas watched the jeep chasing after the convoy and climbed back into the truck. Josh was awake.

'"The mechanic", indeed. Damned cheek! I've got a name as I'll be sure to remind that pompous moron when I next see him. What was that all about, anyway?'

'The gates. That jerk wanted to lock them up.'

'So?'

'So nobody'll be able to get in.' He started the engine and drove beyond the outer gate. 'Nobody's left alive around here but there're still lots of people out there, hungry, thirsty and dying. Back there,' he gestured towards the ziggurat, 'is water, the supplies we couldn't take and shelter. We're never coming back so why can't others use what's left? I'm going to wreck the locks. Where's the hammer?'

He felt a lot better as he caught up with the convoy and took up his rearguard position. Sux to Spode! Behind them and around the perimeter, battered diggers, bulldozers and other abandoned equipment watched them go with the mute reproach only derelict machinery is capable of.

The motorway passing east of the old cathedral city of Gloucester soon appeared and the convoy swung up the northbound ramp at a smart clip. All obstacles had been shouldered aside by many such trains of vehicles, allowing a reasonable average speed to be maintained.

North they went, never stopping, and hardly even slowing down except when climbing the steeper grades. Old Josh had fallen asleep again across the stained front seats almost before the ziggurat had disappeared behind the low hills flanking the lower Severn valley. He fully deserved his slumbers after more than a month of non-stop labour.

The truck engine knocked, rattled and droned; a steady, soporific background noise that hardly altered throughout the whole trip. Gildas held the wheel with a light touch, fighting sleep, as the long convoy held to an unvarying velocity of just under thirty miles an hour. Motorway driving used to be bad enough back in the days when frenetic streams of bad-tempered traffic kept all but the most exhausted of drivers fully awake; now it was far worse. The heat and lack of any interesting scenery caused him to nod off several times. With grim determination he concentrated hard on the featureless rear of the van in front.

No life of any sort was to be seen. Only bleached or blackened vegetation lined the cuttings and embankments. No smoke rose from the chimneys in any of the villages they passed; nothing moved. The whole social collapse had happened far too quickly to allow desert life to spread naturally from the traditionally hot regions further south. Not that the English Channel could have been crossed anyway now the Channel Tunnel was flooded. No gecko, lizard or snake basked on a roadside rock. Everything was dead, very dead. The land had died in the way it had been doomed to from the beginning of man's interference - in torment, screaming violence and apathy. Long live mankind, Gildas mused.

The trip took nearly three hours and they didn't stop once. Surely they should be getting close to Birmingham by now! Gildas thought he recognised the three-lane hill they were climbing. From the cutting at the brow the outskirts should be visible. At its steady, trundling pace the convoy entered such a cutting and began to descend.

The hills fell away to one side and there it was - a sun-baked desolation of ruined buildings shrouded with dusty heat haze in the middle and far distance. But in the foreground ...! A series of huge, flattened toroids spaced far apart ranged across the land like a row of high tension electricity pylons in their regularity. Painted a gleaming white, they marched down the slope of a hill on the right, crossed the motorway and continued across lower ground out of sight to the left. Four silvery rails, suspended near the centres of the gigantic structures and supported between by frames of spidery metal webbing, connected them. The truck slowed as Gildas involuntarily relaxed his foot on the accelerator to gawk at the scene.

With a grunt and a smacking of dry lips Josh resumed communion with the real world. Ever the mechanic, any change in the engine note bought an automatic and instant response. Stretching and yawning he peered out at the view ahead and grunted again; with satisfaction, this time.

'Good, nearly there. I could use a drink. Can you pass the bottle?'

Gildas groped under his seat and extracted a plastic bottle from a wire container suspended under a hole in the floor. Without refrigeration, it was the only place to keep water reasonably cool in the shade and slip-stream. He passed it over to the old man.

'Josh, what the hell's that up ahead?'

'Launch slip.' Josh guzzled water without looking. 'Big, eh? Maybe you'll see it in action soon if you're lucky.'

They had moved fully out of the cutting by then and Gildas could see almost all the enormous artefact. From high on the hill to his right the hoops swept at right-angles to the ground over the valley floor to another lower range of hills in the distance. Towards the far end they grew progressively larger in diameter, culminating in one enormous circular frame tilted towards the sky. It was at lest two miles in length and a truly impressive feat of engineering.

'To launch what?' he asked, braking hard to avoid running into the rear of the van in front. 'Spaceships or something?'

Josh chuckled. 'You're nearly right. Shuttles, that's what it launches, shuttles. Like what the Yanks used to put satellites up only this is a different arrangement to save on booster fuel which we can't spare. That whole thing is only a big linear accelerator which gives the initial push. It's pretty brutal too, they tell me. Like being caught on the edge of a nuclear blast or getting a hefty kick from a big

239

mule - hence its name. A few have got dead riding it. That's what we'll be going up in.'

'Can't say I fancy the sound of *that*.'

'Either ride the Mule or stay here. There aren't any other choices.'

'Oh I'll go, all right. Where are we heading?'

'Only a short way now. Base is built round an old motorway service area a bit down the hill.' He pointed. 'There it is.'

A small town had been constructed on one side of the road, centred on the service area Gildas remembered from journeys this way in the past. Neatly laid-out rows of huts and warehouses followed a semicircular network of roads. There was no sign of a perimeter fence; not surprising, really. This part of the country had been one of the first to become completely depopulated as starvation and disease forced people towards the coasts. There simply wasn't anybody around to keep out.

With stately grace the line of vehicles pulled off the roadway and into a huge parking area where a group of armed men awaited their arrival. With much waving of arms and shouting the whole convoy was lined up into rows, none of the passengers alighting until invited to do so by the reception committee. As they disembarked, they were pointed in the direction of the large service pavilion, where refreshments were being distributed. Gildas and Josh, being last in the queue, got served last. Scrag ends, as usual. Gildas shrugged, he'd become accustomed to it. Someone sniffed loudly behind him. Turning about, he saw Clare with a smile of greeting on her face. He didn't smile back. A large man in lightweight battle fatigues jumped on a counter and called for order. Conversation ceased.

'You're the last lot in as far as we know; no more are anticipated, anyhow. Just for your information, we're well short of the numbers we expected. From the little news we've been able to get there's been a hell of a lot of unforeseen mortalities.' Groans of despair came from the crowd.

'I know, I know.' He shouted over the hubbub, 'It's the fault of all those funny bugs loose out there, we suspect. And I sincerely hope none of those that any of you might know are among the casualties. The fact remains. A list of those who haven't turned up is posted on the board at the end of the foyer behind you. Wait!' This last was to those who had started to push through the crowd in an effort to see the list. They wouldn't have got far, anyway; armed men blocked the doorway. The speaker continued.

'As you've heard, the schedule's been speeded up. Medical investigations have been overloaded so if any of you have any medical training or experience whatsoever would you please report to the desk in the foyer on your way out; your help is badly needed. That's about all, I think. The men at the door will issue you with accommodation slips which you will hand over to your barrack supervisors, who'll assign you to duties and keep you informed of developments. A map to help you find your way is outside to the left of the main door. Good luck!' He descended from the counter in the midst of a confused silence. The crowd began to move hesitantly in the direction of the door.

Gildas turned to Clare. 'I don't know what half of that was all about. Better get my bed ticket. Coming?'

'I've got it here.' She produced a slip of paper, pushing it into his hand. 'Let's get out of here. I'm feeling claustrophobic. Don't worry, you're not sharing a double with me … yet!'

Gildas thrust the paper into his pocket. Were his thoughts *that* transparent? Knowing his companion, he suspected that may actually have been the case.

'What do you mean ... yet?' he demanded.

Clare grinned. 'I'm beginning to get quite worried about you.' They reached the doors and walked along the foyer, squeezing past the knot of worried people around the "missing" list. A few were already in tears. 'Want to look around first? There's not much to see in the village itself, mind.'

'No thanks. Where's that map?'

'I'll take you to your hut. Where's Josh got to?'

'Right here,' came a voice from behind. 'Give me a look at your docket, son!' Gildas passed it over. 'Good, same as my pad. Lead on, warrior!'

The layout of the place ensured no personnel had to walk very far from the pavilion; all accommodation was central, while storage units formed a wide fringe on the outer edge. A stroll of a few minutes brought them to one of a row of plastic-clad huts, each no different in any way from its neighbours, except for a large identification number painted crudely over the door. The rushing sound of air conditioners surrounded them.

Conversation within ceased as the new arrivals pushed through the twin plastic portals. Suspicious eyes appraised them. It was refreshingly cool inside, almost cold. It smelt a lot fresher than outside, too. Banks of sleeping bunks, four tiers high, formed a continuous line each side of the central corridor. Clare pointed to a pair of empty compartments at the top of the set nearest the door.

'Those two are yours.'

Josh balked. 'I don't think I can get up to the top one, son.' he murmured to Gildas, 'The old muscles aren't what they were.'

'I'll take it.' Gildas knew he had no choice in the matter. 'Where are you staying?' he asked Clare.

'Bottom bunk, same row.' she smirked. 'So you'll have to climb past me every time you want to stretch your legs. I'm a light sleeper too, so be careful I don't grab anything when you pass. Let's have your dockets for my collection or Spode'll go mad.'

'So you're the supervisor here?'

'Naturally. Think they allow talent to be wasted around here? Seriously, though, there's a good reason for it. Josh knows; he'll tell you when you need to know - or I will. See you later; I've got a stint over the medical section.' Grabbing the dockets she marched out into the hot evening air.

'Give us a leg up, mate!' Josh requested, eyeing the height of his bunk with a certain trepidation. He groaned as he was thrust unceremoniously two floors up. Gildas followed him.

'And what did she mean by that bit about a good reason for it? Reason for what? What the hell's going on around here? And where's Emma?' he asked.

'Not now, son, please!' grizzled Josh. 'Allow an old man to relax, will you? Call me in a couple of hours; we'll discuss it then. Better still, we'll all discuss it later if Miss Clare calls a meeting tonight,' *All?* thought Gildas. 'I've got a feeling we're not going to be here very long the way things are looking and never mind Miss Emma. She'll call for you when your presence is required, never fear. Now leave me be!'

He was snoring almost by the time Gildas reached the floor.

A rather puzzled Gildas.

INTERMURAL 5

The result of all the new highly-technological processes since the middle of the twentieth century was the release into the atmosphere of many new gases not found in nature as well as contributing to the overload of ammonia, carbon dioxide and other scorch factor gases. These broke down the Earth's defensive layer of ozone just the same; first at the poles then over the rest of the globe at an accelerating rate. Excessive absorption of ultra-violet, gamma and X-ray wavelengths created yet more problems.

Only two of them are relevant here.

The worst (to begin with) was the decimation of food animals and wildlife. Only those kept out of direct solar radiation or fitted with protective coverings were able to avoid blindness and malignant skin tumours; an almost impossible task. Countless millions of creatures perished, unable to feed themselves; frightened to move. Cattle and most other domestic meat animals were nearly wiped out completely during the fourth decade of the twenty-first century during the weeks after the ozone barrier disappeared entirely between (approximately) the Tropics of Capricorn and Cancer.

This took place just after mid-summer and it was all downhill from there on. People were affected in the same way as animals. Whole townships greeted each new day with rapidly developing retinal cataracts. Blindness requires help and support but the numbers involved were far too large to be assisted so nobody made any serious attempt. Even if they had, it was too late; the stampede had already begun.

Millions stayed where they were, waiting for help which never arrived. Hundreds of millions more headed north in repose to rumours things were better there. Very few went south; the situation was just as bad and there was much less land. Whatever transport became available was commandeered by those who still retained their eyesight and used to ferry those who were blind - at a price. Only Death can alter basic human nature to any marked degree.

What authority was left could only try to keep people alive by using whatever means were locally available. Without vegetables, food animals or fish they were reduced to using seaweed, whatever could be dredged from the sea bed using irreplaceable nets and the bodies of the dead (processed quickly and not very well) by converting tankers and old cargo ships anchored permanently offshore. Old mores and the habits of civilised behaviour had to be abandoned due to the need to live. Luxury items were carefully hidden and only supplied to those who kept things going - a fair enough arrangement when one considers the level of stress they were under.

Throughout all this carnage with death, war, disease, starvation and dog-eat-dog on all sides, a number of individuals had already made plans to get away and start up again elsewhere. Ironically, these were the very people who were directly responsible for causing the mess in the first place - the super-rich and those who had clawed their way into a position of power. With skills refined over many generations of manipulation and accumulation, they gravitated together, with an unforeseen degree of mutual co-operation, to do what was necessary.

For their own benefit only, of course!

The coup-de-gras *would be donated by the planet itself. Not consciously, silly! Planets can't think! But they can alter their internal arrangements, sometimes with frightening speed.*

A bit to the west of the mid-oceanic rift in the Atlantic Ocean an unusually fluid hot-spot finally broke through the lowest levels of a tough bit of lithosphere that had been holding the lid on it for many millions of years. Access was thereby gained to a more shattered and weakened area below a certain section of oceanic crust, which just happened to be bordered on three of its four sides by two long, and very deep, transform fractures and the rift itself. Barely viscous matter, hot and elastic, pushed up at an increasing rate, striving to create a new equilibrium of pressures. Movement intensified the heat; elastic became ever more fluid and half a million square miles of ocean bed supporting a chain of long- extinct volcanic sea-mounts began to bulge. Cleansing and metamorphosis at last.

And about time, too!

Bad luck, really, for all this to happen just as what was left of the human race was trying so hard to get back on its feet and survive long enough to start tackling the appalling mess it had created.

245

CHAPTER 19

The eastern end of the Mule could be clearly seen from the front of the barracks. Gildas wished he possessed a pair of binoculars; it presented rather an intriguing scene. Not wishing to become involved with the other tenants, none of whom had taken any notice of him except for radiating a tangible atmosphere of hostility, he'd soon relinquished the coolness of the indoors for the hotter, yet more isolated and desirable shade cast by the setting sun.

A thick concentration of fine dust in the upper atmosphere ensured a spectacular sunset, as usual. The deep apricot-coloured light tinted the hoops of the massive linear accelerator giving them the appearance of lightly-roasted spare ribs decoratively arranged as a lengthy dining table centre-piece. At the top of the hill to the east sat several large hangar-like buildings and it was here the first hoop was located standing at a severe tilt downhill in front of the nearest hangar.

Something was going on at the base of this hoop. Gildas peered at it as he shuffled his bottom on the hard ground to find a comfortable position for what could turn out to be a lengthy wait. Clasping his hands into a loop he peered through the gap thus created and concentrated on that point.

It was only about half a mile away and clearly visible in full sunlight. The four continuous internal ribbons he'd noticed earlier were close together here and considerably thickened. At their collective ends stood a heavily-built arrangement of girders, which resembled an open-sided lift shaft, and this was exactly what it was if the platform slowly being hoisted to the top was anything to go by. A silvery cylinder lay in a bulky cradle mounted on the platform.

It had to be one of the shuttles he'd heard about. About to be launched, too! He didn't have long to wait. There was

246

no cloud of smoke, no flames from superheated fuel, no noise; in absolute silence the shuttle hurtled from a standing start at a frightening acceleration, whizzed down the slope and raced over the camp, still accelerating. Gildas just had time to notice it was running between the ribbons without touching them. He hardly noticed the craft itself, just a blurred impression of a wingless dart without any distinguishing features. Running around the side of the barrack hut he was just in time to see the take-off as the shuttle seemed to flicker, left the final hoop and rapidly disappeared from sight into the sky almost straight towards the setting sun. A few moments later he thought he saw a small flash of flame in the far, high distance.

And they had to ride to safety in *that*? Gildas quailed at the thought. He wandered back to his seat in front of the hut door. There was a lot to think about.

Thoughts came slowly, and with them, confusion. No stranger to having to adapt to new circumstances, he recognised the signs of cultural overload - a resistance to the pace of change - transformation fatigue? In spite of the necessity for survival he was gradually becoming extremely tired of the need to be always on the alert for danger.

It was the same here, even in this base. The looks of suspicion cast in his direction when he'd first entered the hut behind him boded ill for his sense of security; and yet he seemed quite unable to care about it. Not *really* care. Almost as if a death wish had overtaken his mental processes. Maybe that was why he always felt so tired these days. He remembered going to sleep within range of Emma's death waggon, the ever-present drowsiness at the ziggurat. And what about the drive from there to here?

Too much trouble to stay alive; that must be it. There wasn't much worthwhile staying alive for any more. Gildas lapsed into a reverie of disconnected impressions and gloomy introspection. Self-pity again, he acknowledged to himself, but there didn't seem to be any sensible alternative to just throwing in the towel and giving up.

He knew he was consciously destroying himself.

Shuttles took off at hourly intervals but he lost interest in them after the first two. He was still trying to think constructively when the cold of deepening darkness forced him back into the barracks where the air conditioning had been replaced by heaters. Josh was still asleep. Others in the hut - for the first time he noticed how few there were for the space available - still refused to recognise his presence. Not that it made any difference to his state of mind; he'd become accustomed to being the odd one out since before his school days. He sat on the edge of the bottom bunk and put his large head in his hands, nearly ready to weep.

It was Clare's bunk! The thought intruded like a cheery and very unwelcome guest at a funeral. He was sitting on Clare's bunk! And where the hell had she got to? And why should he care? Despite his miserable confusion he missed the big, jovial and totally amoral woman and now felt abandoned when she wasn't around. He groaned softly; only another thing to worry about. What was happening to him? Maybe he would ask her when she came home.

Now what produced *that* thought?

Came *home?*

He groaned again. Two hours passed. Two more shuttles passed overhead with a thin shriek of displaced air.

'What's happening to me?' he bawled as Clare stamped through the door bringing a whiff of freezing air and antiseptic in her wake. She halted in surprise.

'Eh? What are you shouting for? The neighbours might complain, y'know. Nothing's happening to you that I know of.'

'Forget it!' Gildas got off the bunk, embarrassed at his outburst. 'I'm just feeling a little low at the moment. What's new?'

248

This looked like it could be serious; he was obviously upset about something. Could it wait? She felt very tired; it had been a hard shift at the Med centre.

'Let me sit down first.' She slumped onto the mattress. 'That's better.' she sighed, patting the space alongside. ' Join me! I'm too knackered to ravish you right now; your precious body will remain totally unviolated this evening, I promise.'

Lay off with that stuff, will you?' Gildas squirmed, but stayed close by. 'Hard time with the medics? Think they could find me a job? I'm getting bored out of my skull sitting around here; the other tenants aren't what you might call sociable.'

'I'll ask. Haven't you tried to join in? There's always a card game of some sorts going on here somewhere.' She nodded to the far end of the hut where a group sat on the floor, all holding playing cards in their hands.

'No good at it. Never have been. I'd like something useful to do instead.'

'Well, like I said, I'll ask. Don't think we'll be here for long though. Three days max. Reckon I'll turn in now.'

'What about the meeting? Josh didn't tell me a thing' He's been snoring away up there ever since you went out. What's the meeting about?'

'Not tonight. Haven't got enough information yet. Anyone else turned up in here?'

'Don't think so unless there's another entrance.'

'Pity. We could have done with a bit more help.'

Help? For what?

Clare stretched and yawned. 'So what's your problem? Why are you feeling down in the mouth? You should be full of excitement at the great adventure before you.'

Was there an undertone of cynicism in her words? Taken in the context of what had happened to the world, wasn't his own set of problems a bit insignificant? Was he being childishly selfish?

Yes, he thought. Nothing seemed to be as bad when Clare was near. He thrust that thought out of his mind, fast.

'I shouldn't bother you with this right now, you're too tired. Get a good night's sleep and I'll bring it up another time if it matters as much by then.' He made to stand up but was stopped by a gentle hand on his shoulder. Clare drew him round to face her. Even sitting she topped him by several inches. Two sympathetic eyes looked deep into his.

'It's no bother, honest. Maybe you won't get another chance before we leave. I'll listen if you think it'll help. What's the problem?'

He felt like bursting into tears. She was so much like his mother - and forty years his mother's junior. Hell, she was nearly young enough to be his daughter.

'Tell me.' she prompted softly.

'It's so confused.' He strove to make sense of his previous thoughts. Baring his soul was more difficult than he'd realised. 'I know I'm lucky but I'm not content. Why? I can't understand.'

'When did it start?'

He tried to remember. 'Don't know.'

'When your wife was murdered, maybe?'

'It must have been. I can't remember having the depressions like this before that time.'

'That was the same time we met up, yes?'

Oh no!

'And it's not love, don't give me that!' he snapped.

Clare didn't make fun of him, for once. 'Try to be serious without losing your temper, if you can. I recall you killed your first human being at about that time. Could that have been the trigger?'

'That one was an accident.' he replied tersely.

'Yes, but then there were the others. The three you caught up with? You deliberately snuffed them out like they were less than nothing.' She did not care to mention how he'd broken down at the time. It would not have served her present purposes.

250

'They deserved it. If I could kill them again, over and over, I would.' He quivered in hatred. 'They didn't have the right to go on living.'

Clare was an experienced counsellor with people damaged by combat situations. It was a role she'd learned the hard way, through necessity rather than training, like so many other minor military leaders in the thick of battle. She sensed she was closing in on at least one of the problems screwing up her diminutive colleague. She led him on to the right moment, patiently, remorselessly.

'But you didn't get them all, did you? There's still one out there somewhere. Had you forgotten that?'

Gildas hadn't. 'But how would I catch up with him now the trail's petered out? Likely he's dead by now, anyway. Have to forget ...' His voice broke.

That was it! Now to shock him out of his self-pity. It usually worked.

The world tilted and fell apart.

Gildas sprawled on the floor where he'd been thrown by the impetus of a powerful shove. His teeth were still rattling in his head as he felt a hand grasp the collar of his jacket, another gain purchase on the seat of his trousers and he was lifted unceremoniously from the only scrap of carpet in the hut - in front of Clare's bunk (where else?). He caught a brief glimpse of the card school, all faces turned towards the scuffle, before his head bumped against the hard plastic of the inner door, then the outer, and he was carried face-down into the frosty night.

Clare dumped him on the hard earth at the base of the single step.

'Get up!'

Gildas' head span. He scrabbled to rise. Once more he was seized, with two large hands; around the neck, this time. Vertebrae popped as he was hauled upright and slammed against the hut wall, feet off the floor.

'You pathetic little wimp! What the hell is it with you? It's about time you got your head straight about a few

251

things or you're going to be a very dead wimp as well before too long.' She banged his head against the wall a couple of times for emphasis, taking no notice of his frantic attempts to clutch at her for support in order to remove the pressure from his neck. He gargled something.

Clare looked him straight in the face, eyes blazing, then dropped him like a sack of potatoes to sprawl at her feet. A wry comment about over-reaction sprang to his mind but he said nothing; it would have been too painful at the moment. He massaged his throat hoping it hadn't received too much damage from her gouging thumbs.

'Well, haven't you got anything to say?' she demanded.

Gildas managed a dry rasp before getting to his feet. It hurt and started him coughing. Clare waited impassively. He tried again.

'There was no need for that. I told you to forget it, didn't I? Now you've only made things worse. Leave me alone!'

'No chance.' She reached for him again, but relatively slowly, giving him time to skip aside. He did so with remarkable agility. He'd been humiliated and frightened enough, she decided; sufficiently softened up for the next step. Clare turned and settled down on the edge off the cold step, patting the space alongside in invitation.

'Wish I could but it's not so easy as that. Look, if you're not going to sit down at least come a little closer so I don't have to shout.' Gildas sidled along the wall. 'That's better. Aren't you glad to be alive?'

He considered. 'Yes and no.' he answered evasively.

Clare snorted. 'Forget the yes bit and tell me why you think it's better to be dead.'

'I didn't mean that. Being dead, I mean. It just seems too much trouble staying alive. And for what?' He waved an arm at the world. 'Nothing will be left before long. Look at it out there!'

'That's why we're leaving.' Clare pointed out.

'Yes, but to where? Nobody's told me a thing about what to expect. It's as if I'm so insignificant that I'm just expected to tag along and be taken for granted, like one of the fittings. It's not as if I'd be much use to anyone.'

'I thought Josh would have bought you up to date. I told you to ask him, didn't I?'

'Well he hasn't. Neither has anyone else, including you. I'm fed up of the whole thing.'

Clare was silent for a while. All that he'd said was true. He *was* an outsider, brought along for the sole reason that she'd taken a fancy to the ugly little man and she couldn't explain why. All others in the exodus knew many of the options their future might hold - but not Gildas. And that had somehow been overlooked, especially by her. She *was* taking him for granted and he was also sensitive enough to react against it. He would have to be brought up to date for his own sake - and Emma's - and it would have to be done right now.

If only she hadn't felt quite so exhausted.

She patted the step once more. 'I'm sorry. You're absolutely right. It'll take a bit of time so you'd better have a seat.'

He sat, without a word.

'I don't know where to begin.' she confessed. 'Ask me something you want to know.'

'Tell me about where we're going, how we're going to get there and how all this has been done in secrecy. I'd love to know that for starters.'

'Easy. Up there,' she pointed to the night sky; 'are two big things called star-ships that we hope are going to take us all to another solar system. They're both above the equator in a geosynchronous orbit. One is about three hundred miles to the west of this longitude and the other is exactly half-way round the world from that. With me so far?'

Gildas nodded.

'Right. They've been under construction since before things really started to fall apart about fifteen years ago. They're nearly ready to leave. We'll be travelling in a form of suspended animation the whole way. Only the crews will be woken up at various points en route to check things out and to make sure we're still on the right course.'

'Where to?' Gildas interjected. 'And how do we know there's a good place to land? I thought there wasn't any life out there.'

'I was coming to that. Remember that unmanned shuttle which got lost early in the twenty hundreds? I was only a kid at the time but even I can remember the fuss that was made. It was almost the last one that went up. Well, it didn't carry any satellites or bits of the space station they never completed. It was carrying probes.'

'Probes? To the outer planets?'

'Some went past them - did a fly-by to gather a few extra bits of information and pick up a bit of speed - but their real destinations were the nearest stars. A few of them are not too much different from our sun and planets had been discovered orbiting three of them. There was just a chance one or more of them may have been able to support us.'

Gildas was calming down now he had something to interest him. 'But it's only been, let's see, less than thirty years. If the ships up there were only started just over fifteen years ago there wouldn't have been anywhere near enough time for a probe to get to the nearest star, let alone the others. I'm not completely stupid. I've read a lot of books, y'know. Light speed is out of the question, so is the transmission of information back to here over that distance. Sure you're not having me on and all this is just a gamble?'

'It *is* a gamble, but a calculated one. The probes were very small and only looking for specific information. They used stored power, solar power and solar wind to get up speed enough to use interstellar hydrogen in a small, primitive ramjet. They wouldn't have had to go all the way; meaningful observations could be made from much less than half way to the nearest star. Only one probe has found somewhere where we could possibly live without too much adaptation, so far. Two planets look promising and it's getting better the nearer the probe gets. We know that because each probe was sending out a continuous carrier wave from the time it set out and the information was transmitted along that.'

'Still couldn't have gone faster than light.'

'Oh no? Ever shaken a clothes line? Ever watched how a caterpillar gets around? Both use a ripple along their length. In the case of the caterpillar the ripple goes a lot faster than the creepy-crawly. That's what they used, apparently. The ripple. I don't pretend to be a boffin but they assure me it works fine. They got the info, anyway. Still getting it. It was picked up by the empty shuttle, which was orbiting the moon so we couldn't see it from Earth. The shuttle boosted and unscrambled it then relayed it on. Clever, eh?'

'Very. And Mr Quorvis managed to arrange all this without official interference?'

'With covert official approval, idiot! They could see the way things were going, all right. Guess how many politicians and their families are travelling with us.'

Gildas nodded as if the fact were pre-ordained. 'It figures. Thought I recognised a few faces here and there but couldn't put names to them. Guess we can add on all their cronies, hangers-on and slaves, no doubt.'

'You catch on quick. And that's precisely why your presence is required.'

Gildas didn't see why, or what she was getting at. He said so.

Clare sighed. 'What's *your* main reason for going?' she asked. 'You didn't seem to be so keen at first, then something changed your mind.'

'Because there's just a chance it'll be a better place than this.' he replied loudly. 'A place to disappear, live freely without some so-called authority telling me what to do all the time. Have a decent life away from the rest of the stinking human race. Look what we've done here! We were overpopulated - and that's what brought about this disaster in the first place. We were over-regulated, ordered to do things against our individual judgement all the time on pain of punishment, treated like statistics without any regard for our own fears and requirements. We weren't allowed to have minds of our own. I want to find somewhere where it won't happen all over again till well after I'm dead.'

'All right. Keep your voice down! Leave the ringing pioneering speeches to those who know how to do it properly. I get the message. Are you really naive enough to think that's what you'll be allowed to do?'

'Why not? It *will* be pioneering, after all, unless the probes got it all wrong.'

'Fat chance of that!' Clare waved a muscular arm in dismissal. 'The majority of our fellow travellers value their precious skins too much to risk them on short odds. Those really in the know have got a lot more information than what they're telling us, believe me. I reckon we'll be able to live there all right. Another thing: it's going to be a long trip of well over a hundred years. We'll be travelling in a form of suspended animation of course.' She paused.

Gildas shivered. He hadn't thought of that. He had automatically assumed the ships would be using the same sort of propulsion as the probes. But never mind about side-tracking Clare now he had finally got her to talk. He'd bring the unnerving subject up later on, maybe. Right now he wanted to know more about this apparently probable curtailment of his idea of freedom.

'Go on.' he murmured, subdued.

Clare came out of her reverie. 'They're bound to have thought ahead to what happens if the probes have got it wrong and the place can't support us. Bet they'll simply turn round and come back. We could wake up back here after close on three hundred years. This planet will have been virtually depopulated by then with just a few tribes wandering around trying to stay alive. They'll be easy to control with all the fire-power we're taking along. Either way, the lives of most of us will turn out just the same.'

'Same as what?'

'Same as it would have been if we'd landed up there.' She gestured at the firmament. Stars glared down at them as they sat on the step. 'Those at the top of the heap would simply assume they had the right to tell the rest how to live and what to do and you can bet your boots they've already made sure they've got the muscle to enforce it.'

'How come you object to that? I would, I know, but you'd be one of those at the top of the same heap since your father is one of those supporting the venture.'

'I just don't like the idea, that's all.'

Gildas couldn't make sense of all this. He considered for a moment, then asked, 'Look, Clare. I know you're tired and need sleep but please tell me one thing. Is Mr Quorvis in total control of things or not?'

'Yes and no.' Clare put a hand on his shoulder to forestall the next question. 'I'll explain. He organised the whole thing so he's in control of that aspect. But there are many powerful sources among the colonists who have their own agendas. Think Lemuel doesn't know that? 'Course he does. And what can he do about it?' She rubbed the side of her nose and grinned at him.

'You mean those in charge down here are going to make damned sure they're in charge up there as well and the rest of us'll just have to knuckle under, that it?'

'Right. So Lemuel has been making certain arrangements. All he wants is to live the rest of his life quietly without being pushed around. Just like you. He doesn't want to be in control of anything when we get there and he doesn't intend for anyone to control him, either. Call it anarchy if you like, but there's a whole empty planet up there, maybe two, where there's room for everybody to disappear if they want. And that's a bad scene for the compulsive power maniacs.'

'Making certain arrangements? With who?'

257

Me and my crew, of which you are one, I hope.'

'What about Emma?'

'He doesn't want her involved - but she's got to be. It's a matter of intense disagreement between us. Lemuel and me, that is.'

'Because of her waggon, yes?'

'Because of her waggon. I hope we won't need it, or her, but we have to be prepared for the worst. Not going to be easy to get it there though.'

'And Emma knows?'

'She knows. Looking forward to it too.'

'I'll bet she is. Where are the rest of your motley crew? In there I suppose?' He jerked a thumb at the door behind him.

'The best that money, fear and coercion can obtain. Tough bunch. If they can't sort out any problems then nobody can.'

Gildas made up his mind.

'Then the sooner I meet them the better. Can you introduce me tomorrow? You'd better get to bed now. I'm sorry I held you up.' He looked appropriately contrite - he hoped.

Clare stood up, uncramping cold muscles. 'Notice you said get to bed instead of come to bed. Coward! My blanket's always open if you change your mind.'

Gildas uttered a short laugh. 'You're incorrigible. Go on! Sleep.'

'For a guy with your background to say the word "incorrigible", let alone in the right context, is one of the things I like about you, little man.' Her tone was friendly rather than sarcastic. 'Goodnight.'

Gildas was too slow to dodge as she knocked his cap off and ruffled his hair. Funny. It wasn't so irritating any more.

''Night.' he said.

He remained on the step watching the shuttles take off until close to first light.

There seemed to be no end to their numbers.

258

CHAPTER 20

A gentle shaking of his shoulder brought him fully awake within seconds. He instantly experienced a feeling of imminence about this new day; something important was going to happen.

Instant worry! The seamed face of an old man peered at him from somewhere below the level of his bunk.

'Sorry to get you up so early, son,' said the face. 'Heard you clamber up there first thing this morning and wanted to let you lie but Miss Clare said to hell with that and I was to get you up and about before she got back from the daily situation meeting. She'll be along any minute now.'

'That's OK, Josh. I feel wide awake already.'

Josh continued. 'I'm also sorry about keeping you in the dark about what we're doing. Couldn't stay awake for long enough, unfortunately. Getting old, see? She told me you'd been put in the picture at last. Not before time too, as far as I'm concerned.'

'You'd make a good clam, Josh. Step down and let me get out of my pit.'

He felt strong as he kneaded his stiff legs after the undignified climb from the top bunk. Stronger than he had for a long while - both in body and spirit. He removed his jacket and treated himself to a long series of press-ups. Josh watched in admiration.

'It's been along time since I could do that, son. Didn't realise you had such a good body, either. Pity about the legs.'

'No need to get personal.' grunted Gildas as he reached a score of fifty and collapsed sideways on the small strip of carpet. 'They've got me round for over forty years without letting me down yet. Phoomph! Need more exercise. Do you know any of our hut mates?'

'Yeah. Not that I bother much with them. Unsociable lot. Miss Clare suggested you be introduced in spite of that. Coming?'

Massaging his muscles as he followed the old man, Gildas tried to put a friendly yet neutral look on his face. It wasn't easy with a face like his - but he tried – And there was something he just *had* to ask the old mechanic.

I've been wondering, Josh' he said

'Wondering what?'

'When we first spotted this place from the top of the hill over there you mentioned booster fuel for the rockets, remember?'

'What of it? The Mule can't do it by itself.'

'That's another point. If the Mule's a big linear accelerator it must use a huge amount of electric power so where does it come from? And what about the booster fuel as well as the stuff for the trucks?'

'You don't imagine that the bunch who planned this set-up didn't sort that out long ago, do you?' Lem saw what was needed straight away and got the others to cough up enough cash to do the job over the years We're not far from the North Sea, y'know and back at the beginning of the century they were still pumping plenty of oil out of there so when it more or less dried up nobody could make any more heavy cash out of it and Lem and his mates could get things at a knock-down price.'

'I remember that.' said Gildas. 'It caused a heck of a problem in all the world's stock markets.'

That's right. Well, it should have been obvious at the time that even if they couldn't get high volumes out any more there was bound to be plenty left and a few of the nearest platforms were still there as well as a couple of pipelines to two of the big refineries on the coast less than a hundred miles from here.'

'OK, so that explains the fuel.' said Gildas. 'But what about the power for the Mule? If I remember right the oil-burning power stations closed down when the price of oil went ballistic. Do they use coal or gas instead? I've noticed there were still a lot of electricity pylons around on the way here and at least two them come here.'

Josh smiled. 'Two lines couldn't carry anywhere near enough power to give the Mule its kick. You only saw the ones coming in from the north and west but if you went the other side of the Mule's control building up on the hill you'd see another one coming up from the south and two more from the East Between them they give us more electric power than we could possibly use.'

'So where do they come from?' asked Gildas. 'Old coal and gas-fired stations?'

'Nah!' said Josh scathingly. 'The gas places packed up the same time as the oil ones and the morons ruling this country destroyed the coal capacity last century.'

'Surely not from the wind and tidal installations, though?' asked Gildas. 'Even I know they'd never have been able to give enough output to power that monster, and come to think of it I've hardly seen any that are still working.' Josh sniggered. 'Those bright ideas were just a fad to lull the eternally gullible public into a sense of false security.

'So where from?' insisted Gildas, determined to get to the bottom of the mystery even though he didn't know why. 'It can't be the nuclear stations, can it? They went out of business when all the global warming stuff really began to get going. I remember reading about it.'
*

The card school had been up and running for some hours. Everybody looked bored. There were about twenty of them grouped about the four current players; sitting on bunks or lolling around in indolent postures on the unyielding concrete floor. Gildas reckoned he had never seen so many hard-faced men - and women - all together in one place before. It was strange that he didn't feel uneasy.

261

'Hey-yup folks! You all know me, I think. Now meet a new member of the gang. Called Gildas; he's Welsh. Answers to the name of Gil. Say hello to Gil!'

A few disinterested nods and grunts completed the acknowledgements. One or two even raised a desultory hand in greeting. Gildas beamed at all and sundry; his good mood seemed to be holding. That brain-squeezing session last night after Clare had gone to bed had been *really* worth while.

Nobody smiled back. They'd forgotten him already. He wasn't sure what to do next. He shrugged. Why bother to do anything?

The unmistakable slap of a stiff plastic sheet attracted attention to the hut door. Clare had just entered. She strode stolidly along the passage between the tiers of empty bunks, bearing down on them with the merciless thrust of a tank. The card school didn't even look up. She flashed a quick smile at Gildas.

'All know each other now? All friends?'

Gildas rolled his eyes and kept his mouth shut.

Gather round, you lot. Oy! You too!' Someone snarled as cards were kicked out of a hand. The other players divined the message and gave her their full attention.

'No strangers?' A few heads shook. No.

'Good. The new lad here has been apprised of the situation. He's going to be my second-in-command. Any objections?'

Gildas stiffened.

'Who cares?' A murmur from someone in the shadows.

'Nobody, I hope. Anyway, there's news. We're shipping out tonight.'

A woman who looked as if she'd lost a pitched battle with the moving parts of a combine harvester spoke in a cracked, grating voice. 'What about our big weapons?'

'Still no way we can get access to anything heavy yet, I'm afraid, Heather. No need anyway, as we discussed before. We can't allow ourselves to show our hand till the need arises. Who knows? It may never happen. Maybe we're just wasting our time.'

Heather snorted. 'No we're not, and you know it. Soon as we land we'll be under martial rule. Wanna bet?'

'No bets, but I hope it never comes to that. Secondary arrangements have been made.'

'What arrangements?'

'Look, leave it Heather! What you don't know you can't let slip. Even Gil here doesn't know.' *Oh,* thought Gildas. 'Just believe what I say, huh?'

Heather lapsed into a sullen silence. Several of the others didn't look all that happy either. Gildas foresaw trouble.

'So you've got all your personal weapons?' Clare continued. Nods all round. 'Plenty of ammo?' More nods. 'Right! Anticipated take-off is at nineteen hundred. Muster in the debarkation room just after eighteen hundred and make sure you're all there with whatever personal gear you think you might need - but keep it to a minimum. That's that! Now to more serious business.' She bumped against a fiercely-bearded man with wild eyes, who was sitting on the edge of the nearest bunk. 'Shift!' He silently moved over for her. Even sitting she dominated the little group. She began to speak. Gildas listened with a growing incredulity and started to wonder anew what he'd got himself into.

'I've had a meeting with those in the know and we've finally agreed on a plan of potential operations. As you all know, nobody will be allowed to keep any personal weapons with them when they enter their coffins for an obvious reason; one puncture of the outer skin by somebody who flips their lid and a lot of the passengers get dead. It has been arranged that all our weapons will be stored in one of the empty coffins in our section. There's plenty of empty ones because of those who haven't managed to make it here. And that's another thing; we're all in the same patch on deck seven - far enough away from

263

officer country to be left alone but close enough to the centre spine to be able to get there fast if we have to. Any comments so far?'

One of the former card players chipped in. 'So we're all there is, then?' He indicated the whole group with a wave of his hand. 'No more to come? Just us - against how many if it comes to it?'

'Use your head! Us against all the rest of them, that's how many. But don't forget they've got a few jokers of ours in their pack that we hope they don't know about. And they're heavy-duty jokers too. Don't ask me who, either. No way are their positions going to be compromised for your curiosity - even for such a loyal and steadfast bunch like you lot. Too much depends on them at the other end.'

The man wasn't offended. 'So it's not anticipated there'll be any trouble before we get there, huh?'

'Correct. And that's what I want to discuss with you now.' She lowered her voice. All, including Gildas, leaned forward in the classic conspirator's scrum. He had to hand it to her; she sure knew how to manipulate them.

'According to one of our informants, both planets will have to be checked out thoroughly to make sure we can really survive there, and a place for a temporary base found. At least that's what they say. It should be obvious when you think about it. But what else will they be doing? We can't afford to believe a word of the official line so we think differently. We think it'll be a permanent base in the form of a stronghold and only a few will be shuttled down to set things up. A source of suitable fuel will also have to be located if the shuttles aren't going to be grounded after their first drop. They'll have to be able to get back to the ship for other loads and there's no linear accelerator on board. Too big to take. It'll have to be brute-force chemical propulsion or nothing. All this will take a great deal of time. Suffice it to say that most of the passengers will probably be spending at least a year in orbit before they're woken up.'

A stir spread through the group but nobody spoke. There wasn't any need to; each knew the others were as paranoid as themselves. Clare voiced their collective concern.

'So we'll be vulnerable, OK? Well don't worry about that. Me and Gil here are going to be woken up immediately on arrival. Are you prepared to trust us enough to look after your welfare? That's the question.'

Deep gravelly tones came from the shadows.

'Damn' stupid question.'

It was sufficient answer. Clare nodded. 'Fair enough. So the next time we discuss tactics will be a long way from here in many years time when we've got a better idea of which way things are going to move. Sort yourselves out today and be at shuttle reception on time. Dismissed.' She stood up.

The scarred woman called Heather had to have the last word. As she turned to stretch out on her bunk she muttered loud enough for all to hear.

'We don't have any discussions. We're just given orders. It'll never be any different; there'll always be someone in charge and pushing others around, dammit.'

Others had similar reservations judging by the muted grunts of agreement with which this was greeted. Clare chose to ignore the subdued rumblings of discontent and signalled Gildas to follow her. They wandered outside.

'Got all your stuff with you?' she asked.

'I'm wearing it.'

'Let's get you back on the job, then. Emma's waiting.'

'She's *really* part of your group?'

'So's her father. So are a few you haven't met who are already on the ship to protect our interests. So's Emma's fervent and frustrated lover-boy.'

Gildas stopped short. 'Danhill? That's crazy! How's he going to react when he hears about me and your stupid story about me?'

265

'He already knows. Lem made a point of telling him before we left the Gloucester area. Come on! Don't worry about it.'

This last was in response to Gildas' instinctive reaction. He remained where he was, buried both hands in the thick woolly mattress of his hair and pulled violently. Tufts of black, wiry curls sprouted between his straining fingers.

'Don't worry about it?' he almost howled. 'Between the lot of you you've signed my death warrant as well as fouling up all your own plans. What the hell are you trying to do to me?'

Clare bent so her face was on a level with his. With one hand she began prising his fingers free of his cranial mop; with the other she gently patted his cheek. She couldn't help but smile at his instant panic.

'There, there. Don't overdo it, you're not up to it. Believe me when I say that everything has been planned for a lot of very good reasons.'

Like hell! But Gildas relaxed a little. They walked on.

'Aren't you going to tell me what the reasons are?'

'Thought you'd never ask. When you met Mr Quorvis, did he strike you as a good organiser?

Gildas reflected for an honest answer which would not give implied offence. 'No.' he said, forced to give up an impossible task.

'Well he is, as well as a first class politician. And we're damn' lucky he's on our side. Apparently he's been very much aware of the potential political dangers right from the beginning and set things up to alleviate them. He encouraged Danhill to fall for Emma, for instance, because he needed someone on the bridge in a position of authority. It was made a lot easier because Danhill has delusions of grandeur all of his own. Trouble was with Emma; she simply wouldn't play along. He hadn't expected that. So you came on the scene, enabling Danhill to stay alive long enough to do his job the way we want. You've got to realise that Danhill, deep down, basically wants the same freedom to run his life up there as we do. He only wants to be in charge of it all when Lemuel wanders off into the backwoods in search of solitude. As far as we're concerned, his continued survival depends a lot on how he does it. We've made arrangements about that too.'

Gildas wasn't concerned with future politics. The subject had never interested him in the past, either. But a niggling doubt had been explained.

'So that's the real reason why you need me,' he grumbled. 'A ready-made patsy to distract the attention of one of the lead players in this comic opera of yours and a bargaining chip for later if necessary.'

'That's about it, if you persist in blindly ignoring another obvious reason. Take it or leave it. You want to stay behind instead?'

'No way! You know, when I woke up this morning I felt fine. Thought I knew the way things were to be after our talk last night. I suppose I should thank you for confiding in me - at last. Well, thanks! Now I'm depressed once more and it's all your fault.'

'No you're not. You just need a bit of time to get used to the idea, that's all.' They were passing one of the barrack huts. 'I know what you need. Come in here!'

The hut was deserted. Gildas looked suspiciously at his partner.

'No need to get nervous. My biological requirements have been adequately catered for by one of the medical staff first thing this morning. Get your coat off and shed all your weapons!'

His scalp tingled. He began to feel strong again. Going to one off the bunks he carefully laid down his weapon harness, clinking with knives and guns. He knew what she meant now; he needed action to focus his mind. And she was right.

But that bit about biological requirements and one of the medical staff! Suddenly he trembled with some indefinable emotion. He wanted to smack that superior attitude right out of her; wipe the grin off her face. Was he getting jealous? Perish the thought! Or was she trying to control him with her sex again as she had undoubtedly controlled so many others.

How *dare* she!

He tore off his shirt without undoing the buttons. One sleeve ripped as he struggled yet more furiously. The shirt proved troublesome; he shredded it in his temper. He swung around to face his tormentor, muscles in spasm, face twisted in fury.

She stood on the other side of the central aisle a few bunks down, poised, confident. She had quickly stripped to shorts and brassiere and was leaning negligently against a support post. He raced towards her, arms outstretched, to pummel and punish. She stepped aside; he hit the hard plastic post and fell heavily on the floor. Limbs quaking with an unnatural violence, he regained his feet and flew for her again, ignoring the searing pain from a damaged elbow.

Clare was waiting for him, crouched and ready. They clashed in true combat for the first time.

She'd been expecting this. In fact, she was rather surprised it had taken so long to occur. Perhaps it was because a full night had passed between the humiliation she had deliberately forced upon him and the opportunity for reaction hadn't been available. Whatever the reason, it was best to let him have it out now and complete the rough and ready treatment. Which was precisely why she had provoked him by using the off-hand mention of casual sex as a spur. At the very least it would prove he had *some* feeling for her. She resolved to try not to hurt him too much. It wasn't altogether his fault.

It didn't work out that way. Clare rapidly discovered she was more likely to come out of this with lumps than the other way round. From the moment he closed with her she was on the defensive. He was like a diminutive tornado, a man possessed; using everything he could to inflict some kind of damage. Fists, teeth, feet, even the abrasive stubble from several days without shaving, which he rasped over exposed sections of her skin. No holds were barred and the Marquis of Queensbury would have fainted away on the spot.

A full ten minutes passed in a whirlwind of vicious action as they slugged it out, crashing against walls and bunks, often rolling on the floor, where the heavier woman's weight proved an advantage. It was a bruising contest. They fought to a virtual standstill. Nobody entered the hut.

Then it was over. Now what? Clare sat on the floor trying to ignore a multitude of protesting nerve-ends while Gildas clung with one hand to a bunk-support drawing in great gasps of air with every breath, teeth bared in a grimace of pain. His other arm was wrapped around his rib cage where he imagined there were more than a few breakages - cracks, at least. They watched each other warily. Neither moved for fear of breaking the stasis.

Clare wanted to say "Feel better now?" but desisted in case he interpreted it as sarcasm. A couple of minutes passed.

'You OK?' She had to say *something.*

Gildas nodded. His breathing had slowed to something approaching normal. After a few moments he essayed a somewhat shamefaced smile.

'I'm gasping for a fag.' he said. 'Got one?'

Clare shook her head, using the movement as an excuse to get to her feet. She felt unsteady. She hurt.

'Let's get dressed and head for the feeding room. Play always makes me hungry. There's a fag machine there. Sure you're OK?'

'Hurt my elbow.' He let go the support and showed her his arm. An unpleasant gash showed just above the elbow but there was very little blood running down. 'Ribs hurt too. Sorry about the mess on you.'

It was not an apology about her physical state, as she discovered on looking down at herself. Bloodstains from Gildas' wound were all over her. The beginnings of some impressive bruises were becoming evident, too. Hastily she averted her eyes and began to dress. Gildas tottered across to where his clothes lay.

'Want a hand?' she asked.

'I'll be all right. Would you carry some of this gear for me?'

'Sure.' she hastened to oblige. 'Better call in at the, er, first-aid post to get you checked out. Me too, I think.' She rubbed her neck ruefully, where a large patch of skin glowed a livid red from the abrasion of Gildas' whiskers. It felt hot and sticky. She'd only just managed to avoid mention of the Medical Centre. That might have started him off again. Whew!

'Fags first.'

'Right.'

'And then we'll go to the Medical Centre where there's bound to be an X-ray machine of sorts. My ribs, y'know.' He gave her an unreadable look.

So he hadn't been fooled. Ah, well!

They sat in the almost deserted refectory surveying the remains of an overly substantial late breakfast. The mood was light, almost amiable. Gildas was well into his third cigarette.

The Medical Centre had received them without comment, used Gildas harshly, tended to Clare in tight-lipped silence and thrown them both out with a terse admonition not to waste their valuable time in future. Didn't they know there was an exodus on? Didn't they have enough to do with real disease instead of ... etc, and so on?

It had fallen on deaf ears. Yet Gildas felt no remorse at their displeasure. The feel of a tight bandage across his bruised ribs - no breaks or cracks, they'd told him - had a lot to do with it. That, and the sight of a white-faced Clare

270

nursing a tender jaw from which a tooth had been peremptorily removed. Both her eye sockets had acquired a dark, irregular patch giving her rounded features the appearance of a Panda seen against a strong light. A thin white pad surrounded her neck. Even so, she seemed to hold no grudge against him and had even insisted on carrying both their food trays and getting him a couple of packets of smokes from the wall dispenser.

The strong aura of antiseptic surrounding them had put neither off shovelling down as much food as their systems could cope with.

'I don't think it's a good idea to put me in as second-in-command of your troupe.' Gildas said, fighting an urge to choke on the rancid tobacco-flavoured mix of his cigarette.

'Why not?'

Gildas counted off on his stubby fingers. 'One, they don't know me from Adam and I don't even know the names of any of them except for that Heather woman. Two, they must have someone among them who the majority would be more likely to look up to. To have a new boy jumped on them out of the blue is going to ruffle a few feathers. Seen it happen often enough in work when a chinless wonder straight out of school tries to boss around blokes with thirty years in the job. He gets treated with a well-deserved contempt - so do those who gave him the job; and quite right too. Three, a few may have ambitions for the job themselves and are much better qualified than me. I don't need a new collection of enemies just now; I've got enough on my plate in that department.'

Clare wasn't fazed. 'Hard luck on them. You've forgotten the most important qualification of all, naturally.'

'And that is?'

'I trust you. Good enough?'

'Thanks. If it's any consolation I feel the same about you - except when it comes to judgements about what I should do. That's not to say I've forgotten how you've helped me these last few weeks. Never will.' He took a deep drag to hide his embarrassment at revealing part of his feelings, but he'd been determined to say it as an atonement for his earlier loss of control. She deserved that, at least. Besides, he appreciated her presence and wanted her to know it. He carried on.

'Trouble is, you've ignored the primary consideration, number four.' He stuck up a throbbing index finger shrouded with a protective sheath. 'Number four is I simply don't want the job. I can't give orders and make them stick. Never could. And I don't want any responsibility, either. Sorry, you'll have to find somebody else if you think you'll be put out of action.'

He leaned back on the bench, satisfied he had made his point and there would be no further argument about it.

'All right.' Clare said. 'We'll discuss it another time.'

'No we won't.'

'Another time.'

'No!'

Clare didn't answer. A silence stretched out.

'What do we do till we have to go?' Gildas asked. He wanted something to take his mind off his forthcoming introduction to the Mule.

'If I were you I'd go back to the hut and get to know as many of the gang as I could. Your life could just possibly depend on them one day. Josh'll help; he's responsible for selecting many of them. They're not a bad lot when you get to know them. As for my part, I'll come with you and fall into my pit for a while. Got up early, see? Need a bit of a rest after our little work-out this morning. You're pretty good, y'know. Getting better. Took me all my time to stay alive, I can tell you. Maybe we'll try it again some time.'

No, thought Gildas. *Never again. Not like that.*

'I'll stay here for a while.' he said. 'Be over later. You want waking up any particular time?'

'No need. Not unless something goes wrong.' She got up stiffly. 'See you later.'

Moving a lot slower than usual, she departed the room. Gildas grinned around his cigarette. It had all worked out for the best. He'd figured out what she had been trying to achieve during his brain-squeezing session the previous night. Although he knew what her next step would be it had proved impossible to ignore it as he'd intended. He frowned at the recollection. She was very definitely OK in his book; a great person to know and be with. He'd grown very fond of her. But why, oh why, did she persist in flaunting her irresponsible sexual activities in his face? Perhaps he shouldn't have been so waspish towards her that time in the mountain hostel. A bit more diplomacy should have been on the agenda. Woman-like, she intended to keep rubbing his nose in her imagined rejection.

Never mind all that! Clare had achieved her objective with him and he had been exorcised despite his knowledge of what she was doing. All had worked out for the best and the devils had fled - at least for the time being.

Gildas had studied intensively in his earlier life. He was not unfamiliar with the basic principle of emotional manipulation even though he had a great deal of difficulty using the knowledge.

He would never admit that to Clare, of course.

Still, he felt good. Perhaps he was finally managing to resurrect some self- confidence.

CHAPTER 21

Evening came quickly. A few of the gang left the barracks hut early, more from boredom than eagerness, to join the growing crew in the shade of the entrance to shuttle reception. Gildas also left early, but not to accompany his colleagues. He had one last call to make on Earth; a call to say goodbye to an old and respected friend.

A man in blue mechanic's overalls directed him to an area outside the main site and close beside the original motorway service station. It was a graveyard - a last resting place of transport considered surplus to future requirements. None could be taken to a new world; the mass-factor automatically excluded traditional forms of mechanical transportation. Only the incredibly light push-plate vans were eligible due to their shape as ready-made containers and their independence from petroleum-based fuels, which could be difficult or even impossible to locate quickly on arrival.

Gildas walked slowly between the neat rows of abandoned trucks, vans and buses. The familiar warm odours of oil, grease, diesel and rubber pervaded the area. A smell of the scrap-yard, of the railway station, distinctive and pleasant to Gildas' nostrils. He sniffed in appreciation, knowing he may never experience it again.

It took nearly half an hour to locate his objective; half an hour of sadness and nostalgia. Rounding the end of one of the rows he saw it, a few positions up the next row.

The truck was standing between a large panel van and a low-loader trailer unit. Gildas stopped. Four of the six tyres were completely flat, causing a tilt to the front and side. Like so many of the others he had seen it exuded an air of incredible weariness, a piteous melancholy distressing to gaze upon. Gildas blinked away a tickling in one eye. He shouldn't have come. It hurt to see it like this.

Slowly he walked around the battered, unlovely hulk, noting with sadness each dent, crumple and hole in the ravaged bodywork - overt evidence of so much neglect and violence. The scarred, blotched metal shimmered in the savage heat. He touched it softly, pressed his palm on the searing steel, hammered his fist on a booming panel in a sudden rage at the futility of it all. He felt no pain.

He stopped at the driver's door, hesitated, then reached up to the makeshift handle. The door clicked open, swung on creaking hinges to hit a front stanchion with a solid thud. He looked into the cab where so much death had occurred, where so many had spilled out their life's blood.

The terrible marks were indelibly stained on the seats, the floor.

The key was still in the ignition!

On an impulse he hauled himself up and onto the driving seat. The familiar position only served to increase his sense of mourning. He looked at the key. Would it be appropriate?

Yes it would.

He checked the gear lever was in neutral, turned the key and pressed the starter button. The engine turned, groaning, coughed once and hammered into life. Gildas pressed his foot hard on the accelerator. The engine bellowed. He kept his foot hard on the pedal. The revs wound up and up to a bass scream. The knocking grew louder. Grinding his teeth he forced it to still greater efforts.

The engine had been built to last, and last it had, but it was well past its prime by a very long way. The fan-belt went first. Gildas heard the crack, followed by a metallic slither as the reinforced rubber band whipped around under the bonnet and fell out on the ground. After that, it didn't take long for the engine to overheat and blow the radiator, followed quickly by the cylinder-head gasket. The slack timing chain slapped viciously, threatening to come off its cogs at any moment and the truck began to rock as the now badly-unbalanced engine strained on its mountings. Metal creaked and groaned; dense black smoke rose all around.

It lasted a lot longer than Gildas would ever have believed possible. Then the bearing which had been the cause of the tremendous, never-ending knock for so long finally gave out. An enormous *BANG!* came from under the bonnet closely followed by thick metal snapping, tearing, mangling into an irreparable solid mass of fused and twisted components.

Sudden silence, broken only by the click of overheated metal and the hissing of fluids under pressure.

Gildas leaned back in the seat, forcing the tension from his muscles and mind. It was fitting. The old truck had

275

ended its life with a proper bang instead of the proverbial whimper. It would never again be subjected to the abuse and ferocity of man against machine and other men. It could now rest in peace for ever or until inexorable decay once more returned it to its natural chemical elements.

He was satisfied he'd done the right thing. He patted the worn steering wheel, aware once more of a prickling at the corner of each eye. He dashed his hand across them, angry at this show of weakness. But it just didn't feel *right* to leave the corpse of an old, loyal friend here like this - all alone.

But why had he come here in the first place if not to give vent to such an emotion? To prove he could still be touched? No, it went further and deeper than that. Much further and much deeper. He forced his mind away from such speculations.

He wanted to say something to the truck. Something silly like "Goodbye". But he couldn't say it out loud. He sighed, lowering his head in respect. Simply to acknowledge the thought would have to be enough.

With shocking abruptness, a powerful shock of emotion swept through his entire being; an indefinable mix of sorrow, compassion, pity and a blazing rage at the cruel injustices of life. He trembled with passion, caressing the chipped and faded steering wheel until he managed to regain some sort of composure. Clambering out, he moved softly to the front where there was a bit of shade, leaned close to a jagged, rusty tear and pressed his face against the ravaged metal. `Goodbye.' He whispered softly. `And thank you.'

With great gentleness he closed the door and walked slowly away with brimming eyes, not daring to look back.

`Stupid, sentimental fool!' he kept muttering to himself. `It's only a machine,'

But it didn't work - nothing ever would.

A straggling line of people trudged through the baking evening heat. They were on their way, for better or worse. Few regretted leaving.

Shuttle reception occupied a haphazard group of prefabricated buildings the other side of the motorway from the old service area. It sat on a narrow plateau at the base of the escarpment in an isolated position. The first launching loop towered overhead, leaning out from the hill at an impossible angle; an object lesson in the true meaning of vertigo. Other hoops, more loosely-spaced at this section of the series, continued downhill at lesser and lesser angles from the vertical until they reached the valley floor and stood upright.

Gildas fought primitive urgings of fear at these colossal structures hanging almost over his head, as did several more of those who had been allocated places on the same shuttle. A few could hardly tear their eyes away.

The great journey had barely begun - and still he harboured niggling doubts he couldn't bring into focus. On the up side, he was able to marvel at the enormous change in his outlook over the last twenty-four hours. No longer a victim of oppressive or aggressive flights of fancy, he couldn't help but be thankful to whatever psychological quirk had brought him back to the here and now with all that implied.

It was Clare's doing, of course; intended or accidental, he didn't care. He felt whole again, in control, normal as he had ever been. Being forced to face the knowledge he would probably never catch up with the last of his targets had helped immeasurably.

But he would still keep looking.

That knowledge didn't stop him being scared as hell of the looming mass overhead.

Then it was his turn through the door, following the queue, and fear no longer provided a distraction. One by one the passengers filed past a desk manned by a harassed clerk, who entered their names and numbers in a laptop.

Gildas confirmed his identity in a low voice hoping the number Clare had obtained for him was accepted. The clerk didn't even look up at him.

All had to pass through a detector cage. Everyone triggered the alarm and had to hand their personal weapons to an overly suspicious character in uniform who entered details in another laptop. All weapons had to be accounted for. Gildas crossed his fingers as his turn came.

All day he had wondered how to retain something secretly for his personal defence. Heather's present paramour, a withered slip of a man called James (reputed to go crazy if addressed as Jim) had informed him of the embarkation procedure. Others of the group had proved just as friendly when approached directly. By the time they had to leave, Gildas felt reasonably at home with most of them.

Nobody was called Dave!

But how to keep a weapon undetected? And what weapon would he choose if he found a way?

The knife! The old gutting knife he had already blooded to such good effect. That was it; the only real choice. Small, thin, deadly, uncomplicated and silent. Where to hide it? In a certain body orifice? Gildas quailed at the thought. Even the fact that the knife was not spring-loaded didn't endear him to the prospect. Besides, the detector would surely be able to sense metal though flesh. Not a good idea!

In his hair, his thick bushy mop? The same objection applied. Damn!

Where, then?

The obvious didn't hit him until the last minute. Climbing to his bunk he'd examined the barrel of his rifle. Too narrow. What about the ammunition clip? Yes! Plenty of room in there if he inserted the knife at a certain angle and there was still enough space to snap half a dozen slugs in on top in case the clip was examined. The fact the clip casing was of plastic he deemed irrelevant; it was supposed to be full of metal, after all.

He approached the detector with some misgiving, handing his weapon harness and rifle to a guard standing to one side. It would not do to attract any unwanted attention by going through clean, which was why he had retained a hand gun in one of his trouser pockets. The machine beeped. Another guard with a resigned expression frisked him and sent him back through. The detector remained silent.

Clare, following immediately behind, had to go through three times before the machine held its peace. She took it all in good part in spite of her battered appearance, even going so far as to crack a joke at the chief officer as he handed back her arsenal. All she got for her forced efforts at levity was the fish eye. Nobody laughed.

After running the gauntlet of the detector all embarkees were issued with a new one-piece overall and given two small brown pills to swallow. 'What are these for?' he asked the tough-looking woman in nurse's uniform after he'd choked them down.

'You'll find out!' she snapped ominously. Your next stop is round the corner. Get going!

Gildas rounded the corner and joined another queue wafting outside a door into which they trouped one by one. When Gildas' turn came he was immediately hustled into a steel chair and given a haircut, despite his protestations at not being allowed to choose a style, by a totally bald barber. It was all over very quickly without pain and he rubbed his hair as he got up from the chair to discover he'd been given a full crew-cut hardly half an inch long.

'Did you take the two pills they gave you back there?' enquired the barber with suspicious solicitude.

'Yes, I took them.' said Gildas, suddenly aware of a sharp twinge in his stomach.

'The toilet's through that door there,' said the barber, pointing. 'You'd better get in there pretty darned quick.'

Another stronger twinge assailed Gildas' offal, galvanising him to urgent movement. 'Thanks.' he said and went through the door to find himself at the tail end of yet another queue. A strong organic aroma polluted the atmosphere. Gradually, the queue moved forward as people at the front went in turn through another door. More came behind him, but the flatulent smell never lessened. He found out the source of the pong when his turn came to go through the swing-door to find himself out in the open air on the brink of a huge communal latrine.

The next twenty minutes were indescribable. Finally he found his way back into the main building at the end of another queue lined up in a narrow plastic corridor without air conditioning. The smell of sweat and the midden hung heavy in the air. Conversation was subdued. A door opened at the far end and the passengers filtered through, down several flights of stairs and into a large concrete-lined room. A hundred yards opposite the entrance door an opening to a wide tunnel breached the otherwise featureless wall. It was exactly like standing in an underground railway station - and a lot hotter. The level floor of the room consisted of large plastic plates covered in a non-slip grid pattern. Enormous roll-up doors occupied much of both side walls.

A voice boomed from the tannoy.

'All personnel stand between the two central lines. The two central lines, please. Then please put on the flight overalls you were issued with!'

The crowd obediently shuffled ahead to comply. Gildas saw the lines, a pair of black marks where adjoining plates met, running the length of the room towards the tunnel. He pulled at Clare. 'Come on, over here!'

'I know, I know. I've been here before, more than once.' She shrugged off his hand with some irritation. The Panda patches around her eyes were hardly noticeable. Gildas looked more closely. She had done a good job with some kind of skin cover; it was nearly impossible to see. It was the first time he'd ever seen her wear any make-up - and the first sign of feminine vanity. He grinned. But not before turning away first.

The floor jerked and began to move towards the tunnel. The section already inside the tunnel rose, creating a low step, which sloped up at a shallow angle. It was an escalator. Gildas marvelled. Its heavy construction indicated it had been designed to carry massive loads. A slow journey of several minutes brought them to another "station" where an armed guard directed the passengers through a small door into a gigantic covered space humming with activity. Both ends were open to the air through a wide and very high portal. Rails set far apart passed through the centre of the shed. An enormous gantry crane moved slowly across the ceiling carrying a pallet stacked with grey plastic boxes.

Gildas stopped short after passing through the door, hesitating before being shoved from behind by the others he was holding up. In the centre of the floor, supported by a cradle running on the rails, lay one of the shuttles. Its twin loading-bay doors were spread like a pair of attenuated wings. As he watched, the gantry lowered its load on to a platform level with the top of the shuttles cargo bay and a gang of men began to transfer the plastic boxes, stacking them into the cavernous hold with an efficiency indicative of long practice.

A burly man hastened across to where the passengers stood, uncertain what to do next. Red faced, clothed for a dress-parade ceremony and all too familiar. Gildas did a classic double-take. Oh no! Not here. Not *again.*

Unhappily it was all too true. Gildas had spent a lifetime in the knowledge that he stood out like fangs on a hamster in whatever company he kept. Now was no exception. The Beast spotted him immediately. Their eyes locked.

'All over to the platform ladies and gents! Hope you're looking forward to your trip round the bay in the Skylark. The weather's just right for it.' The Beast's yellowing teeth gleamed wetly in a parody of a smile. He ignored Gildas completely.

Gildas nudged Clare. 'You know that guy?' He nodded towards the Beast.

'Never seen him before. Should I?'

'Thought you might, that's all. He was in charge of the supply depot back in Town. He's the one who supplied those medical drugs to your late colleagues back in the camp. A word to the wise; be careful of him - very careful. He's a bad egg and damn' clever with it. I also suspect he might harbour a grudge against me. I can't understand what he's doing here, especially in a position of some authority. He always seems to land on his feet.' Gildas spoke with some envy.

Clare eyed the Beast who was now conducting his charges across the floor. 'He looks it. Jolly sure of himself too. I'll see what I can find out.' They followed the crowd.

The front section of the shuttle hold was packed with seats from side to side, all facing forwards. A sliding ladder ensured convenient access. The Beast stood alongside a pair of boxes attached to the top of the ladder. Each passenger received an item from both boxes. Gildas's turn came. The Beast looked directly into his face without acknowledgement or friendliness.

'Take one of each.' he recited. 'Face mask and whoopsy bag. Put the mask on as soon as you sit down!'

Gildas dipped into the boxes, averting his eyes from the stony visage and obeyed without comment. It was best not to precipitate the inevitable confrontation here. That was bound to come sooner or later and he had better prepare for it. The Beast never forgot an affront, real or imagined.

Clare was the last in line. The Beast followed her into the hold to sit in the one remaining seat. Within minutes the cargo loading was completed and the doors closed over their heads. Bolts slammed, seals hissed with vacuum and the shuttle began to move.

'Put the mask on, right now!' Clare ordered in a muffled voice. She was already wearing hers. The thing reminded Gildas of the wartime gas-masks he'd seen in the museum but without any eye openings. He fitted it over his face and ears, fastening the Velcro straps tightly. Where were the nozzles for an oxygen supply?

'What does it do?' he asked.

'You'll find out.' came the answer, more muffled than before. 'The easiest way, of course, is not to wear it, but I wouldn't recommend that. I've no intention of clearing up the mess after take-off if you don't.'

He didn't enquire further. Clare was not in the best of moods, apparently.

After a lot of banging and lurching everything went quiet. Gildas had figured out about the mask by then. Almost as soon as he had donned the headgear it began to take on a horrible life of its own, twisting and to match the contours of his face and pressing uncomfortably against his eyelids. He found he could still breathe easily, though.

'Launch in ten seconds; ten seconds from now.' grated the tannoy.

Gildas fervently wished he had taken the trouble to read the pamphlet of launch preparations. Too late now!

The seat tilted to a steep angle, leaving him supported only by the seat belt. He hung suspended at the very edge of his seat.

Someone punched him hard in the stomach. Very hard. His back slammed into the thick, upholstered seat upright. Cries of pain came from all around. Someone was busily being sick to one side of him. *Poor devil,* thought Gildas. *Hope whoever it is has taken off their mask.* Gildas fought his own stomach for control of the situation.

The mask did its job. Acceleration sensors sucked at his eyeballs to keep them from pressure damage in their sockets. A thin, stiff sliver of something warm shot between his lips, sliding over his palate to press upon his tongue as that useful organ attempted to slide down his

283

throat and choke him. He felt severe stress in his bowels and was glad he'd visited the toilet when advised. The pressure increased. It *hurt!*

Gathering enormous velocity with each passing microsecond, the shuttle screamed along between the guide rails. It didn't last long; acceleration ended with a shocking abruptness and for a few moments most of the passengers had their initial experience of free-fall. Then the wings slammed out as the shuttle passed through the enormous final hoop of the accelerator. Half a second later, the chemical thrusters kicked in.

The flight seemed interminable. A near-nightmare of stench, foul noises and uncontrollable bilious attacks. Gildas dreaded the permanent free-fall to come.

There were no windows.

Clare didn't seem to mind. She also had no intention of being engaged in intellectual conversation - or any sort of conversation, come to that. After the first few abortive attempts Gildas gave up and tried to shut out the ghastly surroundings by going to sleep. It didn't work. He had never even travelled in a plane before. Luckily, the trip was surprisingly short.

Deceleration was so gentle as to be barely noticed. The first indication they were nearing their destination was given by the pilot's voice telling them to ensure their seat belts were firmly locked. Only ten minutes later a tiny judder shook the shuttle as it sealed itself to a transit tube. The passengers were ordered to remain in their seats until, one at a time, they were escorted from the craft.

Free-fall hit a lot of them hard. Not so the Beast. He was the first to leave, swimming over the heads of the others as if born to the lack of gravity. A crew from the main ship helped the rest.

Gildas made sure he was the last to leave. Clare simply left him sitting there. With the assistance of two burly men he was guided to the ceiling, on which a strap of wide-mesh plastic netting was fixed. He had wondered as to its purpose; now he knew. Slowly, hand over hand, he entered the transit tube close to the front of the shuttle where more mesh made his progress easier. By the time he entered the ship he was beginning to enjoy the sensation.

His pleasure didn't last for long. The Beast was waiting.

As the outer airlock closed, another opened up at the end of the short passage, where the passengers waited clinging to the webbing on both sides, top and bottom. The vast majority looked extremely unhappy and disoriented. The Beast passed them through the door singly, handing each a slip of paper. Gildas stuck to his position at the end of the line using Clare's broad back for concealment.

His turn came.

The Beast swung from the wall to block the narrow door.

'Welcome, little friend! Nice to see you again. You got something for me?'

'No chance! I found out what you were doing, didn't I?'

'Tsk, tsk. And there was me thinking you were the one person I could trust. Just shows how wrong you can be, don't it? So what are you going to do about it, eh?'

Gildas jerked his head up. Conditions were still weightless. His feet began to swing up in reaction to the movement. He automatically compensated by thrusting them under a strand of the netting. He was through being forced to kow-tow to this guy. He smiled.

'Not a damned thing. The question should be what are *you* going to do about it?'

The Beast sighed theatrically. 'Ho, hum. Not much I can do, when you think about it. I'll just have to add it to my thick volume of horrible experiences and disappointments I've had from the human race. But I can't allow it to be overlooked, y'know.' He wagged an admonitory finger in the manner of a stern schoolmaster. 'We'll simply agree you owe me one, OK?'

They were both oriented the same way, feet lodged under the netting. Gildas had very long arms. He was also aware that Clare had stopped a few yards away waiting for him to join her. It was time to remove an unwanted incubus from his back before it dug its claws in. Best to get it done as soon as possible.

He grabbed the admonitory finger, which was still wagging up and down as the Beast enjoyed his little demonstration of falsely-assumed authority. He pushed and twisted, back and down. The Beast followed, surprise and pain allowing him no room to make alternative arrangements.

Gildas bent to the floor - if it was the floor - he couldn't tell, still holding the violated finger in an unbreakable grip. The Beast hit the bulkhead, falling squarely onto a large globule of yellow goo, where someone had discarded the contents of their stomach. It broke up and drifted around him, slimy and greasy. The Beast blinked in horror and tried to roll away, crying out in pain as Gildas refused to roll with him. He grabbed at the netting to steady himself and to take off some of the leverage. He raised his other hand, clenched it into a fist, then thought better of it.

'I owe you nothing.' Gildas hissed into his ear. 'On the other hand, forgive the tasteless pun, I think you owe me a lot more for putting me in a situation where I could have been killed for your benefit. You're a slob, Frankie-boy. Always were and always will be. Where's my bit of paper? What's it for?'

'Here, take it and go!' croaked the Beast. 'Find out for yourself. I won't make any threats about catching up with you later. You can see the prospects as well as me in regard to our relationship.'

'I'm sure I can. Stay well clear of me in future, understand?'

'Let me go!'

Gildas wondered whether to break the finger. He desisted. See what happened; watch his back; that was the only way to proceed for now. Damaging an official would put him off the ship for sure, either by shuttle back to Earth or through the nearest airlock if the Beast had any say in the matter. He released the finger, using the Beast's chest to kick himself away to where Clare waited; an approving smile on her face.

He glanced at the slip of paper. '"L4, S6, D77." What does that mean?' He thrust the paper at her, catching on the netting for support.

'Simple. All directions on board are given that way. Level 4, Section 6, Door 77, see? Look, on the back, there's a rough plan of the ship.'

'Why? And how do I get there?'

'It's next door to where they want to see me. Medical section. Follow me!.' She kicked off down the corridor.

It was a long way and Gildas's well-developed sense of direction gave up in confusion. There was too much to remember all at once. Many were the victims of unaccustomed free-fall they passed on their way, clinging to the walls or blindly crawling along. Gildas wanted to help them.

'Leave them!' Clare ordered. You can't help them all. They'll just have to get used to it in their own time.'

'Old folk and children?' Gildas was disgusted. 'Left to fend for themselves here, in an unnatural situation? They should have been assisted, or at least all kept together. Where are the natives?'

'Up to their ears in work, that's where. We're getting out soon as we can. Haven't you been listening to what's going on?'

'Not really. Sorry.' Too much had been on his mind recently. The momentous occasion of leaving his own planet had somehow lacked significance. It didn't help his feelings of guilt at being immune to the worst effects of weightlessness. There weren't any windows here, either. He glanced at the ship plan. A small outline of the ship had been printed in one corner

A big, featureless cylinder; an elongated old-type post box; that was his first impression of this great ship being built to take representatives of the human race to the stars. Shuttle docking facilities seemed to be concentrated in a ring encircling one end of the cylinder. He couldn't see how the thing was propelled - no clusters of tubes or flaring nacelles. He'd find out eventually - maybe. The rest of the paper was a sectioned diagram of the interior of the central cylinder. At least the diagram looked easy to follow even if certain sections were blank – possibly for security reasons, he guessed. Folding the paper and shoving it into a harness pocket, he pushed off up the corridor after Clare.

CHAPTER 22

Was there anything worth going back for? He knew there should be no problem about obtaining a seat for a return trip on the shuttle. They left every hour, always empty, to fetch more colonists and construction materials for the ship still being built around him. A single passenger wasn't likely to pose any problem with fuel or flight time. Nothing would have improved - was it worth it compared to an unknown future?

Searing heat, ghastly diseases, barbarism, all growing more intense with every day that passed. Let alone the full-time occupation of finding (and keeping) water pure enough to drink and some sort of food for his belly. No, there was nothing to go back for. All he truly loved was either already dead or close to it. Earth would not recover during his lifetime, if ever. If it did, it would be different, alien. Too much damage had been done for it ever to be the same again.

He remembered that famous blue and white picture of the living planet; a vibrant beautiful globe of life and hope drifting in a black void. If only he could find a window to look out of and see it for himself.

But there were no windows. The ship was being built to strict parameters of function and utility. Luxury and indulgence were *out*. Curiosity occupied a very much lower position on the scale of priorities.

Bet it would be different for the fat cats and the officers. It always was.

Gildas sighed and twisted his limbs yet more firmly in the ubiquitous mesh, which lined all the corridors he'd seen so far. Thinking of the past was a pointless exercise now. Ever a martyr to nostalgia, he found it difficult to concentrate on his likely future. He waited for Clare, barely bothering to acknowledge the steady stream of people moving, with varying degrees of success, to and fro along the Medical Section corridor. She'd been closeted in that room for a considerable time.

His own examination had taken no more than a few minutes. After a short wait in the corridor, the door of room 77 had opened. The outgoing examinee, a middle-aged man whose face was hauntingly familiar, floundered for a moment, grabbed wildly at the mesh and motioned him in with a jerk of her thumb. He entered a small room nearly filled with blank, unpainted cabinets. Within two paces he noticed a slight return of weight and remained motionless until his feet touched the floor. Artificial gravity? Had *that* been developed and suppressed too? He looked down at the floor.

'Only a reverse application of the push-plates. Expensive but very necessary when examining patients.' Doctor Payne sat in a chair beside a narrow desk. 'I remember you. Gildas, right? Clare Masson's paramour?' He turned and pushed a series of buttons on a keyboard.

'That's me, except for that last word you used. Nice to see a friendly face for a change.' Gildas sat on the only other seat, relishing a little weight feebly pressing out his buttocks, while at the same time dreading what was to come. He recalled with horror what this man had put him through back at the bunker.

289

Dr Payne gave him his full attention and smiled; a somewhat predatory smile, Gildas thought. His dread must have been etched plainly on his face. 'Relax, man! We've got all the latest state-of-the-art gear up here. Let's have your left arm.'

'Temporarily, I hope.'

The Doctor gave another ambiguous smile. 'For now.' He pressed a flat pad on Gildas's forearm. It was warm, soft, and connected by a flexible cable to one of the cabinets. Gildas sat stiffly, tensed for pain.

It didn't happen. The doctor studied a small display panel, which had flashed up on a monitor the moment the pad touched Gildas's trembling flesh. Columns of colour moved up and down, then stabilised. The machine chirruped. Apparently satisfied with the information gleaned, Payne removed the pad.

'All clear on the bug front. All vital signs within parameters. Any trouble with weightless conditions?'

'None.' Gildas was heady with relief. 'It's great when you get used to it.'

'You're lucky. Some never do. The number of bruises and contusions I've had to deal with, you'd never believe. Can't train everyone, though. Not enough staff yet. Too busy with construction to bother about wet-nursing.' Payne pressed a few more buttons. A series of numbers lit the screen. He copied them down on a thin plastic pad the size of a postage card.

'Right, you're passed for proper work. The construction gangs need all the help they can get. Don't lose this pad! The numbers I've just put on it are your first assignment. From now on look at it every hour or so when you're not sleeping. My writing will disappear soon and will then be replaced by other times and locations determined by the ship's personnel deployment computer. You can write on it with anything metal to ask questions; just don't press on it too hard. Report to the location given after you've had some sleep. And that's your first assignment - sleep. Look at the card again about six hours from now. OK?'

'I've got it.' Gildas accepted the proffered card and put it in one of his harness pockets. 'That all?'

'Not quite. Let's have your arm again for a few jabs to keep you fit.'

Even *that* didn't hurt. Good equipment here. Wonder why they didn't use it on Earth he thought as the shining metal injector head, looking remarkably like a pepper pot, shot the drugs through his skin under high compression. Payne waved him away.

'See you around. Send in the next victim on your way out, please.'

And that was it. So where the hell was Clare? Gildas was beginning to get fed up of hanging around for her - quite literally. By the time she put in an appearance he'd become nearly numb with boredom.

'That took a hell of a time.' he groused, stretching his seized limbs, drifting gently towards her as he let go of the mesh. The door hadn't quite closed behind her and he caught a brief glimpse of a tall, handsome man wiping his hands with a cloth.

'Sometimes does.' Clare was still not inclined to be communicative. 'Got your billet directions?'

'Here.' he tapped his harness. 'I was only there in a couple of minutes. Is there a problem? What were you doing in there?' He was genuinely concerned.

'Woman's business. None of yours. Come on!' she kicked off along the corridor.

Up to now all the connecting passages had been narrow; no more than five feet wide and just over eight feet high, Gildas guessed. These, as he shortly found out, were the exception. Only certain areas of the ship where a high traffic flow was anticipated merited such a profligate waste of space. After a short journey past several bends Clare entered a side passage, the first Gildas had seen of such a size. It was roughly the same width as the main

291

thoroughfare and square; more of a shaft than a corridor. There was only sufficient room for two people to pass each other. He entertained serious doubts whether two Clares would manage without some drastic compression of certain female protuberances. He followed her kicking feet, afraid of dropping too far behind. He would be lost for sure then.

It was like negotiating a rabbit warren designed by a cubist fanatic. All intersections and branches met at right angles, each with a small local ship plan and location mark attached to a convenient wall. Not much traffic was about; only twice did they meet anyone. It seemed to be a long way to their destination.

Clare slowed quickly without warning, pressing her hands against the mesh for braking. Gildas wasn't looking. The first he knew of it was when his head sank into a pneumatic cushion of soft flesh. Clare kicked him lightly under the jaw. It could have been accidental - he knew it wasn't.

'Not now, little man. Someone may be watching. We're here.' She moved to one side into another long corridor.

The end of the corridor seemed enormously distant, yet from floor to ceiling (or was it wall to wall? with no gravity for orientation it could have been either) was only about twelve feet. Gildas decided to think of them as walls and directed his attention to the only obvious feature - a narrow net placed halfway between the walls, held in place by thin polyester ropes. A few people were slowly groping their way along it on either side in the middle distance.

'What's that for?' he asked.

'To get to your coffin without disturbing anyone else. Let's look at your card. Right, next to me, I think.' She pulled herself along one wall and studied a plaque attached close to where they had entered. 'Other side.' She swung around to the opposite side of the net and set off along the corridor, looking at the numbers marked on the wall. Finding the correct row she headed out to the centre of the room. Gildas followed. The walls, he now noticed,

292

consisted of semi-transparent plates set edge to edge, two high, as far along the corridor as he could see. Behind a few of them he could discern the shadowy outline of a human form. So these must be the famous coffins! Clare swung to a halt, holding onto the net with her feet and beckoned him to join her.

'UN 27, that's yours.' She informed him. "I'm next door in UN 28. Press the blue button!'

Gildas did so with some difficulty. He was much shorter than his companion and had to stretch more to reach the large blue button while trying to retain the correct stance relative to a shifting net in free-fall. It wasn't easy, but he managed. With a soft sigh the translucent door opened to reveal a recess lined with a silky white plastic sheet. They'd chosen the right word, he reflected. It *did* look rather like a coffin.

'This is what we travel in, I suppose.'

Printed in the United Kingdom
by Lightning Source UK Ltd.
129085UK00001B/1-30/P